ALIEN TAKEBACK

Printed in Australia

First Printing: May 2022

Shawline Publishing Group Pty Ltd
www.shawlinepublishing.com.au

Paperback ISBN- 9781922701800

Ebook ISBN- 9781922701855

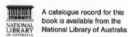
A catalogue record for this
book is available from the
National Library of Australia

ALIEN TAKEBACK

KATE FERRIS

This book is dedicated to all the authors of the world who aren't there yet – have faith in yourselves.

Acknowledgements

Many thanks to my wonderful husband, you didn't always understand but you still believed, and my beautiful children who gave me the strength and fortitude to believe in myself.

1

As I sat huddled in the bush waiting to make sure the coast was clear, I couldn't help but think back to the misadventures of my youth – not that it was all that long ago mind you – there was so much the same and yet so much different at the same time.

For instance, as a child, hiding in a bush meant I was hiding from someone, usually for fun or the thrill of it. You know, kids' games like hide and seek. Now I was hiding to avoid discovery because my life depended on it, as did the lives of my small unit.

You see, I'm in the army now. Not my army mind you, and not the army proper, more like a guerrilla army created to try and win our planet back from the invaders. Right now, we are taking back America, or at least we're trying to. But I flew here from Australia almost two months ago. Seven and a half weeks, to be exact. And yet here I was leading a unit of other untrained soldiers, much like myself, against an enemy vastly more powerful. But there were no two ways about it, we were going to win; we had to.

I use the term unit about as loosely as I use the term soldiers. We would never pass muster in a real army and I'm pretty sure the only time you call a group as small as ours a unit was to make it sound tougher... even navy seals are called a team and they have four; just like us. Well, I suppose technically we were five, if you Include overwatch; can't forget overwatch.

When the first incursion of aliens came to earth, most people thought it was some kind of joke. They landed in New Zealand. They sat there silently for a few hours in their ship, ignoring all attempts at communication. When they finally emerged, they destroyed all the military forces assembled there, like they always do in those movies. No one made it out. They then went on to destroy as many people as they could. The rest went into hiding. Some of them ended up here, with us in America, but not many.

Next place they landed a ship was Papua New Guinea. They did the same thing there. But PNG managed to send a distress signal when they landed. We still don't fully know what had happened in New Zealand at that point, but everyone was taking the silence as a bad sign. We figure they must have left bases set up in the two countries because both ships then moved on.

To Australia, to home. Both ships landed there. One on the east side and one on the west. They moved faster this time. They destroyed our military in a couple of days, but this time they took some damage. A lot of damage. We – well, our military – actually managed to destroy one of their ships. But eventually they won as they had in New Zealand and PNG. They hunted us down. But this time they couldn't get everybody. A lot of people survived and it was going to take them a long time to find us. Gotta love a big country full of wilderness. If they'd waited another twenty years, we might not have had so many survive.

Next, a whole bunch more ships joined the two (well, one by then) already here and they moved on to America. I guess they figured the losses were too great to try and hide their numbers anymore. The seven ships the aliens sent to America, the seven to Canada and the four to South America, were whittled down to eight in the two months it took them to take The Americas. They took out most of the military and government structures – possibly all of it – and at least three quarters of the civilians. But for some reason, unlike the campaigns they launched in New Zealand, PNG and Australia, they didn't hang around afterwards to hunt. They just took off again. Some people wondered why, others just figured they realised they had to be quick – or they wanted to get out before they suffered too many more losses and couldn't re-coup from that.

You might be wondering at this point why the unaffected countries failed to send military (or any other kind) of aid during these attacks. The answer is, I don't know. Speculation was that the aliens somehow stopped the aid from coming. But I don't know how.

After they finished in America, they disappeared. For three weeks. But that three weeks was all it took for the good old US of A to send out calls for help and planes to collect those who answered the call. They got quite a few from Australia, as you can imagine. We over-filled several C-17 Hercules aircraft. You know the ones, the planes they put planes on. The ones that need a whole airport to land ... they are pretty awesome. I don't know exactly how many. But I'm sure I could find out. Someone knows, I guess. Someone knows everything. I do wonder who they got to fly them if – as they said – they had little to no military left.

There were enough people left alive this time; enough people who were talking; for stories to start spreading about what these things were really like. What they looked like, how they killed, you know, stuff like that, stuff a military would want to know. Some of these people had been scared out of their minds and came off sounding like ranting lunatics, but there were enough similarities in their stories for someone to pay attention. Most of them were hushed away for questioning. Whoever was in control in America tried to keep it under wraps, but they didn't get everyone and it soon got out that the aliens were like vampires; yes, I mean as in the mythical creatures we read about in fictional stories.

The news went wild with a few of them. People who had seen them, been bitten and survived, had family, friends or other loved ones die. A couple of people even claimed that like vampires, they could turn those bitten into versions of themselves. Mostly these people were passed off as nuts who were trying to stir up terror as if we weren't all freaked out enough. Besides, the people who were claiming to be bitten and survived didn't seem any different, right?

For three weeks, no news came from any other countries about alien landings or sightings. Some people thought it was over. We were prepared to take action, hence a whole bunch of us jumping on planes bound for America to join the World Army – as it had been dubbed – based in America because they had the guts to start it, I guess. For three weeks, people dared to think maybe we were safe.

They were wrong.

The world woke up one morning to find that in the night, twenty ships had landed across Asia. There were five in Russia and the rest scattered throughout the continent. Obviously, they had many more ships than we had seen so far. Maybe they had been waiting for more reinforcements in those quiet three weeks, I don't know. We didn't hear much of the news coming out of Asia with regards to what was happening. Well, I suppose someone heard it, but the information wasn't passed along to us.

There was a lot we were never told.

I should probably explain who Rochelle is, and maybe who I am might be prudent too. My name is Tyne Cape. I'm twenty-three years old and this is my story. It's an interesting one, I promise you. It's long and some of it is confusing, but I'll try not to leave you with too many questions at the end. Wherever it ends, hope you're still with me then. I think I'll always remember everything that happened since the day the aliens invaded.

Rochelle Parker is my best friend. She's not with me right now as I hide in this bush, telling you my story. She's off somewhere else with her own unit. But that's another part of the story. Rochelle and I grew up together, literally. We were born three days apart (she's older). Our mothers had been best friends since childhood and our dads were on good terms, too. The only real difference in our lives was my dad died about twelve years ago in a car accident, in my early teen years.

We lived next door to each other and we grew up like sisters. We have been close since birth and everything Rochelle did; I did more or less three days later. This includes sleeping through the night, first teeth, first smile, crawling, walking, and first words. Our mothers used

4

to joke we were weird twins. When we finished high school, we both opted not to go on to university. And as far as I know, neither of us has ever regretted that decision. I know I haven't, but obviously I can only be about ninety-nine percent sure about Rochelle, at least until I get another chance to ask her.

The only other real difference we have is we tend to go towards different types of men. I like them big and tough looking, but caring and sensitive. Rochelle tends to go for them skinny and scrawny (in my opinion) but smart and funny always helps too, and strangely enough we are amazing at picking out guys for each other. We always found that rather amusing. After high school, we moved in together. We were both eighteen when we finished, so we got jobs and a small unit around the corner from our parents. After we had lived together for about six months, we decided to start our own business. Which we did together of course, and quite successfully, I might add.

We ran our own DJ/Karaoke business. It didn't pay a whole lot at first, but it supplemented our incomes nicely and covered our nights out. Eventually, it started making enough, we could have it as our primary jobs. No more waitressing; yay! We had what we felt was the perfect life. And we'd probably still be happily doing that if these stupid aliens hadn't come along and ruined everything. I hate them so much. I really hope we win this war.

Two years after we moved in together; once they were sure we were going to survive on our own, and not die in the attempt, our parents decided to up and move to the country. Rochelle's dad retired. They had always wanted to move out bush – as they called it – so they took my mum with them. They bought a huge property with a massive house on it and built a granny flat for my mum so she would still have her privacy when she wanted it. I'm just glad they didn't abandon her. I know she had been scared of that since my dad died.

Oh, another small difference, Rochelle had a little brother. He was born about seven years ago. Not long after we turned sixteen. He was a surprise baby; I don't even think her parents had been trying. They had always been happy with just one kid, the same as my mum. He was partly a prompt for their move to the country. He was autistic and had some behavioural issues.

They weren't able to get proper funding to help out where we lived, so they figured why not shape an environment around him rather than try to shape him to the environment? It worked out great for them. They were all really happy.

When the aliens first landed in New Zealand, Rochelle and I planned, in case they came to Australia. We are not survivalists by any stretch of the imagination, but we just had a feeling we needed to be ready. We spent a good portion of our savings stocking up on non-perishable food, bottled water and fuel for my truck. I miss my truck. It was so awesome. And still fairly new. I wonder if I'll ever see it again. We kept it loaded in the tray from that first day.

When they landed in Australia, after everything we didn't know about what had happened in New Zealand and PNG, we loaded some clothes in the truck too and headed to the farm. It was closer to Central Australia than we were, and they landed on the outer edges, so we figured we'd have time to get there and make a plan before they got that far. We still didn't really know what was going on, which made it hard to imagine we wouldn't be safe. At least for a while.

Rochelle and I had both jumped on those huge planes to America without a second thought, eager for a chance at some payback. We hadn't actually seen these aliens in person, but we had seen enough of the damage they had done and heard enough stories by the time the Americans came and offered to train us.

Once we disembarked from the planes, we were split into two groups and trucked off to two separate army bases, assigned quarters and beds and told we would start training the next day. Just long enough to get over jetlag I guess, for those that got it, anyway. We weren't allowed to leave the base. Not that we had any inclination to, sadly there wasn't much left in America now and with three quarters of their population gone, it was going to take them a while to recover.

Rochelle and I got posted to the same base, Roswell, New Mexico, of all places. We laughed at the irony of the situation. We were in the smaller of the two groups and fortunately got bunked together. We thought it was going to be a blast. We were told we would have six weeks of intense training, including fitness, fighting, camouflage, hunting and I don't remember what else. I really hoped they weren't going to be too harsh on the fitness test. I was by no means fit. But I didn't think they would expect miracles in six weeks. It's not like we were real army recruits or anything.

The first week on the base consisted of intense fitness training. Which we desperately needed. A lot of us weren't sporty or athletic. We were just lucky not to have been caught, I guess. After that first week, they started teaching us hand to hand combat skills. I remember wondering on the plane over, what kind of combat we would be trained in? I hated guns. They terrified me and I despised watching the destruction they could do and yet I signed up to use them. Silly, huh?

But hand to hand suited me well. Rochelle and I had taken quite a few martial arts classes when we were younger. Before we discovered alcohol and the pub and spent too much time working to do much of anything else. We had been pretty good at it, too. We had both been brown belts before we gave it up. We found some of that training came in handy now.

Next came weapons training. I went into it terrified. As I have already said, I hated guns. Still do, actually. It was the main thing that stopped me from ever joining the police force or any armed services. Luckily for me, all the training was with knives. Close quarter combat was what they called it. I excelled in it. For some reason, fighting with knives and other blades really worked for me. Rochelle wasn't quite as good as me, but she wasn't far behind. I was secretly a little proud I had finally surpassed her in something.

So our time continued on for a few weeks. Then they decided to give us a fitness test. I didn't do so great, I thought. Not dismally and honestly, most people only just scraped through because they lowered the standards a fair bit. Rochelle scraped through by the skin of her teeth.

I've never been ridiculously unfit. I mean sure I drink probably a bit more than I should and I don't always eat the right things – well *didn't but you know what I mean – I thought I would be on the lower end of the spectrum but I honestly didn't think I would fail that badly. Rochelle has always been a little bigger than me and struggled more with her weight. She also drinks more than I do and eats way more junk food. And yet she did pretty good and I didn't. Go figure. They offered an intense training course for those of us who were interested. One of the drill instructors quietly suggested I should sign up for it. I signed up immediately. The few others did too. Rochelle didn't bother. She was happy enough with her results. She signed up for more hand-to-hand combat training instead.*

2

Everything seemed clear around me. The only sounds I could hear were the noises of the other three breathing quietly behind me and the very faint sound of static from the earpiece I was wearing. We were all wearing them. It made communicating during battle much easier. Not that we had seen anything resembling battle yet, which just quietly I was grateful for. All was quiet on the western front, as the saying goes.

There wasn't even any wildlife around I could detect. I couldn't hear any birds or the scuffling of insects through the scrub. I wished I had had more time to learn about tracking before we had been shipped out, but this had come up last minute. I don't think it's what they originally intended for us. The earpiece hummed slightly because the others were huddled close by and there was the tiniest amount of feedback. It was a strangely comforting sound.

I rose slowly, still looking around for any other signs of life in the surrounding forest. There was nothing, not even a breeze to rustle the leaves of the trees right now, but I knew that would change soon. It had been breezy earlier, so there was no reason to believe it wouldn't be again. Each unit had a handheld GPS system. So I was pretty sure we weren't lost. That is to say, we knew what our coordinates were.

We were however, on our own. We had been dropped together at the border of the Nevada State Forest and each unit took a different route into and through the forest. Our mission was simple-ish. Supposedly, the aliens were spread out across the forest in small groups called nests. From the information we had, there were many of these nests in the forest. We were supposed to go through and see if we could pick up any signs of life. Human life.

The Elko Nevada base had been attacked. We hadn't known how or by who (for sure) until we got there. Elko had been the bigger of the two bases. They had sent almost three quarters of the recruits there for training. We had been here just shy of seven weeks. Our training – such as it was – was as good as it was going to get for now. We were considered more or less battle ready. At least good enough to be cannon fodder I guess, which I strongly suspected we were going to be. They still hadn't really told us exactly what they had planned for us, but most of the recruits thought we were learning to fight to go home.

About five days ago, an update communication between the two bases had been cut off at the Elko end. We tried for twenty-four hours to re-establish communication and failed to do so, prompting a small group to be sent on a reconnaissance mission to the base to find out what had happened. I was part of that mission, as were the other team leaders. We had already been assigned our units, and combat and weapons training had turned into sparring matches with the other units, teamwork being the main key in this form of training. My team all got along and fought together well. We all respected and listened to each other. Sadly, they weren't coming with me this time.

There were eight of us in the end that went out there. Myself, another three team leaders (there were lots of teams but they weren't all needed), and four of the trainers we had been working with for the past few weeks, at least two of whom I suspected were regular army, but had survived the original alien incursion somehow. I was the only girl who had been made a team leader.

We had flown in by helicopter and landed about one mile out. The rest of the way was by foot. We were armed with the bladed weapons we had been training with. The plan was to get in as quick as we could and ascertain what had happened and why contact had been lost.

There were no lights anywhere on the base that we could see, which wasn't so surprising given the loss of communication had occurred during daylight hours. We couldn't find anyone or anything in the outer buildings, so we headed to the centre, clearing other small structures as we went through. We always broke off in groups of two or three, depending on the size of the building we needed to check. We didn't go anywhere alone.

When we got to the control centre, where communication had been cut, we all went in as quietly as we could. What we found will stay with me until the day I die. As we entered the communications room, we were all struck by the smell. It was the odour that alerted us seconds in advance to what we were going to find.

Blood covered the walls like an abstract painting. There was so much of it that it wasn't dry yet. Then we started tripping over bodies. So many bodies. It was hard to tell how many as they were tangled and it was difficult to tell where one ended and the next one began. They were everywhere. I felt ill just looking at them all. My stomach wanted to empty itself like one of the other team leaders did, but I managed to control it... just.

We found the computers had been mostly destroyed in the attack, but a couple were still working. We radioed back to Roswell and got a copy of the full crew manifest for the base. Then we went about the task of trying to locate every person on that list. We were lucky enough the army was organised. Everyone who had signed up was issued serial number-only dog tags as soon as we landed. So identifying them was at least possible. Although it was time consuming finding the serial number that corresponded with each name on the list.

We flew in another crew of about twenty (mostly medical staff) to help us with identifying the bodies. And yet it still took hours to go through the list and find all the sets of tags we could. There were supposed to be six hundred personnel on this base. And we needed to account for every one of them. We went through the remaining buildings, finding more blood and death wherever we went, but all on the one side of the base. Our only very small consolation was there were many alien bodies in amongst the human ones, so at least we had something to study.

We knew it had been the aliens that had attacked the base, so they were either back in America from somewhere without us knowing, or not all of them had left when the ships did. I personally thought the second option more likely. And although I hated the idea that so many more had died at the hands of the aliens because of incorrect intelligence, it was some small relief to know at least there wasn't yet another unknown faction working against us.

When we had accounted for all the bodies, and God there were so many of them, we consulted the manifest and discovered we were about one hundred people short of what we should have. One of the trainers found a trail of blood heading out the side of the base towards the Nevada State Forest, near as we could gather. Just outside the base boundaries, we found another five bodies. These were seriously mutilated, almost torn in half, as though the aliens had been fighting over them. As we looked out onto the horizon, I thought I could see movement. I pointed it out to the trainer. He and another trainer went to investigate.

They came back with a recruit. She was covered in blood with cuts all over her –we later discovered these were bites – she was wild with fear. We had done everything else we could do here and were told to return to base. Another team would be sent to scout the area, so we wrapped her in a blanket and bundled her into the helicopter with us, back to Roswell. Once we had landed, she was taken off to the base hospital. The rest of us went to debrief the commander on base.

They questioned the recruit before she started getting ill and slipped into a coma – or so we thought – not that we were really told any of this. I found out later through other channels. She was the reason we discovered about these so-called nests. The recruit, along with others from the base, had been taken back to one. She told us she had escaped and the others still had a chance of being alive.

So a plan was quickly put together, to attempt to find and rescue the other recruits and to destroy the aliens we had thought were gone from America. I was a little annoyed at this. I had been hoping to go back home and fight there, to free my own land. Although I was assured that was the eventual plan, this would be a good test.

According to the sick recruit, there were only about fifty aliens left from the group that had attacked the base and they were spread out into smaller groups of two or three in these nests. We assumed the other people taken from Elko would be randomly spread out across these nests also. That was apparently why only four teams of five were being sent in. They thought we should be able to handle it. According to the recruit, the aliens were doing a lot of infighting, so they were unlikely to come to each other's aid.

As it turned out, the scouting mission ended up being us. Us as in the teams belonging to the leaders who had gone to Elko to check things out. It had taken another twenty-four hours to organise before they had shipped us out to our starting point. Here we were, slowly creeping through a forest, trying to find signs of these so-called nests and a trail. Anything that might give us more information. There was occasional chatter over the radio of the other units discussing something they had or hadn't found. And in one instance, debating if this whole mission was a sham based on faulty information. I didn't get involved in these debates. They were pointless and got us nowhere. Although I didn't disagree; as the designated team leader – an honour given to me due to my leadership skills and fighting ability I was told – I didn't want to get involved in these debates, especially when I knew others were listening, but there was one thing I was sure of, there was a whole lot of something going on here that we didn't know.

After creeping along for another few miles, I called a halt on our hunched over travel. We were tired and sore from the way we were walking and there had been nothing around to see that I could detect. I stood slowly and stretched out my back for a short moment and I sensed, rather than saw, the others each stretch out in their own way. I sat on the ground to rest. I didn't want to listen to the chatter anymore. But turning my radio down was sadly not an option. I was the team leader. I needed to be in contact all the time.

The other units called a halt for the night shortly after us. We had all been out here for three days so far and we hadn't been sleeping great. None of us was overly used to sleeping on the open ground, but we made do. As always, before we tried to get some rest, we called out our coordinates so people knew where to look for us if we didn't make contact in the morning.

We set a watch for ourselves every night. It made me wonder what the overwatch boys did, because they were alone out there. They were snipers. Supposedly, they had been sent in to watch our backs if we got into a scuffle with the aliens. Since bullets didn't kill them – unless there were a metric ton of them per alien – I suspected there was slightly more to their mission than we were originally told.

We had only found out about the overwatch at the last minute. We had been told four units of four were going on the search and rescue mission, but there were two extras on each chopper when we were dropped in and they had big guns. Really big guns. The exact type of weapons that make me very nervous, if not completely terrified. And I gotta tell you those guns scared me more than the idea of walking into those alien nests.

Once we had landed and set ourselves up and were ready to set out, they told us who they were and what they were doing there. The idea was they follow about two hundred metres behind us and watch our backs. Since we were yet to find any nests, or aliens, or even a sign any had been there really, they hadn't had a whole lot to do except watch. Our overwatch soldier was call sign Delta Overwatch. Very original right? Since we were team Delta and obviously I was dubbed Delta Leader. The other teams were Alpha, Bravo and Charlie, in case you were wondering.

I had tried talking to our overwatch soldier via the radio, but he was reasonably uncommunicative, which lent more credence to my theory they weren't just there to watch our backs. They had some other secret mission or purpose we weren't allowed to know about. I'm not altogether sure that's a good thing.

◆

The morning after my fitness test, myself and the other people who signed up for the extra training were told to warm up and meet our new fitness instructor over at the flats, which was an area at the far end of the base. We got there before our instructor, which I thought was probably a good thing. It showed we were dedicated, I guess.

When the drill instructor drove up and stepped out of his jeep (yes, he had driven over), we snapped to attention. And then stayed that way in complete shock. Standing in front of us wasn't just any random drill instructor like I – and I bet everyone else – had been expecting. Though he wore the same uniform as us.

We knew him. Everybody knew him. He was famous, after all. His name was Brock Hunter. He was a pro wrestler and an actor. Also probably one of the fittest men in the entire world. So I guess it made sense for him to be a fitness trainer here, if I'd thought about it at the time.

I was pretty awed personally. I LOVE pro wrestling. I watched it on television all the time. Rochelle and I get pay-per-view of all the pro wrestling matches; well we did, I guess I should say now, especially the ones Brock was in. We had even travelled interstate to see the pro wrestling tour when it came to Australia. Brock hadn't made that trip because he was shooting a movie at the time (which was pretty disappointing) but it was awesome just the same.

Wrestling is the one of the times I can deal with men looking all huge and muscly. Body builders are gross, they get too big and they look like they are wearing balloons on their arms; I feel ill looking at them. But don't ever tell them that. They get really pissy and have a cry at you (actually all men do). But pro wrestlers look good. Big and solid but still able to move in a normal looking way. And just between you and me, Brock Hunter is the HOTTEST guy on the planet. And of course, totally unattainable, which just makes him that much hotter.

And now here he was, standing in front of me, well, us. All of us were awed by his body. He was, for lack of a better word; perfect. He carried a lot of muscle on his shoulders and he looked strong, but not like a balloon. It was natural muscle. He had solid legs, too. And his arms looked like they could hold the weight of the world. If I'd let myself, I could have easily gotten lost in fantasies about him and missed every word that anyone said to me; I mean us.

I wasn't sure what to expect from him, but I knew he was here to help us. We all listened intently. So far, our drill instructors had been tough, a few of them yelled a lot. I couldn't imagine Brock Hunter yelling much. He was very soft spoken in interviews and even the louder scenes in his movies always seemed forced. It was the only time his acting wasn't at its best.

As he looked over the five of us, we all stood frozen under his gaze. He looked as though he was sizing us up to work out where to start. I wondered if he had been given files about us or if he was just told to come out here and get us fit. His facial expressions gave nothing away. When he continued to say nothing, a couple of the others started fidgeting under his gaze (I was fighting the fidgets as hard as I could). At the end of the day, we weren't used to this kind of scrutiny. We were just civilians, most of us barely more than kids. And our worlds had been torn apart. As soon as he took a deep breath and opened his mouth to speak, we all snapped back to attention.

"I'd be guessing from the looks on your faces that you know who I am. But let me introduce myself properly, anyway. It is the polite thing to do, after all," he said with a blank expression on his face, but I thought I caught a small smile at the end there. He was toying with us. "I'm Brock Hunter. I am running this course, so I am your trainer for the foreseeable future. I volunteered to be here, same as you. And I will try and get you ready for whatever you might face out there.

You will report here at oh seven hundred hours every morning. I would advise you not to eat a big breakfast before-hand because you will throw it up. I will make sure of it. Make no mistake, I will work you hard. Some of you I think are here because you believe you failed at the fitness test they set yesterday, some are here because it was suggested to you by an instructor, I wouldn't worry about the why too much, it's not like you're getting thrown out or anything, but your results are a good guideline to help you with what you want to work on and that's what I'm here for." He flashed a brilliant smile at us after he finished and I don't know about the others, but I had to hold back a nervous gulp. This was exciting and terrifying all at once.

3

As the last shadows of the afternoon disappeared and became night, we settled in to rest up. I told the rest of my unit I wanted to get a good rest, because I wanted everyone sharp tomorrow. We had already gone too long without some sign of what we were looking for. There had been no sign of the missing recruits and none of the aliens. If we hadn't found something by tomorrow night, then we may as well go home failures. My gut told me something was missing and something big was coming.

I should take this opportunity to introduce my unit. I already told you my designation is Delta Leader. My second in command is Aiden Davis. He is twenty-five, about the same height and build as me – about five-nine and seventy-five kilos-ish – and he aced weapons training. Next is Daniel Jones, he is a chubby kid. Nineteen years old and every bit a kid for it, but he's a good fighter. He was a gamer, sitting in his room all the time playing video games before all this started. He is taller than me, well over six foot – maybe six-five – but as I said, he's a bit on the chubby side. Last but not least is Abigail Cameron, she's twenty; we call her Cam. She is really little, like maybe five-two tops. She wouldn't weigh more than forty-five, maybe fifty kilos with her muscle. And she is quick, really quick. I've seen her fight and I can honestly say the aliens are going to have their work cut out for them when they come up against her. Cam had earned her nickname for a couple of reasons. One is her surname, the other was because she has a photographic memory, maybe even eidetic. I had a feeling I would end up relying on that later.

I respect them. They are smart and about as scared as I am, but they listen and they have good ideas. They were happy enough for me to be named team leader, but I pretty much think of them as equals, and we listen to each other. Once we were divided into units back on the base, they moved us around so we were bunking together as a unit. We actually took the time to get to know each other. We had shared information about ourselves and our lives. We hadn't shared our stories yet, what specifically had brought us here, there hadn't really been time. Although I know Daniel is an Aussie like me, but the other two are American.

Each night we've been out here, after we set a watch rotation, we sit and share what we jokingly call campfire stories. Mostly we just talk. Decompress. We generally talk about anything that did or didn't happen throughout the day. We talk about our theories on overwatch. I haven't told them my theory. I can't bring myself to let my personal fears see light. I don't want them to lose hope that one day we can win this war and have some semblance of normality back in our lives.

We didn't talk for very long this night. We just sat quietly in our own thoughts. We still hadn't found any of the nests we were supposed to be looking for. And we were all starting to feel a little dejected. I think to some degree we were hoping to find something, anything, even if it was just to get some closure. We were a little naïve perhaps, but we were also young and in unknown territory. We thought we were going to be making a difference. Well, we hoped we would anyway, because if we didn't take our world back from these monsters, then who would?

Aiden had first watch tonight. He was supposed to relieve me after three hours, but I heard him creeping into camp trying not to wake the others after only an hour.

"What's up Aiden?" I asked, barely above a whisper. I didn't want to wake them either.

"There's someone or something creeping around out there. I don't know who it is, or even what it is, but it seems to be staying about twenty or thirty metres back. Like it doesn't want to be seen. I just didn't want to wake everyone in case it's nothing. Sorry."

"There's no need to apologise, Aiden. I wasn't asleep and besides, it's my job, I guess... to make decisions about these things." I tried to put some levity into my voice, but God, it was hard. I was nervous.

I didn't want to think about what might be out there any more than Aiden did.

I got up and grabbed my pack. I slept fully clothed as we all did, but I didn't go anywhere without my pack, not even on watch. It's where I stored my knives while I slept. My whole world was in that pack right now and I wasn't going to be separated from it in any way if it could be helped. I would have slept on it if it wasn't full of knives (I carried extras).

We went over to where Aiden had been sitting and sat quietly to watch for a while. It wasn't long before I heard what Aiden had been talking about. I didn't think it was an alien. If it was, it must have been seriously injured because it was moving slow. It could have been some animal, but I didn't think that was right either. The way it sounded and the way it moved were more like a human. A human trying to be quiet and sneak up. And honestly, if we hadn't been listening for it, then I'm pretty sure neither Aiden nor I would have heard anything at all.

I decided I would go over and check it out. Leaving Aiden sitting there watching out for the others, I grabbed one of my knives out of my pack and slowly made my way towards where the noise was coming from. I had gone about thirty metres when I heard someone breathing quietly. It wasn't the ragged breathing full of fear or trepidation I half expected to hear. It was the breathing of someone completely calm.

It was very dark tonight. I could only make out vague shapes at any kind of distance, so was pretty sure the breathing I was hearing came from the large human-ish shaped lump five metres ahead of me. I couldn't make out any features at all, but I could see it was a very large person. Most likely a man. And he was carrying something. Something that looked like it might be heavy.

It suddenly dawned on me who it must be. It also answered a few questions I had about what he did at night. I almost turned around and walked away there and then, but something wouldn't let me, not without making one hundred percent sure I was right.

"Nice night for sneaking up on our unit." I said quietly, but loud enough for him to hear me. "You know, you could have just called if you wanted to talk. I would have answered." Okay, so I couldn't help it, I had to be a smartarse. I was fairly sure of who it was, so the rest just hid my nerves, just in case I was wrong. My knife was in my right hand close to my body, ready to move immediately if it turned out I was wrong. But in the meantime. Smartarse.

He was silent for a long moment and I started to wonder if he was going to bother replying at all. But I didn't need him to answer anymore. I was sure I was right about who it was and I could see he was breathing... normally, so this wasn't some kind of alien trap. I waited a couple more moments before turning away and walking back over to Aiden.

"It's just overwatch, coming closer for the night. Why don't you go get some sleep and I'll take your watch? You can take mine later. I'm wide awake now, anyway." I put confidence into my voice to try and let Aiden know it was normal for overwatch to be coming in closer at night. Even though I didn't have a clue if it was normal or not. But until I found out more, I was going to make them think it was. Aiden looked at me carefully, trying to make sure I wasn't trying to hide some danger from him he should be defending me from. Apparently, he decided all was well, because he shrugged his shoulders and turned back toward the camp. Waving as he walked over to where I had been sleeping before he'd woken me.

I waited for him to fall asleep. His breathing soon calmed down as his body relaxed a little and after another agonising ten minutes, his gentle snoring joined the others as he finally drifted into a proper sleep.

Once that happened, I waited another five minutes before standing up and walking back out to where overwatch had been sitting when I found him. He didn't look as though he had moved at all. I could tell he was awake though because as I approached, he was too still. Almost as though he had turned himself into stone. I waited a moment, only to see if he would say anything this time before I walked right up to him. I had a couple of options on how I could handle this. Instead of being a smartarse, this time I went for direct.

"What are you doing here?" I whispered. We may have felt alone out here, but that didn't mean we were. He didn't move or answer straight away, but this time I waited him out, all the time my head on a swivel, watching out for danger from anywhere. I didn't really think there would be any, but I also wasn't going to be the reason we got ambushed or surprised. Ok so I tried to wait him out, but I'm not the most patient person in the world.

"Well? Are you going to speak? I know you can. I've heard you on the radio." My impatience almost made me dive back into smartarse mode. But as I was opening my mouth to speak again, he looked up. His dark eyes stared straight into mine for a moment, then he opened his mouth to speak. But the comment that came out was one I never would have expected.

"What is a pretty girl like you doing in a place like this?" he said it with a gentle cheeky smile and I couldn't help myself. I laughed. "Sorry. I didn't mean to sneak up on you or scare your sentry, but I wanted to check how well you kept a watch. It's good, by the way. I know the others have done the same test and other overwatches got a lot closer before they were spotted. Charlie managed to walk right into camp without anyone noticing."

"Um, thanks, I think." I didn't really know what to say. I was in a bit of shock. He simply smiled again. Then he unfolded himself from the uncomfortable-looking crouch he had stayed in from before I first came out to see what was going on almost twenty-five minutes ago. "Is that all you came over for?"

"I was ordered to check your watch, but honestly, I've been coming in at night since the beginning. I don't have anyone watching my back out there like you guys do. I like the idea of knowing someone will at least hear me die if I get attacked in the night." He shrugged as he said it, but again, I didn't quite believe him. There was something else going on and I suddenly really didn't like it.

"You don't talk to us much on the radio," I said. It wasn't a question. I wanted to let him know I wasn't some mindless idiot. I noticed things. "The other overwatch boys don't talk much either. Seems wrong to me. Seems like something else going on." I waited for him to mull over what I said. I wondered if he was going to reply. When he did, it was only half what I expected. He was as much of a smartarse as I am.

"Actually, Bravo Overwatch is a girl. She doesn't sound like it on the radio, I guess. And Alpha and Charlie are brothers, fraternal twins, they are two of the best snipers we have left. It's why they are with the two weaker groups."

"Because they are going to need the most help?" I asked, partially hopeful and partially sarcastic. I couldn't help my concern coming to the surface a little. "Why is the weakest group the Alpha group? Wouldn't it have made more sense to make the weaker groups Charlie and Delta?" I couldn't help asking as well. It was something I was going to wonder about later, may as well ask now.

"I don't know why they did that. I think it just fell out that way, or maybe you guys just surpassed them once you were split up into groups and had already been given your designations. We were only assigned our groups the morning we left." He looked like he wanted to say so much more. So I decided to wait him out.

We were sitting by now in the lookout spot I had chosen earlier in the evening. I had started idly wandering back here after he had finally started talking and he had followed along with me. I waited a while longer for him to continue, but as is my way (you may have noticed) I got impatient. So I tried a different tack.

"What is going on? What aren't we being told?" I cut myself off from asking a million more questions. I wanted answers, but something told me the more I asked, the less I would find out.

"I can't tell you much," he said with a sigh, "we don't know much either. But I can tell you we aren't just here for your protection. That girl. The one you guys rescued from Elko. She got very sick. Turns out she'd been bitten while they had her, but they did something to her. She's changed... by her illness. They don't know if it's some kind of infection. They can't work it out. We're not meant to tell you. But I don't think that's quite fair. The others can do what they want with their groups, but I am choosing to do things my way."

"I...," I started and then paused to collect my thoughts. I wanted to know so much more, but right now I had one pressing question on my mind. "We're on our own out here, aren't we?" I paused for a moment, "they aren't going to come get us if things go wrong, are they?"

"No. No one is coming for you. Did you really think they were?" he asked it gently, as though trying very hard not to imply I was stupid. "No, I figured there would be no rescue. That's why I wasn't planning on anything going wrong. I was kind of hoping there'd be a pickup at the other end if we win, though." I answered honestly.

"Have you shared your thoughts with the rest of your group? Do they know?" he asked. I was cautious about answering. He was asking a lot of questions and not answering very many. But I didn't see the harm in answering this one right now.

"No, I haven't told them yet. I was hoping I was wrong and I wouldn't have to, but since it would appear I am right, then I will have to tell them soon. Before we get into any trouble. Is there anything else you can tell me that might help? Anything at all?"

"No, I don't think so. Nothing that will help you. But I do have one more question...if that's ok?" He waited for me to deliberate a moment, when I nodded, he looked at me a little sheepishly, "Can I stay here tonight?" He asked in a put-on whiny voice.

I burst out laughing again. I couldn't help it. It was just the last thing I expected when he said he had one more question. I quieted myself quickly, but I made Delta jump. It was worth it just for that.

"I'm Tyne, by the way," I introduced myself through what remained of my now stifled giggles. I figured he knew who I was already, but I felt I should let him know, anyway. "And yes, you can stay at my place tonight." He seemed to let out a breath – as though he really thought I was going to say no – and then smiled.

"I'm Tim, call sign Delta, which is also my last name. That might be why they gave me that as my call sign," he smiled impishly, "why don't you use your call sign?"

"I don't have one." I replied simply, "I haven't been given a call sign."

"You don't really get given a call sign; you earn one. They all call you 'Boss'. Sounds like a call sign to me."

I thought about this for a moment. When we had first been assigned together, I had told them I didn't want to be their boss, so I'd only issue an actual order when I absolutely had to. Ever since then, they had jokingly called me boss. I hadn't realised they did it on the radio. Or anyone else would have noticed.

I didn't say anything to Delta. I didn't know if I wanted a call sign, really. It kind of implied I was going to be here for a while. And I still believed I was getting out and going home as soon as these stupid aliens were disposed of – to go and dispose of some more back home, hopefully. He seemed to understand my silence and we sat there for most of the rest of the night not saying much, switching off napping every couple of hours, letting the rest of the team get a good night's sleep.

I woke from my last short snooze as the sun was peaking over the horizon. Delta was sitting in a meditative position facing the sunrise, appearing to enjoy the first rays of natural light on his face. To the outside world, I suppose it might have looked like he was asleep, but I could see the natural tension through his shoulders that told me he was very awake and alert and probably could have pinpointed the exact moment I woke up too.

Once he was sure I was awake, he gently unfolded himself from the ground and disappeared into the horizon without a word. I don't know if he wanted me to keep his joining us overnight as a secret, but he didn't say anything, so I took it as a sign he was leaving it up to my discretion. I decided to keep it under my hat for now. I sat up and finished the watch on my own. It only lasted about half an hour, anyway.

4

The next day passed uneventfully, as did the day after that. At night, once everyone was asleep and I was on watch, Tim would come in for the night and we would catch up on all the things we didn't talk about during the day in front of people or over the radio. He started opening up more and wanted to learn a little about the team. I didn't know if I was doing the right thing by telling him, but I think at this point it was useless to worry about it.

After another two days of nothing, we were getting bored on our march across the forest. I realise that sounds ridiculous for a group of supposed soldiers, but there is just no other word for it. We started talking about our lives before the invasion and what we planned or hoped to do afterwards, when we won the war, because there was no option of failure in any of our heads. We were spread out a little on our march and trying to be quiet, so we used the radios on a private channel I had claimed (I hoped no one was listening in on it anyway). My most recent concession to Tim (I know, I should really call him Delta – I'll try and remember from now on) was to let him in on the secret of why he could never hear us during the day, when we were chatting amongst ourselves about unimportant crap – our private channel.

Cam was starting to tell us a story about her mum when I heard a lot of screaming coming over the radio; my radio is duel channel I had discovered, so I could be on our channel but still be listening in on the main one like we were supposed to. Bravo team had walked headfirst into a nest without realising. Now they were in trouble and they knew it. I held my hand up for a halt and froze to listen; Bravo Team was the team Rochelle had been assigned to. They were all screaming, but not for help. They were just screaming at each other. Their leader was shouting orders and it sounded like the others were trying to obey by varying degrees.

Bravo Overwatch (I had to admit, now that I was listening for it, I could tell she was a woman) was trying to help them without getting too involved. She was probably trying to help them a little more than was technically authorised; I was secretly praising her and hoping she didn't get reprimanded at the same time. We heard something that sounded like the high-pitched scream of a wounded animal. Bravo leader was screaming someone was down but we couldn't make out who. The last thing we heard before the radio went dead was the sound of a gun being fired. We knew Bravo Overwatch was the only one carrying a gun, so we knew she had to have been the one who fired. But who or what did she fire at?

Knowing what I knew and didn't know about the overwatch soldiers' real mission, I didn't want to think about what had happened back there. I wanted desperately to get on the radio and call out to Rochelle to ask if she was ok. But I knew I couldn't do that. I had to wait for a report. It was a nerve-racking wait for me in particular. I knew I wouldn't be able to move again until I knew Rochelle was ok (yes, I also know how stupid that is, but give me a break, I'm only human).

It was getting a little late in the afternoon and we were due to stop soon, anyway. I told the others just to make camp here for the night. Bravo Leader still hadn't radioed in to let us know what was going on, but for all I knew, they could have been dealing with injuries (and hopefully finding a safe place to hole up and recover for the night). I could only hope Rochelle was alive and ok.

Camp was quiet that night. We dared risk a small campfire to heat some water for tea. Other than that, we ate our food cold like we did every other night. After the others had bedded down for the night and I had set myself up for first watch, I heard Tim coming slowly in towards where I was sitting.

He must have already checked I had first watch (which I had done the last four nights). Either that or he was going to come right into camp to talk to me anyway, because there was no hesitation as he walked right up and sat down in front of me. He watched me for a moment. We had talked a couple of nights ago about the other teams and the people we had known before this. He must have remembered what I had said about Rochelle being my best friend… my sister.

"She's ok." It was a simple sentence said with the confidence of someone who knew rather than someone who was trying to placate. I looked at him. He held my gaze.

"Tell me?" I asked him, trying to keep the pleading out of my voice (I think I failed).

"They had one casualty. The young boy. He got bitten. Overwatch was ordered to take him out, but she was hesitating – that's not what we are supposed to be here for – I think she was waiting for someone to tell her she misheard. Another one came up behind him and ripped him in half. She shot it in the head at the same time your friend stuck her blade through the back of its throat. Overwatch is pretty impressed with her, actually.

"Bravo Leader copped a few hits. He got cut and scratched a bit. He has a nasty gash on his neck that has needed some tending to and he can't really talk much. His second – I think they said his name was Max – said he may have nicked his vocal chords. Stupid idiot did that injury to himself, too. Pulled his knife up in the middle of a fight and didn't turn the blade away from himself."

I stared at him in disbelief. I had so many questions jumbling around in my head; I just couldn't grab one to start asking. I opened my mouth to start so many times, eventually I just closed it again while I tried to collect my thoughts. Tim waited me out. All in all, he seemed fairly relaxed. Instead of aggravating me (which I would have expected) it actually calmed me down.

"So, what are they going to do now?" I finally asked. I couldn't pin down any other question to ask, and it seemed as important as any.

"They are going to go on. They had to leave the body behind. Maybe we'll be lucky and the aliens will leave it alone so we can go back for it when this is all over. They were only able to move a short distance from the nest before they had to stop and tend wounds, but they are planning on heading out early in the morning. Before first light, if they can."

I didn't really know what else to say to that. None of the other questions rattling around in my head seemed important anymore. The reality of our situation out here really sank in hard with that. Well, as far as I knew the situation thus far.

We sat there in silence for a while. I probably should have been trying to get some sleep or encouraging Tim to do so, but I couldn't seem to gather my thoughts properly to do anything. After about another hour, I looked over at him and he looked as though he was struggling to stay awake. I told him to sleep and prepared to take the watch. My mind wandered.

We were already warmed up as we had been instructed, so Brock put us straight to work going over things from the fitness test. He must have had some information about us because he seemed to already know all the areas we had struggled with. He didn't pay any particular attention to any one person that I noticed, but I assumed he was watching everyone very carefully. At the end of a gruelling two-hour session, Brock congratulated us all and told us we had all done really well and he didn't think it would be too hard to get us up to scratch. Just listening to his calm voice sent my crush into overdrive.

I managed to shake most of it off by the time I got to combat and weapons training later that morning. But it was still there in the back of my mind and it threw me off a little. My instructor appeared to notice and seemed to be working me harder. Rochelle noticed too; she didn't ask then, but the look she gave me said I was going to get drilled later. After a little while, some of the other recruits noticed we had an audience, just one man, hidden in the shadows. It made most of them work a little bit harder and some of them chatter amongst themselves, causing the instructor to yell a bit more than normal.

Rochelle and I just kept working. I knew she wouldn't care who was watching. We were there to work (she had always been like that). I found myself less than curious, mostly because I already had a suspicion about who it was standing in the shadows watching. One of the other recruits nudged me and told me she thought he was watching me, which went a long way to confirming my suspicion (and worst fear) about who it might be. Correspondingly, my fighting got worse and Rochelle really noticed. I tried to pull it together, but my mind was all over the place. Rochelle took a water break and dragged me off to the side of the mats to make sure I was ok.

I told her about my morning training session. About who was running it, it was all I really needed to say, but it was enough. Rochelle knew how strong this particular crush was. She also knew about my self-conscious nature.

*At school around Year Ten, there had been a guy I liked. Rochelle had been the only person who knew about it and we never discussed it at school. Our classmates were brutal at high school and very cruel. And given this guy was on the popular side of the scale, it was better to be extra careful about mentioning it. A rumour started flying around this guy was going to ask me to the school dance coming up. I freaked out. Not because I was excited (although I was a little, I guess) but because I thought someone had found out about my crush and they were playing some kind of cruel trick on me – don't laugh ok, the kids at my school would actually do something like that. They were all very 'mean girls in Carrie' – and I didn't want to be the butt of their jokes, having managed to fly fairly well under their radar for most of my high school life so far.

A couple of days later, I had been paired with him in science. I can't remember what experiment we were doing exactly, but I remember we were using bunsen burners. I remember that part really well because I managed to use that bunsen burner – not deliberately – to do a fair bit of damage. He had looked at me to ask me to show him what the teacher meant about something and I had gotten extremely nervous under his gaze; I had managed to knock the lit burner off the edge of the table, then to make matters worse, in my attempt to fix my mistake I had reached to turn it off, only to turn it right up, which managed to set fire to the rubbish bin it landed next to and a whole lot of other things from there. I had managed to burn down half the classroom by the time we got it under control. No one was hurt, in case you were wondering. But I never looked at that guy again.*

She looked around and saw the guy who was watching us. He was easy to spot by then because half the class was sneaking furtive glances at him when they thought no one else was looking. And if you're thinking this was a class made up of mostly girls, you would be wrong. It was a sixty-forty split with more guys and they were looking just as much as the girls. She confirmed it was Brock Hunter and it looked to her like he was watching everyone. (I think she was lying a little to calm me down). We tried to get back to work and after about five minutes, Rochelle told me he was leaving. I had my back to that side of the room so I wouldn't see him in case he really was watching me.

I took her word for it and didn't turn to look. Instead, I focused on trying to calm my breathing and get back into a good sparring rhythm. It took me a while, but I got there eventually.

Delta's snore brought me out of the memory quickly. To keep myself awake, I went through my bag and checked on all the extra things in there. I carried five spare blades and a bunch of boxing bandages – you know, the kind people wear under their gloves in the ring. They were an added gift that my team had been given. A gift from Brock. He had shown me how to do them up properly, along with a few other tricks I could use them for. It made my pack heavier than everyone else's but it was worth it for the added protection.

There were a few things Brock had made sure of before he disappeared on his own mission. One of them was the extra items in my bag, plus a paper map of this forest we were searching. I had gifted that to Cam to look after. She had been studying cartography when all this had started and she loved maps. She had been putting her memory to good use. I hadn't said anything to her about it, but I secretly hoped she was still using that knowledge.

It was another hour or so before I heard what sounded like muffled screaming coming from the radio headset I wore. I had taken it off my ear for a while and it was hanging around my neck. I placed it back on my ear and heard the most terrifying sounds at this time of the night.

Bravo team had been attacked by the aliens. My heart stopped and a sickening lump formed in my gut. They had probably been tracked from the nest they had cleared. Though how the dying ones had communicated their distress so many hours earlier was a mystery. Bravo team hadn't gone far from the nest because of their injuries. They would have been easy to track. And their watches probably weren't as good as they should have been. Bravo Overwatch was probably propped up in a tree nearby. As far as I knew, none of the other overwatch soldiers came in overnight, at least not the way Tim did.

From what I could tell, the aliens were on top of them before they were even really aware or awake enough to do anything. They were screaming as they died. I sat there frozen, listening to them fighting for their lives. Tears were streaming down my cheeks as I heard Rochelle screaming out in pain. I heard what sounded like three shots fired and then a scream that could only have been Bravo Overwatch. Hers sounded like a death keen as well, so I could probably assume she had been closer than I thought at first if they had found her, too.

I sensed rather than heard Tim rise and come over to me. He must have still had his radio in his ear and the noise had woken him. He put an arm around me in a consoling gesture. It made me cry harder. My best friend had just died painfully, more or less alone and there was nothing I could do. I wasn't there with her, as we always thought we would be. I cried myself out after a while, although I don't remember much of it. Afterwards, I must have fallen asleep.

I dreamed of the conversation Rochelle and I had later on that evening, after my crappy training day.

We were sitting by the door of the barracks. Everyone else was still off in the Mess Hall eating dinner, so we had the place to ourselves, but we kept our voices down, anyway. In the dream, Rochelle's voice echoed a little as she spoke.

"Are you okay?" Rochelle asked me.

"Yeah, I think so... I mean, it's just a silly crush, isn't it?" I tried to be flippant about the situation, but Rochelle saw through me.

"Oh don't even try that with me, girly. This may be a silly crush but that doesn't make it any less real... I remember you dragging me interstate to go and see the wrestling and I remember how bitterly disappointed you were when he didn't make the trip down under with the others," she paused building up steam, "and this is different. He is here in front of you. You are going to be working closely with him for a while. There is a chance you will have to talk to him, eventually. Are you going to be able to handle that?"

"What am I? Five? Of course I can talk to him, he's just a man..."

"Yeah, he is just a man, but you don't really believe that... I've known you your whole life. And you have had exactly two crushes in your life that tied your tongue and left you a mess on the floor... and Brock Hunter is the bigger one of the two..." she didn't seem to want to finish the thought.

"Well, at least I can't burn anything down here..." I said, trying once again to make light of the situation. "We aren't working with bunsen burners and science classrooms."

"Ha ha yeah, I guess so," Rochelle said, finally laughing a little at my weak joke. "I just remember how much that incident upset you. If something goes wrong this time, you can't afford to lose it. I know you have dated guys since then and been fine, but I'm worried that this one might just undo you." I was touched, as I always was, that she cared so much about me... but I suppose that's what best friends were like. I should be used to it by now. I smiled at her.

"I love you; you know that?"

"Yeah, I know," she said, "I love you too."

"Urgh, what am I going to do?" I asked, exasperation colouring my tone.

"It would be so much easier if you could just shut your eyes when you had to talk to him," she looked up at me and continued, "that way you could humanise him a bit more, might help you get some control over yourself... and your crush."

"Yeah..." I paused to think about it for a second, "yeah actually, *that's not a bad idea. I wonder if that would work? Maybe I should give it a try."*

"Can't hurt," she replied, "Unless you're running at the time or something." She finished with a laugh. We didn't say anything after that. We heard the others coming back from dinner, so we returned to our racks. The last thing she said to me before we went to sleep was.

"Tomorrow is a new day."

5

I woke as the very first ray of light brightened the sky overhead. Tim was sitting nearby, watching me and keeping watch at the same time. He must have stayed up all night. I felt terrible. Aside from all the things I was feeling emotionally, I had deprived him of his sleep all night. I don't think there was much chance of us making it far today if we marched. Although I knew we had to move, it was one of the ways to help prevent attack, keep moving. Always. It had been drummed into our heads from the moment we had started combat training.

Once I was awake, I expected Tim to leave like he normally did, but he seemed to be waiting for something. Finally, as I opened my mouth to say something, he spoke himself.

"Are you going to tell them what happened last night?" as he said it, he gestured towards where the rest of my team slept with a nod of his head.

"I have to. I can't not tell them. They will figure it out pretty quickly, anyway. I don't think any of them know anyone on Bravo team, but that doesn't make it any easier... a whole team just got wiped out and their overwatch to boot. It doesn't bode well for the rest of us, does it?"

"Bravo Overwatch was my friend, you know. She never would have pulled the trigger on our own people, no matter who gave the order, even if it was her own father. She would have hated herself too much, so she never would have done it." He paused to look at me. Up until now, he had been looking at the trees. He saw the question in my eye and interpreted it correctly. "Her father is a general. He is the reason she joined the army. We don't know if he is alive or not." As he explained everything, I noticed a tear in the corner of his eye and realised they were probably better friends than I understood.

"Tell me about her?" I asked gently. I knew I would have to return the favour and tell him about Rochelle. But this way I could have a breather first.

"Her name was Tayler Cassidy. She was very tough, tougher than most people thought. And she was a good sniper. She had trouble getting trained because she was a girl. The higher ups didn't think girls could be snipers; even in this day and age, when we are all supposed to be enlightened."

"How did she do it in the end?"

"She conned someone from the sniper unit into training her. Then she used reverse psychology on them and said she didn't need them anyway because she already knew how to shoot. So they tested her and saw how good she was. She was in the unit without question then."

"Who was the brave and possibly stupid one who decided to train her behind their backs?" I asked, although I had a sneaking suspicion I already knew the answer.

"Me!" he smiled broadly with the answer. "I have never regretted that decision. She is one of the best. She became far better than me within a few months. The only two on base better than her are Alpha and Charlie. She was one of a kind."

He asked me about Rochelle, and I told him. We swapped stories back and forth for a while and then sat in silence until the sun actually showed itself over the horizon. My mind wandered again.

I was running around on an oval, kicking a soccer ball back and forth with Rochelle. We were having fun and must have been about eight years old. We were at the park up the street from our houses. Some other kids came over and wanted to play with us, so we let them, but after a short while they got pushy and tried to take over the game and steal our soccer ball. It had been Rochelle's Christmas present

from her grandmother who died the year before, so she was a little attached to it. One of the boys tried to walk away with it and Rochelle, who had already tried without success to negotiate the return of her precious soccer ball, started crying. She tried to avoid confrontation when she was younger.

I however, had no such qualms.

"Oi, you little punk!" The boy holding the ball turned and laughed at me, "give the ball back, you filthy little thief!" Even Rochelle looked at me strangely at that one, but it was something I had heard on TV and it suited the situation as far as I could tell.

"What are you going to do if I don't, shrimp?" He must have been a little older than us, but calling me shrimp was going a bit far. He wasn't that much taller or bigger than me.

"Make you." I said simply. In my head, it wasn't a matter of if he was going to give the ball back, it was a matter of when and how I was going to take it from him.

The group of kids around him all laughed. He was obviously the ringleader of this little group and they were all used to him getting whatever he wanted all the time.

"Whatever you reckon, shrimp, it's my ball now." Taunting never went down well with me. Not sure why, I just didn't have the patience for it. I looked at Rochelle's face again as the boy and his group turned away and continued to walk off and I saw red.

Before Rochelle could think to stop me, I launched myself at the boy and tackled him from behind. His friends were too shocked to do anything to stop me. He managed to roll himself over, only to meet my fist with his face. His tooth cut my knuckle a little, but I barely noticed it. I didn't wait for him or anyone else to recover themselves. I grabbed the soccer ball out of what was left of his loose grip and ran back to Rochelle.

I handed her the soccer ball and then we turned and ran straight home, not looking back to see if the horrible kids were chasing us. As soon as we were inside my front yard, we stopped running. We felt safe here. There were parents close by to defend us if danger came calling. Rochelle tossed the soccer ball gently over the fence so it was safely in her own yard and then pulled me into a massive hug. Tears were still streaming down her face as she choked out the words,

"Thank you... Tyne, I can't believe you just did that." She laughed as she spoke.

Jumping to a new memory, a particularly sad one. It was the day of my father's funeral. It had finally hit me he really wasn't coming back. He was really gone. People were trying to talk at me and nothing was going in. Rochelle was holding my hand tightly. I think she was the only thing keeping me in the world. I felt terrible. I couldn't even help my mum and she was on her own now. Rochelle's mum was looking after her and doing a great job, but I felt like it should be me.

Someone came over to talk to me. I didn't register who it was, but something they said came through loud and clear.

"He's in a better place now, you know." said the disembodied voice. (I still don't know who to be angry at for that comment, so it's easy to remember them as disembodied)

"What the hell is wrong with you?" My thirteen-year-old self yelled at the person. Rochelle gripped my hand tighter to ground me, but this time it really didn't help. "Why would you say something like that? He wasn't sick, or in pain, or anything like that. So why would being away from us be a better place? He died in a car accident, you moron! Some idiot drunk driver smashed into the side of him. Do you think he would prefer that to being here with his family?" It was the first time I had ever called an adult a name. I barely registered the shock of the people around me at my language. I think the disembodied voice must have gone to say something else because Rochelle's voice rang out next to me, her grip tighter still on my hand.

"Piss off mate, keep your stupid comments to yourself," Her voice was even louder than mine and the person standing in front of me fled, probably in embarrassment. More quietly to me, Rochelle continued, "he better not have said anything like that to your mum." We both turned our heads to find her. She was sitting in a chair with her head in her hands, sobbing. Rochelle's mother was sitting next to her, rubbing her back and holding her. Rochelle's dad was standing off to the side and slightly in front of them, like a bodyguard. He caught my eye and nodded his head and gave a small thumbs up without moving his hands from in front of him. I knew Rochelle's mum - though on this

occasion I felt sure she wouldn't punish us – would go spare if she knew he'd applauded us for speaking to an adult that way.

Jump ahead to another memory. We were almost nineteen and trying to plan our birthday party. My boyfriend at the time and I were having problems. He could be a lovely guy sometimes, but he was quite uptight and I was such a calm and relaxed person, it just didn't make for a happy relationship. I was going to end things with him when I saw him next. I think a part of him knew it was coming, but he was trying to hold on.

Our guest list was pretty short, considering. We were only inviting about thirty people. We knew a lot of people, but there weren't many that we considered real friends and even fewer that we considered close friends.

My boyfriend turned up on the doorstep. Rochelle had answered the door. I was in the bathroom at the time. He made polite conversation with her, asked what she was up to. She told him about the birthday party list we were compiling. He must have been looking at it, because he asked about a couple of names on it. She told him who they were. Friends/ex boyfriends/etc. he didn't say anything after that.

I came out of the bathroom and the look he gave me was pure venom. I was taken aback for a second, thinking, what could possibly be wrong? But he didn't make me wait for long.

"What the hell do you mean by inviting your ex to your birthday party? Are you trying to cheat on me? Do you think I'm stupid?" He advanced on me while he was yelling all of this at me. I was temporarily frozen in shock. Rochelle was watching, completely confused. The particular ex he was talking about was one he had met before and gotten along with. But then he did something unforgivable. He slapped me full force in the face.

I slapped him back as I spoke to him. Rage colouring my voice more than I would have liked.

"Who the hell do you think you are to hit me? Over an ex who has been a friend since high school? An ex that you have met many times and gotten along with fine? How dare you..." I ran out of words. I was so angry and upset I couldn't even get words into my brain to spit at him.

"You bitch! You have no right to talk to me like that after what you have done." He slapped me again and I was so shocked I didn't even raise a hand to defend myself. I barely registered Rochelle flying across the room. She punched him cleanly in the side of the head, hard enough to knock him off balance.

"Don't you ever lay another finger on her, you foul, useless punk. If you really believe you can get away with slapping my best friend, then you are as stupid as you look. No matter what the reason." He looked at Rochelle in shock, as though he had never expected anything like this from her. "Get out of our house and don't ever come back here or near her again. You are nothing but a cockroach and if I ever see you again..." She left the threat hanging in the air while she pointed to the door. "My cousin will come around to your house tomorrow and get the rest of Tyne's things. He's a cop, so you might not want to slap him."

He turned and walked to the door. Slamming it behind him as he left. I sank down to the floor in a mixture of relief and shock. Rochelle sat next to me and held me while I cried. We had always been there for each other. It was hard to accept she was gone.

Tim touched me gently on the shoulder, bringing me back to the present. I could see he was a little edgy. I thought he wanted to go before the others woke up. As he usually did. But he told me he wanted to wake them up and get moving early. He was edgy about a possible attack. I was feeling it a little myself, but as we hadn't hit any nests yet, I didn't really see that it was possible. Although now, I supposed they were very aware we were here, if they hadn't been already.

So I rose and went to wake the unit, Tim following a couple of steps behind me. The first thing I did after they were awake was tell them about the attack the night before and the complete loss of Bravo team. They took it well, considering. I introduced Tim to them, by his name and call sign. He then relayed his edginess to them and we all agreed we would have breakfast on the move and get going straight away.

Cam was the first to recover from her shock and she introduced herself as we walked. I had told them Delta (I really have to remember to call him that) knew our private frequency and they were happy enough to talk via the radio like we normally did. Aiden and Daniel followed suit pretty quickly after with introductions. Soon we were all chatting away amiably, although in hushed tones, as though we were a bunch of mates on a camping trip. I could still read a little tension coming off the others and I guess they could probably feel it coming off me, too. Delta however, seemed completely at ease with this new situation.

About half an hour or so into our day's travel, he dropped back a little into his overwatch position and continued to chat as he walked about a hundred metres behind us.

When everyone was about as relaxed as they were going to get, I broached the subject of the lack of alien presence we had come across since we had been out here. I think we expected to have had a scuffle or two by now, at least. The fact that only Bravo had faced any action was a little confusing. It seemed to be fairly vacant out here. The longer it took to find them, the less likely the people we were supposed to be searching for would be found alive – if at all – and that part was concerning.

Cam had taken the opportunity to get out her paper maps and look them over again. She was comparing the map and the GPS and looked a combination of concerned and confused. She told us we were not where our GPS said we were. According to the GPS, we were skirting the edge of the denser part of the forest, but the map said we were heading more towards the centre, though we were still on the outskirts of the forest proper at the moment. The denser part of the forest seemed like a more likely place for aliens to be hiding. As I thought about what she said, I had to concede she was right. Which brought us to the conclusion, if we were going off information supposedly gathered from the girl we rescued (that the nests were in this outer part of the forest) then she may have been wrong... or lying.

I shared my thought with the others and they agreed with me, the whole thing was fishy. Cam was distracted looking at something on her GPS and her map, so she didn't answer right away. When she finally spoke again, what she said shocked us all.

"The GPS is wrong." She stated it with such conviction, I didn't doubt she was right for a second. I waited for her to go on, as did the others. "According to the GPS, we are still quite near the edge of the forest – which probably doesn't mean much considering how bloody big this forest is – but heading toward the centre. But according to the map, we are at least a couple of miles deeper in than that. Bravo team was deeper than us. Alpha and Charlie are a little deeper than us, but a lot closer to us than Bravo team were. But I'm only going by their GPS co-ordinates they are giving us. I can't pinpoint their actual position for obvious reasons.

"It all points towards the aliens and their nests – if that's what they are – being more towards the centre of the forest, which makes sense as we said, but it doesn't explain why the GPS is wrong…" She was about to continue but I interrupted her.

"What do you mean 'if' nests are what they are?" for some reason, the idea scared me.

"Just that it seems strange to be calling them nests. There is no proof there are male and female aliens in each grouping, which is what would technically make up a nest. They are more like clusters or barracks, that's all. Nothing more sinister than that, I think. This is an army whichever way you look at it.

"But if Bravo finally encountered a nest and they were deeper in than they thought they were, like we are, then we have to consider there is a lot of information we don't know. But given what happened to Bravo team, we have to ask ourselves what is going on here and do we really expect to find any of these so-called hostages alive? Which honestly I don't believe we will anymore. The other thing that worries me is I think we may be a little out of our depth here."

"When do you estimate we left the supposed search area pattern?" Delta chimed in. (It was easier to remember to call him Delta now the others knew about him.)

"Some time around noon the day before yesterday. If we assume Bravo wasn't on theirs and neither are the other two teams, then I would imagine all the changes happened at the same time. But I'm sure the GPS tracked fairly well up until then. It's almost as though someone is changing it as we go. But I can't figure out who or how. But the why seems sort of obvious. They are trying to send us somewhere else without telling us."

We were all stunned by what she said. No one could think of anything to say and the silence stretched on. Eventually it was broken by Delta.

"We have gone far enough for today I think, especially if there is some question about where we are going. Find a camp and I'll be with you shortly. I just want to do a quick scout of the area. Something doesn't feel right to me."

I agreed and we started looking around for a small clearing. I saw something up ahead that looked like a ring of trees. It almost looked like it had been deliberately cleared. I paused my walk mid-step. Something didn't feel right. I could sense the others tensing behind me and I whispered quietly into the radio to tell Delta to get into position. I didn't wait for a response before unsheathing my knives. I wasn't going to have time to bandage up or get set up any better than this. I did a quick head check on the others to make sure they were all ready. They all nodded and I walked forward into the middle of the clearing.

6

They were on us almost immediately. We had a little insight into what fighting them was going to be like, thanks to Bravo Team. So we had previously worked out a vague plan as we walked, how to handle it. We were all naturally very calm people anyway, so no one felt the need to panic and start screaming.

"Hell Boss, they are pretty big." Cam said. She was standing just behind me, so I heard her through the radio and over my shoulder as they sprang into attack.

They tried to separate us straight away and we let them to some degree. Aiden and I were the best fighters, so we took one each, leaving the last one to Cam and Daniel. They were still both really good fighters too, but with Cam's height, I worried about her. Daniel seemed to have the same thought and he stuck to her like glue. I couldn't keep track of what was going on visually with the others because my concentration was taken up in the fight. I couldn't afford to get distracted for a second.

The alien towered over me. It had to be at least seven feet tall (I'm not exaggerating). It had long legs, long arms and really black eyes. There were no pupils that I could see, just endless depths of black (like possessed people portrayed on some TV shows and movies). It had very sharp pointed teeth, with two fangs where the eye teeth would be on a human. They were all dripping with what I took to be saliva or maybe venom. The whole effect was terrifying. We had seen pictures of course and been told about their size, but sometimes all the information in the world just doesn't prepare you for the real thing. I wondered briefly if Rochelle had thought that before Bravo's first fight... before she died.

But then the thing went on the attack for real. It raised its large hand and took a swipe at me. I noticed the ends of its fingers were claws rather than nails. They were long and looked incredibly sharp. Luckily, I didn't find out how sharp just yet. I managed to avoid the claws and I pivoted on my right foot, swinging my blade around in a tight arc. The alien jumped out of the way quickly – my god they were fast – and took another swipe at me with its clawed hand. I tried to dodge, but I felt one of the claws scrape down my arm.

I felt an odd tingling I hoped was nothing more sinister than a little blood. I made a quick dart in with my blade and managed to connect with the flesh along its side. It hissed at me and I pulled back quickly as it made a grab for me again.

It swung both its arms at me and tried to simultaneously hit and grab me. I stepped in close and drove my blade up through its jaw as it bent its head to try and bite me. I felt some resistance of the flesh and muscle as I pushed as hard as I could to get my blade right through its brain.

It floundered, arms flailing, still trying to grab at me. I wondered if it was actually dying. I decided not to take the chance and used my second blade to make a deep cut across the back of its neck severing the spinal cord. The flailing stopped almost immediately, though the ragged breathing continued, eventually slowing.

I retrieved my blades and turned away, trusting it was going to die soon. As I turned, I saw Aiden landing the killing blow on the alien he had been fighting. I continued my turn and saw Cam and Daniel were having a bit of trouble landing blows. The alien they had taken on seemed a little bigger than the one I had been fighting and had a longer reach. It was also much faster. I sensed rather than saw Aiden start forward to help them at the same time I did.

I took about two steps when I heard Delta's voice through the headset in my ear.

"Boss." His voice was raised and strained. "Watch your six!" I turned quickly and saw another alien entering the clearing. It was a little shorter than the other one I had fought – though still really tall – but it was far more solid. Its gaze assessed me and it was sniffing the air around it, as though trying to detect something its eyes couldn't see.

It launched itself at me so fast I barely had time to raise my knife before it was on me. Its attack seemed more ferocious than the last one and I was fatigued. My other fight might have been relatively short, but it had still taken it out of me.

"Boss, I'm coming to you." I heard Aiden's raised voice through the radio and with my uncovered ear. I replied to him at a half yell.

"No Aiden, I can hold this one off for a minute. Help Cam and Daniel." As I finished speaking, I heard the report of a rifle. I assumed it was Delta's because I didn't think any of the other teams were close enough.

I didn't really give it much more thought than that. This alien I was fighting was throwing a lot my way and it was taking everything I had to hold it off. It was so fast that I didn't even have a chance to stop defending and go on the attack myself, although it hadn't managed to actually hurt me at all yet (which I counted more towards luck than any particular skill on my part – unless it wasn't really trying).

"Boss, we're on our way," I heard Aiden say again. This time I didn't argue because he had said 'we' so I knew the other fight was over. I just concentrated on the fight. I was tiring fast and I would now welcome the help when it arrived. I sensed Aiden behind me and I ducked right down and rolled off to the side as fast as I could to get out of the way as Aiden thrust his blade straight into its chest.

The thing kept fighting and Aiden lost his grip on the blade and it remained stuck in the alien's chest; I tried to stand so I could go and help him, but my legs didn't want to lift me and hold my weight just yet. Daniel was at my side a moment later, while I saw Cam launch herself into the air. She managed to grab hold of the alien's arm and swing herself around onto its back, using the momentum of her running jump. She copied the move I had used earlier (although I doubt she had actually been watching) and using the blade in her free hand, she severed the spinal cord through the back of its neck.

It lost control of its arms and legs and fell to the ground, landing in front of Aiden. Cam was thrown off its back and rolled onto the ground. It looked like she hit her head on a log lying nearby. Aiden retrieved his blade from the alien's chest and drove it quickly through its head from underneath the jaw, like I had done. We had been drilled on that move because it was very effective, apparently.

There had been none of the defences we heard about them having. None of the things Bravo team had been screaming about when they had walked into the nest they stumbled across. It was almost as though this was a new nest.

It felt like it was over pretty quickly. There was no panicked screaming. We had been ready for this and we had seen it coming. The whole thing took about ten minutes, give or take and we walked away with only a few injuries. I had a large gash down the back of my arm that Aiden quickly cleaned and threw a dressing on after informing me it was fairly shallow and wouldn't need stitches.

We cleaned and dressed all our wounds quickly before we left the nest. We were hoping maybe it would make us harder to track if the aliens came looking for us. Then we moved on. It was clear we couldn't stop anywhere in the area and it was going to be completely dark in a couple of hours, so we didn't just walk, we ran. Running at full speed in the dense forest was too dangerous, but we still managed to set a pretty good pace. Delta caught up to us before we had gone two hundred metres. I think he wanted to see for himself we were all ok. I thought he would drop back once he had reassured himself, but he didn't. He just kept running along with us. Maybe he didn't want to be at the back on his own (which made perfect sense, really).

We ran until the sun had almost set. We were exhausted and panting. We had changed directions on Cam's suggestions several times and to be honest, she was probably the only one who knew for sure where we were. But we hadn't run into any other nests, so I guessed we weren't any deeper into the forest than we were before. Either that or Cam had led us around anything that could be a nest. We made camp and ate, then using as little light as possible, we double checked our wounds and dressings. Delta was obviously fine, so he helped the rest of us.

It was completely dark by the time we finished. Delta had done a perimeter walk about two hundred metres out while we were setting up to make sure there was nothing in the immediate area. He had told me we were clear as far as he could tell. We would have to keep a very thorough watch tonight. I offered to take the first watch after we had eaten. The others agreed quietly. And bedded themselves down.

After we were sure they were asleep, Tim and I moved off a little back the way we had come. We were sitting about fifty metres from the camp, and we could talk quietly without waking them up.

"You should be sleeping and letting someone else take the watch. You know that, don't you?" Tim asked me.

"Yes, but I've had longer to process everything that happened last night... and honestly, I don't feel too bad."

"Well, at least let me keep watch while you get some sleep."

"Are you kidding me? You've had less sleep than me in the last twenty-four hours. You watched all last night while I cried and slept. I think it's a better idea that you get some sleep and I'll keep watch for a couple of hours. Then I'll wake someone else to keep watch."

Tim didn't say anything (funny how quickly I switch back to first names when the others aren't around), he just looked at me for a short time before he spoke.

"Yes, but I'm trained to go without sleep. You are not." He said it with a shrug, as though it was the most obvious thing in the world. I wasn't going to argue with him, but I wasn't going to give in either. So we just sat there side by side, looking at the darkness around us.

My mind started wandering back to our time at the base before all this became real. Well, more real. I suppose in the end, it wasn't until the moment we walked into that nest a couple hours ago it really became real.

Training with Brock started much the same the next day as it had on the first. I was determined to try and treat him just like any other drill instructor. I succeeded better than some of the others. They kept trying to engage him in conversation as though this were a fun boot camp. I think seeing a famous person here made them forget how serious this was. He rebuffed them quickly and they eventually got back to business.

Once we were dismissed, everyone ran back to the barracks to shower before dinner. I started to join them and then noticed Brock was starting to pack up the equipment by himself.

"Can I help with that, Sir?" I asked, trying to keep the nervousness out of my voice. I had often offered help to the other drill instructors in the past, so I told myself it wasn't a big deal.

"Thank you, Cadet." He continued picking up the various items we had used and I hurried to help him, tripping over my own feet as I went. I opened my mouth to say something to him a half a dozen times, but quickly closed it again when my nerves got the better of me. But come on; alien invasion or not, this was Brock-freaking-Hunter. At least I waited until after training to do it (okay yeah, that was cringeworthy even in my own head). So I held my tongue.

"Something you want, Cadet?" I looked up and noticed he was looking straight at me.

"No Sir. Nothing." I replied as calmly as I could. I couldn't meet his eyes for long. I was too nervous, for far too many reasons. I knew realistically no one could read minds, but people could read faces if they tried and I willed mine not to give anything away.

He didn't say anything else, at least not straight away. We finished packing everything up. As I put the last piece of equipment into the back of the truck, I found him watching me.

"I reckon you're wondering why I was watching you yesterday at combat training." It wasn't a question. It was a statement. And it was accurate. I didn't respond. He didn't seem to need me to. "I was watching you because I was trying to work something out. I would like to have a conversation with you about a couple of things if that's ok. Are you hungry?" I shook my head, wondering where all of this was going. "Okay, come take a drive with me."

He gestured to the jeep he had arrived in. I hesitated only a moment before climbing in the passenger side. He climbed into the driver's seat and started the engine. He drove across the base. It took us a few minutes before we came to a tall gate. I thought this must be as far as we would go, but he pressed a button attached to the sun visor above his head. The gate slowly slid open and I started to wonder where we were going. I just couldn't dig up the courage to ask.

After another few minutes of driving, we took a sharp turn to the left and pulled up in a car park. We were stopped in front of what looked like a giant playground. I realised it was an obstacle course. We had done some training on one on the base, but it had nothing on this.

"What is this place?" I finally asked. My curiosity getting the better of my nerves. For some reason my smartarse side had disappeared (which sucked for me because it left me with very little to say.)

"This is one of the obstacle courses newly refurbished to test and train Special Forces guys before they go into the field." Came the reply. I waited for him to elaborate, but he stayed silent.

"Cool, so... what are we doing here?" I prodded. Glad my voice didn't fail me, or even shake. It helped if I kept my head down, but it made it harder to judge what he was thinking. I needed my brain firing on all cylinders right now, though.

"Well, you and I need to have a talk, and I wanted to do it in private. And I've seen you on the other obstacle course and I thought you would appreciate this one." He seemed to want to say more. This time I waited him out. Instead, he turned to look at me, his gaze asking if I understood. I nodded lightly to indicate to him I did.

"I know you think you're here because you didn't do so well on your fitness test... but that's not really why this course was suggested for you. Some of the other tests and courses they've had you complete have been to try and work out if you're suited for particular roles. You have all been selected because you have leadership potential. They want us, which would be me and a couple of others, to help select which of you should go on to become team leaders for when they send you into the field. Which won't be long from now, so we don't have a lot of time. I have been watching you very carefully in all of your sessions over the last couple of days, although a lot more discreetly than I did for your combat training session yesterday; and I think I'm going to put you forward for team leader. I have a backup in case one of the others doesn't have a good candidate or has a washout..." he paused for a moment and I jumped in before he could continue.

"Are you so sure your candidate will succeed? Shouldn't your backup be for you?" I was honestly curious at his train of thought and also feeling a little nervous that he seemed so certain of me. I was even referring to myself in the third person and I don't do that ever.

"Yes, I'm very sure my candidate will succeed," he said, using the third person, which actually made me relax a little... weird, huh? "Partly because I think she is brilliant, partly because she asks the right questions and also because I am going to offer her extra training, which I think she will be smart enough to take me up on. Fitness, combat, battle strategy. Everything that might help out there and when the teams get assigned, then I will train her whole team along with her."

"That's really cool, but..." I paused, hating myself for needing to ask the next question, "Are you sure? About me I mean."

He didn't speak, just nodded his head, which I saw because I was finally able to make myself look at him. I was lost for words. Meanwhile, he climbed out of the jeep and gestured to the obstacle course in front of us. I joined him to ask a million questions, but only managed to get one out.

"Is this where we are training?"

"Yep. If you can do everything on this course – even slowly – you might actually have a chance of surviving out there. Maybe even killing some of these alien bastards. We'll start with stamina and go from there. I want you to run laps around the outside of the course."

I didn't ask any questions. I just took off in the direction he gestured and steadied into a slow run. It wasn't long before I heard footsteps behind me and realised he was going to run with me. I felt nervous about that and promptly tripped over my own feet, though I managed to stay upright. I had watched other trainers at work and a lot of them just sat back and watched; I wasn't sure if this was better or worse – I figured fifty-fifty. Either way, I was going to trip over my own feet a lot and embarrass myself.

At the same time, I was strangely thrilled that Brock was running with me. It would give me a chance to work on my crush control. I kept thinking of things I wanted to ask him and say to him, but then convinced myself not to. We were here to train, after all. He kept pace with me easily and I figured he was going easy on me, which I appreciated. We talked very little throughout the run. Afterwards, he let me try my hand at a couple of the smaller obstacles on the course. I wish I could say I did them really well, but that would be a bit of a stretch. Although Brock told me I did pretty well, considering.

7

It was late, towards the end of my watch, when I heard sounds over the radio. I had it in my ear, but I hadn't been listening too carefully. I turned up the volume a little and listened in for a minute. I took a second to look at Tim. I realised he had taken his radio off when he went to sleep, so the noise I heard wouldn't have bothered him. I waited for whoever it was to talk again, because I was sure it had been someone talking I had half heard.

"Delta Leader. Lucky numbers. I repeat Delta Leader. Lucky numbers."

That's all it was, but that small, whispered message made me want to shout from the tops of the tallest trees. I immediately reached for the dial on my radio and tuned it to another channel. The channel that corresponded with my... and Rochelle's lucky number. Seventeen, incidentally the channel my team sat on during the day when we were talking amongst ourselves. Tim stirred and I realised I must have disturbed him from his sleep when I jumped with excitement.

"This is Delta Leader." I waited with bated breath for a reply. It came almost immediately. To my great relief, because I almost thought I had imagined that whisper. Tim must have heard me because he opened his eyes and looked up at me from the ground.

"Tyne? It's Rochelle, I'm ok. I was knocked around a bit during the attack but I'm ok; sorry I didn't make contact sooner, but we wanted to be sure it was safe first. I have a message for Tim from Tayler. She is alive. We have a lot to talk about."

I had tears streaming down my face and a smile as broad as a country as I relayed Tayler's message. His face didn't give much away, but he sat straight up and immediately picked up his radio and turned it on. Then he finally looked at the channel my radio was on.

The next few minutes were a blur of information. We discovered the aliens had gotten into their camp because the watch was asleep. They had snuck right up to him and torn his throat out. Bravo leader had woken when they dropped his body on the ground loudly. That was when the shouting had started. Rochelle had woken quickly and rolled away a short distance before she got up and joined the fight.

She had taken out one of the aliens before turning just in time to watch Bravo leader fall under the weight of another two. After that, she was on her own. She managed to get one more alien down before she got into serious trouble. The biggest one had been busy doing something with Bravo leader's body while she was fighting the other one. But just as she was striking the killing blow, it turned her attention to her. It was on her before she realised it was there and it had her down with its teeth almost at her throat before she heard the sound of running feet.

Bravo Overwatch had run in and taken the alien out. They had had a quick conference in which Bravo Overwatch – in tears – had told Rochelle she had been ordered to take them all out when the attack started. Not that she had needed to because the whole attack lasted less than five minutes.

Tim sat still for a long time. He seemed to be thinking. He looked at his GPS frowning and then spoke into the radio quickly and quietly.

"Bravo Overwatch? Rendezvous exactly five miles directly north east of our current co-ordinates, there is a lot more we need to talk about. Do you have us marked on your GPS?"

"Copy that, affirmative. Will rendezvous approximately seventeen thirty hours tomorrow."

"Keep us marked and keep checking your GPS, be prepared for it to be slightly out. I'll explain properly later. Let us know if anything changes, try to avoid nests if you can and keep off the radio unless absolutely necessary. Keep quiet and stay safe."

"Copy that. Out."

We talked quietly for a little while after that, mostly about Bravo team and the attack that had taken most of them. After a while, I started actually feeling tired. I'm sure part of it was the relief of knowing Rochelle was alive and okay.

I slept for a couple of hours before Aiden woke me again for my watch. Delta was sound asleep beside me. I don't remember moving back to camp before falling asleep, so I figured Delta must have carried me back here after I fell asleep. Aiden was being very careful not to disturb him as he woke me. I think the others were all still a bit nervous around him.

Aiden explained to me Delta had stayed awake for his watch and half of Cam's watch (which he woke her for) before finally falling asleep. Cam had passed on through Daniel's watch to let him sleep. I agreed with that and sat up, telling Aiden to go back and do the same. It was only a couple of hours until dawn, so I was happy to finish the watch alone. I felt good this morning. Much as I thought I would be ok without sleep; I felt a lot better having had some. I knew Delta would feel the same once he woke up, too. Trained or not, no one felt good on no sleep. Delta had also kindly informed them that Rush and Bravo Overwatch were alive and meeting up with us in transit, but hadn't filled them in on the details of what had happened to them.

The sun peeked over the horizon in no time, and I found myself waking the others gently. I left Delta till last. By the time I got to him, I found he was already staring up at the sky. He blinked at me when I let my shadow fall over him.

"You feel better this morning? How long was the last watch?" he asked me.

"Only a couple of hours. I feel great, actually. How about you? I know you said you are trained to go without sleep, but surely you do feel better after that. Every little bit helps."

"I feel ready to take on the world, which is handy because I think we'll see a bit more action today. Not that I'll see any, because I'll be up a tree fifty metres away watching you all through the scope of a sniper rifle." he joked. I gave him a dirty look but couldn't help smiling. I definitely felt safer knowing he was watching our backs and wasn't going to follow any orders to fire at us.

It still worried me Bravo Overwatch had been ordered to do that. I was really glad she hadn't. But I was trying not to dwell on it. It made me worry about Rochelle and miss her more. It made me want to forget what we were doing and run straight to her. But I couldn't do that. I had to stay on task. Besides, I wanted these aliens off our planet and if that meant ignoring what I wanted, to go out and kill some, then that was what I would have to do. Besides, we would meet up with Rochelle and Tayler tonight.

When the others were awake and ready to go, we decided to eat while we walked. We continued on the line we had been on the day before. But we spaced ourselves a bit wider than we had previously and kept communications to our private radio channel. We figured it would be the best chance of finding the nests, instead of them finding us. And it was a quick flick of a switch to put us back on the main channel if we thought we were coming across something like yesterday.

It was about two hours into our march when Cam – who was near the middle, on our actual line – called us all to her. We gathered around and waited for her to show us what she had found. I was expecting it to be some sign of a nest close by, but what she said shocked us.

"I'm pretty sure now that our GPS systems are being altered as we go."

"What do you mean?" Delta and I chimed in at the same time. We were almost in stereo.

"Well, this morning we were heading due north-east. Exactly north-east. And I had us on a straight line to the coordinates they expect us to be at tonight..." she paused as if worried about what she was saying next. "The GPS still has us heading in exactly the same direction. But I have a map and a compass – an analogue one – thanks to the Boss's friends in high places and we are heading almost completely due north now."

"Show me?" asked Delta. There was some confusion in his voice, but also anger and he wore the matching expression on his face. But not the kind that indicated he didn't believe her, just the kind that said he wanted to understand and needed to see for himself, also I think he wanted to know who to punish for messing with us. I told everyone to take a short break while they sat together and tried to work out what was going on.

54

They were at it for almost ten minutes before they called me over. Delta pointed to the map.

"This is where the GPS says we are, right? But according to the map and the compass, we are here. We are a lot further north than we should be. We seem to be heading right into the centre of the forest for whatever reason. I just don't know why or how. I mean, if they wanted us to go in there, why not just tell us?"

"So, what are you saying? Is someone messing with our GPS system or is it just seriously faulty? Should we call it in?"

"No, I don't think it's faulty. I think someone is changing it. They never really seemed to want to tell us exactly where we were going, just that we were looking for survivors, but it has always seemed more than that. Because going out searching for survivors never made any sense. Almost like this was a trial run for something else and searching was an excuse."

"Ok, so what do we want to do? Do we assume Rush and Tayler's GPS is still being altered also? If so, how will they find us?"

"I would assume they are adjusting all of them at the same time. So they should still end up at the same coordinates as us if they follow the GPS where we were supposed to meet. It's probably an all-encompassing program they are using to do it, so it would be difficult to suddenly remove one set of systems." Surprisingly it was Daniel that answered.

"How do you know?" Delta asked him.

"I didn't just sit around playing video games, you know. I was actually a computer programmer and a hacker... the video game thing was actually a job. I was working for a company that got sick of people cheating on their online games, so they hired me to destroy cheat hacks. I got paid to make things like bots and cheat commands obsolete. It was a good cover for other stuff that I was doing too... stuff that may not have been entirely legal..." We all looked at him in shock and he laughed. "These things are sadly, completely hackable... which is why the military stopped using them about three years ago. It's not even that hard to do. You can buy walk-throughs online."

We all absorbed that for a moment. I could see everyone thinking hard. Trying to work out what was going on.

"So what do we do?" Cam asked no one in particular. But it was Daniel that answered her.

"Well, assuming we are not just giving up and going home, we have two options. One, we can try and hack the GPS back from here. It's doable and not even that hard, but we could never be one hundred percent sure our coordinates were totally accurate. Also, we would only be able to do one GPS at a time and it would be noticeable to whoever is doing it back on base, so they would know we were onto them and they may choose to try and take us out of the equation altogether. Or two, we can keep going as we have been for now and make another decision when we meet up with the other two tonight. If we go with option one, I think it would be overridden anytime they hacked the whole system again, so we'd have to keep redoing it."

I looked at Delta and Cam.

"We have the map and compass. We know with some degree of certainty where we really are... I'm not ready for them to know we are onto them yet. I suggest we wait until we meet up with Rush and Tayler tonight and look at it again."

"I agree," said Delta, "I think we'll learn more playing along than we will letting them know we know something isn't right. We have the advantage at the moment as they don't know about the map and compass Cam has. But since I'm the interloper here, I'll leave it to you guys to decide."

The others quickly agreed we should go on. We decided to close our ranks a little more than we had been previously, so we were always within eyesight with each other. And Delta walked only about twenty-five metres behind us. He didn't want to be too far back and we hoped we would spot a nest early enough like we did yesterday for him to find a good sniper spot before we launched any attack. If the attack was launched at us, it might not be so easy, but we would cross that bridge when we came to it. If an alien force had followed us from our last nest, then we were all in a lot more trouble than not having an overwatch, anyway.

It was about another two hours' march when we came across signs of a nest. Daniel spotted it first. He was furthest out on our line, so it was possible if we had all been bunched together that we would have missed it. Which I think might have been really bad, especially now we knew they hunted... and knew we were around.

At the same time we came across our nest, one of the other teams walked blindly into one as well. We paused to listen to the fight before going into ours. It took me a moment to work out which team it was.

It was Alpha Team. As what had happened with us, the aliens were on them in a heartbeat. They were in the fight of their lives and they knew it. They didn't seem too scared, but there was a bit of shouting. It mostly seemed to be the Alpha leader trying to get them focused and fighting properly. Everything around me paused for a moment as I listened intently to the battle going on over the radio. I didn't even know anyone on Alpha Team.

There seemed to be four aliens. Instead of trying to take them on individually like we had done, they were bunching together and getting caught up with each other. As I listened to them yelling, I heard their overwatch trying to help Alpha Leader direct them. Between the two of them, they got everyone focused and concentrating on what they were doing. They finally got them separated and fighting without tripping over each other.

It was over pretty quickly after that. The aliens were dispatched and no one in the unit was seriously harmed. And most importantly, no kill order was given to overwatch, which lead credence to my belief that it had something to do with getting bitten (a fact I hadn't shared with my team yet). They got a bit cocky after that. They were boasting on the radio about how they had killed the aliens. That was until Alpha leader reminded them how much of a mess it had started and how easily it could have gone wrong. Delta got on the overwatch channel and told Alpha Overwatch to get them moving quickly, reminding him of Bravo Team.

We got into position after we were sure they were moving on and waited for Delta to give us the ok, then we flicked our radios back to the main channel and advised everyone we thought we had found another nest. All the chatter on the radio went quiet. I couldn't remember if that happened yesterday. I hadn't been paying that much attention to the radio yesterday at all, only enough to know no one else had died.

The defences seemed pretty basic. There were deep holes every few feet, obviously designed for people's legs to end up in, much like rabbit holes in a horse paddock. But if you looked into the bottom of them carefully, there were sharp spikes standing up that would stab straight through the foot that fell into the hole. I didn't imagine anyone would be walking away from that and into a fight in a hurry. Other defences seemed to involve causing a lot of noise. We assumed it was to alert the aliens to an incoming attack. Or maybe to alert them to the escape of prisoners if there were any here.

We managed to bypass the defences pretty easily. No one lost a foot or made too much noise. We crept into the nest and found only one alien there. It was a huge one and Aiden and I went at it together while Cam and Daniel watched our backs. We expected other aliens to be hiding away, waiting for us to relax, but none turned up.

The big alien decided Aiden was more of a threat than me. It turned to face his attack full on and left me standing to its side. I used the advantage it gave me and darted in, managing to get my blade deep in under its arm. I heard a faint pop as I managed to sever something internal. It roared, I assumed in pain, although it was not a sound I had heard from one of these things before. Its arm hung limply at its side, but it decided I was a threat after all. It spun to face me and Aiden ran in and dug his blade right into where the stomach would have been on a human. It bent over forwards as though it was badly hurt and Aiden went in for the kill, but it was feinting and it grabbed hold of Aiden's arm and yanked hard.

Aiden screamed and I saw Daniel come flying in out of nowhere. He copied the move Cam had used at the last nest and launched himself in the air. Instead of using the alien's arm to spin around, he jumped straight up on his back and dug his blade in. He used his own weight to pull downwards and made a long deep gash down its spine. I jumped in and completed a T-shaped cut across its neck severing the spinal cord as we had done every time now, then I jammed my blade up through its lower jaw and into its brain. It stopped moving finally and we were able to turn and attend to Aiden.

The alien had dislocated his arm. It was pretty bad, but Delta called over the radio to say he knew how to fix it. Aiden would just have to put up with the pain for a little while. We couldn't have Delta out of position yet, not until we were sure we were clear. Aiden sat down on a log while we quickly checked the nest over and see if we could find any sign of any other aliens or prisoners. There was nothing. We decided to move on quickly so we could get as far away as possible. Delta caught up with us after only about ten minutes and helped Aiden put his shoulder back in its socket. He used a spare gun strap to make a temporary sling to hold it while we moved.

It was starting to get dark before we reached the rendezvous spot. Once we finally made it there, we set up camp and a watch. No one seemed inclined to go to sleep, though. We talked quietly so the watch – Cam at the moment – would still be able to hear any sounds of approach. We were settled in for a long wait.

Rochelle and Tayler were late. We hadn't had any contact with them for most of the day, as we had decided. They wouldn't have called through unless they were more than an hour late. It was what we had agreed upon during our last conversation this morning. We had decided then it was safer if they stayed off the radio as much as possible. We still weren't sure if we wanted to tell people they were alive.

They were only about fifteen minutes late so far, but I couldn't help worrying. I was so close to seeing Rochelle again, so of course I was stressing it wouldn't happen. (Yes, I am a little dependant on my best friend, but she's family and we've been through everything together.)

I was checking my watch every few minutes. Around the forty-minute mark, I was checking almost every minute. Delta put his hand on my arm, covering the face of my watch. I looked up at him and he just shook his head. I think he was trying to tell me to stop stressing, without making a big deal out of it in front of the others. I was about to ask him if he was okay when Cam held her hand up in a fist to get everyone's attention and silence us.

We all listened carefully for a moment before we heard what must have alerted Cam, the unmistakable sounds of people. They were picking their way carefully through the dense scrub. They weren't extremely loud, but you could definitely tell they weren't animals. I don't think any of us would have heard them if we weren't really listening for the sounds of approach. It made me appreciate how the aliens always seemed to know we were coming. There were four of us marching into their nests and even trying to be as silent as we could. There would still be some noise, probably enough to alert enemies of an incoming attack. That was something we could work on.

I couldn't tell you how I knew, but I had no doubt it was Rochelle and Tayler at the other end of the noise. I kept my seat though and beside me, Delta let out a low whistle. A short answering whistle came back seconds later and we breathed a collective sigh of relief. Delta and I rose from the ground as one to meet them. They stumbled into camp, looking exhausted. It was a wonder they were as quiet as they were, considering how tired they both looked.

We sat them both in the centre of the group and gave them some food. They had told us they lost a lot of their supplies in the raid on their camp. Once they were fed, we told them to get some sleep. Much as we wanted to know what had happened in more detail, they didn't look like they could really stay awake long enough to tell us the whole story, anyway. Let alone be peppered with all the questions we would no doubt ask.

Tayler wanted to talk to Delta for a moment, but Rochelle laid down and fell asleep straight away. Delta and Tayler walked a short distance away to talk but returned fairly quickly. They both looked quite grave when they returned, but neither said anything. They both laid down and went to sleep.

Two hours later, I was still laying staring at the sky, wide awake. I rose and told Cam to get some sleep. I was due to take over the watch next anyway and it was only half an hour early. Within ten minutes of her lying down, she was snoring softly and I knew she was asleep.

Delta rose from the ground as I knew he would and came to join me. I had been fairly sure he wasn't asleep – he never was – just as I had been fairly sure he would want to talk to me. He still liked to give me the choice of how much I shared with the team, even though he knew I would probably share most of it.

"So... what happened?" I whispered to him. He folded himself back onto the ground in front of me – so we could talk without having to look around behind us all the time.

"Something weird is going on back at base. The way Tyler was ordered to take out her own people. If it had been seriously injured people who weren't going to make it, then it would almost make sense..." He looked at my face and appeared to quickly adjust whatever he had been going to say next. "I'm not saying that I would do it even under those circumstances – and neither would Tayler – but since we know no-one is coming to rescue us if something happens... but she was ordered to fire on them all the second time. No matter their injuries, or apparently, lack thereof."

"Were you ordered to fire on us?" I couldn't keep myself from asking.

"No, which is also confusing me. The only reason I can come up with that makes even the tiniest scrap of sense is, whoever issued the order to fire wasn't around at the time of either of our skirmishes. Which tells me it's obviously not a standing order, which gives me more questions than answers, really."

"Yeah, that is a bit confusing. And why are they changing the GPS on us? It's hard enough doing all this because of these stupid bloody aliens in the first place, but now there might be some of our own people against us, too. It's too much." It took me a moment to realise there were tears streaming down my cheeks. I wiped them away angrily, only for them to be replaced.

"Tyne..." Delta began. I looked at him, expecting him to tell me I had to be strong. But instead he continued differently, "It's okay to feel lost and hopeless, we all do at the moment. But we will keep fighting. I'm not saying all of us are going to survive, because that is a promise I can't make. But we – as in the human race – will survive. We're fighters by nature and we will find a way to beat these fuckers." With that, he pulled me into a bear hug. "It's okay to cry if you need to. You're among friends here and we understand. We've all been through a hell of a lot the last few months. It's normal to have a moment of weakness. It doesn't take anything away from your strength." It was like he was reading my mind.

He let me go after another moment and I managed to wipe my face and get rid of the rest of the tears, which had finally stopped leaking from my traitorous eyes. It felt good to get my frustrations and fears out (although I hadn't voiced any of them) and have a good cry. Even though it wasn't what I had meant to do. I vowed silently to myself I wouldn't let it happen again.

We didn't talk much after that. We just kept our watch, throwing occasional comments back and forth quietly, mostly about random, inconsequential things. Neither of us wanted to talk about anything important, though we probably should have. It felt good to just be people for a little while. Sometime later, I let myself get lost in memories again.

The first day of training I had after Brock had taken me for a drive, I was so keyed up I had trouble focusing on breakfast. I hadn't slept great either, a fact Rochelle had noticed although she didn't say anything. I knew that she had a million questions. But she also knew I wouldn't talk about it in front of other people, anyway.

I got to training with the rest of the group. We all warmed up while we waited for Brock to arrive. The other girls in the group were chatting as they worked out how they were going to approach him and try and engage him in conversation. I listened to them and tried to keep the disgust from my face. They didn't try to include me in their conversation, for which I was grateful. I don't think I would have been able to hide it from them for long.

They were so engrossed in their conversation, they failed to notice when Brock's jeep pulled up. He stood in front of the rest of us (who had snapped to attention when he arrived and climbed out of the jeep) and waited. And waited. After about five minutes, one of the girls finally looked up from the conversation to see why all the noise around them had stopped. They looked straight at Brock and their faces fell under his raised eyebrows. He didn't mention anything to them about what he had undoubtedly overheard, but the meaning was clear.

He worked us hard. By the end of it, one of the girls had passed out and the other threw up as he had promised would happen. At the end of the session, he brought us all back to attention. He congratulated us on our excellent (yes, my heart jumped at the word) work and then turned to the girls who were still huddled together on one side of the group.

"You will not be joining us tomorrow. I will arrange for you to join another trainer; details will be given to you later this afternoon."

They looked crestfallen and looked like they wanted to argue, but they seemed to think better of it. They didn't wait to be dismissed, but turned on their heels, red faced, heads hanging down and walked away. Brock dismissed the rest of us, then started packing up the equipment again.

I stayed back to help without comment this time. We worked side by side in silence for a few minutes.

"You have combat training straight after lunch, yes?"

"Yes Sir."

"You don't have to call me 'Sir' when no one is around if you don't want to. My call sign is 'Hunter' same as my surname. You can call me that if you like. It's a little less formal than 'Sir'," he paused for a moment, "and honestly, 'Sir' makes me feel old." I looked at him, dumbfounded for a minute. He smiled at me and I let out a laugh I didn't realise I'd been holding in. He nodded his head once, as though he had made his point. We finished packing up in silence.

"Meet me at the Mess Hall doors after combat training and we'll head out to the obstacle course. I'll drive you out there for the first couple of days, then once I'm sure you know the way, I'll just meet you out there."

I nodded my head in agreement. Then waved goodbye as I headed back towards the Mess Hall for lunch. Not that I wanted to eat too much before combat training, but I needed something. I hadn't really eaten a lot for breakfast. I hoped whatever he would have me doing tonight was going to wear me out enough that I would get a decent night's sleep, regardless of my thoughts.

I managed to nab some sandwiches and a bottle of water when I reached the Mess, then looked around for Rochelle. She had saved me a seat like I knew she would. I sat next to her and smiled to let her know I was okay... and promptly stuffed my face. I hadn't realised how hungry I really was. She smiled at my overfull face, knowing me so well.

As soon as I was finished eating – which really didn't take long considering the three sandwiches I stuffed in - we took our bottles of water and walked out of the hall together.

"You okay?" she asked me as soon as we were alone. She knew I'd had training with Brock that morning.

"Yeah, I'm okay. I need to get this under control. I am going to do it." I said. I hoped I put as much conviction into my voice as I felt at that moment. I had a great learning opportunity here and I would be wasting it if I couldn't get my crush under control enough to be able to take it in properly.

"Good! You look a lot calmer." She smiled at me to let me know that was all the insight she was going to give. I was grateful. I knew she understood me and that half of what I was projecting was pure bravado and that was okay with both of us.

We didn't say anything else as we kept an eye on our watches to make sure we headed over to combat training on time. We started heading vaguely in that direction anyway, with nothing else to really occupy us on base. It made sense to arrive everywhere early. Although knowing how little there was to occupy one's mind, otherwise it was amazing how many people actually did turn up to sessions late or 'only just' on time.

Combat training went much better today than it had two days previously. Our trainer rotated all the pairs, so we weren't working with the same person all the time, which made perfect sense really, because the aliens we were potentially fighting would probably not all be the same.

Rochelle was on the other side of the room, working with one of the girls who had been removed from Brock's session this morning. They were a good match and made a pretty decent fight to watch if one was so inclined.

I was paired with a giant. This guy was twice my size, in weight definitely and in height, almost. I saw it as a good opportunity to learn, because we had been told the aliens were quite a bit taller than us generally. He seemed a little on the clumsy side. And a little slower than I was used to.

But he was strong. Incredibly strong. I found myself actually having to concentrate a lot more than I expected. Which I suppose wasn't a bad thing. I found I rather enjoyed it. I made a mental note to myself to find out who he was. If I had a choice of who my team was, I would request this kid as part of my team.

After combat training, I was sweaty and gross. My instinct would have been to go for a shower before I went to dinner, but I wasn't going to dinner. I didn't have time to shower and I figured Brock wouldn't expect me to come out to training smelling like roses. I had to keep reminding myself I wasn't trying to impress him in any way other than my battle ability.

I jogged over to the Mess Hall suddenly full of energy. There was no-one around. Most of them went to shower before dinner (to be fair, the Hall really stank if we didn't). Brock was there waiting in the driver's seat of his jeep. He raised a hand gently in a wave and I jogged right over to the passenger door, hopping in without hesitation, and we drove off over the base. I tried to pay attention to the direction we were going. If I was going to have to find my own way over here in a couple of days, then I wanted to make sure I wasn't going to get lost.

When we arrived at the obstacle course, I jumped out of the jeep and quickly stretched. I was still fairly warmed up from combat training, but I didn't want to take any chances. I looked towards Brock briefly to confirm what I suspected, that I would be starting with running laps again. He nodded his head once to agree I should begin without him and with that, I took off.

I started to really enjoy my ring when I realised Brock hadn't joined me today. I wanted to look around for him, but I knew I would lose momentum on my run if I did. When I had completed my first lap, I started a second without waiting to be told. I was about halfway through the second lap when I heard the sound of the footsteps I had been waiting for, gaining on me. He was moving very fast. Within only moments, he had caught up and overtaken me. He was running at a good pace and I found myself naturally trying to compete with him. But he held his pace without any apparent effort. I had to work for every bit of speed I gained. I never caught him.

After that lap and another besides, he slowed right down to a brisk walk. And I managed to catch up and slow beside him. He nodded to me. I was panting, breathless and I worried I would get a stitch. He continued walking, not even breathing hard.

"I thought we'd have a go on some of the obstacles today," he said without stopping his brisk walking pace. "I'd like to see what you make of them. And I'm going to do them with you. We can make a competition out of it."

"Can you actually do them already?"

"Some of them, without even thinking, others I might have to figure out alongside you. But I do know the theory. I was never interested in special forces training. It's too much of a full-time commitment and I wasn't willing to give the time."

I was intrigued to hear him talk about his personal life. It's not something I would have asked him myself. I would have been too nervous, but it felt nice he was telling me something so personal. I realised I was getting myself into a dangerous cycle of letting my crush take over my brain again. I pulled myself together and looked over at him, hoping my lapse in sense hadn't shown too much.

His face gave nothing away, but I had the feeling he had been watching me a moment before. He started walking over to a tall wooden wall with ropes hanging in front of it.

"This one is pretty self-explanatory I think," he said, gesturing to the wall in front of me, "you just gotta get to the top. It will help with your arm and upper body strength. Do you want me to go first and show you how it's done?" he offered.

"No, I think I got it." I said. I was trying not to be too confident, but I had used the wall like this over in the other obstacle course. This one was a hell of a lot taller, but it was still the same principal and I hadn't done too terribly on the other one.

"Get to it then," he replied with a shadow of a smile on his face. I didn't stop to analyse it any further than that. I just ran for the wall. He watched me carefully as I climbed using the rope. It was harder than I had expected. I wouldn't have thought the extra height would add all that much work to the climb, but it really did.

I made it to the top, but it was a hard slog. Somewhere around halfway up, I had stopped thinking about Brock watching me and just concentrated on not falling. It made my climb a tiny bit easier. When I reached the top, I sat there for a second, catching my breath and enjoying the feeling of success, before I heard the sound of another person breathing beside me.

I looked over and realised Brock had climbed the wall at some stage, unnoticed by me and made it to the top before me. He was smiling.

"You actually did that better than I expected."

"Thanks. I wish I could do it faster, though."

"That will come with time and practise, just try and keep your upper body higher than your legs. It'll help you when you get to the top. You ready to try again?" I nodded and we went back to work. This time he climbed with me, giving me tips as we climbed.

Afterward we walked over to the jeep and I realised I had missed dinner, but Brock was way ahead of me. He pulled out a cooler that had a selection of sandwiches and snacks and we leaned against the tailgate, eating and talking about the obstacle course.

◆

9

The new day dawned bright and clear. I could even see it through the dense tree tops. I had taken over all the watches for the night with Delta. We had both been wide awake, so letting the others get a decent night's sleep seemed like a good idea.

Everyone woke fairly early, even with the absence of the noises you would usually expect to accompany a stay in the forest. They were a little disgruntled at me and Delta for taking all the watches, but I think they knew better than to complain too loudly. We sat around eating breakfast quietly. No one seemed overly inclined to start the conversation that needed to be had, including me and Delta. It was Tayler who finally broke the silence.

"So what's the plan?" she looked from Delta to me as she spoke. Rochelle looked up from her own breakfast at Tayler's words, watching my reaction.

"I don't know," I replied honestly, "but we can't stop. I think you guys should come along with us. There's no rescue to be had anyway, so you may as well stick with the group." Delta nodded his agreement. I would have stopped there, but something else was on my mind. "And I think... for now... that we should leave you 'dead'." I used my fingers to make quotation marks. "Until we have more information about what is going on back at base, it might be better if they continue to think you are."

Tayler nodded as though this made all the sense in the world. I think she was feeling a little out of her depth, although obviously far more qualified than me and way more experienced, she seemed happy enough to follow along with what I suggested for now.

Rochelle was watching me with a strange look on her face. I could see there was a lot she wanted to say. But she just nodded her head and continued her meal.

"I think for today maybe the two of you should hang back if we come across a nest or anything." Delta said, obviously meaning Rochelle and Tayler. They both nodded.

"Well, let's get packed up and on the move. I want to put some decent distance behind us today if we can." I said. I looked at Delta and he gestured with his head for me to walk a short distance with him.

When out of easy earshot of the others, I turned to him.

"What's up? Why are you benching them?" I asked him,

"It's nothing really, but I notice Rochelle is a little shaky, which is understandable after what she's been through and I thought it might be difficult to hide the fact they are with us if we walk into a nest, if they fight alongside you. It would be an extra person talking and it would be noticed."

I nodded my understanding. I suspected there was something he wasn't telling me, but he would speak in his own time. In the meantime, the reasons he had given me were perfectly acceptable and I remembered neither Tayler nor Rochelle had argued the point when he had brought it up, either.

We returned to the others; they were ready to go. I strapped my pack on properly, so it wasn't just hanging over one shoulder. We checked in with the base and then consulted the GPS and map, then headed out.

It was a hard slog. The trees were getting thicker the deeper into the forest we went and the undergrowth was so thick tripping on hidden roots became commonplace. There were still very little signs of wildlife, indicating to us that although we weren't seeing signs of nests or aliens everywhere we went, their presence in the forest had made itself felt.

It was late morning when Aiden spotted the first sign of a nest. We geared up what hadn't been done and prepared to walk into it. Rochelle and Tayler backed away with Delta and they went to find a nice big tree or two to watch over us, radios turned to mute so they couldn't be overheard by anyone listening in. The rest of us edged forward cautiously.

About another hundred and twenty metres or so further and we came to the lip of what we strongly suspected was the nest. It seemed bigger than the other nests we had seen so far. We edged slowly into it after getting confirmation Delta was set.

Nothing happened when we walked in. We edged further in until we were standing in what should have been the centre of the nest. And still nothing. I looked around, wondering if it was abandoned, but something about it didn't feel right. I looked around on the ground and saw the others starting to do the same. I saw nothing that would help me understand what was going on here. I kicked the ground in frustration and my foot squelched... there is just no other word for it. I looked down and kicked aside more of the bracken and leaf litter covering the ground beneath me.

I gasped in horror as I realised what the thick liquid under the leaf matter was. It was blood, rather a lot of it, by the looks of it. I decided to radio Delta and see what he thought. The others were also sweeping back the leaf litter with their feet now. Trying to ascertain how big of an area was covered, to take a guess at how much blood there was.

"Delta Overwatch, this is Delta Leader." I kept it formal because we were on the open channel.

"Go ahead Boss." He replied.

"There is blood all over the ground here. Lots of it. It's thick enough that it's turned the dirt to mud. But it looks old. It's drying up."

"I hate to ask this because I'm pretty sure I already know the answer, but are we talking about human blood?"

"Yes, I think so." I replied, watching the disgusted look on Cam's face. "It's red, the alien's blood is blueish from what we've seen. My guess would be some of the people taken from Elko were killed here. Or maybe some others, I don't know. There are no bodies. No way to be able to tell what happened. But if I had to guess, I'd say it's probably enough blood for five or six people." I heard someone retch behind me. I think it was Daniel, but I didn't look around, lest I joined him in emptying my stomach.

"What do you want to do?" Delta asked me.

"We'll have a bit more of a look around and see if we can find anything else. Then I think we'll move on. Something doesn't feel right here. I want to get moving as soon as possible."

"Roger that. Let me know when you're ready to move on and I'll head over to... BOSS LOOK OUT BEHIND YOU!"

I spun around to see seven huge aliens entering the clearing from the left edge from where we had entered. The others turned with me. Daniel was nearest them. It was where he had been retching up the contents of his stomach. I thought they were going to walk right past him, but as the last one came level with him, the one in the lead hissed something and it flicked out its arm and knocked Daniel hard on the shoulder. He flew into a tree and hit his head, sliding to the ground in a heap. He was out cold.

"Oh! Crap, we are so screwed!" Cam said quietly beside me.

Unfortunately, as far as I could see, she was right. We were screwed. There were seven of them and now only three of us. I couldn't see a way out of this; but I knew we would have to fight for our lives and hope like hell for a miracle. I think Aiden and Cam must have been thinking along the same lines, judging by the look of determination on their faces. I knew beyond any shadow of a doubt they would fight.

My mind was in three places at once. I desperately hoped Delta, Rochelle and Tayler were under cover and safe. I needed to fight and try to get Aiden, Cam and myself out of this and I somehow had to get over to Daniel to check if he was alive.

The aliens were advancing on us very slowly. Like they were stalking us. It made me wonder how long they had known we were coming... or had they been following us from somewhere else? The leader was the tallest. He looked at me with intelligent eyes. This one was different from the others, like the big one I had fought in the last nest. There was something about it. The intelligence was calculating and malicious. Something lurked in that thing's brain that was a different kind of evil.

I decided that no matter what else happened here and now, I needed to kill the leader. If I managed that, then there might be a chance for the others to get away. I had my blades ready in my hands. I had made sure while we walked that I had spare blades in the sheaths on either leg. My gut had told me something big was going to happen. I was glad I had listened to it.

I started stalking towards the leader, blades at the ready. It stopped its stalking, stopped as though waiting for me. I gripped my blades tighter in both of my hands and broke into a run straight at it. I wondered if I could catch it off guard with a direct attack. It didn't have quite the effect I was hoping for, but at least it was paying attention to me. I hoped Aiden and Cam were using whatever time I had bought them wisely.

I ran straight at the alien and at the last second dropped to the ground and slid across the bloody, leaf strewn ground straight under its legs. Honestly, it was awesome. I still don't quite believe it happened, that I had actually managed to pull it off. As I slid under its legs, it took a swipe at me with its sharp clawed hand. I managed to slice the inside of one of its legs and dig my other blade into roughly where its ankle should be. But I lost my grip on it as I continued through the slide. I slid way too far (taking some of the coolness out of my unbelievable move) and ended up about two metres behind it. I managed to get myself up and turn around at about the same time it did.

I didn't stop to think or look around. I just jumped up and ran straight in for another attack. This time I completely missed. It took another swipe at me and took a gouge out of my shoulder. I screamed, partly in pain, partly frustration and partly in defiance. I was angry. I had been angry all along, but now I was letting it flow through me. I planned to use it to try and get out of this. I could hear chatter going on through the headset and grunts and hisses and other noises coming from around the clearing.

I could hear Cam yelling into the headset, trying to rouse Daniel. I would have joined her, but I was using all my breath to try and keep my feet. The alien launched into another attack and I barely got my defences up in time. I accidentally severed one of its claws in my defensive move (my blades were really sharp). The alien hissed at me angrily and tried to swipe at me again. But thankfully missed. I was tiring and as far as I knew, there were still four or five more to go.

I heard Aiden yell something that sounded like 'he's up'. I hoped he was talking about Daniel, but I didn't have time to look. The alien I was fighting launched itself at me and managed to get me down. I landed on my back with the alien on top of me, but I continued the roll as I had been taught and threw it straight over my head. It landed behind me with a thump.

I didn't have time to get back to my feet because another alien had jumped on top of me as soon as the leader landed on the ground. I barely managed to get my blade up in time to stop it biting down on my shoulder. My blade caught it in the stomach (roughly where the liver would be on a human) and it let out a hissing roar that gurgled a little. I wondered if I had hit something vital with my jab.

I managed to get another blade out of my leg sheath and dig it into the thing's shoulder with my left hand. It didn't go as deep as I would have liked being my weaker hand, but it was enough that the alien jumped back and I was able to scramble out from under it and onto to my feet. But before I could get very far, the leader gave me an almighty shove and I flew across the ground and landed with a thump against a tree trunk. I hit my head, not hard, but enough to stun me for a moment.

I shook my head to clear it and rose shakily to my feet. Both the aliens were now facing me getting ready to launch themselves into an attack, but before they could, I heard a deep angry roar that could only have come from a human. I saw Delta come charging through the trees from the other side of the clearing. He launched himself into the air and landed on the back of an alien fighting with Cam. He scaled its back so fast, I almost didn't believe I had seen it and slit its throat from behind. It fell to the ground hard and fast and he rode it down.

It only occurred to me after a moment I shouldn't have had time to watch that action. No matter how fast it had been, his entrance had caught the attention of both the aliens I was fighting. But now they turned back to me. I saw out of the corner of my eye something else human sized launch out of the trees. It landed on the back of the smaller of the two aliens I was facing off and started stabbing its blade repeatedly into its back and shoulders, anything it could reach.

It took me a moment to realise the shape was Rochelle. She yelled something at me but I didn't catch it. The lead alien had launched an attack at me while I was watching her and I only just managed to duck in time to save myself from getting swiped back into the tree. I screamed at it defiantly and charged straight at it with my blade in front of me. It tried to duck away from my launch, but I was ready for the direction change. I got in under its arms and threw as much strength as I could behind my blade as I jabbed it sharply up through its head from beneath.

I reached down to my other leg sheath and grabbed my last blade to slice across its throat with my left hand. Its blood ran down both of my arms, making everything slippery. I lost grip on both of my blades as it fell on top of me. I lay there for a moment, winded from the weight of the thing. It had fallen rather unfortunately, with its teeth extremely close to my neck. I wriggled away from its teeth as best I could, but I didn't get far.

I could hear the sounds of battle continuing around me. But I couldn't see anything, or move from under the weight of the alien lying dead on top of me. I thought I heard Rochelle yell something, but I didn't catch what it was. I heard the reply from Delta though, as it sounded like it came from right beside me.

"I got her."

Suddenly the body of the alien rolled off me sideways and I found myself looking up at Delta. He offered me a hand to aid in getting up, which I accepted gratefully. I pulled my knife out of the alien's head and the other out of its ankle; from where it had stayed throughout the whole battle, apparently. I looked around on the ground for the one I had used to slit its throat and found it lying a couple of feet from where I had lain.

Delta retrieved my other blade from the stomach of the one Rochelle had killed. He walked over and handed it back to me. I looked around quickly and saw six of the aliens were dead. The seventh had vanished. Daniel was up and walking around slowly. Cam hovered just to his left side, hands lightly outstretched, as though ready to catch him if he fell. He did look a little unsteady on his feet.

"We need to talk and make a decision very quickly." Delta said as I made my visual checks on everyone.

"What's happened? Why did you and Rochelle come in like that?" I asked him. I know I sounded ungrateful, but I was still trying to catch my breath.

"You were going to be slaughtered. Tayler agreed to keep overwatch and I just ran. I didn't know Rochelle had followed me until I saw her jump the alien that attacked you. I think I'm glad she did, though. I don't think we'd have all survived if she hadn't. She's got some salt in her that friend of yours." He said the last part with a massive smile on his face and I finally understood what he hadn't been saying earlier. He had been concerned about her fighting skills because he didn't know her. "The seventh one ran off when I arrived in the clearing. If I had to guess, then I would say it's gone for reinforcements. I imagine we don't have long." He waved the others over while he spoke and flicked his radio back over to channel seventeen. I did the same.

The others joined us. Cam Aiden and Rochelle took up positions of the circle that would give them a complete view between them. Daniel sat down on the ground between us. I put a hand on his shoulder and he looked up at me and nodded to let me know he was ok. I turned to Delta.

"You got the order, didn't you?" Rochelle didn't react, indicating she already knew. Aiden and Cam looked shocked for a brief moment, but didn't break their watch.

"Yes." He bit the words out sharply. "Almost as soon as you engaged. Daniel was down and the three of you were all fighting at least one or two. The others were just standing back, watching. And the order came from some general, not the guy we normally talk to..."

"Skipp," I interrupted him, he looked at me "The radio guy, his name is Skipp."

"I broke off contact. I don't know what they think happened, but I can claim radio trouble or something if I do it soon." He let me absorb that for a moment. "We need to die. All of us. This general wants this unit – and probably the others out here – gone. I don't know why, but if we want any hope of surviving to find out, then we need to vanish. I have a feeling others will come after us if they know we are alive. Maybe the other teams... maybe something else."

"Well, it seems like these aliens knew we were coming. Like really knew. Not just in the sense that they knew people were out here, this was almost like some sort of trap." Aiden added to the conversation. Cam and Daniel nodded in agreement and I wasn't going to disagree, mostly because I didn't – at all.

"Okay, so what's the plan?" I asked him.

"Basically, we wait until that thing brings back reinforcements. Which I don't think will be very long now. And we fight, same as we always do. At a certain point, Tayler will give the word and we start screaming about people being taken out. One by one, we fall... and then I get attacked in my hideaway and as far as they know, we are all dead and we have a bit of breathing room. Then we run like hell for as long as our legs will carry us."

"Where?" I asked him, but it was Daniel who answered.

"North-North-East, or close to it, we stick roughly to the line they wanted us on but off to one side of it. It gets us closer to finding out what's in here that they were sending us after, without telling us." He said simply. I nodded. At the very least, it would do until we could rest and regroup and come up with a new plan. I looked at Cam to see what she thought, since she had become our navigator. She nodded.

"Okay, well you better get back to your hide then before it comes back." I said to Delta.

"I'm staying here," he said simply. I opened my mouth to argue, but he forestalled me. "These things have my scent now. If one of them got through, it would hunt me down anyway. I may as well stay here and fight with you. We don't know how many it will bring back and Daniel is still a little wobbly on his feet. You're going to need me. Tayler will take over my overwatch duties."

"Okay then, how do we do this?" I asked him. I figured he already had a plan.

"I'll call out a name and that's the next person to die. Just listen for Tayler to call out 'now' after you hear you name and then 'take the hit'," he used his fingers as quotation marks. "Tayler has our backs. Don't worry."

"Wasn't worried at all. What about your orders?"

"I'll fake it. They won't know the difference." He smiled. He was going to say something else, but Tayler's voice came over the radio.

"Hey guys, time to wrap this up. There's movement to the north-ish of you. I think they are back. Be ready to move."

"Got it." Delta answered her before I had a chance to. Then turned to me. "You ready for this?"

"As I'll ever be." I said wryly, feeling as though I was delivering a line in a movie. He smiled and switched his radio back to the overwatch channel. The rest of us switched back to the main channel.

I looked over at Rochelle and she winked at me. She looked a little pale, but well enough. Daniel got slowly to his feet and I found myself desperately hoping that there wouldn't be so many of them, that we couldn't handle them and that maybe Daniel wouldn't have to fight at all.

We heard the rustling movements before we saw them coming from north of us. We turned to watch them come through the trees. There were four of them this time. Which meant there had been ten in this nest. I hoped that wasn't a sign of things to come. Ten or more in every nest was going to be a big ask.

I heard Delta start yelling into his radio, starting mid-sentence, as though the radio had just fazed back in. I didn't stop to listen too closely to the words, but I thought I caught 'Delta Four is down' as I launched myself into an attack on the alien standing closest to me.

It tried to take a swipe at me, but I ducked under its arm. I was too sore to try and pull my cool 'once-in-a-lifetime' slide move again – and honestly, I didn't think I could do it again; it was a fluke the first time – but I slashed my main blade straight across its belly. It must have gone deep because lots of stuff started spilling out of the gash I had made (it was very messy). I didn't wait to see if that would be enough to kill it. I slammed my blade up through its head twice as fast as I could and then severed the spinal cord. In the background, I heard Cam's name being called, then mine.

I moved onto my next victim, not realising it was one of only two left and the other one was already injured. Delta and Aiden were playing with it. Cam was right behind the one I ran towards. I heard a quiet voice in my ear saying 'now' and I instantly grunted as though I had taken a hit. I heard the report of the rifle from closer than I expected. I grunted again and gasped with pretend pain as I head Cam let out a scream as she quietly severed the spinal cord of the alien she had somehow mounted without me even noticing. I had to hold in a laugh. It seemed ridiculous to me anyone would believe our terrible act.

I looked around and saw the other alien was down. Delta and Aiden stood over it waiting to 'die'. Rochelle was sitting on the ground next to Daniel, who looked as though he was basking. A big smile on his face, which honestly I took as a sign he was feeling better. Delta said Aiden's name and within seconds I heard another two shots from the rifle and Delta nodded to Aiden. Then he started screaming into his headset that he had been attacked. He took a mouthful of water and really played on the gurgling death scene. It was pretty funny.

We waited a few minutes for the calls on the radio trying to re-establish contact with Delta to stop, by which time Tayler had joined us looking rather proud of herself. Delta and I looked at each other for a moment and nodded. We were good. I turned to Cam, who already had her compass at the ready. She pointed in the direction we should be heading and without a moment's more hesitation, we took off.

We ran for a good couple of hours. It was well past noon when I looked at my watch before calling a halt. Hopefully, we were well clear of anything tracking us, enough to take a break. Either way, we couldn't keep going at a flat out run much longer without stopping. The forest around me was extremely dark. It seemed the further in we got, the darker it became. I was used to the dark in here at night. I had grown accustomed to it pretty quickly. But it wasn't night right now. It was the middle of the day. I knew I was deep in the forest, but the darkness felt unnatural, creepy even. Cam pulled out her map again to check roughly where we were. After a moment, she looked up suddenly with some small amount of shock on her face.

"I think we are near a town!" she paused briefly, "it looks really old. I doubt it's even inhabited anymore, but it might have some structures left that we could hole up in for a little while." She continued on after a brief pause, as though nervous of her next words. "We can maybe get some rest and take some time to heal while we plan our next move. I know they all think we are dead, but eventually we are going to have to make some decisions."

We all just stared at her for a moment, trying to process what she had told us. Eventually, all heads turned to me, and I realised it was up to me to make this decision. I still couldn't get used to actually giving orders. I hadn't really needed to do much before now. It was mostly just things like what time we stopped marching, etc. What was most unnerving was Delta and Tayler were looking to me as well. I had thought with the way Delta had planned everything out before, maybe he was going to take over the leadership of the group. Or maybe Tayler would. They were both far more experienced than me and much higher ranked, but they were giving me the authority and seemed happy to follow me, whatever I decided now.

"Let's check it out," I found myself saying, "Maybe there are people there, maybe not, but Cam is right; there may be structures there, and we do need proper time to rest and heal; somewhere reasonably safe would be good, too." My eyes flicked to Rochelle momentarily. She claimed she was fine when I asked her, but I could see something wasn't quite right with her. She was looking paler than she had before. I got a scowl in return; she knew I was worried and she didn't like it.

Cam pointed us on the small change of direction and we continued on carefully – walking now – I briefly considered sending someone to scout ahead but dismissed it almost as quickly, we were all too wrecked and too edgy to be separated when we had to try and stay off the radio, even with our secret channel, that we were all now on. Instead, we walked along, keeping an eye out for signs of a possible nest in our path. Right now we really didn't want to have to fight anything – or anyone, really.

10

It was another half an hour or so of walking before we began to see the beginnings of basic civilisation. We came across a fence. It was broken, but it didn't look as ridiculously old as I had expected. Of course, the chances of people still being alive here, even if they had been here recently, were pretty slim, given the whole forest seemed to be a hub of alien activity. I just hoped whoever had lived here had gotten out of their own volition. Although given the state of things currently, that seemed unlikely.

Another ten minutes put us in the middle of a very small town. There were only eleven houses, a large hall, an old-fashioned forge and a beautiful big old church. It looked like something out of a novel about olden times. After a quick conference in the middle of the town, we decided to give it a quick search and then select the best place to make our temporary home base.

When we reassembled ten minutes later, our search had revealed all the houses were empty. Some had contained signs of a struggle and a couple also had some blood around, which saddened me more than it should have, given I had expected it. From our investigations we found although the forge was old-fashioned, it looked to have been in good working order and well used until recently – though there was a hole in the roof of the building. The large hall looked to have been used for trading or a market-place and maybe a meeting point for the town.

After our search, none of us had felt good about using any of the houses. Silly as it was, it just felt wrong. The forge and the hall both had an unsealed roof (deliberate on the hall) so we decided to hole up in the church. Although I don't think any of us had religious tendencies as such, it felt better than the other options. I can't speak for the others of course, I am not a religious person, but I suppose I am spiritual. That is to say, I believe in God – yes even now – and I was comforted by the idea of being in His house (even if that was a religious distinction) but it didn't feel evil or wrong to take our troubles in there. Besides, as Aiden pointed out, churches were supposed to provide sanctuary to those who asked for it and in a way, we were asking.

The church was warm and dry and clean, as though its priest or caretaker had just gone out for a stroll and would return any minute. We spread out; carefully completing a search before settling in to tend our wounds before we had a good long rest.

We had many wounds that needed to be addressed. Getting rid of the dirty field dressings that had been slapped on at the time of injury and replacing them with clean ones. The one on the back of my shoulder from our most recent fight was as yet uncovered and judging by the amount of bleeding and pain, probably needed stitches. No one was really confident with them. We had only learnt how to do basic stuff and we probably could work out stitches in most places if we had to, but it was a difficult area, being right over my shoulder blade. Delta looked over it thoroughly and we decided to tape it closed and see how it went. As long as we could give it time to knit and it didn't keep ripping open, it should be okay – we hoped.

After our wounds had all been cleaned and dressed, I noticed Rochelle had disappeared. I had a quiet word with Delta and then went looking for her. The church wasn't an enormous cathedral, like you sometimes saw, but for this size of town, it was huge. The wall behind the altar had a door through it on the right-hand side. It led through to a narrow hallway and a small bedroom with a small bathroom attached. We assumed that would have been where any priest or caretaker of the church would live. It had a second level of pews that were reached by a long staircase that lined the side wall opposite the door to the back. The floor containing them sat about halfway overhanging the lower level. The church and staircase were carpeted with a thick, soft pile of a very dark red colour and the pews looked like they were made of a very pale pine. They were lacquered to a high gloss and honestly looked almost new.

It was up the stairs in the balcony area I found Rochelle. She looked pale and tired. I sat next to her and waited for her to talk. She hadn't really said much since the fight in the clearing, or even since she had joined us, really. I had a feeling she was close to losing it and was operating more on autopilot than anything else. When she didn't speak, I prompted.

"Long couple of weeks," I said. I kept my head facing forward and watched her out of my peripheral vision. I saw a tear escape the corner of her eye.

"I couldn't do anything to save them, Tyne," she said, "they were already dead before I really knew what was happening. They practically tore them in half. This wasn't just fighting or attacking for food, this was revenge." I didn't say anything. She didn't need me to speak. Only to listen. "Where do they get off, coming after us to get revenge? This is our planet, our world they have invaded. We are the ones who get to have revenge!" Oh yeah, she was carrying some heavy anger with her. I understood where she was coming from, but I still had to keep her here in the present with me. If I lost her to her own thoughts, it could be disastrous for all of us.

"Rush, use it! We're not out of this yet. We still have a chance to get our planet back. And we are going to win! I'm not giving up. I'm going to keep fighting until we get that revenge. And so are you!" It wasn't a question, it was a statement, because I knew Rochelle wouldn't give up. She couldn't. I put my arm around her shoulder and gave her a gentle squeeze. She gasped and flinched as though she had been struck; at the same moment, I felt a large wet patch on the back of her shirt. I was about to ask her about it when all hell broke loose downstairs – figuratively speaking, of course.

I looked over the balcony at the sounds of shouting below. A man stood near the altar. He was frozen in place with two rifles trained on him and three other obvious fighters in position, with blades at the ready. He slowly raised his hands in a calming gesture. I took a quick glance at Rochelle, who gestured with a nod for me to go and raced down the stairs to find out what was going on.

"Hey Boss," Delta said as I approached without appearing to take his eyes from his target. "This guy just appeared out of nowhere."

"I didn't appear out of nowhere, although I can understand how it would seem that way to you," he paused as though collecting his thoughts and looked at me as I raised my eyebrows at him. It was the only question I was going to ask at the moment and I think he realised I wasn't going to verbalise it. "I have been here all along. I heard you up here and I waited to make sure that you were human." He looked at me nervously.

"Alright guys, I think he's human; you can relax... a little." They hesitated only a moment before lowering their weapons slightly. The man nodded his thanks. "Mind telling us who you are?" The last was obviously directed towards him.

"Sorry. You're right, I should have probably started with that. I'm Father Tom. At least that's what they call me here; called me." He seemed sad as he corrected himself with the past tense.

"So you're a Reverend then? Or a priest?" I asked, trying to get a handle on what was happening.

"No, not really, well sort of, I guess..." he sighed and then nodded to himself, "Let me start at the beginning. My name is Thomas Harding. But it used to be Father Thomas Harding. I used to be a priest, a Catholic priest specifically." He paused again for a moment before continuing.

"You see, I went to seminary school when I was a teenager and became a priest. I was a pretty good one, too. When I finished school, I was assigned to the church of a hospital. I worked there as a priest for a couple of years, performing last rites, marriages and taking confessions. You know all the things priests do. Then I decided I wanted to do more to help.

"So while continuing as a priest, I also decided to attend medical school. I originally wanted to be a doctor, but after six months, I felt the time constraints were taking too much away from my work as a priest. So I switched to nursing instead." He paused in his story again momentarily and I took the opportunity to break in. I never was very patient.

"So what did you mean when you said you used to be a priest? Did you quit to become a nurse?"

"Well, aahh..." he hesitated before continuing, "No, I didn't quit. While I was doing work placement for my nursing degree – approved by the church, of course – I met a woman. She was a nurse at the hospital where I was working. I started having improper thoughts about her and one day while we were alone together... I kissed her.

"She was scandalised, knowing I was a priest and all. I realised the error I had made and went straight to my superior and confessed my sins." He paused again for a moment, as though bracing himself for what he was about to say.

"He went to the others to help decide my punishment."

"I thought Catholics were all about forgiveness?" Tayler broke in.

"Yeah, not as much as they like to advertise. After discussion, they decided that I should leave the church. I wasn't kicked out exactly, but I was told I wouldn't be given any new assignment. With that, they pretty much turned their backs on me.

"I was depressed and I took what little I had and I ran. I ended up in Vegas. I was lost and confused and I ended up in a casino. I lost what I had and a lot more besides, I ended up owing some very bad people a fair bit of money. They came to collect and of course, I couldn't pay.

"The guy took pity on me because I was a priest. He ordered his guys to take me out of town and make sure I didn't come back. One of them was heavily religious and knew of a place for me. They brought me here. They left me in the town here, uninjured and alive on the condition I never headed back to Vegas. I thought this place was some kind of commune when I first came here." He gave a small chuckle and looked up at us. It was a thought a couple of us had voiced ourselves. "It's not, I mean, it wasn't. These people just don't... ah... didn't want to be around others. They grow most of what they eat themselves and almost everything here is done on a barter system. They were told when I was dropped off here that I was a holy man, but not what kind. The townsfolk put me up in the church and started calling me Father Tom. I have been here for four years now."

"The townspeople ever find out the truth about you?" Delta asked.

"I told them after about three months. I told them I had lost my title and almost my soul. They were very forgiving. They wanted me to stay, anyway. They said I was the best priest they had ever had and they wanted to keep me – although I think my nursing degree had a lot to do with that too – I've been living in the church here since I arrived." He looked around at each of us. He seemed on the verge of saying something else when another sound reached our ears.

It was a dull thumping sound. Like someone falling down a flight of stairs. Which I realised was exactly what it was. Rochelle. She had been upstairs still. She had obviously tried to come down and fallen.

I rushed over to her. That was when I realised something was very wrong. Rochelle was very pale, even paler than she had been when I was sitting with her. Her skin was warm and clammy. Her breathing was shallow and laboured. She was sick, really sick. It took me a moment to register that Delta had followed me over to where Rochelle was until he shoved me gently out of the way and picked her up off the floor. I opened my mouth to ask him what he was doing, but I didn't get the words out.

"Priest is a nurse. Maybe he can help." He said as he moved past me with her in his arms and carried her toward the front of the church where the priest still stood.

"Priest," Delta said in a rough but quiet voice – the one he used when he was concerned. "Can you help her? You're a nurse, right?"

"Yes, of course I can try. What's her name?"

"Rochelle." I put in, finding my voice at last. "Her name is Rochelle. I think she had a wound on her shoulder. It felt wet and she flinched when I gave her a hug right before you appeared."

Delta placed Rochelle gently on the ground and Tom knelt next to her. Together, they rolled her onto her side so he could look at the wound that I thought was on her shoulder. It went straight down her shoulder and it was bad. It looked like something sharp but wide had torn down her back in two places. It took me a moment to realise they were claw marks. And they were very red. Beneath them, higher up on her shoulder, was an older circular wound that also looked like it needed a good clean.

"The wounds are getting infected pretty badly. How long ago were they inflicted?" Tom asked me.

"Umm, I don't know, but I assume during our last battle with the aliens. So a few hours ago, maybe." I replied.

"They may even be going septic. I've never seen a wound do this after only a few hours. The aliens did this." It wasn't a question, but as he looked at me again and I nodded and shrugged. "She's burning up. We are going to have to try and cool her down. Do you guys carry penicillin with you?"

I shook my head and Delta informed him we weren't allowed to because they didn't have time to train us on correct dosage for specific things. We weren't trained medics, after all. Tom nodded to himself and jumped up from the floor with a lightning quick motion and ran behind the altar where he disappeared. Delta and I looked at each other and I noticed Aiden walking over to the altar to see what was going on. He stood there for a moment, just staring and looking very lost and confused. Then he jumped a little and the surprise on his face turned into a smile.

Tom reappeared from behind the altar with a small cooler bag over his shoulder. He knelt again next to Rochelle and opened it. He started fiddling with vials and bottles in the bag before asking if Rochelle was allergic to anything. I informed him she had no known allergies. He didn't hesitate and filled a needle from one of the bottles that he had dug out; I managed to make out the first few letters on the bottle and it started with PEN, so I assumed it was penicillin. He injected it straight into the fatty part of her leg. Then he prepared and administered another injection into the vein in her arm, which he informed me was morphine.

Once he had done that, he instructed us to roll her onto her stomach, which Delta and I did, while he put on gloves and got some other things ready; he cleaned and stitch the wounds on her back. It was complicated work (at least it looked it to me) and it took him over an hour to stitch her up and dress the wounds, but he did a really good job.

While he worked, we asked him how he had avoided us when we searched the church. Aiden chose that moment to reappear as Tom explained there was a section of the basement that could only be reached via a trapdoor hidden under the altar. Aiden put his comments about how cool it was down there, after which Tom explained when they had heard about the aliens, he and the townsfolk had hidden down there to avoid being found. It had worked and after they had heard the extent of the attack, most of the townsfolk had decided to leave to seek safety elsewhere. Obviously, there had been no contact since, so he didn't know if they had made it, but I could see the fervent hope in his eyes that they had found safety. He had heard the aliens come through the town but hadn't come out of hiding to find out what they had done. In that moment, I did not want to be the one to inform him seventy-five percent or more of America's population were suspected of having been killed.

He finished stitching up Rochelle's wounds and asked if anyone else needed stitches. Delta and I looked at each other briefly and I gave him the smallest shake of my head. We had agreed to see how my shoulder went and I didn't want to go through another dressing change if I didn't have to. (Yeah, I was being a sook, but I didn't care right then.)

We told him we had taken care of everything else for now and Tom nodded thoughtfully to himself. If I had to guess, I'd say he probably knew we were nervous about trusting him. He didn't say anything as he cleaned up the mess he had made. Instead, when he finished, he offered to show us his little hideout. Aiden smiled as Tom led us to the altar and lifted the curtain at the back. Underneath was a very cleverly concealed trapdoor. It opened outwards with two doors that met in the middle. When it was closed, you couldn't tell there was a door there at all. It was set up to look exactly like the rest of the floor. He took us down the ladder so we could see the rather large room below it.

It was about the size of a decent master bedroom. There was a small cot in one corner and a couple of small cabinets with drawers in them. There was plenty of floor space available and Tom suggested we all bunker down there rather than stay up in the actual church. I got the impression he was taking guesses at what we were doing. But he was guessing right if he thought we were hiding.

I agreed that sleeping down in the hidden room would be preferable to the alternative, especially if the aliens came looking around again. After the decision was made, we set about the difficult task of moving a still unconscious Rochelle down the ladder. (Delta ended up carrying her down there by himself using what I think is referred to as a fireman's carry – it was the only way we were fairly sure wouldn't burst her stitches since we didn't have a stretcher or backboard to strap her to.) Tom decided she should use the cot and had quickly run around putting fresh sheets on it while we carried her down.

Afterwards, we cleaned our presence out of the church as much as we could and set a watch rotation. We decided to set a two-person watch. We were all getting very tired and we didn't want to run into the same problem Bravo team had, being caught off guard. We had enough people to keep a dual rotation and Tom offered to take turns keeping guard with us. We accepted, though I secretly decided he would only be on watch with me, or maybe Delta. It wasn't that I didn't trust him – or the others – but I had a feeling there was something he wasn't telling us and I hoped maybe I could get him to open up with some one-on-one time, but I didn't tell anyone about my suspicions. I didn't want them casting judgements on something I wasn't sure about. I was pretty sure Delta would be thinking along the same lines as me. We seemed to think alike on a lot of this stuff I had noticed.

11

That night while I sat watch with Delta, I turned my radio up. I had left it down for the last few hours since we had 'died'. I knew Delta had kept his on the overwatch channel so he could keep tabs on anything that happened. He hadn't mentioned anything to me and honestly, I hadn't asked, but I figured nothing had happened that was super important.

I was surprised to hear a lot of chatter going on. Not fighting type chatter, just conversation. The kind that hadn't really happened much at the start. Having been out here for weeks had taken its toll on everyone. Although I noticed that overwatch weren't joining in much, except to half-heartedly remind them to keep it down and pay attention every now and then.

They were probably thinking they were near the end of their search. I wondered if they had figured out the glitch with their GPS systems yet. I hoped they had and were just being smart enough not to talk about it over the radio.

Delta assured me the overwatch twins had figured it out through things they said. We just hoped they hadn't figured out anything else yet. Much as Delta trusted them, we weren't ready for them to know we were alive just yet. It was almost midnight when Delta and I traded off the watch with Aiden and Tayler, who informed us if we were going to go on from here, she wanted a new call-sign. Delta laughed. I promised her we would find one for her.

When my next watch came around, I found I had slept for almost twelve hours. Delta and Tom had taken my watch and Tom was staying up with me for the next watch as well. Delta went off to sleep after telling me to keep my radio on both channels so I could hear everything. He hadn't asked me to listen in on the overwatch channel before. I was curious as to why, but I didn't want to ask in front of Tom.

I ate some food that had been prepared earlier, at some time in the middle of the night I guessed, given that it was still very early in the morning. Tom informed me with Delta's permission, he had given Rochelle another heavy dose of penicillin and another dose of morphine, but she hadn't woken up yet, although she had stirred a few times (he suspected around the same time the first dose of morphine had worn off) he was taking it as a good sign her brain was still active and we had started treating the infection in time.

After I had eaten, I went and sat by her for a while. About an hour or so later, a sudden loud voice through the radio made me jump. I felt the wound in my shoulder tear open again, but I ignored it for the moment. I walked quickly to the other side of the room as I listened. Part of me wanted to pace anxiously, but I kept it under control. I didn't want to wake the others.

Alpha team had walked into a nest. The shout through the radio had been overwatch, letting them know they were about to get jumped from behind. To their credit, they reacted quickly, from what I could tell. I heard Alpha leader barking orders to his team. The fight lasted only about twelve minutes and at the end of it, Alpha team was one man down.

Alpha team had learnt from Bravo team's mistakes – just as we had – and they didn't stand around and talk. They moved and kept moving. I had been facing the wall while the battle was going on and paid very little attention to what was going on in the room with me. But I turned suddenly at the slight sound almost right behind me, my fists half raised to defend myself because I stupidly hadn't picked up my weapons; any of them (although what kind of attack I expected down here that would have gone unannounced by Tom eluded me, and I didn't think Tom had any malice in him.)

Tom stood behind me with one hand raised, as though he was going to place it on my shoulder. His face was somewhere between concern and shock – probably at how fast I had turned around – behind him on the floor I saw he had his medical kit unpacked and set up ready as though to care for a wound. That was when I remembered jumping and tearing my shoulder open and I finally allowed myself to become aware of the pain and the wet feeling that probably meant I was bleeding quite a lot. I realised Tom must have noticed the large wet patch on my black shirt and set everything up first rather than disturb me while I was listening to the radio.

He had paused in the act of reaching toward me to get my attention rather than speaking. Like me, he was trying not to disturb the others who were sleeping. He dropped his hand to his side, gesturing at the medical kit.

"Let me have a look at that and try and fix it up, please?" I studied him for a moment. He had been forward enough to get everything ready, but he seemed like he would genuinely leave me alone if I said no. He really was just asking. I decided to trust him a little bit more and nodded my head as I walked over to where he had set up the kit. I sat on the floor and realised – rather awkwardly –I didn't have a singlet on under my shirt. Both of mine were among the things we had washed in Tom's little laundry room the evening before – prior to setting a watch and turning in – and were hanging up drying. While I was comfortable enough to be in only my bra while Delta was tending my wounds earlier, it felt altogether different to do it in front of Tom. I figured the feelings probably had something to do with the fact he was a stranger and a priest – sort of – rather than my own issues.

I told myself to stop being so stupid and compromised with my brain by turning around so my back was to him and started to remove my shirt. It had stuck to my shoulder in a couple of places, so I figured maybe it had already been bleeding before I ripped it open again. Tom had to help me remove it gently from the wound. He also asked me to pull my bra strap off my shoulder so it didn't pull on the skin while he was stitching me up. Then he gently prodded the wound with gloved fingers.

"This is a pretty bad cut and it has a fair bit of dirt and stuff in it – fluff from your shirt, I think – what did you do it on?" I sat quietly for a moment, not wanting to answer.

"Tyne? You still with me?" It was funny, but I hadn't realised he knew my name.

"Yeah sorry, I was thinking, um, I got a decent scratch from an alien during our last fight and I ended up spending a bit of time on the ground fighting after that, too."

"Yeah, I'd be guessing so. It's going to leave a pretty bad scar and I'm going to have to open it up a little more to clean it and repair the edges so the stitches will hold."

"Scars I can deal with."

"I'm not sure I can give you any morphine, though. I don't have a large stock here and I think your friend is going to need more before she is up and about. I have a little bit of local anaesthetic though. It's old, but it should at least help with the pain while I clean it out."

"Whatever you got, I'll deal with."

"You're not from around here, are you? I mean, well... you're not American... how did you end up in the middle of the Nevada state forest?"

"I volunteered..."

"Huh? What do you mean, you volunteered?"

"After the big attack here, the Americans sent planes to Australia and asked for volunteers to come and fight. Our country had been abused and abandoned by then and people were already rebuilding. There wasn't much Rochelle and I could do there and we were both so angry. So when someone came and said we could fight back, neither of us gave it much more thought. We just jumped on the plane." I didn't bother to elaborate on the fact we had both lost everything and had nothing left to keep us in Australia (or for us to go back to even if we survived this). "Why didn't you leave, really?"

"Part of it is that I really have nowhere else to go..." he paused for a moment. I couldn't see his face, so I didn't know if he was going to continue. "But another part of it is I had somewhere safe to hide in case anyone came back. I almost gave up hope there for a while. Until you came along..." he paused again," "Can I ask you something?"

"Sure," I said carefully, wondering what he wanted to know and if it would be something I was able to or willing to answer.

"You searched the houses around the town, didn't you?" I nodded my head. I suddenly had a stomach dropping feeling I knew what was coming. "Well, I was wondering what it looks like out there?"

"Haven't you been outside since all this started?" I asked him, a little surprised.

"Well yes, I've been out there, but I couldn't bring myself to go into any of the houses after the others left and the aliens came through. I know that sounds bad." His hands stopped moving on my shoulder for a moment and I realised he had finished stitching and putting a fresh dressing on. When he finished and I couldn't avoid it anymore; I turned to face him.

"We found nothing really..." He went to say something, but I held up a hand to stall him. "There are no bodies or anything, but there is a lot of blood. I hate to say it, but I don't think a lot of people got out. I think they were killed... or taken." I watched several emotions cross his face. Finally, he seemed to settle on anger. It was strange seeing anger on a priest; but given the situation, it was a safer emotion than pity or sadness. Anger might make people act without thinking sometimes, but it did make them act instead of freezing up. Something told me that before long, he was going to need to act.

I looked up from his face and over his shoulder, straight into Rochelle's eyes. Happiness shot straight through my heart as I saw a smile come slowly to her face. She looked much better than the last time she had been awake.

"Hey there," she said, her voice gravelly from sleep. "How long was I out? Where are we? This doesn't look like a hospital – or the church. Who's that?" That last one included a nod toward Tom.

"Hey yourself, you probably shouldn't talk too much. You've been out for over half a day. We've given you two doses of penicillin and morphine. Do you really think we were going to get to a hospital?" She shook her head sheepishly; I think she knew I was testing her to see what she remembered; if anything. "We are in the hidden basement of the church and for the record, getting your unconscious arse down here was not so easy." She laughed at that. It was a stronger sound than I expected. It made me feel relieved she seemed to be feeling better.

"I'm Father Tom, or just Tom, if you prefer. This is kind of my church. I've been hiding here since the beginning." Tom spoke up before I could answer the other question. "Tyne? I'm going to go check the church and then get some sleep. Do you need me to wake the next watch for you?" It was very formal, as though he wasn't sure how to act around a new person. I realised I hadn't really seen him interact with anyone else in the team. Maybe he was like that with everyone.

"No thanks Tom, I can do it. Are you sure you should be going up there?" I asked him. I tried to put as much innocence into my voice as I could. I still felt he was hiding something and I hadn't worked out what it was.

"Delta and I took turns to do it during our watch and the other watches did the same during their turns. I'll be fine." I thought I heard him whisper something else to himself, but I didn't quite catch it. Rochelle looked like she wanted to say something, but I shook my head as subtly as I could to silence her. I knew if Tom was going to tell his secret, then he needed to do it on his own terms.

He went off to check his church and Rochelle raised an eyebrow at me. We held a hurried, whispered conversation about everything that had happened in the last sixteen-ish hours while she had been out. She asked me about my thoughts on Father Tom and I told her I was cautiously optimistic. I was about to elaborate on that when we heard Tom coming back through the trap door and down the ladder. He nodded to us as he walked over to his blankets. He lay down facing the wall away from us and appeared to fall asleep rather quickly. We didn't talk about anything important while we waited. Once I was sure his breathing was rhythmic and signalled actual sleep, we quietly continued our conversation.

We had just moved back onto other topics when I heard a crackling buzz over the radio. I turned the volume up again – I had turned it down a little after Alpha team's fight – so I could hear what was going on.

Charlie team was on the border of a suspected nest. They were hashing out a quick plan. I don't know why they were doing it on the radio. Maybe they were hoping for some input from Charlie Overwatch or something. He wasn't really giving much input, though. Alpha leader was trying to give them tips for fighting with injuries. Everyone was sporting a few by now. It was the same stuff we had all been taught in basic training. It was almost as though he was trying to remind himself as well as them.

And then suddenly it was all on. They were yelling at each other. It sounded like chaos, but then it became semi-organised chaos. It took me a moment to realise Charlie Overwatch was helping them. He seemed to be giving them his bird's-eye view of everything in the fight. A couple of times, he called out a number and told them to turn around. There seemed to be a never-ending supply of aliens. Every time they killed one, it seemed like another one was there to take its place.

As I listened to the battle unfolding and taking longer and longer, it felt like they had walked into an ambush, just as we had. As soon as I had that thought, one of them fell. From what I could hear, there were two aliens feeding on him. The last thing I heard him scream was begging someone to kill him. The next sound I heard was the report of a sniper rifle.

Rochelle was watching my face. Suddenly, she reached out a hand and wiped a tear off my cheek. I hadn't realised I was crying. I had my microphone muted to stop the temptation of speaking to them.

Alpha Leader was yelling into the radio for them to get out, to run. His cries were falling on deaf ears. I don't think it would have made a difference; they didn't really seem to have anywhere to go. They were swamped, trapped and they had no escape. It was only a matter of time before they all fell.

Charlie Overwatch shouted something into the radio at the same time someone else yelled something. They cancelled each other out for a moment and the next thing I heard was a pained scream. I wasn't sure who it had come from. I heard another shot as a hand landed gently on my shoulder, furthest from Rochelle. I looked up and saw Delta standing over me. Rochelle was lowering herself back onto the cot gently. I hadn't even noticed her get up, but I realised now she had gone to wake him.

Delta had his radio on as well and he looked sad, but as if he was waiting for something else to happen. There wasn't any more screaming. The radio had gone silent. I didn't want to think about what that meant.

Then a whisper came through the radio. I realised it must have been on the overwatch channel, because Alpha leader didn't react.

"It's over. They're dead, they're all dead." There was silence for a moment. I wondered who Charlie Overwatch had been talking to, even though I technically knew the answer. I could see Delta's hands shaking as he tried to restrain himself from replying. Finally, a reply came from Alpha Overwatch.

"Charlie, are you secure?" I raised my eyebrows in question at Delta. I somehow expected something different since he told me they were brothers. He just shook his head at me for a moment and held up a hand to tell me not to talk.

"Yes, I'm secure. I'm on the move."

"Head towards my location and rendezvous with Alpha team." He read off a bunch of coordinates and I saw Delta checking his GPS. They confirmed a time that they would meet up and signed off. There was no comment or interference from back at base, although I assumed they were still monitoring all our transmissions. I hadn't heard an order to fire on them, so whoever was giving that order obviously wasn't around.

Delta came and sat in front of me, while Rochelle was still beside me on the cot and showed me the GPS. Alpha team was heading on a path that would run parallel to the village we were in. They would pass us about seven kilometres to the west. I just hoped no one on Alpha team was a map nut like Cam; we knew by now their GPS wouldn't show the town, or even where they accurately were. But with no map, I knew they wouldn't discover our little hiding place. We were planning on holing up here for a while yet. Provided the priest didn't mind us hijacking his church basement for a while longer. We had healing and planning to do and we wanted and needed time to do it in relative safety.

Delta and I had a quiet conversation about Charlie and Alpha. He wanted to find a way to contact them, but we had no way to do it safely via the radio. Rochelle tried to keep up with us, but she was still very weak and fell back asleep.

Delta didn't stay awake long either but he woke Tayler before he went back to sleep so I wasn't sitting the watch alone anymore. She was really happy when I told her Rochelle had been awake for a while. She seemed genuinely concerned for her. I liked that she cared so much.

12

The next twenty-four hours went by much like that, two always on watch and the rest sleeping as much as they could. The next time Rochelle woke, she managed to get up for a while and walk around. Tom gave her one more shot of antibiotics before declaring she should be all good. The only other thing that happened was he changed mine and Rochelle's dressings. He was very, very quiet afterwards and I wondered if there was something wrong.

Late in the morning the next day, Delta woke me for my watch and informed me Alpha team had been taken out shortly after Charlie Overwatch had caught up with them. When Alpha team had started fighting, Alpha Overwatch had been ordered to fire on them. He had flat out refused and as the next member of the team had fallen, he and Charlie both had supposedly run in to render assistance, but contact had been lost shortly afterward and they were also presumed dead. He seemed sad when he relayed the information, as though he wished there was something he could have done. I assured him there was nothing any of us could have done to help them, at least not without exposing ourselves. I didn't ask him if he really believed they were dead and a big part of that was because I really wasn't sure I wanted to know the answer.

Toward the end of my watch, I started getting bored (I had sent Tayler back to bed to get some extra sleep – she hadn't been sleeping well). I woke Aiden and Rochelle and told them I was going for a walk around the town.

As I wandered through the town, I tried to imagine what it would have been like as a functioning operating place. I imagined happy, smiling people who didn't want for anything. I'm sure my imagination was inaccurate, but it was my dream, after all.

I came to the outer edge of the town, near where we had entered and found a nice shady spot just inside the tree line, where I decided to sit for a while. I needed to think and to plan my next move. Our next move. Part of me wished Delta was here for me to talk this out with. But a much bigger part of me wished for Brock. Somehow, I felt sure he would know what to do. It was not lost on me. I was now in charge of the fates of eight people (yes, I included Tom in that. Our fates felt tied to him and his now). Delta and Tayler had more experience than me, but they seemed to be looking to me to lead them too. (Funny how quickly I had reverted to calling him Delta now I had put my mind to it, also having a Tim and a Tom got a bit confusing.)

And I also felt a strange sense of responsibility for Tom. He had sheltered and hidden us and although I still felt sure there was something he wasn't telling us; I felt as though I owed it to him to protect him.

My radio was on, but I had it turned right down. I had been sitting out in the trees for about half an hour or so; it wasn't until I heard Rochelle's voice saying my name repeatedly that I paid any attention. I had switched the channel over to our private one when I had left the church. After all, the only people on our private channel were with me in the town. And if they needed to contact me, I wanted them to be able to.

"Yeah Rush I'm here, what's up?" I asked her once I had turned up the sound again.

"There's some funny chatter on the open group channel I think you should hear."

"Okay, I'll switch over, over." I had to laugh to myself as I said that (I had done it on purpose, we kept things pretty informal on our private channel) I knew she would have gotten the joke and would be laughing too. I flicked my radio back to the old group channel and listened.

I felt as though my prayers had been answered. I immediately wanted to look at the sky to see if there were shooting stars around I had been unknowingly wishing on.

"This is Hunter. If anyone is reading this, I have a message, over."

That was the whole thing, but it was Brock. My heart leapt probably a little more than it should have. Especially in the current circumstances. But I couldn't help getting excited. I wasn't quite sure how to respond without giving away that I was – we were – still around to anyone else who may be listening. I couldn't remember if I had ever told Brock my lucky number. I had to hedge my bets and hope I had and that he would recognise my voice, because I wasn't going to be repeating myself.

"Hunter, switch to lucky numbers." I waited with bated breath, hoping desperately I hadn't just made a huge mistake, especially without consulting the others.

"Hunter switching to lucky numbers." Came the reply. I breathed a sigh of relief before switching back to our channel and waiting. I didn't have to wait long.

"This is Hunter, Tyne, is that you?" There was a nervousness in his voice I hadn't expected. I wondered if it had been there before and hadn't noticed it, or if he had kept it buttoned up being on a very public channel.

"Yeah Brock, it's me."

"I can't believe it's really you, how? I mean, I didn't think you could be dead, not really, but still. Why have you..? What the hell is going on out there?"

"It's a long story. But yes, we are alive, well some of us, my team is alive although we are sporting quite a few injuries, we have a couple of extras including two of the overwatch soldiers." I paused for a moment before continuing, but he broke in.

"What overwatch soldiers?"

"They were assigned to each team. They were supposed to be watching our backs when we fought to provide back-up apparently... at least that's what we were told. They are snipers."

"That makes no sense. Bullets barely hurt these things. They just pass right through and then they heal quickly."

"Yeah, that's what I thought, too. But they were with us, anyway. When push came to shove with Bravo team, overwatch was ordered to take them out."

"What?!" He almost screamed into the radio. "What happened? Is your friend okay? She was on Bravo team, wasn't she?"

"Bravo Overwatch didn't take the shot. The team was pretty much already gone, anyway. She ran in and took out the last couple of aliens instead. She found Rush afterwards and together they got the hell out of there. After a while, they contacted me. Then they joined us. We got into another fight and when our overwatch was given the same order, he also refused to shoot. He came in and helped us instead and we all decided we needed to die and go offline. Overwatch did a spectacular dying scene." I said with a smile coming to my face, remembering Delta's death acting.

"What about Alpha and Charlie Teams? Are they with you or are they really dead? I've been listening in for a little over twenty-four hours, so I heard some of what went on in the other battles."

"We think they might actually be dead. They aren't with us. Their battles were pretty bad from our end and we haven't heard anything from them at all, not that we could make contact with them without giving ourselves away, anyway. Overwatch went offline a while ago and we only have a vague guess at Alpha team's last coordinates."

"Do you think they could have done what you guys did?"

"Honestly, I'm hoping that's exactly what they've done, but I don't think so. Maybe one or two of them are alive, but not many. We know Charlie team was completely wiped out except overwatch... it still leaves the problem of how we would contact them though."

"I would imagine that they will find you if they are alive."

"I don't know if they will or how they would know to look. We're pretty off the beaten path here. I don't know if they will feel the same way about being ordered to fire on us. Charlie Overwatch wasn't ordered to that we heard. We don't know what happened out there."

"I would imagine they would feel much the same as you guys do. No soldier or sniper wants to fire on his own people. It goes against everything they are trained to do."

"Yeah, I guess so. Anyway... you said you had a message. Who for? And what is it?" As much as I didn't want the conversation with Brock to end, I knew I had to do the right thing.

"The message was for you, actually. I didn't want to believe that you were dead. You're too good for that, so I figured it was worth a try."

"You mean you trained me too well?"

"Yeah, something like that." I heard him chuckle. "Listen Tyne, I know what's going on here... well, not all of it, but I know some of what you're up against."

"What are you talking about?" I asked him. I was a little confused. He had left base around the same time I did (a little bit before) on his own mission. I wasn't even sure if he really knew what our mission was. Because it had changed from one day to the next.

"I need to know where you are and how many people you actually have with you."

"What is going on? Why does it matter? They all think we're dead, so there's no help coming." I was instantly on the defensive. I felt bad. I was nervous about trusting him, but right now, I was nervous about trusting anyone who wasn't here with us.

"There is help coming! At the very least to get you out!" He said, pretty convincingly.

"Who is going to come help us? They don't even know we are alive... do they?" I asked him. I didn't believe the army would send help, even if they did know we were alive. I didn't want to get my hopes up about the other option that jumped into my head.

"Me! I am coming to help you! Now I need to know where you are so I can get to you. I will explain everything when I get there. I don't know everything you've been through, but I imagine you are having some trust issues right now but please, you trusted me before... trust me now." It was about then I realised I was no longer alone. I turned, almost fearfully, to face whoever or whatever was behind me.

It was Delta. I wondered briefly how he always seemed to know when I needed him to turn up. He watched me for a moment longer, searching for something in my eyes, maybe. Then he nodded his head. I realised then he must have been listening to us on the radio. He was telling me it was okay to tell Brock where we were, but was it? I trusted Brock with my life – mostly – I'd had to, otherwise all of his training would have done me no good at all. But telling him where we were meant I was trusting him with all of our lives and there was still a chance that someone at the base would find out we were still alive. I wasn't sure we were ready for that yet.

Brock had never lied to me though and Delta seemed to think it would be okay if we told him. So… I chose to trust in the two main men in my life at the moment (well, in my mind anyway). The one I had very strong feelings for and the one I had trusted to have my back out here in this forest and had helped keep me alive for the last couple of weeks.

"How well do you know the Nevada State Forest?" I asked Brock.

"I know it, okay. Lots of fun facts about that forest and you know me and my useless trivia." I laughed… I did know him and his useless trivia.

"Did you know there's a town in the middle of it? That's still inhabited. Well, was until the aliens came along, anyway."

"Actually, I did know that. It was set up to seem like a kind of commune. But it's more just a bunch of people who hate the big bad world. It's on that map I made sure was in with your stuff."

"Can you find it? We can't give you exact coordinates. Our GPS is a little unreliable at this point in time."

"Yeah, I can find it… Tyne, are you okay? Really?" There was genuine concern in his voice.

"I'll survive Brock. There are eight of us here. We're holed up in the church."

"I'll be there in about twenty-seven hours, give or take."

"How?" I asked, "I thought your mission was halfway across the country or something?"

"I borrowed a car. It's very fast, and the owner wasn't using it anymore. I've been heading in your direction for two days already, but I didn't want to make contact until I was sure I would be able to get there soon."

"How did your mission go?"

"Surprisingly, not a total bust, but not what I expected at all. I'll tell you about it when I see you and Tyne… don't worry, okay? Everything is going to be alright. I know that underneath all that self-control you seem to exude, you're terrified, but it's going to be ok, and I won't tell anyone you're alive or where you are. I know that had to be playing on your mind the whole time we've been talking. Trust me, I don't want you found any more than you do before you're ready."

"Thanks Brock."

"But Tyne... if you do come under attack again, by the aliens that is... do me a favour... Don't get bit. Brock out." And with that, he was gone. I turned my radio back down and tuned out anymore possible conversation that would let me give into the fear Brock knew was bubbling under the surface. I looked up at Delta.

"You didn't come out here just to eavesdrop on my convo. You could have done that from the church... like Rochelle probably did. What's up?"

"For starters, are you insane being all the way out here on your own? What if you had been attacked? We haven't been checking the surrounding area very well since we've been here. There could be aliens anywhere. I know you're good Tyne, and you have great hearing and your instincts are incomparable for what we are facing out here, but that was dangerous." He paused to take a deep breath. (I had the impression that he was trying not to yell.) "Please don't do it again."

"You really came out here to growl at me?" I asked him. I wasn't shocked or surprised and even if I had been, he was right. It was stupid and dangerous for me to be out here by myself, or at all, really. No matter how much I needed air and to think.

"No, but it was a good excuse... I'll use it next time too, especially if you do this again. I did come out to make sure you were okay and it did need to be said. I would never do it in front of the others. They have chosen to follow us, well you, but they shouldn't see us argue even about something like this. I would never undermine your authority like that."

"Why?" I asked and he opened his mouth to answer, but I held up my hand instinctively knowing he hadn't quite understood the question – not that I had phrased it well – I went on. "Why do I have this authority? Even you and Tayler listen to me... you both have far more experience at being soldiers than I do." He studied me for a long moment before answering (I think I was right about him misunderstanding the question).

"Because you have good instincts. Exceptionally good, as I said before, everything you have done since I've been around you is to try and save and protect the people that have been with you, because you have good training for this situation. Because of Brock Hunter, his reputation and the fact that he trained you personally – which means more than any of the others got – and because you have kept fighting even when it seemed hopeless, be honest you still would have fought if you'd been facing those last seven alone; you'd have charged in anyway, wouldn't you?" I nodded. "At the end of the day, Tayler and I are soldiers. We do what we are told... mostly. You have shown me that with the right information you will make the best decisions for the group and your goal is to actually destroy the aliens and get out alive, currently it doesn't seem like our bosses are trying for that so... I'll follow you. Into battle, out of here to safety, whatever you decide to do, especially with this new information that is coming. I have a feeling you will use it better than anyone else could hope to."

"Okay..." I didn't really know what to say to that. I was honoured and terrified all at the same time.

"Having said all that though, there is something I have done I should tell you." He paused and I watched him warily. "I thought of a way to contact Alpha and Charlie Overwatch if they are still alive and assuming they continue on their current path, which I think they will."

"What? How? Did you send out a message on the radio?" I suddenly felt strangely elated. Hope began to rise. They might actually be alive, at least a couple of them.

"No..." He seemed a little nervous, "Tayler and I went for a walk last night while Cam and Daniel kept watch. We went out to roughly where we figured their previous path would have passed by the town and tied a rag to a tree."

"A rag? How will that let them know where we are?"

"It's an old sniper trick. Red rag tells them to change directions. Yellow means go straight. So I tied a red rag right in their path where they couldn't miss it and a yellow one on a tree fifty metres away, heading them directly toward town. Then another yellow one every mile or so to let them know they are on the right track."

"Do you think it'll work?"

"If they hadn't already passed by the place I tied the red rag, (which from their last known coordinates they shouldn't have by the time I did it) and assuming of course they are actually alive, then it will work alright." I stared at him in stunned silence for a while. I didn't know what to say. I probably should have been mad that he and Tayler had taken such a risk; even though they had gone together – which, as he pointed out, I hadn't taken anyone with me. – Although I had also desperately wanted to find a way to make contact with Alpha and Charlie if they were alive. I let all this flow over me, then I asked the question that came to mind first.

"How long do we wait?" If Delta was surprised by my lack of reaction, he didn't show it; other than looking slightly calmer than he had a moment before.

"Well, I figure we're here for another two or three days at least. Waiting for Hunter, finding out what he knows, letting him get some rest and then making a plan. If they aren't here by then, I would guess they aren't coming."

"Okay then. Sounds like we have the beginnings of a plan." I couldn't help smiling.

"Now, are you done risking your life out here?" I saw the smile on his face. He was trying to make a joke about it now. I'd noticed he was like that when things got too serious, unnecessarily. But when things got bad, he was all over it.

"Yeah, I guess I'm done. I'm hungry too. But I think now that we've had a couple of days' rest, we could all use some exercise."

"We were thinking of talking to the priest about taking some food from the houses. There's still power here. I assume a generator somewhere; so there should be some that's not spoiled and we're going to need to replenish our food if we're going to go on. In the meantime, we could all use some real food."

13

We walked back to the church to find Tom and ask him. I thought he'd put up more of a fight about it, but he agreed quite readily. He said he didn't want to see it all go to waste. He seemed to have accepted now that most of the townsfolk were probably dead.

He came out with us and found boxes to carry food in, but he wouldn't come into any of the houses. I saw the pain on his face at the very thought of seeing the damage and possible blood inside and I vowed to myself, if we survived this, I would come back (hopefully with Rochelle) and help with the clean-up. I didn't think Tom would ever be able to do it (at least not by himself) and I wouldn't want to make him.

We managed to get quite a good haul of preserved and frozen food. Tom had been the one to keep the town's generators going after everyone left and the aliens came through; given they were in the church, so there was quite a good stock. Tom seemed to be okay with taking a harvest from the vegetable gardens outside the houses himself. So we had quite a few potatoes and carrots especially, as well as some greens.

We made our way back to the church with the boxes full of food to cook up and eat and Delta and I decided we would wake everyone up for a full proper meal once the food was ready. I secretly hoped my cooking skills were good enough to please everybody. (Rochelle has always told me I put too much pressure on myself for that type of thing.)

The meal was planned out well and was going to be ready late afternoon. Most of us were awake long before that. It seemed we had slept ourselves out the last couple of days. Add that to the smell of real food and it was hard to keep us down. Daniel and Cam offered to go out into the town and keep a watch further out for a while. I think they just wanted to escape the confines of the church for a little while. I didn't blame them, especially after being outside for a while myself.

Tom checked my wounds again and declared that despite the delay in stitching and proper cleaning, they were healing well and I'd probably be okay. (I think he was trying to have a joke with me – to let me know he was okay – and I appreciated it after the afternoon we had just put him through). Afterward, he went off in search of Rochelle to check her wounds. Everybody else had already had their dressings removed, although Aiden's shoulder was still strapped from his dislocation; but he had almost full use of it. We had also had our clothes washed and dried (we each carried one spare set of clothes and they had all been dirty and bloody). So effectively, we were ready to go whenever we decided what to do.

The smell of food was wafting through the air telling me it was almost ready, when Tom came back, he looked confused and concerned about something, but before I had a chance to ask him what was going on Cam's voice across the radio called me and Delta out to the middle of town. I met up with Delta on the way out there and we greeted Cam coming back towards us at a quick jog.

"What is it Cam?" I asked her.

"Someone is coming towards town, from the direction Alpha team would have passed by us."

"How many are there? And where is Daniel?" Delta asked her. Cam looked at him for a moment before answering.

"There are two, as far as we can tell. Daniel is following them in. They appear to be human. They also don't appear to be taking many precautions."

"Okay Cam. You can go back to the church if you want. We'll go out and meet them." she looked at me like she was going to argue with me but changed her mind, instead she handed me the large hunting knife she carried at her waist.

"Just in case." Was all she said as she walked away already on the radio, telling Daniel that Delta and I were going to meet our 'guests' when they came into town.

I looked down at the knife briefly and then realised I hadn't grabbed mine when I had come out of the church. For the first time since coming into this forest, I was unarmed. My blade was a little different in shape to Cam's but around the same size and weight, so I could work with it if I needed to. I appreciated the gesture either way.

We walked as far as an open space close to the edge of town. We decided to wait there. I wondered briefly how far out Daniel had gone that he'd been able to give us this much notice. I should probably say something to him, but then again, I had to admit our watches up to now probably hadn't been quite adequate.

I tried to contact Daniel via the radio, but all I got back was a series of clicks. They were – Delta informed me – morse code, which I had a moderate understanding of (I studied it back at base but I couldn't remember everything) but Delta was obviously much better. He informed me Daniel was saying he was all good. He must have been close behind them to not risk them hearing him respond.

So we waited. It only took about another seven or eight minutes before we could hear sounds of them coming through the trees. They were definitely human. I hadn't heard any aliens make that much noise, even when they were severely injured or hurrying.

They broke through the trees and instantly stalled, so despite the noise they were making, at least they were watching where they were going and who or what was in front of them. The first thing I noticed about them was Delta was right about them being twins, but not identical. One of them was about two inches taller, but they both had the same shockingly blue eyes and the same haircut, although different colours. The taller one had dark blonde hair and the other had very dark brown, almost black.

They wore identical expressions on their faces – awed and a little confused as they came through the broken fence until they saw Delta and me standing there. They both looked at me for a moment before focusing on Delta, at which time their faces broke out in identical huge smiles.

"So glad to see you are alive, brother. We thought the worst until we saw those flags." said the taller one, walking forward and holding his arm out, which Delta grabbed and then used to pull him into a hug.

"Good to see you too, brother. Sorry about giving you a scare. But it was necessary. I wish we could have told you what we were doing." Delta answered.

"Yeah, we saw the flags out there and it all clicked into place pretty quickly." The other brother joined the conversation. "How long have you guys been here?"

Delta looked at me for a moment as if suddenly remembering I was there.

"Guys, this is Delta Leader. Most of her team call her 'Boss'. She's pretty much the one calling the shots here now. She has amazing instincts. She's stubborn too. We would probably be dead for real if it wasn't for her."

"Hey, I'm Cain," the shorter one held out his hand to introduce himself, "This is my brother Adam," he said gesturing to his brother, "Most people call us Cain and Abel." He smiled at me as I took his hand and shook it, then I shook Adam's hand as well.

"I'm Tyne. It's nice to meet you. I'm glad you guys made it out. I'm sorry your teams didn't."

"How many of you made it out? Where are the others hiding?" Adam asked (I suspect more to Delta than me, but Delta stayed silent and allowed me to take the lead).

"There are eight people here at the moment, seven of us, and someone we... found... when we got here. We have been hiding in the church." I tried to watch their faces as I spoke to gauge what they might be thinking.

"Eight? How did you even end up with seven of us? Each team only had five, unless... someone from Bravo team survived. The calls about lucky numbers... that was someone from Bravo, wasn't it?" Adam looked confused for a moment. Then he was all business again. "How many of them survived? Who?"

"Tayler Cassidy survived - Bravo Overwatch – and my friend Rochelle Parker, I think she was Bravo three or something. They have been with us since late the day after they all... 'died'," I held up my fingers in quotation marks as I said the last part. "Tayler didn't want anyone to know they had survived yet and Delta and I agreed with her." At that point, Cain must have gotten impatient to ask his question because he broke in.

"Is there room in your church for three more? And who the hell did you find all the way out here?"

"Three? What do you mean, three more?" Daniel walked out of the trees at that moment and looked at me.

"You got your radio down, Boss?" I nodded, "Rush says grubs up."

"Okay Daniel, go eat. We'll be in soon." He headed off toward the church as I turned back to Adam and Cain. I said nothing. I just raised an eyebrow and waited for someone to answer my question.

"Well..." Cain began, before pausing to look at his brother, who nodded. "Someone else from Alpha Team survived..." He paused again, but I just waited for him to continue. "Alpha Leader made it out of that final battle, too. He is a little banged up... and honestly, he's a damn pain in the arse, but he is alive."

"Why isn't he with you now?" Delta asked. He looked angry. I remembered he had heard the final battle Alpha Team was in. He had only given me the 'highlights', but I wondered if something else had happened. Something he hadn't told me.

"He didn't have as much faith in your flags as we did, and as Cain said, he is a bit banged up, so we hid him in some trees and said we would contact or come back for him once we knew it was safe." Adam said, clearly more comfortable talking to Delta than to me. But that was a problem for later.

"Have you guys got a private radio channel organised?" I asked.

"No. We were going to use Morse code, or an abbreviated version of it," Cain informed me, "or just go and get him." Something in his voice told me he thought going to get him was a much better option.

"How far out is he?" asked Delta.

"About halfway between here and the red rag," Adam answered, "I'm happy to go back and get him."

"I'll go with you,"" said Delta. He looked at me briefly and I nodded in agreement. I didn't quite know what he was trying to tell me, but I went along with it, anyway. I trusted Delta. I didn't think he would do anything to jeopardise us.

"Okay, I'll get this one fed," I said with a smile at Cain, "how long do you think you'll be?"

"Depends on how injured he is. But the march alone will be about two hours." Delta said, looking at Adam.

"He's not too badly injured, but he will slow us down coming back... and he's lazy." Adam informed us.

"I'll go grab my stuff." Delta said, already jogging toward the church.

"Grab some food for both of you as well. You need to eat." I called after him. He waved to show he'd heard me. I looked at Adam and Cain. I found myself desperate to make conversation. "So... I gotta know..." I started.

"Me, by three minutes," said Cain, "and no, they had to change it." Adam laughed at his brother. But turned to me and actually smiled.

"We get asked that a lot, as you can probably guess. My name was going to be Abel but the Office of Births, Deaths and Marriages wouldn't allow it. They even questioned our parents' names on the application... Dad always said some religious nut got hold of it."

"Oh, don't tell me..." I started to ask.

"Yep, Adam and Eve. Well Evelyn, but everyone always called her Eve. So I got Dad's name and Cain got to keep his."

"Wait," I paused after processing what they had said, "Did you say the Office of Births, Deaths and Marriages?"

"Yeah, we were born in Australia, Melbourne actually," Cain informed me, "Dad moved there when he was a teenager and met and married Mum. Then, when we were about three, they decided they wanted a different life. So we started travelling. They eventually settled down again, in America just after we turned five... Mum didn't want to home school us."

"Did you ever think about going back? Even for a holiday?" I asked them.

"Maybe one day," Adam answered, "but we wanted to serve our country first, the one we spent most of our lives in."

Delta jogged back into view at that moment. He carried his rifle and one of my spare hunting knives in a sheath strapped to his left leg. (I hadn't known he was left-handed.)

"Borrowed this," he stated when he saw me looking at the knife at his side, "figured it was about time I started carrying and Cam told me you had spares."

"Whoa," said Adam, "I might have to get myself one of those." I reached behind my back and grabbed the knife Cam had given me and handed it to him in its sheath. I hoped Cam wouldn't mind, but I knew she also carried a spare. I told him I didn't have a strap for it, but the sheath would sit in his belt.

He thanked me as he took it. Delta and I confirmed times and agreed to half hourly check-ins on the radio, then they left. They wouldn't be back before dark, but they were hoping to make it to Alpha leader's hiding place by then at least and would decide what to do from there.

Cain and I stayed and watched as they walked into the trees. Once they were lost to sight, we turned and I led Cain through the town and into the church. When we walked in, Rochelle jumped up – with an energy and agility she shouldn't have had yet after her injuries – and brought us a large plate of food each.

We accepted the food gratefully and walked further into the church to find a place to sit and eat. I noticed Tom watching Rush with a strange look on his face, as though he was trying to puzzle something out. I made a mental note to ask him what was wrong later, when we were on watch together.

About an hour after we had eaten with two check-ins from Delta done, I told everyone to go off and get themselves some more rest. They had all been awake for a few hours now. Cain offered to stay up with me, but given he had less sleep under his belt than any of us, I told him to go off and get himself some. Rush stayed up with me for a while and we sat talking just like old times.

Eventually she started yawning and I realised she had been up for the whole day, given how sick she had been only a two days ago, it was no wonder she was tired. I scolded her gently for staying up for so long and told her to get her butt back to bed. She looked like she was going to argue, but with a jaw-cracking yawn, realised it wasn't going to work. She waved to me as she covered her mouth for another jaw-cracker. I waved back and looked at my watch. Delta was about seven minutes overdue for a check-in. I decided to wait until the ten-minute mark before I made contact. I made it to nine.

"Delta, come in." I spoke into the radio as quietly as I could. Even though I was up in the balcony of the church and the others were all sleeping in the hidden basement room below, I didn't want to risk anyone overhearing there may be some kind of problem. There was no response, so I tried again, "Delta, you're ten minutes overdue for check-in. Come in please."

"This is Delta," came the reply at last, when I was about to make the call for the third time. "Sorry Boss, we have reached the place where Alpha leader was left. It's pretty closed in around here and I couldn't hear properly. I had to walk back out of the trees to make contact."

"Is Alpha Leader there?" I asked, "Is he ok?"

"Yeah, he's here. He's not in a great way, but that could be hunger and thirst also. They ran out of food and water a while ago. We've fed him and given him some water, well Adam is doing that now and we're going to work out a way to move him."

"Is it safer to stay where you are for the night and move in the morning?"

"We'll assess that properly, but I don't think so. There seems to be a lot of movement around here at night. It all seems to be smaller animals right now, but if this is some kind of animal highway, then it might only be a matter of time before the bigger ones come along. Not to mention the noise would disguise an alien raiding party from us until it was too late."

"Any sign of them in the area?"

"Not that I've seen; the animals being through would imply not, at least not recently enough to be obvious, but that doesn't mean they won't be through at some stage. Especially at night."

"Okay, how long do you think it'll take for you to get back here with Alpha Leader?"

"He's got an injury to his leg that may hinder us a bit. Have to figure out if he can walk or if we need to rig something and carry him. Which I actually think will be quicker and probably safer."

"Okay, let me know when you head off and stick with thirty-minute check-ins."

"Will do. See you when we get back, hopefully in a few hours. I think we're all going to have our hands full with this one." Delta said the last part very quietly, as though worried he would be overheard.

"Oh goody, just what I always wanted, a difficult teenager." I laughed back at Delta. I felt sure he was laughing along with me. We signed off after that and I sat back; still laughing to myself about the difficult teenager thing, when I noticed a movement on the stairs. I was still sitting up in the balcony, though I'd paced in the small space while I was talking to Delta.

I reached down beside me to my hip to grab my hunting knife – which I had replaced after getting back and telling Cam where hers was – I didn't think it was an alien, but that didn't mean I shouldn't be prepared. I slid off the pew I was sitting on and into a crouch on the ground. I held my knife at the ready and called out quietly.

"Who's there?" I asked the staircase.

"It's just me," came the reply quickly. I thought it was Tom, but the church echoed a bit at night. He walked up the rest of the stairs and I saw it was in fact him. There was something different about him, but I couldn't put my finger on what it was. "I was supposed to do the watch with you. Rochelle woke me, but when I came up, you were talking on the radio, so I didn't want to disturb you."

"It's ok Tom, we were just doing a check-in and Delta was a bit late."

"He's okay though? He's coming back soon?" Tom seemed apprehensive. I decided to puzzle it out later and just reassure him for now.

"Yes, they are all fine. They will be coming back hopefully in a few hours and then I suspect there will be someone else for you to play doctor to."

"Ah yes, Cain told me about... Alpha Leader, is it?"

"Yeah, Delta said he's got an injured leg, but I don't know how bad." Tom just nodded. I suddenly remembered I had been wanting to ask him something. "Tom, are you okay? You have been rather..." I searched for a word to accurately describe what I wanted to ask him, "pensive since this afternoon, pretty much since you were checking Rochelle's wounds." He didn't say anything straight away and I started feeling nervous, "Tom, what is it? Are her wounds not healing well?"

"Her wounds are healing. Great actually... too well, in fact. I can't puzzle it out. They are almost completely healed. As in, they almost look like scars already. That kind of healing should have taken weeks, even for a fast healer. It... unsettles me." As Tom spoke, I took in his appearance again and finally realised what was different about him. He was armed. I had never seen him armed, in the whole time we had been here, it worried me a little.

"Tom..." I started carefully, "Why are you armed?"

"It seemed prudent." It was all he said, but I felt there was a lot more to it. I was torn whether I should try and get more out of him. He beat me to the punch.

"There is something I should tell you."

"What is it Tom?" I asked as lightly as I could, but my insides started knotting themselves up with wariness.

"I know I should have told you this sooner, but I haven't been completely alone out here this whole time. There is another... person... around." He said person in a way that made me simultaneously cringe away and curious to know more.

"I haven't seen anyone else here, Tom. Where are they hiding?"

"Well, that's the thing. She is not in town. She's not staying here at all. But she was originally from here, sort of."

14

"Okay Tom. Start from the beginning and this time don't leave anything out." I tried to keep any anger out of my voice, but it was a struggle. After all, I'd had a feeling there was something he wasn't telling us and he didn't know us at all, certainly not enough to trust us with secrets he may have kept. I tried to keep that in mind. But this was bigger than I had thought and now we may be in danger.

"It was about three days after the aliens came through. I was still hiding in the basement... A girl walked into the church and sat in the front pews. She just sat there and prayed. I didn't come out of the basement and I honestly don't know if she knew I was there or not. But she prayed for hours." He paused as though waiting for me to say something, but I waited him out. I had told him I wanted to hear his story before. Now I was finally getting the rest of it, I wasn't going to interrupt him. "She comes back and sits for hours, every ten days or so. I still don't know if she knows I am here. I haven't revealed myself at all, but... I recognise her." He paused again and took a deep breath. "She moved to town about six months before the invasion. I don't know her back story. She hadn't really opened up. But I know her name is Selena and she used to pray a lot even before the aliens came."

"If you know this girl and she was a member of your town, why haven't you approached her?" I had to ask. I was never very good at waiting for the end of a story.

"Tyne... you don't understand... after the attack, I should have latched onto anybody who walked in here. As I did with you and your team. No one is more ashamed of that than me. But... I got this vibe from her, from the moment she walked back in those church doors. I don't think she's quite the same, not quite human anymore. Sometimes I think I hear her sniffing as though she's an animal or something trying to sniff something out – like they do – she has never spoken as though she thinks anyone is here and she has never come with anyone – or anything – else," Tom looked about as shaken as I had seen him and of course I knew who 'they' were.

"Tom, is there something else? You look scared."

"Tyne, I've been trying to count the days, but I've lost track a couple of times... I think she'll be here tomorrow. I don't know what she's doing or what she's smelling – if that's what she's doing – but I'm sure this place is going to smell different with ten extra people in it. What if..?"

"Tom, you can't live your life for what ifs. We'll just have to cross that bridge when we come to it. Brock is on his way here, but it doesn't look like he'll make it to us until after dark tomorrow. We just gotta hope that Delta, Alpha Overwatch and Alpha Leader are back by morning."

"Do you think they will be?"

"Well, Delta is due for his next check-in any minute now, so we'll have a more up-to-date answer on that one very soon."

Tom seemed happy enough to let it drop for the moment, but I could see he was still stewing on it. We continued the watch in silence until Delta's check-in.

"Delta Leader, this is Delta Overwatch, come in."

"This is Delta Leader. How are you guys doing?"

"We're trucking along. We created a sort of litter thing. So we're carrying Alpha leader for the most part. He wants to walk some but only seems to be able to manage about five minutes at a time, so we're trying to make as much ground as we can while we are carrying him. We're all tired though. I would estimate we will still be about two and a half hours out. If we can keep him from trying to walk too much. Make sure the priest is ready with his med kit when we get there."

"Will do. You guys got enough water?"

"Yeah, but we're completely out of food.."

"That's ok we saved you some."

"How are things back home?" I laughed at his use of the word home.

"Things here are quiet for now, but we may have company tomorrow." I gave him an abridged version of the story and we agreed if he thought they weren't going to make it back by first light, they would change course and come in from a different direction. Tom couldn't give us much idea of where she was coming from... or going to when she left, so we just had to wing it and change the smell if we could. We signed off after that and Tom and I went back to our silent watch. We didn't really have anything to talk about. As I sat there, I realised I felt very comfortable with Tom. I think I had even before he finally came clean about what he wasn't telling us. Although that hadn't been what I expected either, I didn't feel as though he had lied to us about anything. I understood his delay in telling us about the girl. He had to figure out if he could trust us, too.

"How bad do you think the guy's leg is?" Tom asked me suddenly. I considered my answer before I decided to be blatantly honest.

"Well... I don't know, Delta didn't go into detail, but if he says it's bad and be ready, then I would guess it's probably going to put a kink in any plans we may make to move on soon."

"Fair enough. I might go and get everything ready now then. Where do you want me to set up a treatment area? I assume you would want to constrict it to a small place rather than all over the church, like last time."

"Well, how soon after first light can we expect Selena? That was her name, wasn't it?"

"Yes, that was her name, and honestly... I don't know. I wasn't great at keeping track of time before you came. But I would guess maybe mid-morning-ish. Why?"

"Just trying to figure on having enough time to clean everything up based on Delta and co not getting back until after first light."

"What about my original bedroom? Because I can lock it and we can always move him downstairs like we did with Rochelle."

"Good idea Tom. Do you want some help setting up?"

"Nah, I'll be okay. You need to keep your watch anyway and the room is at the very back of the church, can't see anything from there. It's why I never hid in there." He shrugged his shoulders. "Do you want me to wake someone else to come and watch with you?"

"No thanks Tom. I'm okay for now and it won't take you that long to set up, anyway. You are the king of organised." He smiled as he walked down the stairs to go get his med-kit and set it up.

Delta was early for our next check-in, telling me they were doing well for time but were carrying Alpha Leader most of the way, because he was tiring quickly. I told him Tom was ready for when he arrived. Tom was walking back up the stairs to join me as we spoke – Delta signed off so they could continue their journey. I was starting to get a little apprehensive about them getting back. I wondered how bad Alpha Leader's leg really was and what other injuries he may have. I hoped Tom would be up to the task of looking after him. I didn't voice my concerns aloud, instead I asked the question foremost on my mind in the moment.

"What are you going to do after we leave, Tom? You can't really stay here..."

"I know. I am just loathe to leave the place that gave me sanctuary when I needed to be rescued."

"You could always come back here, you know... I mean, after everything is over. It might not happen next week, but we will beat them. We will win our planet back. We're a stubborn bunch, us humans and we don't give up easily."

"I'm seeing that more and more the longer I'm alive. I will most certainly come back here. But I fear that if I do leave now – or soon – I won't be back for a very, very long time. And I need to resign myself to that fact before I can make any decision. This will no longer be my church, my home, my safe haven. As you said, us humans are stubborn and we don't give up easily – even when it may be for our own good." He laughed at his own joke.

"That is very true." I laughed along with him.

"What are you going to do, Tyne?" Tom asked me suddenly.

"You mean after all this is over?" I asked him.

"No, I mean now. When you immediately leave here..."

"I don't have enough information yet to make that decision. But I have thought about the fact that this 'army' we joined..." I used my fingers for quotations when I said army – I seemed to be doing that a lot lately – "tried to kill us, for what reason I don't know. And I do wonder if that will sway my decision."

"What do you feel? I mean, I know you are waiting for more information, but if you had to go right now, what do you feel like you would do?" I felt like Tom was pushing me for a reason, but I couldn't puzzle out what it would be.

"Right now, if I had to choose, I think I would go on. Try and find out what is going on around here and kill as many aliens as possible in between. I want to go home. But I need to do this. I need to be here right now." I sat and thought about what I had just said. I wondered if this information Brock was bringing us would make a big difference to what I felt I needed to do. Tom looked strangely satisfied and I realised I had given him the answer he wanted. Now I just had to figure out why he wanted it. He looked like he was about to say something, but cocked his head to the side to listen instead. I heard what he must have heard only half a second later. We both crouched down from our seats and peeked over the balcony. Someone was walking around the church. For a moment I thought they were looking for something, but after a moment I realised they were pacing, as though stressed. I indicated to Tom I was going down the stairs to try and see who it was. I was fairly sure it was one of us down there; we would have noticed if the door had been opened, but sneaking down was good training for me anyway and I figured I may as well take what I can get. I made it down the stairs and into a row of pews before he spoke.

"Your good Boss Lady, but I'm not some wet behind the ears recruit." Cain turned and stared straight at the spot I was hiding in the pews, "I've been doing this a long time and I had an advantage... I knew you and the priest were here somewhere."

"We are up in the balcony. Would you like to join us up there? There is room to pace if you wish." I said, rising and starting to head back to the staircase. Cain nodded and followed me back up to the balcony.

"Have you heard from them? Are they ok? Did they find Alpha Leader?" He asked me, suddenly in a rush.

"Oh Cain, I'm sorry, I forgot you didn't have our private channel set on your radio and Adam would now. Yes, they are fine. They found him and he is alive. They are more or less carrying him back. His leg is pretty bad. They are making good time." I told him.

"When are they due for the next check-in?" Cain asked me. He seemed instantly calmer just hearing the answer I had given him.

"They are due for the next check-in, in about five minutes, channel seventeen. As far as we know, it's unmonitored."

"Thanks," he said as he looked down at his radio to find the dial. We finished our walk up the stairs and joined Tom on the balcony as Cain turned the dial on his radio to get the right channel. I silently prayed they wouldn't be late for their check-in. I didn't know if Cain would be able to handle waiting even longer to speak to his brother than he already had. I hadn't spent much time around the two of them yet, but I had spent enough time around twins to recognise these two had the trademark closeness some sets of twins instinctively have.

"Boss, come in." Delta was right on time.

"Go ahead Delta." I told him, looking at Cain briefly.

"We're making excellent time here; we've made up a lot of what we lost. I anticipate we'll only need one or two more check-ins at this stage, then we'll be seeing you."

"That's awesome Delta. Is Adam around by any chance? Cain would like a word with him."

"Yeah, hang on." There was a pause in which I assumed Delta was telling Adam to get on the radio.

"Cain? What's up?"

"Just wanted to know how Jase was. Is he a lot worse than when we left him?" I assumed Jase was Alpha Leader. I hadn't known his name before now.

"Yeah, he's not good, Cain. You better prep them as much as you can. I know Delta hasn't been able to say much to Boss because he's been around us a lot. But he's asleep now. We haven't told him how bad his leg is. He can't see it properly, so we're trying to keep him distracted. I thought he was starting to clue in, but he stopped asking questions."

"I'll tell them don't worry, Adam?" Cain sounded nervous.

"Yeah?"

"Did we make the right decision... to leave him there? Should we have made him come with us?"

"I don't know Cain... I..."

"From what I can see, it wouldn't have made much of a difference." Delta broke into the conversation. "He will either survive his wounds or he won't. The few hours won't have made much of a difference. His bleeding is minimal and without a proper hospital… no offense to the priest, but it would always have been hit and miss."

"Thanks man. See you when you get back." Cain looked a little calmer. I signed off with Delta and turned to Cain.

"I take it the final decision to leave him was yours?" He nodded. "So tell me… How bad is it, really?"

"Honestly, I was concerned he wouldn't be alive when we got back. The wounds aren't deep, they don't even look that bad but, there are quite a few of them and they just look wrong. I can't explain it. I have no medical training at all, but I got a bad feeling when I looked at those wounds." Cain seemed a little shaken talking about Alpha Leader's leg. I wondered how weird they could look, then I remembered back to the conversation I had with Tom about Rochelle's shoulder and back. Something healing rapidly would look weird, I guessed. Especially to the untrained eye.

"Hey Cain," I asked slowly, "Did Jase get bitten or scratched by the aliens at all?"

"I'm not sure, but I guess it's possible. Adam was watching him. My focus was on the other side of the nest, where the other two were. Watching them die while orders to kill them were getting yelled in my ear." He sounded defeated now. "If Jase is still asleep when they call their next check-in through, we can ask Adam. He might have seen something. I don't know if it's worth asking Jase. He may not know. He was pretty out of it after the attack. I don't know if he was really aware of everything afterwards."

I nodded quietly; it wasn't much, but it was a small plan. I vividly remembered Brock's warning about getting bitten and some nasty suspicions were starting to form in my mind. Nothing I was willing to share yet, but I was starting to put things together.

Rochelle came up shortly before the next check-in. I half-heartedly admonished her for not getting more sleep, but she reminded me it was morning and the next watch should have started a while ago and I was the one who should be asleep. But there was no way I could go to sleep now with everything going on. I needed to see how bad these wounds of Jase's were.

We didn't get to ask Adam anything during the next check-in. Jase was awake and they were only about twenty minutes from 'home' anyway, so I figured we may as well just wait and speak to Adam when he wasn't able to overhear. No point in scaring him any more than was necessary.

By the time Delta radioed through to tell us they were entering the town, we had been joined by Tayler. She told us the others were all awake downstairs as well.

We unbarred the church door just as Delta and Adam arrived and directed them straight through to the back of the church to the room Tom had set up for treatment. I didn't like the look of Jase when they brought him in. He was almost grey and his skin was clammy and he was shivering. He wasn't asleep, but he wasn't really awake either. He was pretty out of it and as I watched Tom work; I started to understand what Cain meant when he said it wasn't bad, but it didn't look right. I watched Tom's face as he looked over the wounds and cleaned and dressed them. I watched as he drew a massive dose of antibiotics into a syringe and injected it just above the wounds in the injured leg. He gave pain killers as well and I watched as Jase slipped into a somewhat comfortable unconsciousness.

I saw out of the corner of my eye Cain pull Adam aside to talk to him. I hoped he was asking about what we wanted to know; what I wanted to know. They both turned to me as I glanced at them again and Cain nodded his head. I wasn't sure exactly what the information meant yet, but at least we knew now. I had to find Rochelle and talk to her. It wasn't going to be an easy conversation.

After we had Jase squared away, we decided to move him downstairs to recover. We were all going to have to move down there soon, anyway. It was after sunrise now and Selena could be arriving soon. We moved him as carefully as we could and then Adam, Cain, Tayler and Delta, (it still amazes me how quickly I switched back to calling him by his call sign after using his name for so long – yet the others remained first names probably because that was all I had ever really known them as) went out to what we deemed quickly on a map as the four outer corners of the town (we basically used North, South, East and West for obvious reasons) where they climbed up high trees and made themselves comfortable. Much like they had done on overwatch. They would be staying there for the better part of the day, or at least until Selena had been and was well and truly gone. Most of the rest of us stayed down in the hidden room under the altar. Rochelle and I stayed in the church for the time being. Tom felt he needed to stay down with Jase to monitor him. It was going to be a long day for everyone.

15

Rochelle and I sat up in the balcony – as I usually did when I was on watch – waiting for Selena to arrive. On the off chance the sentries missed something, we would at least be hidden if we couldn't get to safety. It definitely wasn't the plan, though. When someone radioed in to say she was on her way in, we were going to get to the room under the altar as quickly as we could but stay up near the door so we could hear and see as much as possible if there was anything to see or hear.

After a while, Rochelle started looking nervous. I was about to ask her what was bothering her when she spoke:

"Tyne, I want to talk about that last fight, the one we lost, but I think it's going to be hard to get through. I know you want to know what happened from my point of view and I know you are deliberately not asking because you are worried about upsetting me… but I think I'm ready now. I need to be ready." I didn't say anything, worried if I interrupted her, she wouldn't be able to get her story out.

"We were resting. It was so stupid. We should have gone further before stopping, or maybe we should have kept going after we had patched ourselves up. But we were so tired, fighting them really took it out of us. We set a watch; but I think he must have fallen asleep. He was dead before anyone even woke up. I opened my eyes and saw his body dangling from that alien's hand, as though he was a bag of rubbish. It took me a minute to realise I wasn't dreaming. By then Bravo Leader was up and trying to fight, but he was injured too and he was moving slowly from sleep and probably pain. The other girl was already dead, too. She hadn't even made it off the ground.

126

"They were so vicious. They tore them apart like they were made of paper. There was blood everywhere. I could see it spraying from the wounds. That wasn't even the worst bit..." she paused and took a deep breath. I waited for her to go on, "the worst bit was they started chewing on the edges of the wounds and drinking the blood, like some kind of weird... vampires, but not even like they were really hungry, just snacking for the hell of it. I mean, I know we knew they did that, but it's totally different seeing it for real. It's almost as though up until that point, my brain had thought that part wasn't true. I think I must have flinched when I saw that, because suddenly they noticed I was there when maybe they hadn't before.

"They were on me before I had time to process that I was on my own. I fought them as best I could and I managed to kill a couple of them and wound another one. Then one of them scratched me down the back. Its claws didn't feel like they went deep, but it hurt so much Tyne. I couldn't even breathe for a minute, then it realised it didn't have a good grip on me, so it lunged again and sank its teeth into my shoulder. It's a little hazy. I remember going down with that thing still on me. I remember it being jolted loose when I landed on the ground, then I heard the gun go off twice and a yell and it was over. They were dead.

"Next thing I really remember is Bravo Overwatch checking my pulse, then trying to lift me onto her shoulders. I came too enough that I was able to understand we needed to move and move fast. She guided me as best she could, but she was trying to keep an eye out at the same time. There didn't seem to be anything following us, but we'd thought that before. I remember running for a long time and then, when we finally thought we had gone far enough, I slept. Tayler helped me climb a tree and she kept watch while I got some rest. When I woke up, I felt much better, so I told her to get some rest. When she woke up, we decided to move again as far as we could, then we climbed another tree and tried to make contact with you." She finished her story with a shrug. As though it was a simple tale she was telling instead of one of the scariest experiences of her life. I knew better, though. I could see how shaken up she was. I hoped this would be something we would both survive, physically and emotionally. Then something occurred to me.

"Rush..." I said gently, a little unsure how to proceed. "Are you sure you were bitten?"

"Yeah... why?" there was no hurt or accusation in her voice, just confusion.

"Because I got a good look at your wounds when Tom cleaned them up and stitched them... and there were no bite marks on your shoulder. Or anywhere, not even a scar from healed ones. And the only scratches were the deep ones from our battle and a healed scratch that looked months old."

"The scratches Tom stitched were from the battle we were all in together; but I was definitely bitten. I wonder why there were no marks. Even Tayler saw me get bitten. I asked her to check the bite for me while we were on our way to meet up with you guys. She said they looked almost like a human bite mark but with long incisor marks. Like a dog . You don't think anything bad is happening to me, do you?"

"I'm sure it's nothing. You're a very fast healer. You always have been, remember when you broke your leg? It was only like four and a half weeks before the doctors couldn't even see where the break had been."

"Yeah, you're probably right. I'm just good at getting better." But she still looked concerned and I had a hard time trying to convince myself nothing was wrong because I was pretty concerned myself. I remembered what Tom had said about her healing too fast. She was a fast healer, but this seemed a little extreme and even if she had just healed that fast, there still should have been some kind of mark, even a scar, anything that showed there had been an injury there less than a week ago.

We sat in silence for a few minutes. Rochelle opened her mouth to say something a couple of times but didn't speak. Finally she took a deep breath, but as she opened her mouth to speak again, we heard Adam on the radio.

"Boss, this is Alpha. Come in."

"Go ahead Alpha."

"I've got some movement in the trees here. I think it's the girl. I'm going radio silent. Get into position and stay safe."

"Copy that, you too, keep an eye out guys. You never know what else is creeping around out there."

I got four replies and signed off. Rush and I got up and descended the stairs into the main church. We joined the others in the hidden room under the altar and closed the door behind us. After Rush vacated the ladder, Tom climbed up and sat next to me on the top rungs so we could peek through the side of the raised area together. It was something Tom had shown me the other night when we were on watch together. It was disguised as a mirror so the people hiding could watch what was going on in the church without being seen themselves. It was how Tom had seen Selena in the first place and how he had seen us to know he felt safe to approach us.

I vaguely wondered what this room had been put here for in the first place, as I had several times before now. I had asked Tom, he wasn't sure; but his working theory was just to hide people, maybe illegal immigrants or people hiding from the law. Churches are notoriously used as a place of sanctuary. How much better would it be if the people after you didn't know you were there in the first place? Then at least they might not camp outside waiting for you, so you could never actually leave.

We had to wait almost fifteen minutes before the doors of the church opened. A slight girl in a dirty white dress walked in. I say girl, but in reality, she was probably my age. She just seemed younger. I couldn't quite put my finger on why, but there was just something about her. Everyone below us was sitting as silently as possible, looking up at us. They seemed to be barely breathing. We were all on edge, waiting to see what would happen.

She walked right up to the front row of pews, knelt, blessed herself and then sat down. She picked up the bible and placed it on her lap, then just sat there. She closed her eyes and faced upwards to the ceiling, as though praying. I thought I could see her lips moving, but I wasn't completely sure. Though I had been warned about the sniffing by Tom and had been expecting it, it still took me by surprise when she suddenly drew in a loud breath that could be described as nothing else but scenting. It was just the same as animals do, as well as vampires, werewolves and other strange creatures in the movies. Given that she was human as far as we knew, it was entirely possible she had just seen a lot of movies and developed the habit of copying them.

She turned her head to look around the church suddenly, as though she felt like someone was sneaking up on her. Still sniffing as though she had caught a scent, which in reality, she very well could have. It would have been impossible to remove our entire scent from the place while we were still here. Suddenly, she stood and Tom froze. He glanced at me quickly and shook his head to indicate she hadn't done anything like this before and I already knew from his previous experience with her, he had been expecting her to stay much longer.

She walked to the doors of the church and opened them wide. Then she just stood in the doorway, staring out at the town. Tom was watching her confused and fascinated at the same time, but then his face changed to worry, which I admit I had already gone to... she was standing in front of the door as though waiting for someone. It seemed like a very strange thing to do. After a while, she came back into the church and sat back down in the front row.

She stayed there for about an hour never moving, never speaking. She didn't even open her eyes. I almost would have thought she had fallen asleep if she hadn't continued the occasional sniffing. When she had finished whatever it was she was doing there, she rose rather gracefully from her seat, knelt again, blessed herself again and walked slowly towards the door. She pulled one of the doors closed before stepping outside, where she paused. She turned and faced back into the church for a moment before speaking.

"You can't win. She knows you're coming." It wasn't a threat, just a simple comment made as though in passing. Her voice was a little deeper than I had thought it would be and there seemed to be a second voice speaking through the words as well. It gave me an uncomfortable feeling. Given the look on Tom's face, I would say it gave him the same feeling.

We waited after she walked away until we had confirmation she had actually left the town, then we emerged from the hidden room and sat in the church to talk. Tom and I told the others what we had seen, which honestly wasn't much. Then we all decided to get some rest. We had a day ahead of us and depending on the information

Brock was bringing, we could be in for a long night, so getting what sleep we could now seemed like a good idea. We had already altered our schedule for the watch, so we went off to do what we needed. I needed sleep. I hadn't been getting enough of it lately and I decided that no matter what, I was going to get some today. I ended up sleeping most of the day. The others didn't wake me for my watch, which annoyed me a little, but in a way I was still grateful. My sleep was plagued with dreams, both good and bad, although nothing serious enough to wake me, apparently.

Rochelle and I were back on the base. We were both covered in scars and Rochelle's eyes were different than I remembered; her irises were black now. They had always been dark blue, but now they were indistinguishable from her pupils and they were bigger; there was very little white in her eyes at all now. I accepted this information calmly, as though it was the norm now.

We were playing cards – snap, I think – on the floor of our small cottage. Again, this was a difference I accepted as normal, because obviously on the base we had lived in a barracks. We were pretty evenly matched playing snap; we always had been. And we were happily playing back and forth, winning one or two hands in turn. I had the feeling we were waiting for something.

Brock walked into the room, maybe from the bathroom. He sat on the floor behind me and wrapped himself around me so I was sitting in between his legs. He laid his hands gently on my shoulders and sat watching our game, smiling serenely as we continued our even play. It felt comfortable and safe, like something we did all the time.

Rochelle offered to let him play the next round, which he declined, as I knew he would. He said we play too rough when other people are involved; we get too rowdy and violent. I vaguely remembered going through several decks of cards in our pursuit of winning. Rochelle just laughed knowingly when he declined and accused him of being a sook, which he laughed off.

We played about ten more rounds before anything happened to change the situation. Tom walked into the room from outside, where I knew he had been keeping a watch, though I failed to remember what for.

"They are coming," he said calmly, though I noticed he looked disturbed. I didn't ask him about it, which surprised me. I figured my dream self must have already known what was bothering him.

Brock unfolded himself from the floor and went to sit at the table. Rochelle and I packed up our cards and joked around about how one day we would make Brock play with us again. He sat at the table watching us and laughing. He seemed perfectly at ease.

We heard laughter approaching from outside and a strange hissing noise I couldn't identify. Delta and Tayler came in, followed by Cain and Adam. They all nodded at Brock as though to answer an unasked question.

He rose from the table and I instinctively went to his side. He took my hand and we walked outside together. Standing out in front of our unit was Selena, which was strange enough, but standing next to her, holding her hand tenderly, was an alien. Six and a half feet tall, dark greenish grey skin, black eyes, just as I remember them being. My eyes took in the sight but kept returning to the clasped hands between them.

I had questions – lots of questions – but my overall demeanour was completely calm. I didn't expect an attack or anything, even with an alien standing right in front of me. The alien smiled. At least I think that's what it did, then it spoke:

"Thank you for having us. We really appreciate the invite. Selena has so few friends, it's nice to be able to get out once in a while." It spoke English, but with a thick accent belonging to no language I knew and there was a really strong hiss to its voice, making it hard to understand. Its mouth didn't form words the way a human mouth did, so lip reading was also out. I made sure I listened carefully to each word it spoke, so I didn't have to ask it to repeat itself. I didn't want to appear rude. Or insult it.

Selena smiled shyly up at the alien as though still unsure how the whole thing had come about, but in that 'I can't believe my luck' kind of way people have when their long-time crush finally notices they exist.

"It's good to have you here. We're sorry that we couldn't do it sooner." Brock spoke as though he meant it. The whole situation was extremely surreal. "The others are running a little late, so we have to wait for them before we can head over."

The alien nodded and looked lovingly down at Selena. He (somewhere along the line I had decided that it must be a 'he') had the strangest look on his face. The adoration that was shining through there was beyond anything I had ever experienced. Selena apparently felt the same because her own face absolutely glowed with love. I felt like I should look away for fear I was witnessing something private.

The sounds of running footsteps drew our attention. Coming up the road, we saw Cam, Daniel, Aiden and Jase. Apparently, this was who we were waiting for. The team was all here. My team, the one I was fighting with in the real world right now. By another strange coincidence, I knew that to be true just as this was my current reality in the dream. It was a freaky experience.

We all turned to welcome them and make introductions. I noticed Jase had the same blackness to his eyes Rochelle now sported. They seemed to have an interesting awareness of each other too, not in a relationship sense; this was something completely different. They moved in sync, but not like they were doing it deliberately. Like they weren't even aware of it.

Once the final introductions were done (apparently the alien had not previously met the four who just joined us, although he and Jase shared the same synchronicity that Jase and Rochelle shared), we all turned and headed off at a jog together. Brock led the way and when we stopped, we found ourselves at the special forces obstacle course he and I spent so many days training on before mission had sent me out into the forest.

There was a BBQ there and Brock set up food and started cooking, while the rest of us had a play on the equipment like big kids.

Suddenly, clouds rolled in, dark and ominous, but not like it was going to rain, more like the kind of clouds that inspire fear in movies. We all looked fearfully at the sky. I noticed out of the corner of my eye the alien pull Selena close to him as though to shield her.

There was a rush of wind from the north and when we turned to look in the direction it had come, we saw something that made my blood run cold. There was another alien standing there. I think this one was a female. Except she was over eight feet tall. Her hair was long coils of black rope that hung down her back, her skin was a bluish shade of grey, unlike the alien with our group who was more greenish. Her eyes were black like all the aliens, except the very edges of them were tinged with red. She was fifty feet away, but then, without seeming to move, she was suddenly ten feet away. Brock moved forwards as though to speak to her, but the alien with us stepped in front of him and pushed him back. With its back to us, it held its arms out as though to protect us all from attack.

"They are my friends. You can't hurt them." It stated clearly and with a force of conviction for some reason I couldn't comprehend.

"They will never be yours. They are mine and I am waiting for them. They are mine now and they will always be mine." She replied in a raspy hissing voice, almost unintelligible, but I had heard her words in my head at the same time. Behind me, Selena gasped out a sob and collapsed on the ground. The alien with her turned and cried out in a guttural roar. The female swung her long arm and it seemed to grow even longer as, like a whip, it swept us all aside as though we were garbage.

"MINE!!" she screamed again. I heard it in her hissing voice and in my head and I finally began to feel afraid... she reached toward me and...

◈

16

I woke with a start to find Delta gently shaking my shoulder, telling me it was late afternoon. I tried to get my brain to function, but it took me a moment. I stood up and thanked him for waking me; he told me I still had about half an hour until my next watch, so I decided to go for a walk around the town to wake myself up properly. Afterwards, I took my watch and hoped I wouldn't have to wait too long for Brock to arrive. Delta told me he had checked in and was apparently a little ahead of schedule.

It was well after dark when Brock finally arrived. He told us he had driven most of the way in a 'borrowed' car and then, when the trees had made it too difficult to drive, he had run the rest of the way.

We gave him a good meal and loaded him up with water. I tried to get him to rest awhile, but he wanted to share the information he had with us first and sleep afterward. We sent out wide sentries like we had when Selena had come – though only two this time – and radioed up so they would still be able to hear everything that was said. Then we sat back to listen.

"So when I found out you guys were being shipped out early, I kind of lost it a bit," he paused and looked straight at me. I remembered his reaction well. "Sorry!" I nodded at the unspoken stuff in the apology. "I requested a mission of my own so I wouldn't have to be on base if something happened to you because I didn't agree with you going out there yet, or at all really, but there wasn't much other choice." He paused again and gave that a moment to sink in, but I could tell he was collecting his thoughts.

"My mission was to go and check out reports of suspected alien activity in other areas around the country where there hadn't really been attacks the first time. The first couple of places were dead ends. There was nothing to be found anywhere and I started wondering if there was anything to these reports at all, but in the third place on the list I struck gold, so to speak.

"I found a young man who had seen the aliens stalking around the town. Well, he found me technically; he told me his story quite willingly; I think he had been alone for a while and needed someone to talk to.

"He and his mate had been out looking for food. A lot of the country has gone back to a hunter gatherer type lifestyle. They had come across an alien stalking a girl. They hadn't been able to get to her before it attacked. But they were able to beat it off her before it killed her. They weren't sure she was going to survive, but they took care of her, anyway. She recovered, but was different. She healed from her wounds too quickly and didn't move like a human anymore. She was too fast and looked a little different. She started going off food, but was starving. No matter what they did, they couldn't get her to eat anything.

"One day, out of the blue, she turned around and attacked the two of them. The man I met got out of her reach in time, but his friend wasn't so lucky. But the friend took her with him when he died. The good news is the human/alien hybrids... they die easier than the aliens. They aren't quite as fast or as tough and they don't instantly know how to fight when they turn. They still only know what they knew before with regards to fighting; but they do have one thing in common... they drink blood and eat people." Tayler interrupted at this point.

"Are you saying there are more of these hybrids out there?"

"Yep. I would guess probably quite a few more. They seem to leave a couple here and there. It's what happened to that girl you guys found taken from Elko. She has become one." Again, he paused and looked at me directly. "I checked with Skipp. She is alive for now. The scientists are poking around. They have some plan to try and find a cure. It seems like maybe they have known about this situation for a while. Takes a victim about ten days to make the change.

"Anyway, this guy, he told me he'd been messing around on the radio a couple of weeks back and he had got onto someone who said they were from China. They said there had been a setup like this over in a forest in his country. Little nests everywhere, getting closer and closer together until you get to the centre. The guy he spoke to in China didn't know what was in the centre. All he knew was anybody who went in there didn't come out again and there was a lot of alien activity in the central hub.

"I asked Skipp about that too and they have spoken to people in the Chinese military who have confirmed it. They said the nest is shaped like an anthill, with alien activity getting more concentrated toward the centre. Skipp told me they seem to have the same set-up here in this forest. They knew a lot more about what was going on in here than they ever let on. This was never a search and rescue mission for you guys. This was a test. They just didn't want you to know. I think they were worried you wouldn't go. They always intended to send you into this forest. The aliens coming out and attacking Elko base just brought the timetable forward. That didn't happen in China. They only knew about the nests from drone footage and people trying to go in there.

"They've been keeping a map of all the places where each team uncovered nests and Skipp managed to send me through a photograph of what they have." He rooted around in his pack and pulled out a large piece of paper with a map printed on it. There were markings all over the place that I assumed were where nests had been uncovered. "As you can see, it's shaped like half a mandala. That's all we've had so far, but we are guessing it goes in a full circle.

"You guys were placed all along one half of the circle, by the looks of it. Which means it's huge. But based on this and the information we got from China; we expect what's around the other side is more or less the same." It was my turn to interrupt now. I had been looking at the map Brock was showing us of the nests our teams had come across (a few of which we had cleared) and sorting my head through everything Brock had said, combined with everything I had seen and heard myself.

"It's a hive!" I said, somehow sure I was right. "And the central hub is where the queen is..." I got a few confused looks, but Tom, Brock and Rochelle looked like I already had them convinced.

"Remember what Selena said?" Tom seemed to be asking the room in general, "she knows we're here and we can't win. 'SHE' must mean the queen. That means we were right about Selena, there is something wrong with her... she's a hybrid"

"Selena?" Brock asked with a raised eyebrow. I realised he hadn't been filled in on our visitor. So we explained about Selena, her connection to the town and her strange behaviour. But Brock spoke as soon as we finished. "She can't be a hybrid!" It was a simple statement, but it shocked us all into silence. "There is no way a hybrid would have left Tom alive all this time. They are mindless and uncontrollable. All they want to do is eat. But there is another possibility." We asked him what he meant. "It was something else I heard from that guy I met and one other guy. I didn't really believe it and Skipp hadn't heard anything about it but... she might be a... well he called it a familiar, but I thought maybe he might have watched a few too many television programs before all this happened, but it's as good a word as any for now. They are kind of like obsessive followers, but not completely of their own free will, either. They have also been... altered; but not by being bitten as far as I can tell. Sounds more like some kind of hypnosis.

"They are happy to follow the aliens. They have a little of the strength, speed and extra senses, but none of the blood lust. They are still effectively human. The guy I met thinks they were here before the invasion, to pave the way and make it easier for the aliens when they came. It's hard to explain, but apparently they have some kind of mental connection with the aliens, or maybe only to the specific one who turned them into a familiar. Although as I said, I'm not really clear on how that happens and that guy didn't have much light to shed on the actual conversion hence, I was sceptical of their existence."

"They didn't expect any of us to survive..." Cam's voice was hard and clear and there was no question in it, a statement of fact. Brock answered her anyway.

"I don't think so. Skipp doesn't think so either. He is pissed off, mostly with himself. He is in the inner circle a little more than most and has a massive security clearance, obviously being the radio operator for the entire unit. He says they kept it real quiet, even in the inner circle, but he's upset with himself because he thinks he should have worked it out sooner. He contacted me as soon as he could after the first skirmish and told me something didn't seem right. I was in the middle of a hunt at the time. I asked him to find out what he could and get back to me. Twenty-four hours later, all hell had broken loose and he called me as soon as he was alone and told me what was happening, and what had happened. That's when he gave me the radio channels. It was around that time I met that guy.

"It wasn't long after that I started heading back this way. He travelled with me for a while. I tuned into the radio as often as I could, but I was trying to get information from him and it was distracting. Just after I left him, you guys walked into your final battle. I couldn't contact you at the time because you were busy and I didn't want to distract you, or immediately afterward because they were listening, so I waited. Not long after that, Charlie and Alpha team were gone too. I knew the channel wouldn't be monitored anymore, so I just waited and listened, hoping for some sign that someone was alive.

"Somehow Skipp managed to get me a recording of your final battle in full. It was both channels concurrently. I hadn't heard the overwatch stuff the first time. He had flagged a particular section he thought I should listen to. He said it might be what I was 'looking' for." He saw us looking at him in surprise and correctly interpreted our confusion. "Oh um, the internet is still working in some places. We, well someone has managed to restore it..." He paused for a moment to let that sink in. "Anyway, I listened to the recording and heard a voice belonging to a person who, to my knowledge, was already dead." And he looked straight at Tayler. "I don't think anyone at headquarters even heard it. But Skipp and I heard it. That voice only said one word – 'now' – a few times and that was the moment everyone in your unit suddenly started dying; one by one, every time she spoke. Then it was all over. I waited a few more hours and got a little sleep before trying to contact you."

"Does Skipp know we are alive?" I asked him.

"Yes, unofficially. I talked to him after I made contact. He knows how many of you there are and that I was meeting up with you. I didn't tell him exactly where yet. He told me not to, just in case someone was listening. He is glad you are alive. I know I promised I wouldn't tell anyone, but I trust Skipp with my life. He's not just anyone. He won't tell them."

I nodded my head. I was thinking hard. I suggested everyone go off and get some rest. Brock looked like he wanted to argue, but I could see he was exhausted, so I put my foot down. He went off with the others to get some sleep downstairs. Tayler and Aiden went to relieve Tim and Adam who were on watch and I went to go sit up in my balcony again (yes, I call it my balcony now). I needed to process everything I had just been told. I think I had already decided what I was going to do. I just needed to plan it out.

I had been up there by myself for about thirty minutes when I heard footsteps on the stairs. At least two people were coming up to join me. I figured Tom and Rochelle were the most likely suspects. I was half right. Tom was there, the other one was Adam.

I hadn't really spoken to Adam much since they had been here. He had gone to bed shortly after he and Tim had gotten back from collecting Jase and then gone straight out on watch when he woke up. Overall, I had spent more time talking to Cain, so I was a little surprised when they sat on either side of me and sandwiched me into the pew I was sitting on. We sat there in silence for a while until I got sick of waiting for someone to speak. (I have told you many times now I am rather impatient.)

"So... what's up, guys? Not that I don't enjoy a good hug as much as the next person, but you're practically sitting on top of me." Yep, smartarse to the end, me. To his credit, Adam actually laughed. But it was Tom who spoke.

"So, did the new information change anything, really?" He was referring to our earlier conversation, which, judging from Adam's lack of confusion, he had been given the details.

"No, it doesn't really change much. It's more or less along the lines of what I was thinking... although the turning people and the familiars stuff is a little bit of a surprise and I'm a bit annoyed they didn't want to warn us or tell us anything about it... but I kind of figured something big was further into this forest and we may have to go there and either find out what it was or try and destroy it."

"If you are right and it is a hive, then the queen rules all." said Adam.

"Yes. That's what I was thinking. If the queen is taken out then maybe, just maybe, we'd stand a chance against them. Kind of cut the head off the snake type of thing." I answered him.

"So... you are going to try, aren't you? Tom said you were, but I didn't know. You could just walk away. You know, most of the world thinks you are dead."

"No, I couldn't, even more so now because I know the truth, or at least what we think might be the truth. Either way, we know they are never going to leave on their own. At least not until we are all dead, I would assume. I'd like to think we have something to live for other than being a meal for something else. Seems like we might actually be onto something with this queen stuff. Makes sense to try. Who else is going to stand a chance? I'm already here. I may as well keep going."

"You plan to go on your own?" Adam asked me.

"I don't know. But I can't ask anyone to follow me; an inexperienced nobody, on a mission that will in all likelihood fail and result in the death of anyone who tries, can I? That's not fair, is it?"

Adam didn't seem to have an answer for that.

"When will you leave?" asked Tom.

"I don't know tomorrow, maybe. Thanks to Selena we know which direction to start. I'll take the GPS and Cam's maps with me and head straight to the centre of the hive. Shouldn't be too hard to find; by the sounds of it, it's going to be pretty big."

No one really had much to say after that. We all sat in silence for a while. Adam started yawning and excused himself to go and get some sleep. Tom followed shortly after, looking deep in thought. I was a little lost myself or I might have noticed that Tom didn't head to the door under the altar but around the back where his bedroom was.

I sat up in the balcony by myself pretty much all night. I dozed a little, but mostly I tried to imagine what was going to happen if by some miracle I actually made it as far as the nest. I tried to imagine what the queen would be like. My imagination took me back to all the science-fiction I had seen. I imagined her to be a cross between the queen out of the movie Aliens and the queens of the wraith out of Stargate Atlantis. I dozed off thinking of those images and woke after what felt like only a few minutes, hearing someone else coming up the stairs.

This time it was Rochelle. She had something on her mind and it didn't take her long to let me in on it.

"Tyne? How long has it been since I was bitten? I've been trying to work it out, but I was unconscious for some of it. By my count, it's been about six or seven days."

"Yeah, that sounds about right." I said quickly, counting the days in my head. I suspected I knew what was coming, but I wanted to let her get it out.

"Tyne, am I going to turn into a crazed vampire zombie?" Her voice broke a little at the end.

"I don't know, but if you do, we'll take care of you. We'll get you back to the base and they will find the cure."

"I don't want to turn into one in the first place."

"I know Rush, but all you can do for now is fight it. Do you feel any different?"

"Not really. I actually feel pretty good. Tyne, how do you plan on getting me back to base when I turn? You're going to try and get into the hive." There was no accusation in her voice or on her face. It was just a simple statement of fact given by someone who knew me better than anyone. "You going to tell them?"

"Of course I am. I'm just not going to ask any of them to risk their lives and go with me."

"You'll never have to ask me. Just promise me something..." She looked up at me from under her eyelashes; I hadn't noticed her head drop; I nodded my head slightly, a little worried about what I might be promising. "Promise me that when I turn, if I can't be controlled, if I'm really not me anymore... you'll take me out before I hurt anyone?" I looked at her and saw the fear in her eyes. It was a fear I had never seen in her before.

"I promise, but Rush... are you sure you wouldn't prefer to just go back to base and see how they are going with a cure?" I already knew the answer, but I felt it would be remiss of me not to at least ask. She actually did think about it for a moment before shaking her head.

By now, the sun was starting to peek over the horizon. I heard people starting to move around downstairs, emerging from the hidden room. I stood and Rochelle followed suit, knowing what I was thinking without me saying it, what I was doing (as she always has). It was time to tell the others.

They watched me coming down the stairs with Rochelle in tow. They all wore different expressions, most in varying degrees of expectation. I was surprised to see Jase sitting in the pews alongside Adam. Last time I had really seen him, he hadn't looked healthy. I hadn't expected him to be up and around yet. He looked surprisingly good, considering. He smiled at me tentatively. I smiled back as best I could. It felt more like a grimace, but that was owing to what I was thinking about obviously, not to him.

17

"'Sup Boss?" asked Aiden. He was always one to try and remove the tension from a situation and my typical reply, obviously given that I can never help being a smartarse, came out before I could stop myself.

"The roof, the sky, some clouds and eventually you get to outer space. Beyond that, you'd have to ask NASA... or the aliens; rumour is that's where they hail from." I smiled when I said it and instantly relaxed. Whatever happened now, I knew I would be okay.

"Okay guys," I began with the serious stuff. I was about to flick my radio to open mic but realised everyone was here. The sentries were standing in the doorway of the church. "You all heard what Brock told us when he got here. Sounds to me like destroying this Queen – or whatever she is – might be a big step in getting rid of these things, but who knows. I don't even know if it's going to be possible to get there, or if I'm right about it being a hive, but I've decided that I am going to go and try to check it out, try to kill this Queen."

"When do we leave?" Cam asked me.

"We?" I asked her.

"Yeah, we..." added Daniel and Delta at the same time. Delta continued, "You really think we're going to let you go without us? We're a team!" He smiled as he said it.

"I'm not going to ask anyone to come with me, let's be honest, from everything we've heard and guessed this is going to be very difficult, maybe impossible, but I want to give it a try. They already think we are dead, so I don't think they will care. I was going to leave now but I think sunset might be better, cover of darkness and all that. No point in waiting any longer than that. It'll give you all a chance to think it through. Now I am going to go and get some proper sleep before I go." I left so much unsaid, but I figured they would all make their own decisions. Much as I didn't want to be responsible for risking anyone else's lives with my crazy mission, it was nice to know at least some of them were thinking they wanted to come with me. I hoped they would think it through properly before they tagged along.

I slept for a few hours and woke to the smell of cooking. I wandered back up the ladder, unable to ignore the smell and go back to sleep. I found everyone sitting in front of the door to the church, enjoying the afternoon sun. They all looked refreshed and relaxed, not at all like people who were about to undertake a dangerous and difficult mission... so maybe they had all decided to stay behind after all.

Brock got up when he saw me and walked over to me with a big bowl of something that looked like stew. He handed it to me.

"Could we go for a walk?" he said.

"Sure." I said. Anything to put off for a few more minutes to find out how many people I had to say goodbye to. It's funny. I was prepared to go by myself on this suicide mission, but knowing even a couple of them might come with me had somehow made it harder to say goodbye to the rest. We walked slowly so I could eat as we went. If not for the bowl, you could almost call it a romantic stroll.

We walked all the way to the edge of town, more or less to the spot I would pass through when I left later on today.

"I'm going to let Home Base know we're alive before I leave here. I hope they will do the right thing and bring in the ones who stay behind." I suddenly blurted out.

"Tyne, everyone is going with you. No one wants to stay behind. You have earned their trust and their respect; they will follow you anywhere. You won't even have to ask. You're a good leader, a natural leader." Brock replied, to my surprise. I blushed at the compliment and then he continued. "I'm coming with you too... if you'll have me."

"Of course I'll have you, but wouldn't you rather lead? Or maybe Delta, you both have more experience than me." I asked him honestly, already suspecting the answer.

"No, I want you to continue to lead and so does Delta, but we are both more than happy to help you or talk things through with you if you need it. But remember Tyne, you have really good instincts. It's why you were picked to lead in the first place, well part of it anyway." I didn't say anything after that. I just quietly finished my stew. When I finished, Brock took the bowl from my hands and put it down on the ground.

"Tyne, I owe you a massive apology." He said. Suddenly serious.

"What for?" I asked.

"For so many things. I am sorry for what happened when I found out you were leaving. I'm sorry for leaving without saying goodbye and for not believing you were up to the task." He paused after that to give me a chance to respond. I, however, got lost in the memory of the night before he had left the base.

We had gone for a run to work out a stitch in my calf. I had just been told we were headed out to Elko in the morning to check why communications had ceased. I told Brock as soon as I arrived for our afternoon training session. He was very quiet afterwards.

I was on edge, both excited and nervous and I wanted to talk it out with him, but he didn't seem to want to talk, in fact he had been keeping my training so intense I hadn't even had a moment to collect my thoughts enough to start a conversation.

I stopped running as we approached the jeep. My leg felt much better and I was very warm and puffed. I needed water. I pulled my water bottle out of my backpack – the one he made me carry everywhere I went – before turning around and noticing he had also stopped but hadn't followed me over to the jeep. I called out to him as I opened my water.

"Brock, are you ok?" He slowly lifted his head to look at me, his expression was confused and upset. He seemed to snap himself out of whatever was bothering him and walked over to me.

"Yeah, I'm fine," he took a deep breath before continuing, "you are doing amazing with your training. You are looking really good, too. I

would say you get a solid pass!"

"Thanks!" I said brightly. I glowed under his praise. My crush was still going strong, although I think I did a pretty good job of hiding it most of the time these days, but sometimes I was still a little star struck.

"We should celebrate... and I've made you miss dinner again..." he said, still looking a little lost in his own thoughts.

"Umm, sure. But what are we going to do to celebrate? I don't see any pubs around here." I joked. Brock didn't reply, just gestured for me to get into the jeep. We jumped in and he drove toward the officers' cabins. He stopped in front of one near the very back and turned off the engine before getting out. I followed him, not sure what to expect.

He walked to the door and opened it, gesturing for me to enter ahead of him. Lights flickered on above me as I walked into a cosy little two-room cabin. The lounge and bedroom were in the same room – though there was a curtain to separate the bedroom that was currently drawn back – and there was also a kitchenette that didn't look like it had been used much. In the back corner of the room was a door, slightly ajar, that appeared to lead into a small bathroom. I can tell you, the officers had it a lot better than us, even in this tiny cabin.

Brock walked back over to me and handed me a glass. I took a sip and found it contained scotch. Good scotch by the taste of it. He downed his in one gulp and went back to the kitchenette to pour himself another. He also started rooting around in the fridge. I figured he was looking for food and left him to it while I sipped my scotch and stared around the room. It was very neat and tidy. The bed was made with sharp corners, military style. There were a couple of items of clothing hanging on the edge of the washing basket, but other than that, not a single thing was out of place. It was all very military. I supposed he didn't spend a lot of time in here. I figured his upbringing had a lot to do with it, too. He had grown up an army brat, the son of a major. She had taught him to be shipshape. He also told me he had been a reservist before he got into wrestling.

The smell of onions sauteing got my attention and I wandered back over toward the kitchenette and saw on the bench the ingredients for hamburgers. He had meat patties already frying off as well, but I'm a sucker for fried onions, so that's probably why they caught my attention. The hamburger rolls were already toasting in the grill, but the thing that stood out the most was the half empty bottle of scotch on the bench near the stove. As I watched, he downed his glass again and refilled it straight away. I didn't know how full the bottle had been when we'd started, but it looked like Brock was hitting it pretty hard.

The burgers were ready in next to no time and Brock took them over to a little table I hadn't noticed before in the corner. He went back for the bottle of scotch and his glass, which he drained again as he walked over. I had finally finished my first one – I have never been a big drinker – and he refilled my glass while he was refilling his own. We ate in the same silence we had been in since we climbed into the jeep. It was definitely the strangest celebration I had ever been to.

We moved to the small couch after dinner and Brock asked me if I wanted to watch a movie or listen to music. I'm normally a music girl all the way, but since we weren't talking much anyway, I decided on a movie. I picked an old-ish army movie (Air America) which made Brock laugh.

"Why would you pick that? It's so old." He asked me.

"I like that movie. I used to watch it with my dad when I was a kid. It's a good movie!" I replied, vehemently defending my choice. Brock held his hands up in mock surrender. "You know my favourite TV show as a kid was MASH." I continued, glad to finally be talking.

"Really?" Brock seemed completely surprised, "it was one of mine too. Mostly because it annoyed my mom. She hated that they could turn something like a war into a comedy."

"She must have hated Dad's Army and Hogan's Heroes too then?" I asked him.

"Even more than she hated MASH. It was funny to me as a kid to put MASH on and turn the start song up really loud. I could always hear her hiss from the kitchen. When I was feeling especially cheeky, I would run in with a shovel and pretend I heard a snake."

"Was she happy when you joined the reserves?" I had never had the guts to ask him questions about his past before, but this felt like more of a social style setting so I figured I may as well feed my interest a little... my crush probably had a little bit to do with it.

"Nope, she was really mad. She said I wasn't taking it seriously if I only went reserves. I did it anyway. Then one day I discovered wrestling and the rest is history." He shrugged his shoulders as though everything else in his life was that simple. "Did your parents like that you were a DJ?"

"They weren't thrilled at first, but when they saw how well Rochelle and I did at it, they warmed up to the idea. I have no idea what they would think about all of this." I finished, gesturing vaguely around me. (I always referred to my mum and Rochelle's parents as a combined unit. Brock was used to it; it took me a moment to realise he had started doing it too.) Brock stayed silent after that. We had already talked about my family (bio and extended). I suddenly realised he had finished the bottle of scotch. He didn't look overly drunk, but some people hide it really well.

"Are you scared?" he asked me suddenly, interrupting my silent assessment. I nodded, but couldn't find my voice to answer properly. He raised a hand to my cheek and held my face gently as he continued, "Don't be. You are good, you are really good. Just don't let your guard down and you will be fine..." He had moved steadily closer while he spoke and when he finished, he gently placed his lips against mine.

The kiss was beautiful and soft and deep and I could have gotten lost in it forever. It was over far too soon. I looked up into Brock's eyes and saw something that looked like regret there. He opened his mouth to speak, but I cut him off. I didn't want to hear him apologise. My heart was racing a mile a minute and my crush was suddenly in overdrive. I didn't want to hear him burst that just yet. I wanted to hold onto it for a little longer. As I looked around for something to talk about, I looked down at my watch. My reaction to what I saw was genuine.

"Oh crap, I'm about to miss curfew. I'd better get back," I rose quickly, "thanks for dinner and the celebration." I said it with a smile. Brock finally closed his mouth and smiled back. I leant down and gave him a quick peck on the cheek, then I turned for the door and walked out before he offered to drive me back to my barracks – I wasn't sure if *he should be driving – I thought I heard him whisper something behind me, but I didn't turn; it sounded something like 'please be safe'. I ran all the way back to my barracks, knowing I didn't have a hope in hell of beating curfew – but I wouldn't have made it if Brock had driven me either. But when I got within sight of the door, I saw someone standing there holding it open. I thanked the lord silently. Cam smiled at me as she let me through, but didn't say anything.*

That had been the last time I had seen Brock. He hadn't been there in the morning to see us off as I had expected him to be. The guy outfitting us had told me – when I quietly asked –he had left on his own mission at first light.

I came out of the memory and realised Brock was waiting for me to respond.

"You didn't think I could do it? You didn't say that." I was a bit shocked, especially having remembered our parting with a fair amount of fondness; even if I had run away from what I thought were going to be sad words to hear.

"No, I didn't say that and I it's not really an accurate description of what I felt either. I was scared plain and simple, scared for you... and scared I wouldn't see you again."

"You're sorry you kissed me?" I asked; even as I did, I still wasn't sure I wanted to – or was ready to – hear the answer.

"What? Is that what you thought? Is that why you suddenly bailed?" He asked me, clearly stunned.

"You looked like you regretted it and I didn't want to hear it at the time. I know you have figured out I have a pretty big crush on you." I replied, shrugging. I didn't see the point in denying it anymore. Even if I was still a little embarrassed.

"I didn't regret kissing you. In fact, I probably would have done it again if you hadn't noticed the time and run off and I probably would have tried to convince you to stay with me, which would have been breaking so many rules. I regretted I didn't do it earlier and I was taking advantage of you, of your crush on me..." he paused and looked up at me again, "Yeah, I knew. You don't hide it as well as you think you do. You were definitely better behaved about it, though. So, it did take me a little while to clue in. I also felt bad because I was about to ask you to turn the mission down, not to come out here."

"Why would you ask me to give up my chance to get some revenge? You knew it was what I wanted to do."

"Because I didn't want to lose you! You don't hold the monopoly on crushes, you know." He said, exasperated.

I stared at him, stunned. I really didn't know what to say. He watched me for a moment as I tried to process what he was telling me; my brain just didn't seem to want to get itself in order.

"Come on Tyne, say something... you're killing me here." Brock said in a small voice and I finally found my voice.

"What do you mean, I don't hold the monopoly on crushes? I know there are a lot of other girls that have crushes on you..." I said stupidly. I was still having trouble with my thoughts. He decided to show me what he meant. He leaned down and kissed me. It was a kiss, much like the first one we shared. Though a little rougher, it was just as deep and over too soon, although I had lost all sense of time while he was kissing me. It was probably only a minute or so; but it felt like time had stopped.

Brock didn't say anything as he gently pulled his face away from mine. I couldn't think of anything to say either. I just stared at him. My mind was going a mile a minute, though. He liked me, he really liked me and it wasn't just a reaction to something. I could see it in his eyes. He had real genuine feelings for me. We stood there for another minute, just looking at each other. Then he bent and picked up my bowl, grabbed my hand and we walked slowly back to the others. That was when I remembered what he had said about everyone coming with me. Hope started to build in my chest. Could he be right? Did I really not have to say goodbye to anyone? The thought made me both happy and sad. I was scared I might get one or more of them killed with my crazy mission, but I was thrilled they cared enough to come with me. I already loved Rochelle for joining me, but I had always known deep down that she would.

We reached the others and found them cleaning up. They were erasing all traces of us from the church and the town. Tom was nowhere to be seen, though. I wondered if he was going to come out and say goodbye before we left. Brock and I joined in the packing and cleaning. Someone had already been down to the room under the altar and collected all our belongings and we committed to resetting our packs and checking our blades and other weapons. Most of us also changed into our clean clothes, something I don't think we were really planning on doing again. I started wondering how long it would take to get to the centre of the hive, barring the nests we might have to fight our way through. I asked Delta and Brock and together we looked through Cam's maps to try and work it out. We estimated two to three days, depending on how many of the nests we could actually avoid. But if they kept getting closer together like we feared, it would be a fine line to walk to get between them with enough clearance not to be noticed, especially with so many of us now.

We made a vague plan of action, knowing we would have to adapt it on the fly. I appreciated their help. I didn't feel quite so guilty about leading everyone in there, now I had someone to bounce ideas off. When everyone was packed and ready, I turned to look at them all.

"Hey guys," I paused. I wanted to say something awesome or inspiring, but I couldn't think of anything. I'm not really one for public speaking. "Thanks for coming with me on this one. I didn't expect you to and I appreciate the support. I really hope we make it through this and maybe even kill this queen or whatever she is. Maybe, just maybe, we might make the difference in winning this war and getting rid of these things for good. But even if we fail, I'm still glad you guys are willing to come along for the ride."

They didn't say anything, but Brock and Delta both saluted me (which honestly felt kind of cool) and Adam and Cain quickly followed suit. Then the others, even Jase. I felt bad for him. It was a fair fall from grace for him; he went from running his own team to being the lowest man on the totem pole in mine. But he seemed happy enough. As we made ready to head out, I went looking for Tom to say goodbye. I couldn't find him anywhere. I walked back out to the others. It was time to call in and let everyone know we were still alive.

18

I hadn't told anyone else what I was going to do, not even Rochelle with regards to calling in to tell them we were alive, but they didn't seem surprised when I turned my radio on and flicked it back to the open channel we had previously used. I didn't know if it would still be monitored regularly, but it was our best bet. Besides, Brock had at least told Skipp, so there was a pretty good chance he at least was listening.

"Home Fifty-one, this is Delta Leader. Come in Home Fifty-one." I said into the microphone and then waited for a reply. It took almost a minute.

"Delta Leader, this is Home Fifty-one. You're still alive? Over."

"That's affirmative, although our ranks have grown a little, all of Delta Team is alive, all four overwatch soldiers and one member each of Alpha and Bravo teams. Over." I gave the numbers and there was a short pause before a different voice came over the radio.

"Delta Leader, this is Skipp. Is Brock with you? I need to know if he made it. He's been out of communication. Over."

"Yeah Skipp, he's with us. Look, we need to talk. Over."

"Yeah, we do. I realise you guys have a lot going on and you called in for a reason, but a lot has happened here, too. Can everyone hear me?"

"Yeah, we're all online."

"Okay, first of all, we've had an interesting twenty-four hours here at base. General Smithe has been removed from command. He is the one who gave the order for you to be killed during your battles. He has been replaced by General Korby. Turns out General Smithe was working for the aliens somehow. We're not sure where the connection came from, but he seems to have been infected somehow during the first attack on America. Either way, he's pretty firmly indoctrinated. We are sure he is what Brock was calling a familiar... did he tell you about them?"

"Sort of. We actually met one here. It's a long story, but finish yours first." I said, looking at Brock, who shrugged. But we didn't get a chance to say more than that because a new voice broke in on the radio.

"Delta Leader, this is General Korby. I wanted to apologise to all of you personally for the actions of General Smithe. Although I take it the overwatch soldiers didn't act on their orders to shoot anyone?"

"Not really Sir, no. They seemed rather upset and appalled by the idea, to be honest and I will fight anyone who tries to reprimand them for not following those particular orders...." General Korby cut me off.

"You have nothing... rather they have nothing to worry about from that. There will be no repercussions for not shooting their own people. We are glad of course, that we have as many of you left as we do. Where are you? We will arrange for a helicopter to come and bring you in."

"With all due respect General, we aren't coming back yet..." I let that sink in for a moment. "We know you suspect the ring of nests to be some sort of mandala with a big nest at the centre. We have a theory that it might be a little more than that."

"What do you mean?"

"Well Sir, we think that it's a hive. Like with bees or ants or something to that effect. We think what is at the centre is a Queen."

"How have you come to this conclusion?"

"Well, it was a combination of all the information, from you, from China and from this girl who came here; we think she might be one of those familiars. She came through here, but she sensed us and when she was leaving, told us, 'She knew we were here and that we wouldn't win.' We deduced the rest from there."

"So, you think this 'She' that the girl mentioned is a Queen of some sort?"

"Pretty much. Does that fit with what you know so far, General?"

"It's as good of a theory as any. I'm happy to go with your assessment, but what does this have to do with you not coming back to base?"

"Well General, we're going after her or it. We have talked it through and we think we are the best placed to give it a go."

"I'm guessing there isn't much I can say that will change your minds on this. Would I be right in that assessment?"

"Yes Sir. We just wanted to let someone know we were alive and we were going to try. Honestly, I didn't expect to be talking to a general when I first called in. I just wanted someone to know where we were headed. I'm not really asking permission, or willing to take other orders right now, pretty sure I speak for everyone here on that one for the moment, Sir. Sorry." I added that last word to placate him. I'm not even sure I really meant it.

"I'm not going to try and talk you out of it. I can hear the determination in your voice. It goes against the army rules and regulations, but I won't stop you, you're not really regular army, anyway. Do you need anything dropped to you? Is there anything we can do to help?"

"Yeah, we are going to need our GPS systems fixed. You can do that from your end, right? And maybe a supply drop."

"What's wrong with you GPS units? They are working fine... what kind of supplies?"

"I'm turning my GPS on now and you tell me where it says I am. Someone was messing with it from your end we think, our techie says hacking, but we have maps with us as well and we figured it out so we stopped using them a while ago, and then turned them off after the last battle."

"We have your GPS registering you around thirty-five clicks directly east of a small town that sits in the forest there. I'm tempted to ask you to detour quickly and check if anyone is alive there."

"They aren't, only one still here is the priest, and we are currently standing more or less in the middle of the town... so you see my problem with the GPS Sir?"

"Yes, I see the problem. Skipp informs me he is working on it now and should have it fixed within the hour. In the meantime, keep using your maps and your compass and let us know your coordinates every hour. Now, back to supplies?"

"More weapons, knives especially, some medical supplies and some ration packs would be good. We are taking some food from here, but it won't last long and we were already running low on ration packs before we got here."

"Done! Once we get the GPS fixed, we will schedule a drop and send through the coordinates. Do you think you can last twelve to twenty-four hours?"

"Yes, we can manage that. We'll let you know if there is anything else we need in the meantime."

"Right you are, Delta Leader. Good luck and we'll talk to you soon. Out."

"Thanks General. Out." when I signed off. I turned to look at Brock. He smiled at me before I turned to the others. "Okay guys, are we all ready to get going?" They all nodded their assent and we turned as one and started walking.

When we got to the edge of town, we found our way blocked by Tom. He was no longer dressed like a priest, instead he wore black cargo pants and a black shirt. Across his chest was the string of a bow and at his hip was a quiver full of arrows. Another quiver hung over his left shoulder.

"I would like to come with you if that's ok? I'm not great at hand-to-hand combat, although I can box a little. But I am really good with this." He gestured to the bow strung across his chest. I won competitions all through school and seminary college. I stopped competing a few years ago, but I never stopped shooting. My aim is impeccable, and I can fire under pressure."

He looked straight at me as he spoke. Clearly, I was the one he was asking.

"How close do you need to be to get a good shot?"

"A perfect shot within fifty yards, but I'm pretty good out to one hundred and still okay out to two. These arrows won't travel that distance very well though and this bow isn't powerful enough to push them. I would need a good compound bow for that. Moving targets present a little more of a problem, but still doable." He smiled tentatively at me. I think he already knew what I was going to say. He was intuitive like that.

"Okay, we can always use more people watching our backs. But you stay on overwatch and you follow any overwatch directions you are given, from any of them or me." Tom smiled and nodded.

"Here," Jase stepped forward and handed Tom a radio headset, "I found a spare in my pack when we stopped the first night. I kept it with me, just in case. You're going to need to be tuned in to hear those directions." Tom nodded his thanks. He joined the group and we walked out of town together, off toward whatever waited for us in the centre of this forest.

We had been walking for about an hour, Cam and I were in the lead with the map and compass, Daniel was behind us, walking with Tom, trying to reset the GPS from our end while Skipp worked on it from base (Tom was helping guide him because he wasn't really looking where he was going). I heard footsteps coming up behind us (me and Cam) slightly faster than the others, as though trying to catch up with us. Tayler appeared on my other side.

"Hey Boss, can I have a word?" she asked. Cam dropped back without a word to walk with Daniel and Tom.

"Sure Tayler, what's up?" she opened her mouth to answer me but before she could speak I suddenly had a thought, which I voiced. "Or now that we are officially on mission again – sort of – should I be calling you Bravo?" She cringed a little.

"That's actually what I wanted to talk to you about. Remember when we arrived at the church and I asked you about getting a new call-sign?" I nodded and waited for her to continue, because she clearly had more to say. "Well, we aren't really four teams anymore and I'm not going to be 'Bravo Overwatch' anymore. I think it would be better for everyone if Adam, Cain and I got new call-signs." I looked to the sides where Adam and Cain had suddenly appeared, drawn in from the deep flanks by the conversation. One after the other, they nodded at me.

"What about Delta?" I asked them, because it became apparent to me this conversation was going to become a group one. I spoke into the radio, giving in to the inevitable; so everyone could have some input.

"Delta's call-sign was always Delta. It was just a fluke he ended up on Delta Team." Adam informed me.

"I've never actually had a call sign," Tayler added.

"Personally, I'd like to go back to my previous call sign." Cain added, "Well, mine and Adam's, if he wants it back, too."

"Yeah, I always liked Cain and Abel." Adam agreed.

"Doesn't using your first name defeat the purpose of a call sign?" I asked them.

"Only if it bothers you. I happen to like my name - even with all the religious connotations that it represents - I was rather happy when it was given to me as a call-sign originally." Cain informed me.

"Okay well, that's Cain and Abel sorted then." I said, "Anyone else want a call-sign while we're at it?"

"Yeah me." Aiden piped up.

"I wouldn't mind one either," said Daniel. "And Tom could probably use one too."

"The priest already has a call-sign, ready-made for him and everything." Piped up Delta, finally joining the conversation.

"I do?" asked Tom. I could hear the amusement in his voice and I guessed that he, like me, already suspected what his call-sign was.

"Yes!" said Delta simply, "You are 'Priest'. You can take care of any... religious needs we have, too."

Tom laughed at the first and I turned in time to see him nodding his head, I assume to the second. I don't think he was disappointed with his call sign – even if Delta was being predictable – in fact; I think it bolstered him a little and made him more confident in the choice he had made to come with us.

"Daniel's call-sign should be 'Techie'," Cam said suddenly, "Because I think he has just worked out the GPS."

"Hell yeah! I like that," said Daniel ecstatically. "Oh and yeah, I got the GPS to factory reset. So it should be all good now." He was triumphant.

"Tayler is really tough and her last name is Cassidy, so what about 'Butch'?" asked Rochelle. It was the first time she'd had input into the conversation. I suspect she was still dwelling on the conversation we'd had about the possibility of her turning.

"Hey Rochelle... you know I'm not gay, right?" said Tayler with a laugh. Rochelle laughed too.

"Yeah, I know that. But 'Butch' means tough and powerful to me.

Straight women are just as tough and powerful as gay women. And you are both." She finished.

"Hmm..." Tayler mused on that for a moment. "You know what? I think that's the best compliment I've had in a really long time. I'll take it... and the call sign, too." She said.

"It does suit you!" said Delta with a laugh, "you do know this is not how call signs usually come about, right?"

"You do know we're not really in the military, right?" I replied in my typical smartarse self, "I figured as much, but since we're a little out there in more ways than one, we may as well do it our way."

"Well, that's everyone, isn't it?" asked Cain.

"No!" Replied Aiden. "I'm still hanging here."

"Well, Aiden," Tayler began, "I've seen you fight; you dance around so gracefully. Your style is very much like my own and I think we would fight really well together..."

"Oh, I think I know where this is going..." said Delta with a laugh.

"And well, you're always so happy..." Tayler continued, "sort of sunny almost..."

"That's true," I said.

"Aw... Tayler... are you asking me to be your Sundance?" Aiden said with a laugh.

"Well, yeah actually... I was..."

"I would be honoured. I think we will work very well together. But I just gotta say... you do know I am gay, right?" Everyone laughed at that.

"Are you really?" Cam was surprised.

"Um, yeah... why? Is that a problem?" Aiden replied (I could hear a little defensiveness creep into his voice).

"Huh... No, no problem... It's just I never got that vibe from you." We all laughed again and though we tried to do it quietly, it was a beautiful, calming sound. One I hoped we could all hold on to, because I didn't think we'd be having a lot of reasons to laugh in the coming days.

19

We walked for another hour or so. The darkness of the forest was becoming deeper the further in we went and the later it got. It was very late afternoon now (we had left earlier than I had originally planned). It would start getting dark for real soon. We had shared sporadic conversation while we walked, but all had been silent for a little while now. My radio suddenly came to life.

"Delta Leader, come in, over," said a voice I recognised. "This is Home Fifty-one."

"This is Delta Leader." I replied.

"I've been asked to check if there are any last-minute additions to your supply drop tomorrow?" Skipp asked me.

"Yeah actually. Arrows, lots of arrows and a heavy-duty compound bow and spare bow strings." I informed him.

"Did Robin Hood come to town and join your band of merry men?" Skipp asked me.

"Yep, but he is woefully under-armed. We could use some spare radios too, if it's not too much trouble, our batteries are all running pretty low." I replied, then added, "And Skipp…"

"Yeah."

"I'm not 'Delta Leader' anymore. It's just 'Team Leader' or 'Boss'. We are no longer 'Delta Team'. We are just a team. The team, really if I'm correct in assuming we are still the only ones out here?"

"Yeah, you are. I think they want to see how far you guys get. Someone has floated the idea of bombing the whole forest, but General Korby isn't willing to do that. Especially with you guys out there." Skipp told me.

"Well, at least someone is kind of on our side. Half of us have new call-signs too." I told him.

"I heard. You know that's not really how things work, right?"

"You know we're not really in the army, right?" I replied, my smartarse side just wouldn't be contained on this issue.

"Touché," he replied with a laugh. "Your supply drop will be around eleven hundred hours tomorrow. Can you wait that long?"

"Yeah, all good. Send through the coordinates to Cam and we'll be there. Hopefully, you don't drop it in the middle of a nest or anything." I joked.

"Roger that. We'll do our best. Safe travels 'Boss', over and out." He signed off. A few moments later, Cam and Daniel confirmed the drop coordinates had come through.

Cain and Adam had faded off again after our conversation about call signs had tapered off. Cam was walking beside me once again. Daniel on her other side, holding the GPS and conferring with her.

Brock came up from behind to walk at my side. I had the distinct impression he wanted to reach out and hold my hand; I had the same desire, but like him, I was trying to be professional.

"We never really finished our conversation earlier." he said.

"We didn't, did we?" I said. "Honestly, you kind of left me in a bit of shock."

"Sorry about that." he said. I looked around and realised Cam and Daniel had faded back. I guess to give us what privacy they could for our conversation.

"My feelings for you have grown far beyond a crush," I started after a deep breath. Admitting this was terrifying, but I figured why not? We may not make it out of here, so why lie? "Now that I've gotten to know you. But I never considered the possibility that you... I mean, that you could even feel anything for me."

"What am I? A robot?" he asked me.

"No... but I'm a nobody and you are this amazing human being who is so far beyond my league I could not ever hope to compete." I gushed.

"I hate when people talk about others being 'out of their league'. I prescribe more to the theory that anyone can fall in love with anyone at any time, no matter what." he said, looking at me earnestly.

"Well, in that case... hang on, did you say love?" I asked.

"I did. I don't know if we are there yet but we definitely have the potential, if we can get out of our own ways and give it a chance... I think we both suffer from the same lack of confidence when it comes to starting a relationship..."

"Is that what you want?" I interrupted him, suddenly nervous.

"Well yeah... I think I'd like to give it a go." he said with a shy smile.

I didn't say anything. I really had no words. I just reached out – very unprofessionally – and took Brock's hand. He seemed to understand what I wasn't saying, because he smiled down at our clasped hands and then at me. It would have been the perfect moment for a kiss, but we were both too professional for that (besides, it's really hard to kiss romantically while walking through a darkening forest teeming with hostile aliens).

We walked along in silence for a moment. I turned to say something to Brock when I heard a branch crack ahead of me. I instantly froze. Brock froze beside me. I put my hand up to signal to everyone else to stop. I stayed still and listening hard. I heard another snap of a branch or a large stick. There was something ahead of us.

I didn't see any other signs of a nest in the area and I knew if the others had seen something, they would have said so, no matter what conversations were going on at the time. Whatever was ahead of us sounded like it was making too much noise to be an alien, but we weren't taking any chances.

"Cain, Abel, can you get into position? Tom, what about you?"

"No problem, Boss," came the reply from Cain, followed quickly by Abel. I turned to see if Tom had heard me, but he was nowhere to be seen. Tayler pointed over her shoulder and slightly to the right, indicating Tom was already making his way to a good spot (hopefully up a tree).

She was making her way over to stand near Aiden so they could fight together. Cam and Daniel were stowing their maps and GPS gear and getting ready. Rush was making her way towards me, as was Delta. And Jase was standing in the rear, by himself. I didn't like that he was fighting by himself. Delta turned to see what I was looking at and saw Jase standing at the back by himself. He took stock for a moment and then retreated to where he had been. Rochelle looked from him to me. I could see she was trying to work out where she was most needed. Finally, she decided – surprisingly – to go back with Delta and stand on the other side of Jase.

I signalled everyone forward. And we walked slowly ahead. When we broke through the trees some thirty or so metres later, we walked straight into a large clearing. Standing in the middle was a single alien. It was a big one. My instincts were torn between charging in and holding back a little to see what was going on.

Once we were all in the clearing, I stopped completely, trying to figure out what was going on. I stared at the alien and it stared straight back at me. Suddenly, I could hear a hiss coming from either side.

"Oh fuck!" I heard Tayler exclaim quietly.

I heard Cam gasp at the same time. I looked around quickly to see what they were looking at. On either side of us stood a small group of people. Humans, or at least what used to be human. There were three on one side and four on the other and one more large alien behind each small group.

The humans looked wrong. A couple of them looked vaguely familiar, like they might have been on the plane with us. Their eyes were black, like the aliens. No whites what-so-ever. Their teeth looked longer than normal and sharper than human teeth. Their bodies looked a little bulkier than they should have, but at the same time, as though they were malnourished. They all wore a look of hunger on their faces. It was almost identical. It was truly the most terrifying thing I had ever seen.

Before anyone could say anything else or react in any way, they charged. It was a complete mess. Though we had decided to fight in pairs, it almost went out the window when it actually started. Brock charged straight at the large alien in the centre of the clearing. I went to follow him in but was waylaid by one of the humans. It charged at me blindly, reaching out with its hands and gnashing its teeth as though it couldn't wait to sink them into my skin.

The bandages I had strapped around my wrists offered some protection. And probably would have been fine against normal human teeth, but they wouldn't stop much in the way of these things; besides that, it's not really what they are there for. They are meant to give extra support to my wrists while I'm in combat (Brock's idea) and they do work, but right now I found myself wishing they were a little thicker.

I managed to hold it off from its first attempted attack. It only managed to scratch me a little with fingernails that felt more like claws but thankfully were still fairly short; therefore, didn't do much damage. I swung my blade around and managed to slice down its arm. I heard a shot ring out from somewhere.

"You can shoot the hybrids. They go down." I heard Abel yell into his radio. The next thing I knew, I could hear multiple shots going off.

"Shit, that one was close, Abel." I heard Tayler say.

"Sorry Butch. You moved faster than I expected." Abel replied.

I was still struggling against my hybrid attacker. Mostly, I was staying on the defensive. I couldn't seem to get an angle to go on the attack, though I was always looking for the chance.

"Has to be a head-shot guys," Cain yelled after a moment, "anything else and the bastards get back up. Delta, watch your back!"

"I got you!" yelled Rochelle.

"Thanks Rush." Delta replied.

I was getting frustrated with my inability to get a good hit on my attacker. I let out a guttural yell. I wanted to swear, but I couldn't think of a single word to convey my feelings and I didn't have time or breath for a whole paragraph. The thing charged me again and again. And every time I barely managed to get away without severe injuries and only managed to land glancing blows myself. I could hear Brock nearby, grunting and cursing periodically with the effort of the fight. I wanted to look around, especially when I heard him hiss in pain; but I was still struggling with my own problem.

The hybrid charged me again. I couldn't get my arms up in time. It was going to be able to do some serious damage to me. I did the only thing I could think of. I ducked. And the hybrid ran right into me and then fell over the top of me. For a moment I stayed crouched down on the ground, confused; it may have been a mindless killing machine, but it had shown much better coordination than this so far.

It took me a moment to realise it wasn't getting up. I finally turned to look at it and saw a long arrow shaft sticking out of the side of its head. Everything clicked into place.

"Looks like I have a guardian angel. Thanks Priest." I said. I was seriously impressed with how well the new call-signs were sticking.

"No problem Boss, you ducked at the perfect time." Tom replied.

I laughed to myself and looked around to see who could use me the most. My eyes naturally gravitated towards Brock. There was a long line of blood down one of his arms and as I watched, he took a backhand to the side of the head. He didn't go down, but he was in trouble. I ran over and launched myself into the air, as I had seen Rochelle and Cam both do on occasion. I managed to get a foothold against the hybrid's knee. It wasn't much, but it was enough to get me up to drive a blade straight into its head.

It started to fall before I could get out of the way. Its arms were flailing around and knocking me aside. Brock was behind it and managed to sever the spinal cord, so all movement stopped immediately. He looked at me briefly and smiled, then his attention was taken by the rest of the fight. Cam and Daniel (sorry 'Techie') were fighting two, a hybrid and an alien together, Aiden and Tayler... I mean Butch and Sundance; had two hybrids on them. They all moved with the same speed. They both had their backs to where Abel would have been, so he didn't have a clear shot to take. Strange how his call-sign came more naturally to me than some of the others.

Delta was fighting another hybrid and Rush was stuck between his fight and Jason's, which was with another alien. He wasn't fighting very well, but he was holding his own, which was something I suppose. I had questioned myself earlier on the sense in bringing him along. He was still wounded (though healing fast) and obviously in pain. Maybe I really should have considered leaving him behind; but I just couldn't make myself turn him away and leave him there alone.

Though he was fighting wounded, the alien was clearly having some trouble getting the upper hand. It really looking like they were dancing around, toying with each other. I saw Rush try and get in there to help him, but she was blocked at every turn, too. It was a strange thing to watch.

I was distracted from this fight by movement out of the corner of my eye. Another two aliens had entered the clearing. They seemed to survey what was going on and started edging towards Cam and Techie (ha... I did it!). I saw Brock come running up behind them to take them on. I went to join him but went down after only two steps. Something had swiped my foot out from under me.

I turned and saw an alien and another hybrid behind me. The hybrid must have been sneaking up on me and then dived when I started moving. It clawed its way over me very quickly when I went down. I started crawling away, but it took hold of my legs and the alien advanced on me as well and stood over me. I aimed an extremely hard kick at the head of the hybrid to get it off me and rolled myself over. I had dropped one of my blades, but I managed to get the other one around to drive into the alien's ankle.

It hissed violently, but stepped away long enough for me to climb to my feet. The hybrid was still on the ground behind me. It looked a little dazed. I must have kicked it right in the head. I turned and kicked it in the head again full force, just to make sure it stayed down a bit longer. The alien swiped at me from the side. It managed to connect with me, but it didn't scratch me. I swiped at it with my blade and managed to get a small cut in on its arm.

I reached desperately to my leg sheath for another blade; but I found my left one empty. The hybrid that was now getting up from the ground must have removed it when it took me down. I looked around on the ground for my two missing blades while reaching across my body with my left hand to my right leg sheath. Thankfully, the blade was still nestled there safely in its holder. I managed to pull it free in time to notice the hybrid charging me. I side stepped, spinning and swung my blade around as I followed through. I managed to slam the blade into its back between the shoulder blades.

It slid right in down to the hilt, a little too easily. I think I must have missed anything vital. I also managed to lose grip on the blade as it spun quickly away from the pain. Instead, I used my fist to land a solid punch to its shoulder. I had been aiming for the head but it was taller than I had expected now it was standing up, so I altered my aim at the last minute to make sure I hit something. It fell backwards into the alien and they both stumbled.

I heard the sounds of the others fighting around me. The fight seemed to be building up rather than winding down. How many of these things could there have been here? And they were so close to the town, why didn't they attack? Apparently 'She' knew we were coming, so why sit here waiting? Was she really that confident she was going to win? She didn't feel the need for a pre-emptive strike.

The alien and the hybrid had both righted themselves and I saw them line up to face me. Side by side they looked more formidable than anything I had yet faced, but then again, that could be because I was exhausted. This fight was taking too long and I was tiring; we all were, maybe more so than normal because almost all of us were carrying injuries.

Suddenly, half the hybrid's head vanished in a spray of blood. It fell to the side. It took me a second to realise either Cain or Abel must have finally had a clear shot and taken it out. The alien turned to look at it, then turned back to me. There was a look of intense anger now painting what little features it possessed. And I wondered if somehow this alien and hybrid team had actually belonged together. The realisation this might be a thing gave everything we had seen and heard so far a completely new meaning.

I tried to compute the possibilities while I concentrated on the alien, but I found I wasn't quite as capable as I'd like to be doing more than one thing at a time right now. I was so tired. I felt as if I wasn't totally running with adrenalin from the current situation. I wouldn't be able to lift my arms. The thought scared me even as it convinced me to keep fighting. I finally spotted one of my lost knives on the ground just behind the alien. I charged and dropped into a roll so I could get past it. As I did, I sliced my blade across what should have been the Achilles tendon on a human. The alien roared loudly and for a few moments, I heard nothing. The sound rang in my ears and I cringed at the idea of yet another weapon that these things seemed to possess against us.

The alien stayed upright and I turned to face it again, armed with two blades. It swung at me and I jumped back to dodge, then launched myself forward again, trying desperately to dig my blade into anything that would hold so I could pull myself up and sever its spinal cord like I had so many times before. In my exhaustion I missed my mark by a lot. My blade sank deeply into its chest but didn't seem to grab on anything solid like bone.

"Boss, look out!" I heard Cain yelling into my ear. I tried to turn my head back to the alien, but only got far enough to see a swinging arm. It collected me across the middle as I tried to duck, but didn't get down far enough. I flew backwards and started to feel something solid catch my body. Everything went black.

20

It was what we had come to call 'Team Day'. The day we would be divided into teams. The teams we would be in out in the field. We would begin training in those teams from now on. We would all move into the same barracks as a team and doing most things together as a team. When we had woken this morning, we had been told to pack our belongings to be moved. They were all piled at our feet.

They hadn't really explained to us how this would be done… if they had already picked the teams and were just announcing them now, if we got to pick our own teams or if it would be a name-out-of-a-hat scenario. I personally thought it was more likely the first or last option. If we got to pick our own teams, it would feel like sport at school.

The team leaders were called to collect our gear and line up at the front of the room. There were fifteen of us. I did the maths quickly in my head. It meant if we were being divided evenly (which made the most sense) then we would be in teams of four. I could work with a team of four. Some of the trainers – including Brock – were standing at the back of the room. I felt oddly comforted by their – his – presence. My musing was halted by a man walking up and standing in front of us. He had an official-looking clipboard in his hand.

"When I call your number, collect your belongings and step forward and join the team leader whose hand will be raised, because I called their number first. After everyone is assigned a team, you will be given your new barrack assignments. You will have the rest of the day off. I suggest you spend some of that time getting to know your team. You will begin training with them first thing tomorrow morning. You will be doing everything with them from this point forward."

He looked around the room at everyone briefly to make sure he had been understood. Then he looked back down at his clipboard. I looked over at Rochelle and she nodded and smiled at me. I smiled back and then looked at Brock. He was watching me... maybe to gauge how I would handle this whole situation. He nodded once, before my attention was called back to the man with the clipboard.

He started reeling off numbers. Not too fast, but fast enough that some people were scrambling to keep up. At the end of each lot of four, (yes, I guessed right) he paused to wait for them to form around the team leader with their arm up and move off to the side together. Rochelle was assigned to team five. I was a little disappointed we weren't on the same team, but she had some good people with her.

I was the ninth team leader to be called forward. I watched carefully as the other numbers were called. There was a girl who was probably about my age. She was a little on the short side and skinny, but fit. You couldn't really call her anything but little, though. But that was okay. I had seen her on the obstacle course and she had been pretty quick, which would serve her well in a fight.

The next called was a guy who was about my height, though considerably more solid. He looked like he could handle himself pretty well and I was confident he would be an asset. He smiled at me tentatively as he walked over with his things to join us. The final member to join my team was the giant I had been paired with in combat training a few days earlier.

He was as big and hulking as he had been then. I already knew he was a good fighter, so I had no concerns. He took us all in as he walked over, but didn't smile. He wore a look of determination that didn't quite suit the current situation, but didn't concern me much. I had figured out the other day when we were training, he was very shy; he hadn't spoken to me the entire time we fought. Once he got close, I realised (given we were in a calm situation, not a combat – or training – one), he wasn't actually twice my size. But he was a lot bigger than me. His height and solid stature (okay chubby, but who cares, I knew he could move) was a boost to our rather shortish team.

I smiled at him as we moved over to the side of the room to clear space for the next team being called. Once all the teams had been organised, we were given our new room assignments. We walked over to our new barracks (which was the room next door to the old one for me). The layout was different. Instead of all beds lined up along the walls at regular intervals; they were in groups of four, two on each side of the room. And each group of four was separated from the others with old-fashioned medical screens. There were four groups of four beds in our barracks. So we each had far more room to move. And the screens gave us privacy to be with our own team. They obviously wanted to encourage us to spend time together.

Rochelle's team was in the same barracks as us, but on the other side of the room, there were two teams in between us. Though I doubted we would have much time together like we had previously enjoyed, at least we could still see each other across the room. I laughed at the thought of how childish I sounded, even to myself.

The other teams were unpacking their stuff loudly. They were all shouting across the room. Two fights broke out within about five minutes of us all entering the room. It was chaos. My team had picked a cot each and was unpacking their belongings. We weren't really talking or even looking at each other, but at least we weren't yelling and fighting.

It was up to me to do something about team building. I was the team leader, after all. I walked over to the tall one and told him unpacking could wait, then I went to the girl and the other guy. I told them all the same thing and indicated they should follow me. We walked quietly out of the room together through the chaos that was the other teams still unpacking and yelling. I left them to do things their way and I took my team off to do things my way.

We walked out of the barracks and across the courtyard muster area. They – my team – followed me meekly half-way across the base, to the side of the obstacle course. I could see the tall guy looking apprehensive when I turned to look at them.

"Well, here we are. I thought it would be nice to get away from all the noise in there and get to know each other in the fresh air."

"Are we going to run the course?" asked the girl.

"Um... wasn't really the plan, but I suppose we can if you really want to. I was just planning on climbing up one of the walls, sitting there and having a chat. Do you want to run the course?" I asked her because she really seemed keen to go.

"Kind of... I feel like I need to move, you know..." she replied. The shorter of the two guys murmured something that sounded like agreement.

"Well, ok... we can do a lap. Start here and when you're done, meet me up there." I pointed to the top of the tallest wall. I picked it because I knew it had a decent platform we would be able to sit on comfortably.

I turned and took off at a steady, slow run. I heard the others following my lead. We went through the obstacles one by one. Everyone seemed happy to go at a nice, even pace. It was a relaxing way to complete the course. The girl had kept pace with me the whole way around the course, but towards the end she charged ahead and flew up the wall with a speed I gotta say was really impressive. The guys both jumped ahead of me right at the end and took the wall with ease themselves. I followed them up, not breaking stride at all and landed on the platform above the wall a few seconds after them.

"Why don't we start with introductions? Because I'm not going to be calling everyone by number. I'm Tyne." I didn't wait to start the conversation. No one seemed breathless, so there was no need to.

"I'm Aiden," said the guy who was about the same height and build as me.

"I'm Abigail, said the girl."

"My name is Daniel," said the tall guy quietly as he blushed. I suspected he would take some time to warm up to us and feel comfortable..

"Well, that's a start," I said with a laugh. "I thought that would be more difficult." They all laughed with me at that. "Why don't we all just start with what we think our strengths and weaknesses are?" I suggested.

What followed was a couple of good hours spent talking, . We got to know each other a little and I'd like to think at the end of it we all felt a bit more comfortable with each other.

We went back to the barracks afterward, all a bit less apprehensive about what was to come and with the intention of unpacking our *belongings, hoping the other teams had sorted themselves out by now. When we walked in the room, the chaos was less but still present. The team in the section immediately next to us had bruises on their faces and looked like whatever argument had been starting when we left the room had come to blows. I looked over at Rochelle, who just shook her head at me. I made a mental note to ask her what had happened later on.*

I opened my eyes. Cain was shaking me gently, trying to wake me. I didn't know for how long. There was an odour of window cleaner in the air. Cain breathed a sigh of relief and Tom put a small bottle back into the side pocket of his medical pack.

"What was that?" I asked him.

"Just some smelling salts. After I checked your head and was fairly sure you didn't have a fractured skull, we figured waking you up as quickly as possible was the best idea." He replied. I nodded in agreement and was glad to feel my head didn't hurt too much. I was going to have a headache for a couple of hours, but I knew I couldn't take anything for it.

"You okay?" Cain asked me. I nodded again.

"What happened?" I asked him, feeling a little lost.

Cain told me the whole battle from start to finish had been a mess. Not through any fault on our part, but just the sheer number of aliens and hybrids that had been there. Fights had raged all over the clearing and it had been hard for overwatch to keep up. It had been a bit easier once Abel had figured out the hybrids could be killed with bullets. Although Cain admitted he had taken shots at the aliens too when he could – apparently he was pleasantly surprised with the results – the bullets were never going to kill the aliens, as we had already known; but if they hit the right spot, they threw them completely off balance for a moment, which was sometimes all the person fighting them needed.

All counted, we had killed eleven hybrids and six aliens. Cain told me that after I had been knocked out by the alien, it had turned away from me, as though it either thought it had killed me or didn't care. Aiden had taken it on, having been the closest when Cain had called out to me. He had jumped the alien and fought hard against it. He had managed to take it down but sustained an injury doing it. The fights had been going strong. Cain had given himself over to keeping a watch on the area immediately surrounding me while the other two kept up what help their bullets and arrows could give for everyone else.

Lucky thing he was, too. About five minutes after I had been knocked out (which happened around the fifteen-minute mark – it felt much longer to me – apparently) Cain saw something sneaking over to me. It was another hybrid he didn't recognise as part of our current fight. It had crept out from the side of the clearing as though it had been hiding there. He watched it for a moment.

It had grabbed me and tried to drag me back out of the clearing and Cain had taken a shot at it. He had missed its head but managed to clip its arm. Instead of retreating back into the forest, it had turned, looking straight at the place Cain was hiding in the trees. He shot it right between the eyes. Another had quickly replaced it and he shot that one straight away.

Brock tried to get over to me but had been thwarted when another alien appeared alongside the first one he was fighting, so he was fighting two at once. Cain had started taking what he called 'pot shots' at them as a distraction and give someone else a chance to get over and help Brock, which, eventually Rush had done. Finally, the last alien had fallen and Cain, Abel and Tom had wasted no time getting out of their respective trees and rushing to the clearing to check we were all okay.

The fight had lasted thirty minutes from start to finish. I'm probably not the only one who felt as though it had gone a lot longer. Tom had gone off to start cataloguing and treating injuries as soon as I was awake. Brock had a slice (from an alien's claws) down one of his arms that needed dressing, although Tom decreed it didn't need stitches. Aiden had his shoulder dislocated again, which Delta put back in for him before I had even woken up and he and Tom were now working out a way they could strap it so – hopefully – it might be prevented from happening again.

Daniel and Cam were examining the dead hybrids. We were fascinated by them and they had taken it upon themselves to find out what little they could from the bodies. Rochelle was looking at them too, a strange mixture of awe and disgust on her face. I knew what she was thinking. I made a note to ask her about it later and make sure she was okay.

Jase, I noticed, was very pointedly not looking at them. His eyes were dark and brooding. He stood with his back to them, almost – but not quite – as though he were watching the trees.

"That friend of yours is a superstar fighter!" Delta said, walking over to me. He was being a little too casual. "Glad you're okay. Was she that good in training?"

"She wasn't too bad. We were pretty evenly matched, I think." I told him.

"Did you – by chance – ever see Jase fight?" he asked me.

"No, he was in a different combat training class to me. I only saw him on the obstacle course. He wasn't too bad."

"Hmmm... Okay."

"What's up Delta?" I was suddenly concerned.

"He didn't really seem to want to fight... he ended up taking on one of the aliens, he avoided the hybrids like the plague... and when he did fight, his eyes looked like they changed. I know it sounds completely crazy, but they turned black."

"Black?" I asked him, unsure if I'd heard him correctly. "What do you mean, black? Do you mean like his irises?" I'd heard of that happening to some people when they got really angry (Rush and I had gone to high school with a girl like that. Her temper had been astronomical). But even as I asked, I could see by the look on his face he meant something different. That look also made me suddenly dread the answer.

"No, not just his irises. The whites too. His whole eye was black. Kind of like them..." he pointed at the dead hybrids nearest us on the ground. "I only saw it for a moment at first, so I thought maybe I had imagined it, but after the fight I looked at him again and they were still black. They seem to have gone back to some semblance of normal now. But they seem darker now than before."

"Crap!" was all I could think to say. (Yes, very intelligent I know.)

"I think we need to be careful and keep a close eye on him..." he seemed like he wanted to say more.

"What is it Delta? Spit it out." I was starting to stress out a little and it was causing my headache to get worse. I didn't mean to snap at him, but it came out that way.

"Rochelle... Rush... her eyes changed, too. Only for a moment with her, but it still happened. She was different, though; she couldn't wait to get at the hybrids and take them out. She's carrying a lot of anger Boss, the kind of anger that gets people killed. Her irises are still black." he added almost as an afterthought.

"Are you still willing to fight with them?" I asked him. He considered my question for a long moment.

"Her... yes. I think she's been altered somehow by her bite, but I am sure she is still on our side. She saved my neck back there a couple of times and a few others to boot. Him... I just don't know; I want to keep him with me because I feel the need to watch him, but I don't think I trust him. He fought the alien okay, but the way he avoided the hybrids... even now, he won't even look at them. I just don't think he will put himself between one of them and one of us if it comes down to it."

We both mused on that for a moment. Brock walked over and noted the looks on both our faces. He became instantly concerned.

We filled him in quietly on our conversation. All the while, I was watching Jase out of the corner of my eye. He was staring off into the forest. You would almost think he was watching for an attack... if it weren't for the fact he was staring into exactly the direction we would be heading... exactly where we suspected the nest was. The way we would be heading when we were finished here.

A moment later, I realised someone else was watching him, too. Rochelle was staring at him from her position on the ground, where she knelt near one of the hybrid's bodies. She held something in her hand, which I was curious about; but it was her eyes that concerned me the most. Delta was right, her irises were as black as her pupils had been before. There was just no distinction. She was looking at him as though she were listening to him talk. A look of mingled confusion, anger and something else I couldn't quite pick on her face.

She stared at Jase a moment longer before he turned and looked at her. Something passed between them, but I couldn't make any sense of it. Anger crossed her face for a moment before she looked back down at the body in front of her and he turned back away. I puzzled over the interaction for a moment before Rochelle looked up and caught me watching her. She smiled and shook her head. I think she meant to tell me there was nothing to worry about. Or maybe that she wasn't turning yet. Who knows?

By the time we had finished cleaning ourselves up and dressing wounds, dusk had passed and darkness had well and truly fallen on the clearing. The effect of darkness on the place was startling. It had already been a bit creepy, but darkness exaggerated the feeling a hundred-fold. We left the clearing together at a slow jog. Maybe we all wanted to run, but we were still tired and sore from the fight, and we could barely see two feet in front of us. We wanted to put as much distance as we could between ourselves and the clearing before we fell from exhaustion. We ran well into the night, even when it became too difficult due to darkness and exhaustion.

21

We made it to the drop site with plenty of time to spare. I was glad because we all needed a break. Delta and Brock took it upon themselves to watch for trouble. There wasn't much discussion between us. We were still tired from moving late into the night, getting clear of that nest. And we had set off almost at first light this morning after only three rotations of a watch. I had been edgy during my watch and talked about it with Rush, who had been on watch with me. She agreed with me that the forest felt different now.

I had wanted to ask her about the strange interaction she'd had with Jase in the clearing after the fight, but I had seen Jase's eyes open not long before and I was sure he was awake. I didn't want him to overhear anything. I think he already suspected we were concerned and watching him, but I didn't want to confirm that for him.

His behaviour had grown increasingly strange in the last few hours. Since we rose this morning, he had barely spoken to anyone and seemed to be getting lost more and more in his own thoughts. I continued to hide my concern as best I could. It was difficult, as my level of concern was growing rather than shrinking. I'm pretty sure Brock noticed, probably Delta, too. But like me, they kept their concerns to themselves.

Even now, as I watched Jase out of the corner of my eye, he was staring off into the distance, still – as always – in the exact direction we were heading. He once again looked as though he was listening to someone talking.

Rochelle wandered over near him and stared in the same direction for a moment. I wondered what she was doing. Rochelle had always been one to look after the little guy. She cared about people and if she saw someone struggling with something – even something she didn't understand – she was the first to go and offer what comfort she could and try to help. She said something to Jase. He nodded his head but didn't turn to look at her at all, nor did he make any other acknowledgement someone was there with him. If I hadn't seen her lips move and his nod, I would never have believed anything had been exchanged between them.

"Ten minutes till drop time." Cam called softly to us through the radio. We were very deep in the forest now and agreed where possible, we would keep our voices low.

We ate a little food while we waited. We were counting on the supply drop for more but were still being sparing with it. We didn't know how much they would send or how long we would need to make it last yet.

Rochelle walked away from Jase and across the clearing. She sat down on the ground and closed her eyes. It looked like she was meditating. She had been known to do that from time to time when she was especially stressed out about something. I briefly wondered again what was bothering her the most right now.

I was interrupted from my musing by the sounds of helicopter blades thrumming in the distance. I admit I hadn't given much thought on how they were going to do the supply drop. But given they were able to give such precise coordinates, a helicopter made sense. I didn't think it would have enough room to actually land, so I assumed they would be dropping it from some height. I hoped anything breakable was well padded.

"Team Leader, this is Drop Ship. Come in." A voice came in my ear, cutting through the sound of the helicopter blades slightly.

"This is Team Leader, go ahead Drop Ship." I replied.

"Are you on-site?" The voice asked me.

"Yes, we are here, awaiting drop."

"Clear the immediate area, take cover in the tree line. The drop is heavy. After we've completed the drop, your instructions are to unpack and leave the area as soon as possible. We suspect the drop could draw attention to your position, so we want you to move on quickly. We are going on from here to scout ahead what little we can for you. We'll let you know if we see any immediate danger. Other than that, your orders are to continue as you were."

"Copy that," I said, waving everyone out of the clearing, "unpack and move on ASAP and you are going to scout ahead for us." I did a visual check of the clearing to make sure everyone had moved out of the way. "Drop site clear and awaiting drop."

"Copy that, area clear, thirty seconds to drop."

Suddenly, the helicopter was right above us. It was very loud. The sound of the blades rotating echoed through the clearing, making it sound as though it was surrounding us as well as above us all at the same time. The trees surrounding us seemed to amplify the sound. It came to a halt in mid-air above us and hovered. There was a large pallet hanging from the bottom of it, swaying a little in the breeze.

As soon as it was steady, there was a loud click and the pallet started falling. It only had to fall about fifty metres; but it picked up a bit of speed on the way down.

"Package released." Came the call as it fell.

"Package received." I answered once the pallet had made final contact with the ground – it bounced a couple of times first.

"Copy that, package received. We'll go snooping for you. Good luck guys. Out." With that, the helicopter rose a little higher and moved off to the north-east.

Once the buffeting winds caused by the rotor blades of the helicopter had abated, we all moved forward quickly to unpack the pallet. It was well secured and it took all of us working with our blades on the ropes to open it up. Made sense though, since they'd had it hanging from a helicopter.

Once we opened it up, we each resupplied ourselves with food and weapons. There was a great supply of food, which I was grateful for. A few spare blades, spare ammunition for the rifles and a new radio for each of us, including Tom – Skipp must have realised there was actually an extra person with us.

Also, for Tom was a fantastic new compound bow and three bunches of metal shafted arrows, all of which he assured me were of extremely good quality. The other item included – which also became

Tom's – was a bigger and more extensively stocked medical kit. It even contained some antibiotics, in pre-loaded doses that looked like epi-pens. It also included pain killers in tablet form and pre-loaded syringes, designed for single use. There were lots of bandages, plenty of wound dressings and sutures, with a note that said, 'any stitches will do just stop the bleeding', which made me very happy that we had Tom because at least he knew how to suture. Finally, it contained a few pre-loaded syringes with huge needles in a case that Tom informed me were adrenaline needles designed to go straight into the heart if needed. They really had thought of everything with this med kit.

The whole unpacking and re-packing process took about twenty minutes (what can I say? We move fast). During that time, we heard nothing from the helicopter. We were just finishing our final check of the clearing to make sure we hadn't left anything behind when the call came in.

"Team Leader, this is Drop Ship. Come in." There was an urgency in the voice that hadn't been there last time we spoke.

"This is Team Leader, go ahead." I was aware everyone around me had frozen. They had clearly all heard what I had in the pilot's voice.

"Don't follow your previous path. There is a large group heading toward your position on a direct line from your destination. You'll need to detour."

"How many is a large group?" I asked him.

"We don't have an accurate count, but we estimate between maybe fifteen and twenty."

"How far out are they? How long do you estimate we have?"

"They are about seventeen miles from your position. At the speed they are moving, I would say you have maybe twenty- or thirty-minutes tops." As he finished speaking, I could hear the helicopter passing overhead again, only slightly off the side this time, as though they were deliberately not flying right over us. It faded off into the distance.

"Thanks Drop Ship. We'll alter our route. Safe flight home."

"Roger that, Team Leader, safe travels. Out."

I turned to Brock and Delta.

"Any thoughts?" I asked them.

"Well... we have to assume even if we manage to evade them now, they will pick up our trail and follow us, eventually." replied Delta.

"One way or another, we have to face the fact we will probably have to fight them at some point." said Brock.

"Yeah, but I don't think I particularly want it to be right now. So, let's avoid it for as long as we can." I said. They both nodded in agreement. "Cam, Daniel, get us a different path out of here as quick as you can."

"Already done," replied Cam.

"Lead on," I told her and she and Daniel turned and jogged out of the clearing and into the trees. If I had to guess, I would say we were heading almost directly due north. It would make our journey to the central nest longer, but at least we were still heading in, more or less, the right direction.

We all turned silently and followed them. I had faith they would get us away from here. I could only hope it would be quick enough. We moved as fast as the path they had chosen through the forest would allow us to. We didn't stop, we couldn't afford to. Not if we didn't want to face those aliens. We kept moving throughout the day. Never stopping for more than a few minutes. We heard no sounds of pursuit, even as the day wore on. I breathed a little easier, as for the moment at least, it looked as though we had outrun them.

We took a longer break in the late afternoon. We had managed to find a small clearing that didn't look like it had been inhabited by any aliens, so we felt fairly comfortable stopping here for a while. We had seen signs of two nests that we had given a wide berth. We hadn't seen or heard any indication of pursuit from them, either.

Rochelle came over to sit by me. My bit of soft grassy ground must have looked very inviting to her. She sat right next to me and placed her head gently on my shoulder. She let it rest there. It was a gesture I recognised from her. She did it when something was troubling her that she couldn't work out.

"Tyne..." she began and then took a deep breath. "I think there is something wrong with Jase. In fact, I know there is... and with me, too."

182

"What do you mean? What do you think is wrong?" I asked her, although I was sure I already knew the answer.

"We're turning..." she said simply. I waited for her to go on. "I can feel it happening now. But at the same time, I still feel like me. I don't have to fight it hard most of the time. The only time I struggle at all is during battle and even then it's more that I feel stronger and I want to use that power for our cause... but I'm scared I wouldn't be able to stop."

"And Jase?" I prompted her gently.

"Jase is struggling to hold onto himself a lot more than I am. I think he's losing the battle, Tyne." she stated nervously.

"Why do you think that?" I asked her.

"Well, I can tell you it is definitely a queen we are facing." She paused briefly before continuing. "She speaks to us... in our minds. I can shut her out. She doesn't hold any power over me. I ignore her easily. I'm not even sure she's actually aware of me. But Jase... he can't shut her out. And she is speaking to him directly now. She is definitely aware of him. With me it's almost like I'm overflow; I'm only hearing an echo of her. Maybe that's why she has no control over me."

"Did Jase tell you this?" I asked her, remembering back to the non-conversation they had at the drop site earlier.

"No, but I know he hears her. He always looks at her, or in her direction, when she is speaking. And... I think sometimes he replies to her or tries to. It's fuzzy and weak sounding, but it's getting stronger." She sounded scared now. "I saw his eyes change during the battle. I saw them turn black and I asked him about it. He said he felt them burn. I felt mine burn too. I think mine changed then. And that was when I started hearing her voice in my head. I'd be guessing it's when he started hearing it, too."

"You felt your eyes burn?" I asked, intrigued.

"Yes, it felt like they were on fire for a moment. It felt like it passed over me and I saw only a shadow for a moment and then my anger spiked up. It was still directed at them, but I couldn't control it. It was like something was egging me on, making me fight harder. But I was able to direct it where I wanted to. I think Delta noticed..."

"He did," I told her. "He mentioned it to me."

"Tyne, am I different? Do I look different? Am I turning in to one of those things?" Despite her earlier confidence in explaining to me what was happening, she wanted me to confirm it for her.

"I don't think you're different on the inside, Rush," I said tactfully. I took a deep breath before continuing. "But your eyes are a little different... I'm sorry." I quickly added because she put her head into her hands and started crying in earnest. Delta looked over at us. I just nodded to let him know everything was okay. He looked away again.

I looked over at Brock. He was keeping watch back the way we had come, with Cain. They stood lightly apart, staring into the distance as though completely lost in thought. At the other side of the small clearing was Abel, watching the direction we were heading. Cam and Daniel were sitting off to one side. They were resting with their backs against trees as though they didn't have a care in the world, but I knew they were watching the forest for signs of danger.

Jase was off to the other side, a little nearer to Abel. He was also watching the forest. But in the exact direction we needed to start heading if we wanted to go straight for the central nest again, where we now knew, almost for certain, there was a queen waiting for us. He again looked like he was listening to something, or someone, in the distance. I wondered about what Rochelle had told me.

"Rush," I asked her gently. "Is she talking now? Can you hear her?"

"Yes, she is talking now. It sounds like she's trying to speak to a lot of people at once. I can tune it out very easily. Jase is struggling more. Tyne, what do you mean my eyes are different? What do they look like?"

"Are you sure you want to know right now, Rush? I can't have you falling apart if you don't like the answer." I asked her. I felt bad about the possibility of keeping it from her, but I needed to make sure my team stayed whole for now. She deliberated on that for a moment.

"Yes, I'm sure. It's scary, but I think it's worse knowing I look even a little bit different and not knowing exactly how." She replied. I looked down at her face, making sure in my own mind she was telling the truth.

"Your irises are the same colour as your pupils. They aren't blue anymore; they are completely black. But they don't have the emptiness and hollowness of Jase's eyes. If we were using it to judge how far through the change you are, then I would guess he is far more gone than you."

"But how is that possible? I got bitten long before him." she asked me.

"I have no idea Rush. I have no knowledge of how this whole thing works. The concept alone is terrifying. But if I had to guess, I would say it might be something to do with the infection you had when we finally made it to the town, because those wounds occurred well after your bite." She nodded her head. "We won't really know until we get back to the base and get you checked out."

"Or until I turn and you have to kill me?" she said in a flat voice.

"That is not going to happen, Rush. You are going to keep fighting it and you are going to win. Because you are a strong, amazing woman. And you can do anything you set your mind to." I filled my voice with as much confidence as I could.

"You know that's almost word for word what you said to me when Eric dumped me and tried to tell me I was never going to succeed in life." She said with a good long laugh.

"Yeah, I know. But it's just as true now as it was then. And it fits." I said, laughing with her, glad I pulled her, at least some of her, out of the funk for a moment. She smiled at me and gave me a big hug. I hugged her back.

"Hey Boss," Tayler said from behind me. "We should probably think about moving on. We probably still want more distance between us and that drop site before we stop for the night."

"Yeah, you're probably right. Round everybody up and let's get on the move again." I said, as Rochelle and I rose from the ground and settled our packs on our backs again.

22

We moved on for another three hours, alternating between jogging and walking. Eventually, though, we had to take a break. We had been on the go since first light and after such a late night, it was starting to tell on all of us.

Rochelle and Jase seemed to be struggling the least – I assume because of the changes they were undergoing – but even they seemed to be succumbing to exhaustion. I called time as darkness started to settle over the forest.

We settled in for the night and set a watch. I went over to sit by Aiden. He had been very quiet since the drop site. We all had, I suppose, but Aiden's silence spoke louder.

"Hey Sundance, what's up?" I asked him, trying to keep it light.

"Hey Boss, the sky is up." He laughed at his own joke. A joke I had made many times myself. His voice was a little slurred, as though he was drunk and I noticed he was sweating a lot. More than even our long exhausting journey could account for.

"Aiden, are you alright?" I asked him, starting to get seriously concerned now.

"Not really," he slurred at me. "I don't feel so good." I took a good look at his face as he spoke and saw he was rather pale.

"Are you in pain?" I asked him carefully.

"Yeah, my shoulder hurts. And my arm is a little numb. But mostly I just feel sick." He looked at me then and I realised his eyes were a little strange. His pupils were dilated. I also noticed his breathing was shallow and rapid.

"Priest..." I called, a little bit of panic creeping into my voice. "Tom,

I need you over here now." I looked around as I spoke to see him materialise out of the almost complete darkness surrounding us.

"I'm here Tyne. What's wrong?"

"Aiden is sick Tom, really sick. And he said his arm is numb and his shoulder hurts a lot."

"Okay, let me take a look at him. We'll sort him out." Tom assured me.

He sat Aiden down on a nearby rock and told him to remove his shirt. When Aiden struggled to comply, he asked me to help him. Once we got the shirt off, Tom set about checking the strapping on his shoulder.

"This is too tight. His arm has swollen, but not from the strapping or the dislocation. Something else is going on here, but either way, we need to remove this strapping for now. It's cutting off the circulation in his arm." With that, he started pulling at the strapping to remove it as gently as he could. Aiden hissed a couple of times but otherwise stayed silent.

Once the strapping was removed, we could see the swelling in his arm. It was extensive. Tom set about examining his shoulder, checking if it was still in the socket properly. I turned on my torch to make his job a little easier and as I did, I saw something on his arm. It looked like a cut. I pointed it out to Tom, who looked at it critically.

"A small cut like that shouldn't cause something like this, but I think you might be onto something." He cleaned the wound thoroughly and examined it again. "Aiden, I'm going to have to dig this out. Are you going to be okay with that?"

"Sure Doc, s-no problem. Wha-s it?" Aiden slurred back at him; he was getting worse.

"I don't know yet. Do you know of anything you might have gotten caught in here?"

"No, maybe, dunno. Tay might know though." He mumbled back again.

Tayler was on watch at the far end of the clearing, so I walked over to where she was leaning with her back against a tree. She looked utterly relaxed, but I knew if she was anything like Delta, she was coiled like a spring ready to strike at a moment's notice. If she heard me coming, she gave no sign until I was right next to her.

"Sup Boss?" she asked me.

"Did you see Aiden get cut or anything in that last fight?" I asked her.

"I don't think so, but if he had, then wouldn't Priest and Delta have seen it when they strapped him up?"

"It's possible they missed it, it's underneath his arm. Anything you can remember would be helpful. He's really sick and we can't find anything else to account for his symptoms. He's sick like Rush and Jase were."

"Okay, let me think a second." She said, looking thoughtful. "He almost got bitten at one stage. I thought I got to him in time, but maybe I didn't."

"Bitten? By an alien? Or by a hybrid?"

"A hybrid. I had just landed a blow on the alien we were fighting and I saw it sneaking up behind him. I ran over and shoved it out of the way. I didn't think it actually got that close. I can't think of anything else though... Boss, is Sundance going to be okay?" She asked me.

"I don't know, Tay; we barely know what happens when you get bitten by an actual alien. Getting bitten by a hybrid is a whole other thing. But he seems to have some kind of infection and we can't find any other wounds at all. Tom will do what he can for him."

"Yeah, Priest will get him through it. Look what he did for Rush and Jase. I'll come over and check on him when I finish my watch. Thanks Boss." she added.

I nodded to her and picked my way carefully back across the clearing to where Tom was treating Aiden. Rochelle had joined them and was holding Aiden's hand and the torch for Tom while he tried to dig out whatever was in the wound.

"Tayler says he almost got bitten by one of the hybrids, but she didn't think it actually made contact. It's the only thing she can think of."

"Well, that would explain this then." said Tom triumphantly, pulling back a little from Aiden, clasping the tweezers tightly in his hand. He placed the contents of the tweezers into my quickly gloved hand. It looked like a shard of a tooth. It was sharp on one side and rounded on the other. It looked like a human tooth. Or part of one, anyway.

I held it in one hand, turned on another torch to give Tom more light, so he could stitch the wound closed. He did another quick search in the wound to make sure there were no other fragments left inside. Aiden flinched and hissed as the tweezers prodded the wound. Finally, Tom seemed satisfied there was nothing else in there and started suturing the wound. Then he administered a shot of antibiotics and one of the preloaded morphine syringes dropped with the supplies. Aiden mumbled something no one understood and fell into a deep sleep.

"I'll give him another dose of antibiotics at first light and a smaller dose of morphine if he needs it. We'll leave the strapping off his shoulder for now. Hopefully, we don't get into any battles until we can put it back on. In the meantime, I'll stay up with him and make sure he's alright through the night. Is that going to cause a problem for the watch rotation?" He asked me.

"Nah, it's alright Tom, we'll work that part out. Are you sure you'll be okay through the night?"

"Yeah, I'll be okay, besides no one else has the training I do, so they'd only have to wake me up if anything went wrong, anyway."

"Okay, Tom." I left it at that. He finished clearing up his first aid kit and sat down on the hard ground next to Aiden' head. Rochelle rose from the ground and stepped over to me. Together, we walked around the perimeter of the clearing. not talking, just enjoying the quiet for a moment.

We swapped out the watch rotation to omit Aiden and Tom and after that, the night was uneventful. We neither saw nor heard any sign of the pursuit we had been warned of. We didn't speculate too much on why that was, there were just too many reasons.

Brock woke me at what he told me was dawn. The forest was still completely dark around us. I looked at my watch and rose from the ground. We decided to let everyone sleep for another hour. I went to check on Aiden and Tom.

Tom was fine. Tired, but fine. Aiden was awake, though still groggy. He refused another injection of morphine, explaining his pain wasn't that bad, but agreed to take a couple of tablets. Tom insisted on the injection of antibiotics. He still looked very weak, but there was more good colour in his face and he wasn't drowning in sweat now. He

189

assured me he would be fine when it was time to move on.

I waited until the sun was high enough to lighten the surrounding forest. I spent a lot of that time pacing. For a little while, Brock paced with me. We let our professionalism slip enough to hold hands for a short while. I found that although I hadn't realised I needed it; I felt comforted by the short contact. Rochelle paced with me for a while when she woke also, though I felt her watching Jase out of the corner of her eye the whole time. I asked her if everything was okay and she told me he was getting closer. She didn't elaborate, but I knew she meant closer to being able to contact the queen.

We woke the others gently when the time came. Tayler jumped up immediately and went straight over to check on Aiden, as she had done before she had gone to sleep after her watch the night before. I don't think we felt as refreshed as we would have liked, even after such a quiet night.

We were all sluggish when we set off. Something seemed to be agitating Jase. I could hear him sighing occasionally. Rochelle was walking with me. I turned to ask her what was bothering him, but she just shook her head at me. She seemed to be listening to something and it took me a moment to realise she was trying to keep track of his ability to contact the queen.

The day stretched on. Still no sign of our pursuers, and we were moving slower every hour. No matter how many breaks we took. We just couldn't seem to get anywhere. It was as though something was weighing us down. And it was getting stronger and stronger the further we went. I wish I could explain it better. The only one who didn't seem to be struggling with an invisible weight was Jase. Rochelle was struggling a little less than the rest of us, but she obviously still felt it, too. Aiden was struggling more than the rest of us, but I couldn't be sure if that was because of the infection he carried or the oppressive weight that seemed to be pulling us all down little by little.

By late afternoon, none of us seemed to be able to fight it anymore. We found a clearing deep in the trees, where it was already getting dark, even though the sun was nowhere near the horizon. We set up camp, set a watch and sat down to eat together (the watch sitting at the outer edges of our friendly circle).

Rush sat near me. She didn't seem to want to be too far from me at the moment. It was as though she was using me as some kind of anchor, maybe an anchor to herself. Jase was sitting on the ground, away from the rest of us as much as he could. He was staring toward her again. As he always seemed to be doing now. He didn't even seem to blink and I could have sworn his eyes were darker than they had been this morning.

Aiden was already asleep. Tom had made him take more pain killers when we had stopped and decided to give him one more shot of antibiotics. Tayler and Delta both sat by him. Tayler was leaning into Delta's side. They weren't talking, just using each other as leaning posts.

Darkness fell even more quickly this deep in the forest. It wasn't long before we could barely see each other in the enveloping blackness. Those who weren't on watch prepared to sleep. I lay on the ground, quietly thinking. I was exhausted, but for some reason I couldn't seem to fall asleep. I listened to the sounds of everyone else sleeping. There were no other sounds from the forest, no wildlife or insects and tonight not even any breeze to rustle the trees surrounding us.

By now I was used to the virtual silence surrounding us, but that didn't mean I liked it. Rochelle and I went camping when we were in primary school a couple of times. I remember the sounds of the forest back home at night. No matter how late I was awake listening, there was always some creature to be heard lurking around and, in a way, it had been comforting. It was what forests were supposed to sound like at night. The silence here was just eerie.

Rochelle and I were waiting excitedly for the bus. We had never been camping before and the Girl Scouts promised us an adventure. We had joined because our sports teacher at school had talked about it. There were seven other girls with us and two scout leaders. We had waved our parents off as soon as the leaders arrived at the hall. We were ten now,

way too grown up for our mothers to be hanging around waiting with us.

We had managed to convince our parents to buy us our own tent to share. We also had brand new sleeping bags and a large backpack, each full of the clothes and food we had been told to bring. The bus finally arrived and we loaded our things onto it. The third scout leader joining us was driving and we set off for our two-hour trip up into some mountain somewhere that Rochelle and I were too excited to have remembered the name of.

We sang songs on the bus ride. We stopped once at a rest stop so everyone could go to the bathroom and finally reached the mountain. We unpacked the bus and put our packs on. Rochelle was stronger than me, so she was carrying our tent. We hiked for about an hour before setting up camp.

We sat around the campfire for a while, telling stories. It was fun, but eventually we were all yawning too much to finish a sentence. The scout leaders told us to go to bed. There were about fifteen minutes of noise from people getting ready for sleep. Eventually, quiet settled around us.

Rochelle and I lay holding hands in the darkness. We listened to the sounds of the creatures in the night. We heard the scrapings and slithering of small animals through the undergrowth and later on larger animals moving around. I lay awake all night, listening to all the different creatures shuffling past our tents. Rochelle fell asleep at some stage. And her breathing added nicely to the noises surrounding me. It was one of the greatest nights of my life.

The noises around me changed, bringing me out of my memory. There was the sound of something moving just outside our clearing. Something rather bigger than we had heard any time recently. I looked around the dark clearing, trying to get eyes on our watch, to make sure they were okay. I could see Abel and Tayler; they were both on their feet already looking towards the sound.

My eyes finally found Brock at the other end of the clearing, also on his feet and closest to the direction the sounds were coming from, I saw Cam. I didn't notice her at first. She wasn't on her feet but crouched behind some scrub. She looked like she was ready to launch herself into the forest at a moment's notice.

I rose from the ground and crept as quietly as I could over the Cam. She looked around briefly when I joined her and shook her head. She didn't have any idea what was out there, apparently. We both waited edgily for the attack I felt sure was coming. I heard Abel swear and spin around. There were noises coming from behind him now. I was torn about where the attack would come from. Then there were noises roughly in between where Brock and Tayler were both watching. Tayler raised her arm and I saw the flash of a blade in a tiny sliver of moonlight that shone into the clearing.

I assumed Brock was also armed and ready. I couldn't see him at all from where I was crouched with Cam. I could see the others – the ones who were awake – setting themselves up quietly around the edges of the circle, as if to cover all the angles an attack might come from. The noises sounded like they were coming from all around us now. Everywhere I looked, I saw someone standing at attention, listening hard for something they had heard.

Something flew past my head and landed with a soft thump on the leaf littered ground behind me. I turned to try and find what it might have been, but I couldn't see anything. I head other soft thumps coming from around the clearing. I heard someone curse, but I couldn't tell who it was.

After about five minutes of the soft thumps coming at us, all the noise surrounding us suddenly stopped. There was complete silence. The only noise to be heard was the sound of the people in the clearing breathing. We waited frozen, sure – well I was –the attack was coming now.

But nothing happened. After a while, I heard someone creeping softly back to the centre of the clearing. I patted Cam on the shoulder to let her know I was going, only to be replaced by Daniel before I was more than a few steps away. When I got back to the middle of the clearing, I found Cain sitting on the ground. Blood was dripping slowly down his chin from a cut on his cheek.

"You ok?" I asked him even as Tom arrived with his first aid kit to treat him.

"Yeah, got clipped by a rock. I don't think it's too serious. Just a bit of blood." He replied.

"Anyone else hurt?" I asked quietly into the radio. I didn't want to yell across the clearing in case there was still something out there listening.

"I got corked in the thigh, but there's no blood. I've had worse." Brock said from behind me, causing me to jump slightly. I hadn't realised he was that close.

"Okay, anyone else?" I received eight 'I'm okay's', I should have had nine. Then.

"Tyne?" Came Rochelle's voice clearly through the radio.

"Yeah?"

"He's gone," she said.

"What?"

"Jase is gone."

23

"What do you mean, gone?" Abel asked Rochelle.

"After everything quieted down, I went to check on him. He was curled up on the ground when it all started; but he was gone. I did a visual check of the clearing because all of his stuff is still here. But he's just not here." she said.

"You did a visual check? It's pretty dark... how do you know you didn't miss him?" Cain asked her.

"I didn't miss him..." she said quietly. "I can see pretty clearly in the dark now." She continued on self-consciously. She was looking nervously around at everyone now, as though she were expecting someone to attack her.

"How clearly?" Tayler asked her, curiosity open on her face.

"I can see faces clearly enough to distinguish features; I can clearly tell who is here. I can see the trees around the clearing easily. I can even distinguish individual leaves. But I can't see colours really, everything just has many shades of a grey-ish shadow over it; kind of like in the movies, when everything at night is blue-ish-grey." She answered in a rush, she was wringing her hands nervously. It's always been one of her nervous ticks and it was oddly comforting to see her doing it now.

Tayler nodded to herself.

"Should we go after him?" Cain asked. I didn't know who he was asking, but it was Rochelle that answered him.

"I don't think so... he can probably see better in this darkness than me, certainly much better than the rest of you – no offense – his pull is much stronger... he had a big advantage over us there."

She looked at me as she spoke, imploring me to say the rest for her.

"He's gone. Isn't he?" She nodded sadly and I continued to make everyone else understand. "I don't think there is much of Jase – as we knew him – left."

"What do you mean?" Abel asked me.

"Come on Abel, we've all seen what he has been like. We've all watched him losing the fight to stay human even if we haven't talked about it." Cain said gently. Rochelle flinched a little, just the same.

"Ever since that nest with the hybrids, we've been losing him more and more since then." added Delta just as gently. "We knew we were losing him. We could all see it." Abel nodded. He knew. But it sounded to me like everyone was trying to convince themselves as well.

"What about Rochelle though?" asked Tayler. There was no accusation in her voice, just curiosity again.

"I don't feel the pull the way I think Jase did. You remember how he was always looking toward where we think the queen is? How he always looked like he was a half a step away from heading in that direction? I don't feel it like that." Rochelle told her. "I feel the presence, but I don't have any great desire to run off and join her."

"What do you mean, the presence?" Abel asked, his voice also full of curiosity now.

"I can't really explain it. I feel something emanating from over there. And if I pointed my finger, I could say with certainty I was pointing straight at her. But I have no desire to go to her. The only desire I feel regarding going there is to kill her and protect you guys."

"For something you can't really explain, you explained that pretty well." said Abel with a laugh.

Everyone else laughed too. I breathed a quiet sigh of relief. I had been gripped by a sudden fear that because of Jase running off, they would all be less accepting of Rochelle. They all knew she had been bitten, just as Jase had. There were no secrets in this team. Everyone knew everything, but people can be strange when they suffer a loss, as we had done and I was constantly reminding people we were not a well-trained army unit.

"She's still with us, by the sounds of it," said Delta, "That's good enough for me." He gave a decisive nod that invited no argument.

"I wonder..." Tom began, obviously thinking out loud. "If the reason Rochelle is having no trouble holding onto herself is something to do with the conversion process being interrupted."

"What do you mean, it was interrupted?" Rochelle asked.

"Tayler told us you got bitten on the night your team died, right?" Both Rochelle and Tayler nodded solemnly. "But you were in another battle after that, in which you sustained more severe wounds, which then got infected. These were the wounds I treated you for..."

"But you treated Jase too, so wouldn't that mean his process got interrupted too?" Tayler asked.

"Yes, I did. And no, not necessarily. The wounds I treated Jase for included his bite. They were all sustained at the same time. I mean, I'm just speculating here. I certainly don't know enough or almost anything really about the process. I'm just wondering if the fact Rochelle got re-injured and then treated for those injuries – with some pretty serious medications, I might add – had something to do with it. Jase never got as sick as you did, Rochelle. I had to give you a few doses of antibiotics to fight your infection. I only had to give Jase one dose and that was mostly precautionary. He probably would have been fine without them, but given how long he was walking around with open wounds and how sick you had been from similar wounds, it seemed prudent at the time." We all sat thinking about this for a while.

"But what does that mean for me?" Rochelle finally asked.

"I have no idea, I'm just speculating again, but the fact you haven't succumbed to the same... call that Jase did can only be a good thing." He smiled at her encouragingly.

"What about me?" Aiden asked suddenly. I hadn't even realised he was awake. He had been so quiet I thought he must have gone back to sleep after all the commotion, if he had woken up at all.

"No clue," said Tom with a grimace, "Sorry Aiden, but you were bitten by a hybrid. That could be completely different. Although you were sicker than Jase for such a small wound, it was quite badly infected, probably from the tooth sitting in the wound for so long."

"Great. So Rochelle gets super-powers and all I get is an infected bug bite." We all laughed at that; whatever tension was left in the group due to our conversation, evaporated in an instant.

"Okay everybody, I think the fun is over. Let's try and get a little more sleep and head out at first light." I said. No one argued. We were all still pretty tired.

The rest of the night passed by without incident. It seemed like the disturbance in the night was designed purely for Jase. Whether he wanted it or not.

As first light became visible through the trees, we once again packed up our camp site and consulted our map, compass and GPS. We decided to change direction from the way we had been heading for a while. Now that we were unsure of what Jase had told – if anything – the aliens.

We had briefly discussed Jase's belongings and decided it wasn't safe to leave them here. But we didn't really want to be carrying them along with us constantly. So we decided to carry them for the day and leave them at the next camp.

We were now heading north-west, at least we would be for the first half of the day. Even though there had been no sign of any alien activity since the strange occurrence of the previous night, we moved at a fast jog for the first couple of hours. There seemed no point in making things easier for anyone who might have been trying to follow us.

Cam and Daniel were leading the way – as always – when they came to an abrupt halt. I was only a short distance behind them and I almost walked into Cam when she stopped. I lost my balance a little and she reached back and caught me without thinking. I swear sometimes, she seemed to see things before they happened.

"There's a nest up ahead." said Daniel quietly as I opened my mouth to thank her and ask why they were stopping.

"How far?" I asked him.

"About a hundred metres or so I think," he said, "doesn't look like a big nest, but we've been mistaken before."

"Okay. Get ready." I told him and Cam and then into the radio I said, "Guys, we've got a nest up ahead. Techie says it doesn't look big, but we've been fooled before. Get ready; we're going in."

"Roger that," said Brock from close behind me.

"Roger that!" echoed seven other replies. I could hear them arming themselves and stowing away anything they wouldn't need in the coming fight.

"Everyone ready?" I asked after a minute. I got a nod each from Cam and Daniel and seven other replies via the radio.

I took the lead from Cam – who was happy to relinquish it – with Brock at my side and we crept slowly forward. I didn't need to be pointed toward the nest. Now I was leading, I saw the same signs that must have alerted Cam and Daniel to its presence.

I broke slowly through the trees into what should have been the centre of the nest. It was a nest alright, a broken one by the looks of it. There was a lot of blood around and lying in the middle of the clearing was a large alien. It had been injured badly, but it wasn't dead. It watched us come through the trees and hissed violently at us. It tried to get to its feet but seemed to be struggling from its wounds.

Brock walked up to it and it tried to swipe at his legs. He jumped back quickly and slipped in something wet that looked like mud (but could have been anything). I didn't want to think about what it might really be. The alien managed to push itself up onto its arms and took another swipe at Brock. He stepped quickly out of the way again and when its arms stilled for a moment; he stepped forward and slice his blade quickly and deeply across the back of its neck, severing the spinal cord. His other blade came up under its chin and into its head. It died instantly, but left me wondering who had left it alive in the first place, and why?

There was movement in the trees on the other side of the clearing. I directed Delta and Rochelle to check it out. They crept quietly over and I heard scuffling and a thump before Delta emerged, dragging the body of another dead alien out of the trees after him into the clearing, followed by Rochelle, one of her blades sticking out of the alien's throat.

"This one was left injured, much like that one." Delta said as he dropped the body he dragged on top of the other one. He retrieved Rochelle's blade, which he then handed back to her without a word. "But this one was mobile enough that it was trying to crawl away. Looked like in that direction." He pointed to the way we'd been heading all day, which was nowhere near the direction the queen was supposed to be. I puzzled over that for a moment, but couldn't make any sense of it.

"Do you want to keep on this line, boss? Or are we changing direction?" Cam asked me. I looked at my watch to see it had only been three hours since we had set off that morning.

"I think I want to keep this line for a little longer, especially now that we've come across a nest." I liked the idea of giving ourselves a little longer before we walked into the lion's den, so to speak. "Let's go." And we started jogging slowly again in the direction Cam pointed.

After a while, I dropped back a bit to check on Aiden.

"How are you doing, Sundance?" I asked him. (I was trying really hard to use call signs now. I hoped it would make it easier for me later – like when we got into the big fight).

"I'm actually feeling really good today. The pain in my arm is completely gone. I feel like I could run forever and fight anything." He told me with a big grin on his face. He looked bright and refreshed, as though he'd had a week of early nights and late mornings. Which is to say, he looked far better than the rest of us.

"That's good to hear." I said, making a mental note to ask Tom what he thought about the miraculous recovery.

Rochelle came up to run at my side. She didn't seem to want to talk, just be there. I think Jase running off bothered her more than she was showing. But I knew Rochelle and she would talk about it when she was ready. In the meantime, I would just let her be.

We passed wide of another suspected nest and paused to discuss if we should clear it. I felt we should try and clear everything we came across. That had been our original mission, after all. Cain and Abel were sceptical, not because they didn't want to complete our original mission, but because they were keen for the bigger fight to come. They wanted to get to the centre nest and kill the queen, which they deemed very important also. I could see their point, but the idea of leaving any of these things alive out here made me angry beyond belief. We weren't going to be able to eradicate them from our planet if we walked by just because there was something bigger or more important to do.

Whether for good or bad, we decided that while getting to – and killing – the queen was important to us, our original mission still stood and so we diverted off our line and went for the nest.

24

It was another small one, although at least the aliens were alive for us to kill this time. So there were no additional puzzles we couldn't work out. There were three of them and I swear these things were getting bigger every time we came up against them.

Rochelle ran forward as soon as the aliens made a move toward us. I could see what Delta had meant about the anger she was carrying when she fought. It was obvious in her stance and movements. That was about as far as I thought about it, because suddenly I was in the thick of it. These aliens weren't just getting bigger, they were getting more vicious. They were gnashing their teeth and swiping their arms around indiscriminately. I wanted to watch Rochelle fight to see if she was any different to how I remembered, but one of the aliens had decided to target me aggressively. No matter how much I dodged or weaved, I couldn't manage to land a hit. Out of the corner of my eye, I saw Brock trying to get in behind it. Finally, he ducked and went into some kind of somersault and managed to knock it off balance. It only lasted a moment, but it was enough for me to get in and take a quick swipe with my blade across its ribs.

It hissed violently at me, whether from pain or anger I don't know and I didn't much care. Before I got the chance to set myself again and try for another strike, it started swinging its arms again. Brock stabbed at it from behind but missed. It swiped at him and managed to connect enough to send him to the ground. In the half second it took me to make a quick check where he landed, the alien managed to get a good swipe in on me too.

I went down hard, landing near enough to its feet to be in danger of being stood on. Butch came out of nowhere (see I really am trying), jumping over me and slamming her shoulder full force into the alien's chest. While she did that, she brought a blade up and stabbed it in the chest. It was hissing continuously now; it was almost loud enough to drown out other sounds of fighting still going on around us. Brock was back on his feet, taunting the alien to come at him. Tayler was doing the same on the other side.

I had managed to regain my feet, but before I could get back in the fight, Sundance came springing up out of nowhere from behind the alien and drove his blade into the back of its neck to sever the spinal cord. Instead of the usual swipe we tended toward, he jammed his blade in deep and twisted it hard. I heard a sickening pop sound and the alien fell, well and truly dead.

I stumbled over, catching my foot on a tree root and stood with the others, a little dazed. I looked around me quickly to see the other two aliens were also down. The whole thing was already over. It had taken less than seven minutes. Rochelle walked over and slung her arm across my shoulders. She seemed exceptionally calm and happy. Delta followed her over, also smiling.

"It saw my eyes... the big one and it tried to control me. I could hear it... feel it trying to give me orders. And I was able to shut it out with absolutely no hold on me. It got distracted, because it couldn't control me and Delta was able to wipe it out... too easy!" Rochelle gushed at me. She was practically bouncing on her feet.

Cain ran into the clearing from where-ever he had been standing as overwatch, his rifle slung over his shoulder. Abel and Tom were close on his heels.

"That was AWESOME!" he just about yelled as he came to a stop in front of us and held his hand up to Rochelle for a high five.

"Thanks," said Rochelle, going a bit red in the face. (I made a mental note to ask her about that later.)

Cam and Daniel joined us too, walking over from the body of the alien they had taken together. Cam had a small cut on her cheek Tom immediately turned his attention to.

"Where to from here, Boss?" Daniel asked me, "is it time, do you think?" He gave me a meaningful look that was echoed by everyone else as we stood in the clearing amongst the bodies of the aliens we had just killed. I knew what he meant, what they all wanted to know.

"Yeah, it's time. Point us at her and we'll kill everything alien we come across on the way there." I said. There was a silly quiet cheer at my words. I think at both that we were going after the queen and that we would be killing many aliens along the way.

"We can probably expect to see more hybrids along the way," said Brock in a quiet, commanding voice, "So be ready. I don't think we can realistically expect to save them at the moment, or even try to. So don't hesitate, we've seen firsthand how vicious they are. I know I was having second thoughts the whole time we were fighting the last lot. I assume a lot of you were also. I hate to be the one to say it, but we can't save them." He gestured to us as a group as he said 'we', "Not right now, maybe not ever. But they will try and kill us, so we have to be prepared."

"Brock is right," said Delta, "Overwatch, if you get a shot on a hybrid, don't hesitate. I hate to put one person over another, especially when they were our people; but right now, if it has to be a choice between us and them, we need to focus on us."

"What about Jase?" Abel asked quietly. I knew what he was thinking. Jase had been one of us, literally from our base. Ours even more than the ones we were searching for from Elko. We had fought together – more than once, in some cases – he had been part of our team. I didn't know what to say.

"Abel..." I tried, "If there was a way... I mean, I know how you feel, we all do... if there was a way to secure him and go back for him later, then I'm sure that anyone here would try. But I just don't see how we can..." I stopped again, unable to finish what I had been trying to say.

"We may not even see him," said Aiden, "maybe if we don't, we can go find him afterward or something..." I had to get control of this before it spiralled any further.

"Abel, I'm sorry, but if we come up against Jase, then – much as it pains me to say it – I think the order stands. In the meantime, maybe just hope and pray we don't run into him." I felt a tear running down my cheek as I finished. Abel nodded and I knew he understood all the things left unsaid. He reached over and wiped the tear off my cheek. I sensed rather than felt Brock stiffen beside me.

"It's okay, little sister. We're all in this together." He said. He gave Brock a sideways glance and quickly dropped his hand.

Rochelle stood up from where she had been crouching on the ground and stretched.

"Let's get out of here. I don't like standing around." As she spoke, I looked at Cam and Daniel. They already had their maps and compass out to plot our path. Rochelle stood for a moment, staring off into the trees.

Cam and Daniel didn't need long to point us in the right direction and we left the clearing behind us. We didn't run or even jog this time. We walked at a decent speed, though.

We didn't encounter – or even see signs of – any more nests as we walked. Cam and Daniel had put us on a perfect straight line directly toward the queen. Which meant the walk should take another two or three days, depending on how many nests we came across in the meantime and how fast we moved between them. We knew we would encounter more nests eventually and probably a lot of them the closer we got to the centre.

Luckily though, we were nest free for the rest of the day. We were able to find a small clearing before dark where we set up camp. We sat around talking for a while about our pasts and things we wanted to do with our lives after the war. It had been a while since we'd had a night like that and the first we'd had as the complete group we were now. It took a while for everyone to settle into sleep. I was keyed up because we were finally heading toward the queen. I think to various degrees that fact was on everyone's minds.

Abel had volunteered for first watch, along with his brother. Aiden and Tayler had also volunteered. They sat or stood at the four points of the clearing. Being such a small clearing, we probably could have gotten away with only three or even two people on watch, but so deep in the forest and with what had happened the night before, we weren't taking any chances. We weren't going to be caught out by complacency.

I was lying in the middle of the clearing with Brock on one side of me and Rochelle on the other. Brock had reached out to take my hand as soon as we were lying down. He had held it in his until we fell asleep, when his grip loosened.

On my other side, Rochelle had wriggled closer in her sleep and flung an arm over my stomach. I, however, was wide awake. I managed to extricate myself gently from under Rochelle's arm and get up. I walked over to where I thought Abel was sitting.

When I arrived where I had last seen him, he was nowhere to be found. I called out to him quietly but got no answer. I heard a rustling noise coming from the bushes a short distance away. As I considered what to do, I felt a hand rest gently on my shoulder. It was sheer will that kept me from screaming loudly. I didn't manage to contain my gasp, but at least it was only slightly audible.

I looked at the hand and the angle of the wrist attached showed it was reaching down from the branch of a tree above me. I looked up into the smirking face of Abel. He held a finger to his lips, then he crooked it at me to indicate I should follow him up the tree he was sitting in and keep quiet.

I nodded my head to show I understood and watched him vanish back up the tree again. I followed. I found to my surprise, he had climbed quite a way up. We were almost twenty odd metres off the ground. I've never been afraid of heights, but it was still disconcerting.

"Geez Abel, I didn't know you were a monkey!" I said quietly as I joined him on a thick branch where he seemed to have made himself a little seat. It overlooked the clearing and also gave a fair sight of the surrounding forest in the area that he was meant to be watching.

"Yeah, that's me, monkey magic," he said with a laugh, "I'm okay, Boss. I know you were worried."

"I'm not," I said honestly, "I'm about as far from okay as I can be and for so many reasons. I have been lucky with my unit... I haven't lost anyone that I came out here with, but when Jase disappeared..." I let the sentence hang there for a moment.

"Boss... Tyne," I registered the uncommon use of my name, "We all knew there was a chance we would lose people coming out here and you're right, you have been lucky not to, but you can't blame yourself for anything that has happened. After what Hunter told us when he arrived, we knew Jase might turn, same as we know there is a chance Rush might… although I personally don't think she will," he paused for a moment, "I think we all saw Jase changing. Even if we didn't say it aloud, we were all watching him."

"And now he's gone… I just didn't expect it to be so sudden," I said to him. "In a way, I'm glad he just left the way he did. I don't know how any of us would have coped if he had turned and attacked us in the camp."

"We would have dealt with it if we'd had to. You know that." He replied.

"Yes, but it would have destroyed us. It was hard enough fighting the ones in the clearing and they were strangers," I mused aloud, "are you all watching Rochelle the way you were watching Jase?"

"No," Abel answered with a shrug, "We don't need to."

"Because she is showing none of the signs Jase did, except the eyes?" I asked him.

"Well yeah, there is that…" he paused and then looked at me fully, "But for me, it's her attachment to you. While she still holds that strong bond with you, I don't think we have anything to worry about."

"Huh…" I must admit I was stumped. I hadn't even thought of that. But it was different, as Jase had been detached from everyone before he turned fully. Rochelle was still very much attached in that human sense.

"You know…" said Abel slyly, "My brother has a crush on your bestie…" He smiled a very cheeky smile.

"Really?" I asked him.

"Yeah… but don't tell him I told you. He'd kill me. He only told me because he was trying to puzzle out the relationship between the two of you. But I saw the way Hunter looked at you – and me – when I wiped that tear away earlier." He let that hang there for a moment.

"We walked along the other day holding hands for a while and yet you notice a look?" I asked him.

"Have you noticed how often you and Rochelle hold hands when you're walking?" I shook my head. "It seems to be a normal state for the two of you… She's held hands with Butch too. It's clearly not a relationship thing with the two of you. And I know Butch is in a relationship, too. So that makes it a friendship thing, maybe a close friendship thing."

"Yeah, we're not afraid to hold hands, but we are like sisters." I said, amused at his insight. "But how do you know who we've formed that kind of friendship with?"

"That's easy... Look at what Rush and Butch went through together. You couldn't go through something like that without becoming close..."

"Like you and Jase?" I asked, looking at him sideways.

"Yes. But not as close as you guys. Or Butch and Rush even. We had no connection prior to the fight where the team was killed. Butch was already in contact with Bravo Team. Maybe not as much as Delta was in contact with you guys, but she was already building an attachment," he paused for a moment, "I will do what needs to be done if it comes to that. I won't like it, but I'll do it."

"I know you will," I assured him, "so how did you know Brock and I were close?" I asked.

"Well, a few of us knew he hand-picked you as a team leader and he trained you himself. That also builds a connection."

We sat in silence for a while. I was quietly mulling over how intuitive Abel seemed to be. The rustling down in the bushes continued. Finally, I asked him.

"Abel, what is that? It scared the crap out of me before, but you don't seem all that bothered by it, so it's obviously not something we need to be concerned about."

"What? Oh that... yeah, I've checked it out already. It is a very large family of field mice. They are the first wildlife I have really seen since we came out here. I didn't want to scare them off. I was just keeping a closer eye on that spot, to make sure nothing bigger came through there."

"Is that how you knew I was there?" I asked him.

"Pfft... I saw you coming the moment you stood up," he informed me. "I knew you would want to check on me privately. Make sure I was okay. I saw that look in your eye earlier."

"Yeah, I'm still hoping we never see him and I don't have to make the call. To make the choice between us and him. I don't want anyone else to have to make the call, either."

"I understand how you feel. But we have to face that it may come, we are going in. We need to get this queen. It may have been a self-imposed mission, but they got behind it back at base and we need to see it through. I don't much like the idea of having to make the choice between Jase and us either, but we might. I'm sorry... Hey Boss, can I ask you something?"

"You just did." I said, laughing. He just looked at me. "Sure, ask away." I said.

"You seem to have some trouble with call-signs and names and stuff. I'm just wondering why you seem so comfortable with mine?" I thought for a moment.

"I think it's because in my head it is your real name and everyone else calls you Abel... plus it suits you better than Adam does. I can't explain why. It just works."

"That makes no sense at all," he said with a laugh. "But thanks for telling me."

"It's funny, I came up here to check if you needed comforting and you end up comforting me." I said, adding to his laughter.

"Yeah well, strange times and all that. Now I'm comforted, will you please go and try to get yourself some sleep?.."

"Yes sir." I said with a mock salute. He smiled.

"And Boss..." I paused and looked up at him. "You're doing a good job. I'm glad I chose to follow you. We're going to get her and we're going to end this," he said emphatically.

I nodded my thanks to him and climbed down the tree. I had planned to go and check on the others who were on watch also, but I was hit with such a weight of sudden exhaustion that I stumbled back to my little possie on the ground between Brock and Rochelle and fell asleep.

A while later, I became aware of whispered voices above me.

"She hasn't slept properly in days. I'll take her watch." said a woman's voice. I think it was Rochelle's.

"Yeah, we can divide it between us, let her sleep. She's too busy worrying about everyone else, she doesn't look after herself properly." said a man, which struck me as a weird thing to say, given that we were in a forest hunting aliens and there weren't a lot of opportunities for self-care out here.

"Let her sleep. She's going to need it. And she's had less than the rest of us lately." said a third voice, another man.

The voices died away and I felt a hand brush the hair back from my face. A soft kiss was planted on my forehead and a whisper in my ear of "Sleep."

25

Our last good night's sleep seemed like a lifetime ago. It had only been about twenty-nine hours but given the amount of nests we had fought our way through, it was telling on us.

We had moved through the night, thanks to Rush's excellent night vision. I felt as though we had probably missed a nest through the night, but we wouldn't have been able to fight in this kind of darkness, anyway. It must have been a new moon because absolutely no light was filtering through the trees. Our eyes adjusted enough to the darkness, enough to follow Rochelle and pick our way through the trees and scrub.

We had come across a small nest around dawn. There was just enough light to see clearly to fight. There had only been three aliens in there and they were quickly dispatched. It had given us a nice boost and seemed to reset our energy levels for a while. But it would be a while yet before we could stop.

We seemed to have now entered a cluster of nests. We had already cleared three since the one at dawn and at the rate we were going, we were expecting to come across another one any time now. I wondered how far we were from the central nest. We had to be constantly on the move at the moment, so there hadn't been a real chance to ask Cam and Techie to check. Moving either to leave a nest we had just cleared or moving towards a new one. Stopping to satisfy my curiosity wasn't exactly high on my priority list.

Up ahead of me, something moved. Cam was at my side and she stopped dead at the same time I did. We both went into a crouch and I sensed rather than saw the others crouching behind us. There were no signs up ahead of a nest, at least none of the ones we were usually alerted by. But there was no wildlife around here anymore – the exception being Abel's family of field mice – certainly nothing big enough to cause the kind of movement we were seeing.

I watched the spot carefully, waiting for more movement. Hopefully something that would give away what was up ahead. Nothing happened. I found a heavy but short stick and lobbed it into the bushes ahead, but again, nothing happened.

There was a rustling about ten metres to the left of the original spot. Then a moment later Cam nudged me as the bushes to the right of her moved, though these looked as though they were being deliberately shaken.

Then there was a shout from behind us. I turned and saw aliens emerging from the trees on either side of us. There were six in all, three on either side of us. I heard Cam gasp and turned quickly to see one ahead of us. That made seven. I had told everyone to stay fully armed and on alert, so at least I knew they were ready to fight.

As if in answer to that thought, the sounds of fighting broke out behind me, as the alien in front of Cam and me charged. Cam and I charged straight back. It was already swinging its long, powerful arms before we were in range. Its claws connected with my arm, but didn't do more than scratch the surface of my skin. Cam slammed her blade into the chest of the alien. It hissed at her violently and I took my chance to attack while it was focused on her. I stabbed it hard through the back.

I was aiming for its neck, but my thrust had fallen short, probably because I rushed it. The alien spun quickly and backhanded me. I didn't fly through the air as I had on other occasions, but it did knock me down. I used my off-hand blade to slice at the backs of its ankles.

It tried to swipe at me again, but I was able to scoot back out of the way in time. Cam was behind it in a heartbeat. Slicing across its spinal cord and dropping it at her feet. She grabbed her first blade out of its chest and slammed it heavily through the top of its head. She looked at me, breathless for a moment.

Then she grabbed her blade out of the alien's head and turned to the rest of the fight. I was momentarily amazed watching her. I had seen her fight dozens of times now, alongside her and sparring opposite her, but she never ceased to impress me with her determination and abilities.

She linked up with Daniel as I joined the fray after retrieving my blade from the alien's back and ended up with Abel. The overwatch boys hadn't had a chance to get away and find positions in trees. That's the beauty of being ambushed, I guess. Abel had his blade out and his rifle slung across his back. But the weight of it was slowing him down.

I jumped into the fight and thrust my blade into the shoulder of the alien he was fighting. I held on for dear life as the alien, hissing and thrashing around, tried to throw me off. I dropped my other blade while I was trying to hang on and couldn't reach my spares while in constant motion. I screamed in frustration. Abel called something to me I didn't catch. The next thing I saw was his blade flying toward me through the air. By some miracle, I managed to snatch it out of the air. I didn't hesitate once I had it in my hand. I swiped the blade across the alien's neck. It was a weak swipe, but it managed to sever the spinal cord. The alien went down. It wasn't a clean fight or a pretty one, but at least I got the job done.

I landed with a thump on top of the alien as it fell and set about retrieving my blade from its shoulder. I had jammed it into the shoulder pretty hard and it was stuck in the bone – or whatever it was these things had inside them – and it required a bit of work to edge it back out.

When I had managed it finally, I stood up panting and started as the blade I had dropped appeared in front of me. I took it and handed Abel's blade back to him, then I looked around. The final alien was falling under Brock's weight.

We had beaten the odds and won in an ambush situation and we had done it without losing anyone. Without any serious injuries at all, really. We had been lucky so far. Luckier than we had any right to expect. Brock or Delta would say it wasn't luck, it was skill, but given what we were out here doing and the situations we were regularly facing; I struggled to believe there wasn't some luck involved. We weren't exactly trained professionals, as I kept reminding them both (and everyone else).

As though in answer – and contradiction – of my thoughts about luck, I heard a rumble of thunder in the distance.

"Anyone got a weather radar handy?" I joked with the others as we all turned to face the direction it was coming from. I could detect a faint whiff of freshness on the air I associated with a coming storm.

"Yeah actually," said Daniel suddenly, "There's a weather app on the GPS. I'll turn it on." He pulled out the GPS and started fiddling with the buttons.

"Hey Boss?" Cam began, "I know we are on the site of a battle, but can we just rest here for a bit? We're exhausted." I looked around at everyone else as she spoke. There were a few quiet nods and murmurs of agreement.

"We can stay for thirty minutes," I told them, "then we really need to get moving again. I feel like maybe we're not out of the middle of this little cluster yet. Set a watch." They nodded solemnly; I knew they understood my edginess about staying still. I'm sure they all felt it, too.

I sat myself down on the ground heavily while we waited for Daniel to finish playing with the GPS. It took him about seven of the precious thirty minutes I had allowed us to stay here.

"I've got it," he said triumphantly. "The weather forecaster on this is vague. It depends on information available to the satellites and stuff, much like the GPS does." He explained all of this with the tone of a man trying to put off giving bad news. I was impatient for the news he was withholding.

"Out with it Techie," I said, trying to make my voice both gentle and commanding. It wasn't his fault I was tired and frustrated.

"Sorry Boss," he said. "Looks like we are in for a hell of a drowning. Doesn't look like the thunderstorm itself is going to hit us, more just pass us by, close enough to hear it. The rainy aspect of the storm, however... is going to find us."

"Crap!" Tom said. Which pretty much summed up what I was thinking.

"How bad is it going to be?" I asked.

"Looks like it's going to rain for about a day, maybe a day and a half. It won't be super heavy, but we are going to get wet."

"This tree cover is pretty thick; it should give us some protection at least." Tayler said, looking up at the roof of the forest as she spoke.

"Maybe it'll hinder them a bit too." said Aiden.

"Did you guys train for wet weather combat?" Delta asked me.

"I did some. All of Delta did a little thanks to Hunter (see I'm doing much better now), but as a general rule no, they didn't train us to fight in the rain." I told him. He grimaced a little.

"Well, at least you've had something..." he turned to Brock, "did you teach them about foot control in the wet?"

"I taught them the basics. They weren't too bad, but there is a difference between what I can do with a hose, some mud and sand and this," he gestured around himself. "This thick leaf litter is already slippery and it's only going to get worse wet, but they've been doing okay on it so far. Hopefully, we'll get lucky and the rain won't change things too much." He thought for a moment. "With wet weather combat, I mainly focused on weapon control. At the time, that seemed more important. We only had a couple of sessions for it."

Delta nodded his head. Everyone stayed quiet after that, all lost in thought. Maybe trying to remember what we had learnt. I tried to recall everything. My mind went back to our first team training session with Brock.

I had taken the lead in jogging over to the obstacle course. Aiden, Daniel and Cam had followed along. We trained together as a team every day, but this would be the first time with Brock overseeing us. I hadn't told them about that part yet. I wanted to surprise them.

I heard an audible gasp from Cam as the obstacle course came into view. I smiled to myself at her obvious awe. We ran right up to the border of the obstacle course before we stopped.

"This..." I paused for dramatic effect, "is where I train most nights. It's the special forces obstacle course." I finished.

"Cool," said Aiden. "Is it always so wet?"

I looked at the course again and saw that everything was very wet, as Aiden had said.

"No, it's not, but you need to learn wet weather combat and we don't know how long we have to get you as ready as we can to fight in all conditions." Brock had appeared from behind one of the obstacles with a hose still in his hand.

"You're Brock Hunter!" exclaimed Daniel. He didn't usually speak unless spoken to. I caught the tone of awe in his voice, which told me Brock had another fan. Cam also looked a little awestruck, but she didn't say anything.

"Yeah, that's me," said Brock. He was trying to sound aloof, but I knew he still found people's reactions to him here a mixture of uncomfortable and amusing. Today I think he was leaning towards amusing. A thought backed up by his next words or rather, the tone of them. "And you are?" he smiled a half smile while Daniel gaped at him for a moment, apparently lost for words.

"I'm Daniel." he said finally. Brock laughed.

"Relax Daniel, I was trying to be funny. Didn't Tyne tell you I was a joker?"

"No, she neglected to mention that, around the same time she neglected to mention you would be training us. I think she wanted it all to be a surprise." Daniel told him. He was visibly relaxing and getting bolder by this stage.

"And are you surprised?" Brock asked. He was playing now, I could tell; he did it to me all the time.

"A little... I'd like to know how she pulled it off," Daniel said.

"Pulled what off exactly?" I asked him. He'd lost me a little bit now.

"Convinced him to train us. I know he worked with you on the team leader selection, but how did you manage to get him to continue with us?"

"I never stopped training Tyne," said Brock, "we've just been keeping it quiet and we've been doing it in our own time. I offered to show you guys a few things. You're all going into this war woefully undertrained. It's not your fault or even theirs really..." He gestured back toward the main part of the base, "It's just a fact. I have the ability to impart some extra knowledge that you wouldn't otherwise

get and I'm willing – offering to share it with you. Hopefully, it will help you in some way, give you an edge on the aliens and keep you alive."

Daniel didn't say anything straight away. He simply nodded while he processed what Brock had told him.

"Well, thanks," he finally said, a smile breaking out on his face. He turned to Cam and Aiden. "We're getting trained by Brock Hunter." His voice had an edge of awed kid in it. Cam smiled shyly and Aiden broadly.

"I'm Aiden," he said to Brock. Brock nodded a greeting and turned to Cam.

"Cam," she said, then added, "Abigail Cameron. But everyone calls me Cam. I prefer it."

"Okay then Cam, done deal. Aiden, nice to meet you. Now, who is going to be the quickest up that wall?" We all took off at a run. I expected it to be a breeze. I had climbed this wall a couple of times a day recently but I found my feet slipped on everything. I couldn't find purchase with them. The others were having the same problem. Finally, I slipped completely and found myself in the mud, where I joined Daniel who had fallen before me and Aiden and Cam, who quickly followed.

I heard a long loud laugh behind us and we all turned to look at Brock, who was doubled over most unprofessionally. I caught his eye and gestured with a mud-soaked hand to the wall for him to go on ahead of us (and subsequently show us how it was done).

He walked over and started to climb. I watched his feet as he went and saw how he was using the toes of his boots to dry a patch of wall before each step. I got myself out of the mud and copied him. I saw Cam was already up and climbing using the same method. She was climbing faster than me and made it to the top first. Aiden and Daniel made it up only a few seconds after me.

"How did you get that so quickly?" Daniel asked Cam.

"I only needed to see one step..." she replied, blushing. "I have a photographic memory. It's the other reason people call me Cam... as in Camera."

"That... is awesome!" said Brock enthusiastically, "you should get a lot out of this."

"Yeah, but I'm small, so the others are going to be better fighters than me," she said, blushing again, at having admitted to him something that had been bothering her (probably for a while).

"Not necessarily. I can show you how to use that to your advantage. We may not have a lot of time together, but I will teach you everything that I can," he smiled, "But for now, we work on wet weather combat." And he proceeded to teach us everything he could about fighting wet.

It all came flooding back to me as I came back to myself and found Hunter and Delta giving a quick tutorial on the main points Brock had covered with us.

Rush was listening intently and somehow I knew she would need no more instruction than this. She seemed to process things much faster these days.

I looked at my watch and saw we only had five minutes left of the time I had allotted for us to sit here. I alerted the others and suggested we all get ready to go. Brock and Delta wrapped up their lesson as we readied ourselves to march on.

We left the site of the ambush a few minutes later, with thunder still rumbling in the distance. Just as the first drops of rain began to fall.

26

The path ahead of us looked clear. It was still drizzling and although only half the water made it through the trees, we were all quite soaked. My shirt stuck to my skin, covered with a mixture of both blood and water, but I didn't bother changing it. Everything in my pack was damp and I honestly didn't see the point of getting another shirt in the same condition.

My boots trudged through the damp leaf litter on the ground, feeling heavier than they should. Cam and Daniel were just ahead of me. Delta trudged along at my side. He seemed to want to talk about something, but he hadn't found the words yet. We were all very tired now. We had marched through the night again, though we hadn't come across as many nests now that we were through the cluster we had encountered.

"Boss," he finally began, "we need to talk about finding a way to get some solid rest..."

"Yeah, I've been thinking about that too," I told him, "we've been going full tilt for a while now."

"About forty-three hours and only a couple of short stops. It would be fine if we weren't fighting as well."

"What can we do?" I asked him, "Do you have any ideas? We are maybe a day away from the central nest. I can't imagine we are going to find anywhere safe to stop for the entire night and sleep."

"Trees..." was all he said. I looked up and realised he may be onto something. We would still have to set a watch obviously, but I had yet to see an alien climb a tree. So maybe, just maybe, they couldn't. It was a big thing to hang our safety on, but Delta was right. If we didn't at least try, then we were going to be worse than useless when the time came to fight the queen.

"Okay," I agreed, "give it a couple more hours until it starts getting dark and we'll look for some good trees to try and get some rest in."

Delta nodded. He seemed satisfied. Hunter walked up on my other side. He took hold of my hand for a brief moment and gave it a squeeze. I probably should have stopped doing it, after all, it was very unprofessional and this was serious business, but I was too comforted by that small gesture to give it up.

"Might be time to think about a breather," he said, "and maybe have some food."

"Yeah, you're probably right." I said and into the radio, "Hey guys, let's call time for a few minutes. I'm betting you're all as hungry as I am." There were a few murmurs of agreement and an outright laugh from Rush.

We found an area off to the side of our line, well Cain found it; where we could all sit for a few minutes. We didn't talk much; we were all too busy eating.

"Boss?" Cain asked me after a while. "Not that I don't love pretending to be superman and all but..."

"We need some proper rest, or sleep before we try and get into the central nest, I know. We've been talking about it." I didn't specify who 'we' were, but it didn't seem to matter. They all looked up at me as I continued. "I hope no one is afraid of heights." Cam gulped audibly, but Daniel threw an arm over her shoulder and whispered something in her ear. "Delta suggested we take a nice long rest off the ground."

"Trees?" Abel asked.

"Trees." Delta and I confirmed in unison. Cam went a little pale. Daniel squeezed her shoulders again.

"We plan to keep going for a couple more hours until it starts to get dark and then start looking for somewhere."

Everyone agreed. We wrapped up and prepared to be on our way. Cam and Daniel took the lead again, and we followed them into the trees.

"Once more into the abyss," joked Brock. He was walking at my side again. Delta had gone back to walk with Rush. Those two seemed to have teamed up well as a fighting pair. Much as everyone else was. Tom was the only one alone, although I suppose he was part of a trio with the twins. I didn't like that he didn't have a partner to watch his back. As I was thinking this, he came jogging up on my other side.

"Hey Boss," he said.

"Hey Priest." I replied. It felt for a moment like an everyday stroll.

"I just wanted to thank you for letting me join your team. The more I think about it, the more I realise I couldn't have stayed in that church alone any longer."

"No problem. How are you going with everything?" I asked him. I planned to get around to asking everyone today.

"Not going to lie, taking that first shot was hard," he paused for a long moment. I waited for him to finish (see I can learn patience). "Especially on something that was human, or used to be, at least. But I had to save you and the others. You're still human now. It got easier every shot, I'm ashamed to say."

"What about the shots you've taken at the aliens?" I asked him.

"That is less difficult. I know it doesn't really do any good, but it seems to distract them for a moment and gives someone the upper hand, so it's worth it."

"How are you going for arrows?" Brock asked him from my other side. I knew he'd been listening, but I don't know if Tom had really thought much about it. He gave the slightest start, but collected himself easily.

"I've only permanently lost two. One got stuck..." he paused for a moment with a grimace. I didn't need to ask where it had gotten stuck. "And one flew wide when the target moved quicker than I expected. I didn't want to venture too far to try and find it when we needed to move on so quickly."

"Was that when you swore?" Brock asked. I could hear the suppressed laughter in his voice.

"It's not funny Brock." I told him, trying to sound stern. (I was doing better with the call-sign thing, but I still missed occasionally)

"It's freaking hilarious... have you ever heard a priest swear? It was funny, would have been funnier if we hadn't been in the middle of a fight." Brock informed me, laughing in earnest now. Even Tom was laughing. "Sorry Priest."

"That's okay. When you put it like that, it's pretty funny." He said through his own laughter.

"It would have been funnier if it hadn't almost hit me, too." Said Daniel, turning around to speak. "Still pretty funny though, tell me something... where does a priest learn such profanity?" His tone implied disbelief, but his cheeky smile gave him away.

"Oh, you pick things up here and there." Tom answered him, voice dripping with sarcasm.

We all had a laugh at that, then Aiden's voice came over the radio.

"We've got something over here. I think you should come check it out, Boss." There was an edge to his voice that implied something more than another nest.

"Okay. I'm coming. Everyone else take five." I said into the radio. I looked at Brock. He turned and followed me over to where Tayler and Aiden were. The sight that greeted me when I got there was one I can never unsee.

We had found Jase. He was lying face up on the ground. There was dirt and leaf matter all over his front. When I asked, Aiden informed me they had turned him over. His black eyes were staring up at the sky, covered in a film I associated with death in the movies. If I had to guess, I would say he had been dead for a few hours. His skin was cold to the touch.

His teeth were bared and looked like they had been when he died. His eye teeth were elongated and looked like fangs. His face, mouth and neck were covered in blood and bits of something that looked eerily like flesh. There was something in his mouth that looked like more of the same. He looked as though he had been killed in the middle of eating.

The whole picture made my stomach roll and I am not ashamed to admit I stepped away quickly and emptied it in the bushes. Tayler followed me over and rubbed my back while I settled my stomach back down and tried to get control of it.

When I had mastered myself, I walked back over to Jase's body and continued to examine it. There were scratches down his chest and his shirt was almost shredded. Looking at his hands, I wondered if he had inflicted these wounds upon himself.

His fingers were longer than standard human fingers were and his fingernails had converted into claws. I wondered if that had already been happening before he left us. I had never thought to look, even after we saw what the hybrids looked like once fully turned. I made a mental note to check Rush's fingers the next chance I got.

Jase's claws were also covered in blood and bits of skin and hair. Some of the marks on his chest lined up with the shape of the claws on his hands, but others looked a lot bigger, as though they were inflicted by a full-size alien.

I rolled him over for a moment to have a look at his back. There were more claw marks there. But he definitely couldn't have done those to himself. I couldn't explain what I was looking for to the others, partly because I was not sure I knew myself and partly because I wasn't entirely sure I wouldn't empty my stomach again if I opened my mouth.

Finally, I found what I thought I had been looking for. One of the scratches on the back of Jase's neck wasn't a scratch so much as it was a puncture mark. It looked as though an alien had poked a claw straight through the back of his neck. From what I could tell (and I was just guessing) it looked as though the puncture would have severed the spinal cord and continued up into the brain stem. It looked like a very deliberate wound.

I wondered what had happened to make one of the aliens turn on Jase. I also wondered if he had been moving in the direction he was facing (back towards us) when he was killed. Was he trying to get back to us? Why? There were so many questions.

I was about to open a radio channel to call the others when I looked down and noticed Jase's feet. Yes feet. He had, for some inexplicable reason, removed his shoes and socks. His feet were scratched up and bloody, as though he'd had them off for quite some time. I think I half expected his toes to have turned into more claws, like his hands had. That would at least explain the removal of his boots and socks. There was dirt and leaf litter and scratches running halfway up his calves as well. He looked like he'd been in the wars. All in all, the effect was just outright disturbing.

"Hey guys," I finally said into the radio, "You should all come and see this... but be prepared, it's pretty bad." I stepped back and waited for the others to make their way over. When Abel appeared out of the trees on my left, I put my hand gently on his shoulder and gave it a small squeeze. He looked me right in the eye and I think in that moment he knew what he would see, if not the full extent.

They all exhibited varying degrees of shock. Cam followed my lead and emptied her stomach on nearby bushes. Daniel held her hair and rubbed her back as much as Tayler had done for me. Priest looked sickened but curious at the same time as he bent to examine the body.

Rush stood back, watching the scene in front of her with a distressed expression on her face. Delta and Cain stood on either side of her, trying to look detached (and failing). Delta had a hand on Tayler's shoulder, who was standing on the other side of him with her back to the scene of Jase's death.

"Do you think he died here?" Daniel asked no one in particular.

"Yes," said Brock, "There's evidence of death all over this clearing. Including the puddle of blood that he's lying in." As he finished, I could hear his voice breaking a little.

"He definitely died here," echoed Tom, "there are no drag marks anywhere and with this wound in his neck, he didn't make it here on his own." He indicated the same puncture mark on the back of Jase's neck I had noticed. "This killed him pretty instantly."

Silence greeted his words for a moment.

"Okay, let's get away from here. There's nothing we can do here anyway, besides speculate on what happened and that doesn't help us in any way." said Delta finally.

"Should we bury him?" asked Aiden.

"I would love to say yes, Sundance, but we don't have the time or the equipment." Delta answered him.

"Let's go." I said with a final look at Jase's broken body. Daniel pointed us in the right direction and we walked slowly away. Rochelle paused and knelt by Jase's body for a moment. Cain stopped with her. I wondered what she was doing until I remembered her after the fight with the other hybrids. She removed Jase's tags from around his neck carefully and gently lowered him back to the ground. Cain handed her something, which took me a moment to recognise as a shirt, which she used to cover Jase's face. Then she pocketed the tags and rose to follow us. Cain guided her gently with a hand on her back. She seemed comforted by his touch.

We walked in silence. I don't think any of us had expected quite this outcome for Jase. I know I hadn't. I had thought it would be one of us that would end up killing him during a fight on the way to the queen; although I had hoped – as I told Abel – that we wouldn't come across him at all.

We only walked about another half a kilometre or so before Cam pointed out signs of another nest up ahead. Silently, we prepared ourselves for the fight. This nest looked like a big one. I couldn't help thinking this might even be where Jase was running from.

Once Cain, Abel and Priest were set, we walked forward through the trees and into a nightmare.

There was a nest here all right. Full of hybrids and aliens alike. These were the first hybrids we had seen since the big nest not long after we left the town. They stood frozen in the same way. Watching us as we watched them. But these ones were different. They were covered from head to toe in wounds, scratches, and bites; by the looks of it, they had been fighting amongst themselves. It seemed as though their uncontrollable nature – the one we had been warned about – made it hard to keep them together in a group this large. Even as they stood watching us, I could see one or two of them eyeing the others as though wanting to get back to some argument or fight they were having prior to our arrival.

"Boss," Cain's voice came over the radio, "I got a good spot here. I can take at least a few of them out without pausing."

I did a quick head count. There were nine hybrids in front of us and I had to consider the possibility there were more hiding off to the sides as there had been last time. Behind them stood eight aliens. I wondered if this nest was meant to be this big or if we had caught them in transit. It was the most aliens and hybrids we had seen in one place. If this was the new normal, then we were in a lot of trouble.

"Roger that Cain. On my mark..." I replied quietly. The hybrids snapped their attention to me. "Now!" I yelled before the hybrids charged.

I heard five shots and two whooshes in quick succession. So I knew all three of the overwatch boys had found targets. Five of the hybrids fell. One stopped and looked at its arm, which now had an arrow sticking out of it and another jumped at Brock as the shot rang out. It took the shot in the chest, which threw it off balance. Thankfully, that helped Brock rather than causing more trouble for him. He was able to get a blade up to thrust it into the hybrid's throat as it landed on him.

I heard more shots from both the rifles and the bow and the fight continued. Eight of the nine hybrids were down now and Daniel was in combat with the final one. Trying to get it turned around to give the boys a clear shot.

All this had taken only a few minutes, in which the aliens had seemed happy to sit back and watch. Until the hybrids were taken out with such speed. They obviously hadn't expected that. They all attacked at the same time and suddenly we were in the thick of it together.

A large alien advanced on me, swinging its arms wildly. I wasn't going to be able to get a safe chance to attack it the way it was moving. I was forced to stay on the defensive. I backed slowly away as I dodged, stepped and jumped accordingly. I felt something fly past my ear and saw an arrow appear in one of the alien's swinging arms. It paused its swinging and looked curiously at the arm for a moment. I saw my chance to attack and took it without hesitating. I knew what hesitation would cost me now. I struck with both blades, then pulled one out and tried to swipe across the back of its neck to sever the spinal cord, but the arms had started swinging again and I was thrown off violently. I landed halfway across the clearing on top of a body, one that was still moving.

I tried to roll out of the way as I saw Rush coming in for the attack, but I just managed to get myself tangled.

"Move left." she shouted at me and I realised she meant my head just in time. I pushed it as far to the left as I could and I felt her blade nick my ear as she thrust it into the alien's neck. It stilled as her blade went down to the hilt and severed the spinal cord. I managed to roll off with the aid of a harsh shove Rush gave me before she ran off to go help someone else.

I took a second to collect my bearings before I ran back the way I had flown, to try and find the alien I had been fighting.

I knew I had given it a killing blow, but without severing the spinal cord, it would take a while to die and it could still do a lot of damage in that time. I couldn't afford to let that happen.

I finally spotted it. It and another alien had ganged up on Hunter and were taking it in turns to swipe at him with their claws, barely missing him as he ducked and weaved around them, trying not to get hit.

I charged in without thought and managed to get a good swipe across the ribs of the one I hadn't stabbed before.

"Nice flight?" Brock asked me, "Thought you weren't coming back... shit!" He swore as he grabbed my arm and pulled me close to him as the other alien barely missed my head. The swipe was strong enough that would have broken my neck instantly. I used his pull as a push off and launched myself at the other one again. I managed to get my blade through its throat but couldn't push it deep enough to sever the spinal cord from the front, as Rush had done to one earlier.

I swung my arm back as far as I could and used all my force to give the hilt of the dagger, still sticking out of the alien's neck, another shove. The blade pushed in up to the hilt and I felt a sharp pop as it sunk through the spinal cord and severed it. The movement stopped at once and I was tempted to take a rest, but I heard a heavy thump and a loud grunt behind me that could only be Brock. I turned and watched for a second in horror as the alien I had already stabbed, opened its jaw wide to sink its teeth into Brock's shoulder.

I screamed in rage and flew at it. I jumped, rolled over its back and managed to get my arm under its chin and pull it with me through the roll, so it moved off Hunter and landed on the ground beside me. I landed sprawled on the ground very unceremoniously and if Brock hadn't collected himself as quickly as he did, I would be dead. He threw himself onto the alien's back and used his blade to sever its spinal cord. It fell to the ground with a thump. Unfortunately, landing on my legs.

27

It took a few moments – and Brock's help – to untangle myself from the dead alien. I looked around and saw there were still three aliens up. Rush and Delta were battling one, Daniel and Cam another and Aiden was fighting the third alone. I looked around to see where Tayler was, while Brock ran straight over to help Aiden.

"Butch?" I called into the radio. "Butch, where are you?" I waited with bated breath for a reply. I saw Delta pause in his swing for a moment and look around.

"C'mon Tay, where are you?" I said aloud, though more to myself than to anyone else.

"Here," came a weak reply finally, "I'm here." Stronger now. "I'm under a body."

"Where?" I asked her. I saw Delta do a quick scan of the area and almost cop a fist to the head for his trouble.

"I don't know," she answered me. "Sundance and I were near the centre of the clearing."

"Okay, hold on, I'll find you." I told her and began running to bodies, one at a time, rolling them over and checking beneath them.

I found her under the sixth one I checked. It was a particularly large alien and had fallen on her in such a way that one of her arms was pinned beneath her. There was no way she could have gotten the alien off herself. I grabbed it by both its feet and dragged it off her as quickly as I could. It was heavy and I struggled, even putting all my weight into the pull.

"Boss! Down!" I heard Cain's voice yell through the radio. I dropped what I was doing and ducked instinctively. I felt the air brush past my head as though I had just been missed by a swinging arm. I heard the rifle shot and could swear I also felt the bullet fly by me before it struck the forehead of the hybrid that had come out of nowhere.

I ran to the side of the alien and pulled it the rest of the way off Tayler. I helped her up and made sure her arm was okay. I heard a thump somewhere behind me and turned to see Delta and Rush's alien hit the ground in a mess of limbs. Rush ran off inexplicably into the trees. Delta called after her but was prevented from following as another alien blocked his path. They started swinging at each other and were soon joined by Brock and Aiden. Tayler ran to join them.

"Uh, guys, I have a problem here," came Abel's voice over the radio. "I have a couple of new friends over here who don't seem to like me up this tree."

"I'm on my way Abel," came Rush's voice and I realised she must have either sensed or seen them and run to cut them off.

"I'm coming too Rush, be careful." I added. I looked around quickly to see if anyone was available to join me, but another two aliens had emerged from the trees and were facing the others down. I ran in the direction Rush had disappeared through the trees, following my instincts, until the sounds of hissing reached my ears. I came to the tree Abel was in. I knew because he told me I was below him.

Rush had engaged both the aliens stalking the bottom of the tree. They were both – thankfully – on the smaller side for these things, but no less fierce for their lack of size. I stood for a moment, watching, frozen in awe. Rush was something to watch. I heard the snap of a branch above me and looked up to see Abel also watching.

Rush had always been a good fighter. One of our combat training instructors had called her slippery, despite her more solid frame, but the way she moved now was beyond compare. She may as well have been fighting through glue before. She dodged and weaved and stabbed with a speed I never thought possible for a human to move.

Every blow she landed did damage, no matter how small it seemed. None of the strikes or swings of the aliens landed blows. Soon, both aliens were bloody. It had taken only a minute.

"I know I'm amazing to watch and all but uh... you wanna jump on here and take one of these off my hands?" she asked me quietly, making me jump; I hadn't realised she was aware of my presence. I didn't hesitate any longer. I ran up behind one of the aliens and thrust my blade straight through the back of its neck. I twisted the blade and heard that unmistakable pop again, the one that told me the spinal cord had snapped.

The alien fell at my feet, almost knocking mine out from under me as its legs slipped on the ground. I jumped back out of the way and turned to find Rush again. She was just finishing her alien off with a smug smile on her face.

Abel had gone back up his tree to check what was happening in the clearing. He then jumped down to the ground to join us.

"It's all over in there, lets head in," he said. Rush and I both nodded and turned to walk back to the clearing.

Cain caught up to us halfway there. He arrived at a jog, clearly eager to check his brother was okay. We continued on in silence and entered the clearing at the same time as Tom. He looked more shaken than usual.

"That was intense."

"You can say that again," said Delta, "and I think we can expect more of the same going forward. It's only going to get harder the further we go."

"I thought you'd say something like that," said Tom with a laugh. Clearly already doing his best to regroup and quickly. With that, he wandered off to join Rochelle, who was kneeling down beside one of the hybrids.

I heard them murmuring to each other, but it was too quiet for me to make out what they were saying.

"We need to move on from here as soon as we can," Delta informed us, "I say we move for at least an hour before we stop. Hopefully, we won't come across any more nests as we go."

"Agreed," I said, "okay everyone, we're moving out in five minutes. Catch your breath and be ready to run."

"Roger that, Boss," came nine replies on the radio, although I could hear most of them normally at this distance.

We set off a few minutes later. Rush – with Tom's help – had checked all the hybrids for tags that would indicate they had been taken from Elko. From what I saw, she found two sets. We ran for an hour before we started looking for a few good trees in which we could get some sleep. It was probably another half an hour or so before we found some that looked like they would do the job and set about climbing them and getting ourselves settled.

The night fell quickly, though at least we were able to watch more of the sunset from our extra height vantage. Once the darkness fell completely, there was total silence. It felt oppressive, as though I had fallen deaf suddenly. It had always been quiet here. Maybe it was the thinner air being at a higher altitude, but the silence seemed even more complete than normal.

Other that the painful silence of the forest, the night continued to tick by blissfully uneventful. About five hours into our sleep, watches being changing regularly, there was suddenly a loud squeak and the thump of something falling. I woke, startled. I didn't know how many of the others woke up. I looked across at the branch near mine, where the noise had come from.

Cam was sitting upright, looking terrified. She clung in a death grip to Daniel's arm and his hand was pushed against her stomach, holding her against the trunk of the tree. His other arm was holding onto the thick branch above them. I whispered into the radio.

"Is everything ok guys?"

"Sorry Boss, I didn't mean to wake you." said Cam.

"She got a fright when a spider crawled over her hand and she nearly fell out of the tree." said Daniel.

"A spider?" I asked. I hadn't seen so much as a web lately.

"Yeah, a bloody big one, too." Cam said almost indignantly. "And my knot had come loose, which is why when I jerked back, I nearly fell."

"You know that means I saved your life again?" Daniel gloated at her.

"Shut-up." She said, but I could hear the smile in her voice and something else that sounded like affection.

"Lucky you were there, Techie." I said.

"I was coming back off watch. I was just climbing up to the branch when she woke up. I got my hand on to her just in time." He said.

"Okay, as long as you're both alright. Tie her on properly, will you, Techie?" I added. "And both of you get some sleep."

"Will do boss." They both answered me.

The rest of the night passed uneventfully. We woke early, with the sun. Being up in the trees, we had the advantage of waking as the first rays shone over the horizon. We ate our breakfast such as it was, in our leafy camp and tried to plan out our next move.

Cam, Daniel, and Rush all agreed we were maybe a day to a day and a half total from the central nest. We knew we were in for a long haul until we got there. It seemed to be the general consensus there wouldn't be many chances to stop and rest – if any – between now and then. So, when we left the trees, we had to be prepared to keep going.

We repacked our gear and stripped down anything we didn't need. We didn't want to be carrying any extra weight. This would have included extra food, but instead of ditching it, Delta suggested we pack enough each in our packs and eat the rest – or as much of it as we could – straight away. We would be full and a little sluggish starting out, but the extra calories would help us keep going for longer.

Those of us that had clean clothes changed into them and we left the dirty clothes behind. When we left base, Skipp had given me extra stuff to stow in my pack. So far, I hadn't really looked at it, but now I went through it – with Brock's help – and worked out what I could use.

There were bandages, the kind designed to be worn beneath boxing gloves. Brock now helped me strap them onto my wrists and use them to secure extra blades to my arms. Effectively turning my forearms into weapons in their own right. The extra blades made my arms feel a little heavier, but I felt a little better knowing I had the security of extra weapons… ones I couldn't accidentally drop.

There had been extra bandages in the supply drop sent from the base for us – I assumed because Skipp knew Brock was with us – so the others all got trussed up like I was. Even the overwatch boys. All except Tom. Although he now carried two blades on him, he wasn't confident in his ability with them. That and as he pointed out, a blade attached to his arm and a bowstring probably wouldn't work the best.

Soon we had left behind everything we – hopefully – wouldn't need any more. We shouldered our packs and prepared for what was probably going to be the longest walk of our lives. I took my first step on that walk with as much hope as I could for what was to come.

I had been having a really bad day. I woke early and was unable to get back to sleep. Then during my morning shower, the drains had blocked up and the floor flooded, so my clothes – which had fallen on the floor – were saturated and I hadn't had time to go back to the barracks and get dry ones. So, I had a choice of wet and clean or wet and dirty.

I had almost completely missed breakfast, so I only managed to grab a piece of cold toast before heading off to training with the rest of my team. We had gotten through our first week as a team fairly well. We all got along and were comfortable talking to each other now. But today was just not going well.

We had reached training only to find another team was slated to train at the same time as us. They were one of the teams from our barracks and their team leader was as usual, having trouble controlling them – yes that one – he was not happy we were all there at the same time. I suggested we all train together so as not to waste the time. He liked that even less. He seemed to think this was some kind of competition. Like a game show or a reality show on television. I tried calmly to remind him we were all in this together and we might be able to help each other. He told me I was being childish and stupid.

I kind of lost it at him after that. I yelled, a lot; I called him almost every name under the sun and questioned his intelligence in the biggest way possible; pretty sure I compared him to a flea on an ape's back. Nothing anyone said could calm me down; I realised later, listening to him belittle and berate his team constantly for the previous week, probably had something to do with the way I lost my temper, but I also knew I was being unreasonable. I was having a bad day and I was taking it out on him.

My team finally managed to get me away from him; I calmed down pretty quickly after that. We went off and did our training. I found out later one of the members of his team had dislocated a shoulder during training that morning and I couldn't help feeling responsible for it. I shouldn't have lost it at him like that.

We made it to lunch and I discovered they were serving my favourite food – lasagne – but before I could get a piece I was called out of the mess hall by a very angry superior, who proceeded to chew me out – rightly so – for ten minutes about my conduct with the other team leader in the morning. I accepted it quietly. I was already angry at myself, so I wasn't going to put up a defence; it would have been wrong.

By the time I got back into the mess hall for lunch, the lasagne was gone. As was the pizza and pretty much everything else. The only thing left were a few chips and a wilted pile of salad. I saw the other team leader sitting there laughing with his team, a double helping of everything in front of him. He looked over at me and winked. I pretended not to notice and went to sit with my team.

We had done all of our afternoon training easily enough. It was combat training and we were sharing the room with Rochelle's and another team. They were all fine with training around us. We all helped each other out. Rochelle had heard what happened to me in the morning and checked I was okay. I told her I was – even though I wasn't – and when we finished training, I went for a run. I was feeling sick by now, having not really eaten anything, when a jeep pulled alongside me and started keeping pace with me.

I tried ignoring it for a moment, as I wasn't really in the mood to talk to anyone.

"Tyne?" The sound of my name brought me up short. I hadn't expected to see Brock out here yet. We weren't meant to meet up for training for another hour or so.

"Hey," I said lamely. Then, feeling as though I should probably explain myself a little better, I added, "Sorry, I was a bit lost in thought. I just needed to clear my head."

"I heard you had a bad day," he said. He had pulled over now and climbed out of the jeep.

"You could say that." I told him. I didn't elaborate and he didn't ask for more information. I assumed he either already knew or didn't care.

"I have a briefing this evening, so I won't be able to make training. Feel free to head over to the course anyway if you want to, although it's fine if you want to take a night off. It won't hurt you."

"Thanks. I think I'll go train, anyway. I don't want downtime tonight." He nodded.

"Have a good night, and be careful, don't hurt yourself out there and tell someone you're going." I agreed, then he got back in the jeep and started the engine again.

"Hey Brock," I said suddenly. He looked at me. "How did you know I was out here?"

"I ran into the little one and your friend. They were talking about it. They filled me in on what happened."

"Oh," I said.

"Don't worry about it. Everyone has bad days." He smiled, then raised a hand in a small wave as he drove off.

I waved back, but I don't know if he saw. I still didn't want to be around people, so I headed straight over to the obstacle course. I ran the course through again and again, timing myself each lap. I managed to shave three full seconds off my time as darkness fell. I looked at my watch and realised with a jolt I had missed curfew (and obviously dinner). I swore angrily to myself and started back towards the barracks. I knew I would be locked out, but I was tired enough to risk the trouble I would get in and if I needed to, find a superior to let me in.

When I reached the barracks, I stood at the closed door for a moment as I contemplated which direction to head and find someone to let me in. As I turned to walk away, I heard the door open behind me and a 'psst' sound. I looked back and saw Cam standing at the door, holding it open enough to let a little light out.

I hurried over and she opened it enough to let me in. I could have hugged her. When I looked around the alcove, I saw Aiden and Daniel were standing there also. I could have hugged all of them. I could feel the tears welling in my eyes as I looked at them.

"They haven't done bed check yet," Cam informed me, "you didn't come back for dinner. We were getting worried, but Rochelle gave us a heads up on where you might be."

"Thanks. Have you been waiting here for long?" I asked.

"Only about fifteen minutes." Daniel told me. Aiden meanwhile, held something out to me. It was a sandwich wrapped in a serviette. It was the most ridiculously loaded sandwich I had even seen, clearly made at a table with the food from people's plates.

"You missed dinner." Was all he said. But it made my eyes well up with tears all over again. He looked embarrassed.

They stood with me in the alcove while I bolted the sandwich down as fast as I could, then we went to our cots and got ready to sleep. Bed check came and went and I lay awake for a long while afterward thinking about how my extremely bad day had ended pretty damn great. They really were my team. They had covered for me, fed me and risked getting in trouble to make sure I didn't. It was like they were my own little family. I knew when we went out into the field, we would be strong together. I knew they would have my back the same way I would have theirs.

I smiled to myself at the memory for a moment, as I watched Cam and Daniel walking ahead of me and then I started to feel guilty. How could I have allowed them to come in here with me? I should have made them turn back at the town. We may have been lucky so far, but I could make guesses at what we were walking into and I couldn't see us all getting out of this with all of us alive. I would never forgive myself if something happened to one of them because I had allowed them to follow me.

Basically, I was wallowing in self-pity. Rush walked by my side today. She was energised too, given that like all of us, she'd had a good night's sleep. I could feel her watching me out of the corner of her eye.

"Cut it out." She said after a while.

"What?" I asked her, although I knew what was coming.

"Stop feeling guilty. We all chose to be here. We chose to come here and fight. You didn't make us come here. So just stop." She looked at me again, a stern look on her face.

"Are you reading my mind or something?" I asked her.

"Pretty much, although it's written all over your face. We grew up together. I know you better than you know yourself and I knew you would start feeling guilty. It was just a matter of time. It's in your nature to blame yourself for everything, even other people's choices you have no control over what-so-ever. I followed you because you're you and you're like my sister and I love you and trust you. And a million other reasons I'm not going to bother listing. The others came along for their own reasons, but I can honestly say it was their choice. And don't think for a second they weren't all thinking of coming out here on their own too, even if you weren't." She smiled as she said it.

I nodded at her words. I knew deep down she was right, but I still had guilt rippling through my brain. To try and distract myself, I started to think of other things. I thought about Rush and the changes she was undergoing. Her newfound energy was awesome, but I wondered if it had something to do with the infection she had sustained from the bite. Or if she was just feeling good. So far, she didn't seem to have exhibited any negative side effects other than a violent temper when in battle and the black eyes were a little disconcerting, but the rest didn't seem so bad. And right now, her energy levels were downright envious. I knew how much sleep I'd had to get the energy I had and she seemed to have twice as much on half the amount. Honestly, I was jealous.

We walked on in silence, although every now and then I had to keep reminding myself not to dwell on negative thoughts. Other than that, the walk was peaceful. Two hours passed without incident. Nothing ahead of us or off to the sides showed any signs of a nest. Tayler and Aiden were walking about fifty metres wide of the main group and Cain and Abel were doing the same on the other. Cam and Daniel were leading the way and Brock, Delta and Tom brought up the rear. To anyone on the outside, it must have looked like an honour guard or something.

"Boss," Cain's voice came over the radio, "we got some bodies over here." he said.

Rush and I walked over to where he was. We found three bodies of what we could only assume were hybrids. Their bodies were decayed considerably more than Jase's body had been. These hybrids had obviously been dead for a while. There wasn't a lot left of them. The small creatures of the forest, though we had yet to see or hear any sign of them, were obviously still around somewhere. It was gruesome. We didn't stay to investigate them for too long. There was nothing to find out from the decaying bodies.

28

We started finding more bodies as we continued. At first, there were one or two every couple of hours, but they soon became more frequent. They seemed to be in varying degrees of decay. Some looked as though they had recently died, others looked like they could have been there for a week or more.

None of them, even the ones that looked recently dead, showed any conclusive signs of how they had died. Some of them had scratches and marks on them as though they had been fighting, either with aliens or each other. Others had almost no marks on them whatsoever.

The most surprising thing about finding these bodies littered along our path was there were no nests. It was eerie. As though the forest had suddenly emptied of aliens. I was sure the others noticed it, too. I was just thinking about calling a halt for a while so we could talk about it when we came across another body, right in the middle of the path. As though it had been placed there for us.

It was another hybrid, definitely dead, but still warm as though it – he – had died only moments before we arrived. He was barefoot, as the others had all been. His clothes were torn and ratty. He wore no tags that we could find. Fewer and fewer of the bodies were wearing them. Many of the bodies of the hybrids we were finding must have been taken from other places.

Tom examined him thoroughly and discovered while he had a few scratches here and there, he showed no signs of a wound or wounds that should have ended his life. He even checked thoroughly through the hairline for signs of a puncture wound like the one we suspected had killed Jase.

We had been travelling again now for almost sixteen hours. It was after dark and although the day had been quiet – by which I mean we hadn't discovered any nests and therefor no fighting – we were all getting tired again. I knew we couldn't afford to stop for a whole night again. Not this close to the central nest, but at the same time, we couldn't keep going all night and risk coming upon it in the dark when we would be unable to see clearly.

I had a feeling once we started finding nests and fighting again, we wouldn't be stopping until we found the queen. So, I started looking around us for somewhere to rest for a couple of hours. Brock joined me as I walked a short distance from the body.

"What are you thinking?" he asked me seriously.

"I don't know, but something seems off. Don't you feel it?" I asked him.

"Yeah, I know what you mean. Do you have any ideas?"

"I don't know. I'm just a civilian militia team leader. I don't know about military type stuff." I told him.

"No maybe not, but you have extremely good instincts and you have to learn to trust them more. What are you feeling?" He pushed me. I thought for a long moment before I answered him. I still doubted myself a lot, but I also needed to get this out.

"It feels like a setup. We have been travelling for about sixteen hours, through a forest that up until now has been more or less teeming with aliens and we haven't seen a nest at all. Just some bodies of hybrids scattered around. This one looks like it might have been left here for us, right in our path. And still warm. It just feels like we're walking into something."

"It's funny, I was thinking about that before. It feels almost like we are heading in the wrong direction. Just because there hasn't been any alien activity other than a few dead hybrids. I was wondering if maybe..." he paused for a moment as though unsure he wanted to finish the thought.

"Maybe what?" I prompted him.

"Maybe we should ask Rochelle to try and tap into the queen's thoughts and find out what is going on."

"You can't be serious?" I asked him. I started out shocked, but as it processed through my mind even as I was speaking, I realised it made sense. I just didn't like the idea of Rochelle opening herself up like that.

"Yes, I'm serious and you know it's our best chance of figuring this out. I'm not going to pretend I fully understand what is happening to her and I can imagine it is quite dangerous, but we do need to consider it if we really want answers. I can see in your eyes you know I'm right." I didn't doubt he could. It was a full moon tonight and even though we were deep in the forest, it was considerably brighter than usual.

"Okay, I'll consider it. In the meantime, we should try and rest for a couple of hours while it's quiet. Once we start fighting, I don't think we're going to have a chance to stop and catch our breath much. Let's get everyone to look for a few good trees."

"Cam's going to love you so much when you tell her that part," he teased me. I groaned. I was hoping he would get to Cam before I could, but it looked like he was going to make me do it.

"I hate you." I told him.

"No, you don't." He gave me his most brilliant smile, the one that showed all his perfect – despite years of wrestling – teeth and walked off to go inform the others we were stopping. I did the same in the other direction.

Exactly as Brock had predicted, Cam was less than impressed about being told she had to climb another tree. Daniel held her hand and promised to tie her on properly this time. I left him whispering gently to her that he would never let her fall. I hoped he meant it. In more ways than one.

In the end, I didn't need to make a decision about talking to Rochelle. She brought the subject up with me. We were on watch together. I was too keyed up to sleep and she swore she wasn't tired at all. We were sitting in the lower branches of a tall tree; I hadn't paid attention to what type it was, but it was good and strong. The others were scattered through the two trees on either side of us.

"Hey Tyne," she began.

"Yeah Rush, what's up?"

"Have you noticed anything strange today?" she asked me.

"You mean including the fact we didn't come across a single nest or apart from it?" I asked her.

"I suppose both. I've been trying to work out what's going on. I mean this close to the central nest we should be coming across aliens crossing the road for goodness' sake, not just nests. And this path that we're on looks used, don't you think?" She looked over at me in the darkness.

"Yeah, I guess it does a bit. Kind of like a highway through the forest, probably made by animals before the aliens came, but they definitely used it a lot. And these hybrid bodies. I'm wondering what the go is with them. Why are they dead?" I asked her.

"Tyne, I know you don't like it, but I have been trying to monitor what is going on with the queen…" she paused as though waiting for me to say something. When I didn't she continued. "she has stopped calling the hybrids to her. She still talks to them, but she's not calling them in. I don't know what it means. I wanted to try and dive in a bit deeper, but I didn't want to do it while we were walking in case I get to distracted."

"Don't you think that's dangerous?" I asked her. I was genuinely curious about what she thought.

"I don't know. It could be. I may get sucked into her completely, I guess, but I still think it's a risk we have to take. But I wanted you to be there when I did it. For moral support you know… and because of your promise…" She looked me right in the eye when she said it and I knew she still planned to hold me to that promise she had made me make in the church, it felt like so long ago now.

"We'll need someone else to help keep watch I guess." Was all I said. I wasn't going to stop her. I knew that look in her eye. The one that said she had made her mind up and nothing anyone said was going to change it. As I said it, I heard noises coming from the base of the tree to the right of us, where some of our team was. Rochelle must have heard it too, because she froze instantly. Anything she had been about to say died on her lips.

"Relax, it's just me," whispered a voice through the radio. Delta's voice, to be exact. "I couldn't sleep, so I thought I'd come and offer for one of you to get some sleep."

"You are welcome to join us, but we are both pretty awake up here." I told him. I heard him start climbing up our tree to join us. As

241

he reached us, he used his typical smartarse line, almost the same one he had used on me the first time we had officially met.

"What are two lovely ladies like you doing in a tree like this?"

"Looking for aliens. How about yourself, sailor?" Rochelle teased back.

"I'm a soldier, not a sailor honey, I don't float," he said, laughing. We laughed along with him. "So what you talking about?"

"What makes you think we were talking about anything?" I asked him.

"You're girls. What else would you be doing?" he said with a wink.

"That is incredibly sexist," Rochelle shot at him, "besides boys gossip far more than girls, anyway." He laughed again quietly and nodded his head.

We told him what we had been discussing and his joking turned suddenly grave.

"Do you really think you can do it?" he asked Rochelle.

"It's not without risk I'm sure, but I may as well try. At least we might be able to get some semblance of what we are walking into right now. Because nothing is making any sense. Why aren't there any nests? Where are all these hybrids coming from and why are they all dead? We need to try and find out and it's not like there is any other way. We can't exactly ask anyone."

He thought about that for a moment. I could see he was weighing up the risks in his head. I heard noises coming from the tree on the other side of us. I put my hand on Delta's arm as I saw Rush freeze again out of the corner of my eye. She relaxed a fraction of a second later, so I guessed it was one of our people. This was confirmed when Brock also joined us up our lookout tree.

We briefly explained what we had been discussing and he just nodded his head. He looked over at me for a moment and I could see the understanding in his eyes. He knew I was worried. Rochelle saw him looking at me and smiled to herself, possibly misinterpreting what she saw.

I moved to sit right beside her on her tree branch and Brock took my spot. She grabbed my hands and looked at me seriously, making sure she made eye contact and had my full attention for a moment.

"Remember your promise?" I nodded. "Don't lose me though, okay?" I nodded again. I couldn't seem to find my voice. I felt a hand on my leg and I knew it was Brock and I felt comforted because at least we weren't alone. We had friends. People who cared about us and would do everything they could to help us. Rochelle closed her eyes but kept hold of both of my hands.

"She's not calling them in anymore, but she's talking to them. She is telling them to obey her. Her voice is loud, as though she's yelling. It's never been like that before. It's always been quiet, seductive almost in the past. It's like now she just doesn't care if they want to be with her or not, she just wants them to listen.

"There is pain in her voice. As though she is saddened by the fact they keep dying, but there is also anger. She's projecting quite far now. As though she has many hybrids out there and she doesn't even know how far they are. She keeps reminding them to stop fighting. But it's coming across like an exhausted mother, as though she knows it's not going to work, but she has to say it, anyway." Suddenly Rochelle's voice changed a little. It became a little flatter, a little bit detached. As though she weren't really there with us anymore. It took me a moment to realise she was actually in the queen's head and was directly translating her thoughts. She had succeeded.

"Leave it clear. Yes, that's right, watch them pass, but do not hinder them. Put another body in their path if you have to, but don't let them give up and turn back. She is with them and I want her. She is able to resist me, but not for long, not when she is near. Keep them coming. They will be here soon." Suddenly Rochelle stopped talking and her hands tightened their grip on mine as she went rigid in her seat. I let out a small yelp and felt myself losing my balance on the branch, having no way to hold myself in place.

Strong hands came around my waist and held me firmly. Brock had noticed me falling and positioned himself to hold me in place. Rochelle started shaking violently, almost like she was having a seizure. Her eyes flew open and they were completely black. There was no white in them whatsoever. I could see her struggling and her grip on my hand became painful. I didn't think it was strong enough to break fingers yet, but it wasn't far off.

Her convulsions continued for about twenty minutes or so and the whole time we sat there, her hands gripped mine painfully and Brock used his weight to hold me in the tree. I wondered why Rochelle didn't fall until I realised Delta had manoeuvred himself around and was holding her in the tree much the same as Brock was holding me. After a while, the convulsions lessened marginally and I saw white creep back around the edges of Rochelle's eyes. Her grip on my hand slackened ever so slightly. Her eyes looked as though they were starting to return to normal until suddenly, they rolled back into her head and closed completely. She dropped my hands and went into a dead faint. Delta and I managed to keep her from falling out of the tree somehow and Brock helped steady me.

We tried rousing her. It took almost fifteen minutes before she started showing signs of stirring. When she finally came to another three full minutes later, she was weak and tired, as though exhaustion had finally taken her. I tried to talk to her about what had happened, but she didn't seem able to answer me. She looked confused for a moment, then smiled at me, closed her eyes and fell into a deep sleep. Her breathing was calm and regular and everything else seemed okay. I looked at Delta. He looked concerned.

We decided to carry her down the tree and put her in the bushes to sleep. Delta went and woke Cain and Abel, who came and helped us keep watch. Brock, Delta and I were on the ground with Rochelle and Cain and Abel up the tree with their rifles. The rest of the night passed extremely quickly. We had only intended to stop for three or four hours, but after all attempts to wake Rochelle failed, we resigned ourselves to the fact we would be staying a bit longer.

As the sun crept over the horizon, Rochelle sat bolt upright in the bushes, wide awake and alert.

"I know, I know what's going on," she said, "get everyone ready. We have to move now."

"Rush, what is it?" I said. I nodded to Brock and Delta that I was okay here and they proceeded to climb the trees to wake the others. We had traded off napping a little throughout the night, but right now they were as wired as me. Rochelle sat silent while we waited. She seemed to be collecting her thoughts.

Cain and Abel were the first to join us. Cain tried to inconspicuously stand close to Rochelle. It was sweet and more than a little amusing. I really hadn't imagined him as being shy. He seemed so happy and outgoing with me. But then again, he didn't have a crush on me, I guess, so perspective and all that.

The others joined us before long. Cam had such a look of relief on her face to finally be out of a tree it was almost comical. Aiden and Tayler also came down together. They looked the most well rested out of any of us. Soon we were all gathered together, eating on our feet, while Rochelle filled us all in on what she had discovered.

"She definitely knows we are coming. The reason we have had such an easy time of it the past twenty-four hours is because she made it so. We are in a corridor, one that leads straight to her. She has amassed an army against us to shield her."

"What is with all the dead hybrids?" Aiden asked her.

"I'm not sure. Not completely. She doesn't seem to have complete control over them anymore. But then again, she's not really trying any more. She's not calling them to her, she's just speaking to them. Their aggression seems to be making them difficult to control. They are fighting amongst themselves more than she would like."

"I wonder if that is because she has discovered they are vulnerable to bullets?" Abel mused, more to himself than to us, Rochelle answered him anyway.

"I don't know. But I know she is helping get some of them killed off and put here for us to find. She thinks it'll keep us interested. I don't think she understands us yet. It's like she knows we are coming, but she can't grasp the concept of why. She seems to think we will stop coming if she doesn't entice us."

"So, she's not as all-knowing as we thought," said Tom, "that could be a good thing. If she doesn't know our motivation, then she can't possibly work out what we're going to do next."

"And she wants… me," Rush continued. "But that could actually be a good thing, too."

"How is that a good thing?" asked Cain, shocked into speaking by her statement.

"She doesn't understand me, how I'm resisting her. She thinks as we get closer, she will have more control over me. She thinks that as I'm the strongest..." Delta and Brock were both about to argue, but she held up a hand to stall them. "She has no respect for the strength of humans. She thinks we hide behind our weapons because we are weak. But either way, that's okay. Because she thinks I will be the one to go in after her." She stopped to let that sink in for a moment.

"So... we keep you on the outside and someone else goes in." Said Brock.

"Yeah, but she might expect that..." I added, wondering if she even knew how many of us there were.

"I don't think she does." said Rochelle. Everyone looked at her.

"You don't think she does what?" Delta asked her.

"Tyne wondered if she knew how many of us there were. I don't think she does. None of the nests we've cleared have been able to give her an accurate count on us, because she doesn't know how many of us are waiting in the trees staying under cover, so to speak." She answered him as if nothing strange had happened.

"Boss didn't say anything about that..." said Delta, confused and maybe a little concerned.

"I thought it though." I put in quietly.

"Oh... crap... I read your thoughts?" She looked at me, shocked. Everyone was looking at her with varying degrees of shock and awe on their faces. No fear though, which was good. Rochelle looked more freaked out than anyone else.

29

"So, I guess we can add mind reading to your many new talents." I said. I was trying to make her laugh. It didn't work.

"But that's the first time it's happened. I haven't answered anyone else's thoughts, have I?" Everybody assured her she hadn't. "So, why now? And why just you?" She looked at me.

"Easy," I told her. "We are best friends. We know what each other is thinking half the time, anyway. We always have. This is just an extension of that, probably opened up because of what you did last night." I finished calmly. It actually made perfect sense to me.

"And you're okay with that?" she asked.

"You've been finishing my sentences since we were eight. Reading my mind kind of seems like the next logical step. Even if it was brought about by not so natural means. It's kind of cool, really." I said with a shrug.

"Okay... so, she doesn't know how many of us there are? Can we use that somehow?" Daniel asked. He seemed to have gotten over his shock a little faster than anyone else.

"Yes, I think we can," said Tayler, "who are our strongest fighters other than Rush?" I thought it was sweet she had picked up my pet name for Rochelle until I remembered that she was a professional soldier and Rush was now her call-sign. It had pretty much seen it as her call sign.

"That would be Hunter and Delta," said Aiden, Daniel and myself.

"Boss." said Rush, Cain, Abel, Brock and Delta at the same time.

"Hunter, Delta and Boss," said Tom.

"Okay how about this, we all go in together, except those three, hang back when the fighting starts and sneak 'through the window' to get to the queen, in theory she shouldn't see them coming as quickly as she would see Rush." Tayler said.

We all pondered what she had said for a moment as we ate. I could see a lot of flaws in her plan, but I could see the merits in it also. If Rochelle was correct that she did not know how many of us there were, then we could and should use it to our advantage. It didn't diminish the danger we would all be in, regardless. I was surprised to be counted as one of the strongest fighters in the team. I personally would have put myself somewhere in the middle.

"I doubt we are going to be able to just 'sneak through the window' as you say, Butch." said Delta.

"I'm sure it won't be quite as easy as that no, but if you sneak through as best you can and only fight what you absolutely have to and stick together, you might have the best shot of all of us to get near the queen, and hopefully kill her." she replied.

"It's a good plan," said Cain. "It's the best chance we've got, I think." We all agreed it was the best idea we had and since no one seemed able to offer a better one, it was the one we would go with. We had finished eating by now and it was time to get going. Rush pointed us in the right direction and off we went.

As we walked, I heard Delta ask Rush how long she thought we'd have to walk before we came across something we had to kill. Her reply gave us somewhere between six and seven hours. I hoped to shorten that time; if we could pick up the pace a little and get there before she expected us. It might give us a slightly better chance and anything that gave us any kind of edge could only be a good thing. I mentioned this quietly over the radio and everyone readily agreed. We picked up the pace and started putting more ground behind us as quickly as we could without running and wearing ourselves out completely.

Within three hours of our march, we were starting to see signs of alien activity in the area. They may not be here now, but they had been at some point. Interestingly, we hadn't found any more bodies. I deduced from this the queen well and truly knew we were coming. I wondered how much of a look inside Rochelle's mind she'd had the night before, while Rochelle was trying to poke around in hers.

Cam and Daniel informed us we had made up almost an hour and a half of extra time in the three hours we were marching. I figured that gave us a fair amount of time to play with, so I called for a rest break. We stopped for thirty minutes, during which time we also did final checks to make sure we were all ready to fight at a moment's notice. We planned to ditch our packs once we got closer, but hopefully before the fighting started. They would only slow us down and given we were walking into the end of the line; they wouldn't do us much good in there.

Another hour passed and we were still ahead of schedule. We had slowed a little but were still gaining time. We started seeing more and more signs of alien activity. Eventually, we came upon a nest. It was empty, but it was a big flashing red sign that told us to be on the alert. Soon enough, we would be in the thick of it again.

All too soon we were. We were walking through a particularly dense section of forest when Cam called a halt to our march. I went forward carefully to join her and she pointed ahead. There were hybrids standing among the trees ahead of us. They didn't appear to have seen us yet, but we would only have the element of surprise for a few moments.

We signalled the others and together we walked into view. The hybrids' attention was on us as soon as we appeared. They rushed forward and three of them fell almost instantly. Two bullets and an arrow fired from the trees around us. Bullets continued to fly and at a slower rate, arrows. The hybrids fell one by one. We didn't stand still to watch them fall. Some of them ran at us to attack and we found ourselves quite busy.

Rochelle was darting around as always, being everywhere at once. She was swiping and killing hybrids almost recklessly. Our overwatch boys were doing their jobs well though and it was only a few minutes before there were none left alive. That was when the aliens came. They stepped out of the trees as though they had been there waiting all along.

We didn't wait for them to attack. We just kept right on going. I engaged one with Brock at my side (which he rarely seemed to leave at the moment). It wasn't the biggest alien I had seen and for a brief moment, I allowed myself the illusion this fight might be a quick one; the alien soon proved though it wasn't as big as some of its counterparts, it more than made up for it in aggressiveness and skill. These things always fought hard, but this one fought like a demon possessed. Every time I thought one of us had the upper hand, it brought out a new move we hadn't seen before.

It looked a little different, too. It had strange bumps stretched across the back of its shoulders. It wasn't long before I realised they would make it more difficult to get to the spinal cord to sever it if we ever managed to get close enough. I wanted to get a closer look at the bumps to try and figure out what they were; I thought they may have been some kind of armour, but I got too close, my attention on the bumps and not the arms which caught me off guard for a moment and before I knew it, I had a clawed hand to the side of my face and I was thrown into a tree. I sat there for a moment, dazed.

I could hear voices screaming through the radio and somewhere nearby in my other ear that sounded fuzzy. My face felt damp and it was stinging. I suspected I had some pretty wicked claw marks there as my hand automatically went to my face and felt the stickiness that could only be blood. My head was pounding a little and it was making my eyes feel a little strange. Suddenly, a hand darted out from the side and gently but firmly pulled my fingers away from my bleeding face. I managed to turn my head a bit and looked up to see Tom.

"Priest! What are you doing here?"

"Helping you with that wound so you can get back in the fight. What do you think I'm doing?" Came the sharp reply.

"But you are meant to be in a tree somewhere shooting arrows at hybrids…" I mumbled. My face was stinging a lot now and talking wasn't helping.

"There aren't any hybrids left and you needed help. Hunter and Delta both called me down and they and Cain were watching my back. I'll be fine. I will go back to my tree just as soon as I get you back on your feet. Now, this is going to sting a bit, but it should feel better in a few minutes." he said quickly. All the while, he was removing things from his pockets.

"It already stings a bit." I said sarcastically.

"Let's see if we can do something about that." He set about cleaning the scratches on my face. "These are going to need stitches, but we don't really have time for that now. I'm just going to clean and numb them, put a dressing on them and get you back into the fight." He finished cleaning, leaving my face stinging painfully. Then he sprayed the whole wound with something that made the sting a lot worse for a few moments, then suddenly, the pain was gone completely. I could still feel the wounds on my face, but nothing else.

"What is that you sprayed on my face? I can barely feel it anymore." I asked him.

"It's a topical anaesthetic spray. It won't last long, maybe an hour, but it will get you through the fight. I'll have to give you another spray before I put the stitches in. I'll also have some morphine ready for you, then. But this jab I'm going to give you now." I looked at the needle he stuck into my leg. It was one of the pre-loaded doses of antibiotics. It had a blank label on it. I wanted to ask him what it was for, but there was no time.

When he finished patching me up, he re-packed his pockets and stood with a hand reached out to me. I grasped it and he pulled me to my feet. It took me a quick moment to settle my feet again, but he waited patiently for me to be stable before giving me a salute and turning to the tree I had just vacated the base of. I noticed his bow had been slung across his back the entire time.

"Boss, you okay?" Delta's voice came over the radio.

"Yeah, I'm on my feet again. Priest fixed me up." I answered him. He didn't say anything after that. I looked around for a moment to see where I was most needed. Brock was up against a different alien than the one we had been fighting before. But I couldn't see the body of the bumpy one anywhere.

Rush and Delta were still teamed up. They were battling three aliens between them. But they were fine. As were Aiden and Tayler. Daniel and Cam had been separated and were each tackling two aliens. A third was moving in on Cam, making my decision for me. I ran over to her and put myself at her back, where the third alien was trying to sneak up.

"Hey boss," she said. The aliens had given pause for a moment as I had joined her. I assumed after having lost the two on one advantage. But it was still three on two, so they didn't pause for long. After only a few seconds, we were once again surrounded by swinging arms and clawed hands, trying to grab at us. I ducked a particularly vicious swipe and thrust out and upward with my blade. I managed to connect with something big. I heard a sharp hiss and blood was pouring down my hand. I didn't stop to think, I just pressed my advantage and stabbed again and again in the same area. The alien went down on its knees, and I reached over its head to sever the spinal cord and finish it off.

As I finished my swipe, another alien grabbed my forearm, hard. There was pressure for a brief moment and then nothing. The blade I had attached to my wrist served one of its purposes and when the alien squeezed my arm, it had sliced its own fingers off. It swung at me with its ruined hand and backhanded my shoulder as I tried to duck out of the way.

Cam was at my back again and we fought like that, darting back and forth when we saw an opening but always returning to each other's back. The alien I was fighting swung both its arms again. And I grabbed Cam by the back of the neck and pulled her down with me as I ducked under its swing. We managed to evade the hit and both came up, swinging our own blades violently. That's about where I lost track of most of what Cam was doing, other than when she came and stood at my back again periodically.

I had had enough of this now fingerless alien swinging its bloody hand at me. I dived forward under another swing and jabbed my blade deep into its throat. By all rights, the move shouldn't have worked. But my speed and the fact it was tiring due to blood-loss probably had a lot to do with it. I aimed three quick jabs into its throat before it went down onto its knees. I jumped as high as I could and got myself a firm hold on its shoulder. I managed to pull myself up high enough, using my legs for leverage as well, to get my blade into the back of its neck. I thrust it in as hard as I could, but I didn't get a chance to twist it before I was thrown off.

The alien was down on its hands – such as it had left – and knees, but it wasn't dead. Cam's alien, I finally noticed, was on the ground and she had been joined by Daniel. I turned to try and finish off my alien to find myself face to face again with Bumpy.

It was standing over the alien I had half killed, watching me. I froze under its gaze, wondering when it would attack. It stepped forward slightly, as though getting ready to spring. Instead of launching itself at me, it grabbed the hilt of the blade I had left in the other alien's neck. It gave a sharp twist of the blade and I heard the tell-tale pop of the spinal cord severing. It pulled the blade out with a sharp yank and looked at it closely.

Then it did the thing I expected the least. It tossed the blade back to me gently. I caught it easily, but when I looked up, Bumpy was gone again. I looked around briefly for it but got distracted when I saw something that almost chilled my blood to ice.

Rochelle was down on the ground under an alien's foot. It looked as though she had been fighting two or three at the same time and one of them had gotten the better of her. Even with what I had started to think of as her new super-powers, I worried she always tried to do too much by herself. Now it felt like all my fears were coming true.

I started toward her with a yell that echoed strangely off the trees in the clearing. The alien with its foot on her head turned to look at me, as it sneered (which is the only word I can think of to describe the look it gave me) I saw Delta coming up behind it, arm already raised to swipe with his blade. I watched as the sneer froze on the alien's face as he slammed the blade into its neck and twisted. The sound of the pop was very satisfying and I smiled as I went over to check on Rush. She recovered quickly and ran off to help Aiden, who was fighting two aliens on his own. I couldn't see Tayler anywhere.

The fight went on like that for another five or ten minutes and then all of a sudden; it was over. All the aliens were dead, their bodies were mingled with the bodies of the hybrids who had died before them. It looked like something out of a horror movie. We tended our wounds and moved on quickly. We were close to our final goal now and failing our mission because we were caught unawares wasn't an option for us.

We estimated we were only an hour or so away from the central nest. We tried to use that time effectively as we walked. Sorting our gear as best we could and getting ourselves ready for whatever got thrown at us next. Some of the team even ate a little. I couldn't eat, I was too full of nervous energy. I kept thinking we really shouldn't have made it this far. The thought made me very nervous and I felt sure something bad was coming. Other than what we already knew about. Because it seemed impossible we could actually make it out of here without losing anyone else.

We stopped when we guessed we were about fifteen minutes out. We planned to have a short rest and then walk in, dropping our bags at the first sign of the nest. I felt as though I should say something to them all, but I couldn't think of anything that didn't sound corny or ridiculous. In the end, no one said anything, but we all hugged. It hurt to think this may be the last time I saw some of these people alive and had the chance to talk to them.

After we had all hugged it out, we turned as one and marched on. We didn't bother being quiet anymore. We weren't silly enough to think we were sneaking up on anyone. They knew we were coming. She knew we were coming. There was no escaping that now. So best to go in loud and proud.

We reached a point where the unmistakable signs of the nest were visible and we stowed our gear quickly behind a large tree. Maybe we would be back for it, maybe not, but until that time, here it would stay.

Cain, Abel, and Tom went off to the sides to find trees to 'nest' in, as Abel had started calling it. It only took them a few minutes before they were giving us the all clear. I looked around one last time at my team and took the first step forward with a deep breath.

"Love you guys, thanks for following me." I said at the last moment. I had suddenly realised I couldn't go into this without saying something. No one replied, but I didn't need them too. I looked straight ahead and walked on into the final nest.

30

The battle was thick and fast almost immediately, as I had known it would be, but somehow the ferocity still shocked me. I briefly wondered if they had been going easy on us or if this was a new tactic. I didn't wonder for long. I was too busy ducking and weaving and trying to keep myself from getting killed. I didn't have time to look around at what the others were doing. I just had to rely on my radio to tell me they were all doing okay and still in the fight.

Brock, Delta and I moved together as much as we could inconspicuously. There were times when one of us got caught up in the fight, but we all kept making for the centre point of the nest. As Rochelle had told us to do. It felt as though we were heading deeper into the nest than was actually possible. Cam and Daniel had told us we were almost dead centre of the forest before we entered the nest, so if she wanted to stay in the middle of the forest, how big could this nest actually be?

Of course, as it is the way of things, when I was trying to avoid too many fights and skate through under the radar, it felt as though every alien in the nest stood in front of me. I managed to dodge through most of them without too much effort. A couple I killed quickly, a few Brock took on or Delta, or someone else from my team flew past and dragged their attention away from me, leaving me free to go on deeper into this seemingly never-ending nest. Finally, I saw what I was aiming for and made for it whole-heartedly.

I crouched down behind a tree alongside what I can only describe as a doorway. I called through on the radio to the boys what I was making for, but we had been separated and they hadn't made their way over to me yet. I decided to stop for a moment and wait for them. I stayed crouched down, partly hidden, with my back to the thick trunk of the tree, my blades at the ready and eyes everywhere at once.

It was the first chance I'd had to really look around since walking into the nest. I heard Delta call out on the radio that he was on his way. I tried to look through the blur of movement going on around me for some sight of him. I could see Brock fighting a large alien nearby, but I couldn't see Delta anywhere.

Suddenly, a hand was on my shoulder from behind. I looked over and saw Rochelle, her eyes were wild with what Delta called battle lust. For a moment, I almost believed we had lost her until she spoke.

"Go Tyne, before they notice you. I'll get the others through to you as soon as I can, but you need to go." With that, she gave me a gentle push toward the doorway that I couldn't ignore.

I crouched low and scurried into the entrance. Still looking quickly around me for any sign that Brock or Delta were about to join me. I couldn't see either of them now, but Rush said that she would get them through and I had complete faith in her. No matter how changed she might be, she was still Rochelle. Stubborn, determined, successful and my best friend.

The shouting and sounds of fighting were loud behind me as I scrambled toward the doorway. It was just one large cacophony of noise. That was until I managed to scramble through the arch. Suddenly, all sound seemed to stop. I spun around quickly, thinking all kinds of terrifying thoughts, from sci-fi transport to everyone suddenly being struck down, but the view that faced me now was the same one I had left behind a moment ago when I stepped through. My team fighting for their lives, for all our lives really.

I realised it wasn't silenced completely, rather just extremely muffled. I saw, through the archway, Rush taking over fighting the alien Brock had been tackling. She yelled something at him and he turned and sprinted toward me. Delta joined him from off to the side somewhere and together they stepped through the arched doorway into the almost silent world in which I stood waiting for them.

They seemed slightly unnerved by the sudden quiet as I had been. They recovered fast and after a quick glance outside, they looked at me.

"Which way?" Delta asked me in a whisper. I looked around for a moment.

"Straight down there, I think." I pointed in a straight line from the door. I'm not sure why, but I was struck by a sudden urge to get everything over with quickly. And forward made sense to me.

We walked along quietly but openly. It felt as though we had suddenly walked into a closed-in maze. From the outside, it looked the same as the rest of the forest, apart from the arched doorway. There were pathways off to the sides, but we kept going forwards. It felt like we were walking for a long time. It was hard to tell in here how far we might have travelled. I tried keeping track, but as we didn't know how big this place was, it was hard to guess how far we would have to go. I was starting to feel like this place would never end.

We could still hear the sounds of the fight going on outside through the radio. It didn't sound like it was slowing down at all, but thankfully, it also didn't sound as though any of our people had been seriously injured, either. I prayed that our luck would hold.

We continued walking until we came to a wall of trees. They were so close together there was no way we would be able to fit through them. We didn't talk. The boys just looked at me and left me to decide which way we should go. I closed my eyes for a moment, hoping to get some sense or feeling; I don't know if it worked, but I chose to turn left and we continued on until we came to another wall of trees. We followed the same pattern a couple more times. After several turns, I was starting to get frustrated. I felt like we were going around in circles, even though I had changed direction more than once. My frustration came through when we came to yet another wall of trees and I kicked them angrily.

"It's a maze." Brock said in a low voice, almost in wonder.

"I think you're right," Delta replied with similar reverence. "But there is nothing like this in any of the maps of the forest I have ever seen. It was all surveyed only a couple of years ago. Trees don't grow that fast."

I didn't speak. The revelation this place was an actual maze instead of just feeling like one, hadn't lessened my anger or frustration. If anything, it had been exacerbated.

"The bitch is playing with us." I said. I wished I could read Rush's mind right then, or that she had been there with us. She would know which way to go. As I was wishing it, I heard a noise from down one of the passages. I held my hand up to signal the boys. Both froze on the spot and raised their blades as they looked in the direction I pointed.

We crept as quietly as we could along the passage toward the noise. It curved around as though it were in a big circle. I realised the whole place had been like that and I had a sudden terrifying thought about where we were.

As we rounded the curve some more, I saw movement heading away from us. I couldn't be sure, but I thought I saw a flicker of white. The aliens didn't wear clothing of any kind, so I began to think we may be dealing with hybrids ahead of us. Although they were quieter than any hybrids I had heard before, so maybe just one.

Brock placed a hand on my shoulder and pulled me gently to a stop. Delta continued ahead for a couple of steps and paused; blades ready in his hand. He let out a quick, sharp whistle. The movement ahead stopped for a moment before continuing.

We looked at each other for a moment, confused. If it was an alien or a hybrid ahead of us, then surely it would have returned to fight us once we announced ourselves. We paused where we were until the sounds of movement passed out of earshot.

"So, not an alien or a hybrid." Brock commented quietly.

"Maybe one of those familiars or whatever they are?" said Delta.

"Hey, Delta?" I asked him. "Do you remember what Selena was wearing?"

"Um... not really, a white dress, I think. Why?"

"I thought I saw a flash of white before we stopped..." I paused for a moment.

"You think that is Selena ahead of us?" Brock asked me.

"Possibly... Yeah, I do. I think she is here to lead us to her... to the queen." I told them.

"Willingly?" Delta asked me.

"Who knows? Is there really any way to tell?" I replied. Delta and I both looked at Brock, who shrugged.

"Either way, we go on, I guess. We weren't going to find her standing here talking about it." he said. I nodded and saw Delta do the same out of the corner of my eye. We turned and stepped forward again.

As we rounded the next corner, we came to a large open space. It almost gave the impression of a room. It appeared to be empty, but my senses – and my gut – were telling me the emptiness was an illusion.

I took another small step forward and another. The boys copied me and we advanced straight toward the centre of the area, one step at a time.

As I took yet another step, I saw out of the corner of my eye another flash of white. I turned my head to catch a better look and to see if my suspicion was correct and if it was Selena. But when I looked, there was nothing there.

I heard a low rumble coming from the other side of me and I turned back toward the front. The area was no longer empty. Standing in front of us were five rather nasty looking hybrids and two of the biggest meanest looking aliens I had seen yet. They were both taller and wider than the other aliens. They had spikes on the backs of their hands and smaller spikes up one side of each of their arms. Their legs were thicker and more powerful looking than the other aliens.

The hybrids took a step towards us but stopped at a hiss from one of the big aliens. I gripped my blades tight as I brought them up in front of me. I sensed rather than saw Brock and Delta do the same. We didn't wait for them to make a move. Almost as one, we charged forward at the hybrids. They appeared to brace themselves to meet our attack.

Two of the hybrids zeroed in on me and I had no choice but to take them on as the others made their attacks on Brock and Delta.

The hybrids fought hard and fast and within only a moment, I was almost overwhelmed. I had completely lost sight of both Brock and Delta already and I had no idea what was happening to them.

As I spun and ducked and weaved trying to land a killing blow on either of the hybrids, I managed to get a bit of a look around me, there seemed to be more than five hybrids now and the little of the boys I could see were busy with two or three each.

My fight drew my attention back with a blow to the side of my head. It wasn't hard enough to knock me out, but it did put me down on one knee for a moment. But from there, I finally managed to get a decent hit on at least one of the hybrids. I swiped at the femoral vein on its leg and managed to cut good and deep. I almost got a face full of blood for my troubles, but managed to turn away. As I did so, I lost my balance and threw out my other arm to catch myself.

It was almost my downfall. The other hybrid I was fighting placed its foot down on my hand, effectively squashing the blade I held out of it. I tried to yank my hand free at the same time as bring my other arm around to slash at its legs or anything that might make it move.

It looked down at me struggling and grinned maniacally at me. I could hear nothing except the blood rushing in my ears as I realised the truth that I very well may be about to die. I didn't stop struggling and by some miracle, I felt it step off my hand and was able to yank it out of the way. I rolled over, ready to thrust my blade into the hybrid's throat – or whatever part I could get to quickly – only to find it falling at my feet, as though in slow motion, an arrow sticking out of the side of its head. It took half a moment for my brain to catch up with what my eyes were looking at. In that moment, I heard another arrow go flying past me and thump into something solid and wet.

"Priest, what the hell are you doing in here?" I called through the radio.

"Long story. Just keep fighting." came the reply.

I really didn't have anything to say to that, so I just did as he said and kept fighting. Hybrids were coming thick and fast under the direction of the two massive aliens that stood there. They hadn't moved an inch from where they were standing when we had walked into the room.

"Where do they keep coming from?" I heard Brock ask over the radio. It was Tom that answered.

"From other parts of the ship." He said.

"What ship?" Delta and I asked at the same time.

"This ship. We are on a ship. It's why the forest looked strange. It's a camouflaged ship. Rochelle saw through the camouflage. But she couldn't get you on the radio. I volunteered to come in after you."

A sudden high-pitched whistle sounded throughout the chamber. The hybrids fell to their knees and started jerking uncontrollably. The two huge aliens dropped to their knees also, although they weren't jerking and twitching. They seemed almost bowed in worship.

The hybrids laying on the floor started moaning in unison as though in great pain. Their movements became more violent before suddenly coming to a complete stop. I wasn't going to get close enough to check a pulse or anything, but I was pretty sure they had all just died simultaneously... and painfully, too. The silence after all that moaning was daunting.

After a moment or two, I noticed the two huge aliens were still in the prostrate position, facing away from us. I caught sight of Brock slowly stepping toward one of them, maybe thinking he could take it from behind. I had a feeling that was a really bad idea. I drew a sharp breath. Fairly quiet, but just loud enough to get Brock's attention. He looked at me and I shook my head vehemently. I don't know if it was that or if he saw something else in my eyes, but he stopped creeping forward and even backed up a few steps.

Another flash of white ahead caught my attention. I turned to face directly ahead of me. Out of what seemed to be another doorway – in the direction the two giant aliens were facing – came Selena. She looked completely blank, as though there was nothing left inside her. Her eyes were bloodshot and teary from pain, or something else I couldn't tell.

She staggered forward as though she were in a lot of pain. It almost looked like she was being pushed. She stumbled and fell to her knees and as she looked up and tried to rise; she made eye contact with me and a flicker of life appeared in them. She mouthed something that looked like 'help me'. Then her face went back to completely blank.

As she came level with the two giant aliens kneeling prostrate on the ground, she placed a hand gingerly on each of their heads and spoke. It was the same voice she had used in the church. The one that sounded as though two voices were speaking in unison out of the same mouth. But this time, I was ready for it and could easily distinguish the two. One heavy and thick, slightly deeper than you would expect from someone of Selena's size and stature, the other quieter, timid, a little sad and fearful sounding that I guessed was closer to Selena's usual voice.

"My time has come, my faithful. I have been challenged! I will win the challenge and we will reap the rewards of my victory."

There was a heavy hissing noise in response and the two giant aliens seemed to sink even lower to the ground for a moment, then rose again to one knee still facing the direction Selena had come from. It looked like we were about to meet the queen herself and it was going to be something considerably bigger than anything we had seen so far.

Coming from beyond the doorway, I could hear footsteps. The heavy footsteps of something big. They were moving slowly, as though strolling through a garden without a care in the world. There was only one thing it could be and I watched the doorway anxiously for my first glimpse of her.

I noticed Brock and Delta were both watching the doorway from either side of me as well. Delta looked apprehensive; Brock looked concerned. Obviously, they had heard the footsteps too and like me, they suspected what was coming through that doorway any moment now. The heaviness of the steps seemed to have frozen all of us into place. My gaze flicked again to Selena, but I was able to glean nothing from her blank expression.

Random thoughts ran constantly through my head. I wondered if we were ever going to get out of here. I wondered if we could possibly win here. Could we beat these impossibly huge aliens in front of us? Plus, the queen that had yet to appear through that doorway. Did we really stand a chance of walking out of this fight unscathed, or even alive?

I remember wishing I knew the answers to those questions as I waited for the queen to finally show herself. I glanced at Selena occasionally to see if there was any change in her demeanour indicating the queen was about to appear. Her face was still a blank slate, so I wasn't hopeful of a hint coming from there.

The footsteps were getting close now. My eyes were drawn once more back to the doorway as a large shadow appeared there. Selena became rigid and if possible, her face went even more blank. This was seen out of the corner of my eye as I was almost mesmerised by the shadow emerging in the doorway. But that was when I knew it was time. The queen had arrived.

31

I watched as the shadow unfolded itself from the doorway on the other side of the chamber. As she drew herself up to her full height, I saw in my peripheral vision Delta straighten on one side of me and step a little ahead. Brock mirrored him on the other side. But the sight that caught my attention the most was Selena's reaction. She started cringing away from the shadow. Then she stood ramrod straight, once again with the blank expression on her face. Her breathing was even, and her eyes appeared to be half lidded, as though trying to hear something far away and closing them to concentrate. But she didn't hold my attention for long.

The shadow was vastly larger than the queen herself – thank goodness – otherwise she would have been unstoppable. But she was still the biggest alien I had ever seen. She stood more than eight feet tall. Her legs were slightly leaner than her counterparts, but just as defined with tightly wound muscle groups. Her knees looked more flexible but bonier, her hips were slightly wider (like a human woman) and like the other two aliens in the room, she had sharp looking spikes running down the outsides of both of those legs. They ran right up to her hips. The amount of solid muscle on her torso was more defined than a human would be.

All the aliens looked strong, but the queen looked as though she was made of pure muscle and nothing else. Her arms were the same as the legs, leaner, more muscular, with a bonier but more flexible looking elbow joint, again with the sharp spikes that climbed all the way to the shoulder joints. Her shoulders were something else entirely. They were wider than the other aliens, wider than any human's shoulders I had even seen (wider even than Brock's shoulders). Unlike her counterparts, she also had a line of long, sharp spikes across the backs of her shoulders. They would protect her neck from any attack that way unless it was done just right. I wondered if these were something she had always had or if they had grown since being here. Since we started fighting back.

She strolled towards us, with her head held high, regally, giving nothing away. I expected to see some expression on her face. Of anger maybe, or defiance; at being – as she put it – challenged. But she was just blank. It was unnerving. As she approached us, I noticed the other two aliens slowly shift their orientation so they were always facing directly towards her. Their heads were up now and they were watching her slow progression towards us.

As she came almost in line with the other two aliens, they rose and turned to face us, so they were standing in front of her, guarding her, much the same as Brock and Delta were doing for me. That is when I realised, they were her bodyguards. That was why they hadn't been involved in the fight when we first came in here. They had just let the hybrids play to distract us. To give her time to make her grand entrance.

I'm not going to lie; I was slightly terrified at the sight of her. Especially once it became clear I would be the one fighting her on my own to begin with. The bodyguards were staring straight at Brock and Delta and it was clear – to me at least –they were going to stop the two of them getting anywhere near the queen. But it seemed she wanted to play with us first.

She looked to the side and my eyes followed her gaze to Selena. As the queen's gaze fell on her, Selena's back went ramrod straight, as though she were suddenly lashed tightly to a pole. Her face was still blank, though the tears that had been welling since she appeared, leaked from the corners of her eyes. She took a deep breath and her face took on an expression of awe as she began to speak.

"So, you are the one who disturbs me." The double sound of Selena's voice was loud in my ears. There was no real question in it. I didn't answer. Selena's face contorted in some strange expression I couldn't read. The face of the queen finally showed some emotion. "Why do you always try to fight back?" She paused to see if anyone was going to answer. We didn't. Selena looked me right in the eye. "You do know, don't you? You can't win. We are more powerful in every way. You may destroy a few of us, but that will not help you. This planet is ours now…" Selena was shaking her head slightly as she spoke, mirroring the queen's movements as though subconsciously. "We took it and we are keeping it. And why wouldn't we? It has such an abundance of good food. Your resistance is but a minor annoyance. Little gnats biting at us to irritate us. You can't possibly beat us."

Her anger showed now, plainly on her face – and on Selena's – as she voiced the last few words. I was getting ready to fight, gripping my blades tightly in my hands, mentally checking my spares. Trying to be ready for the moment this fight got physical.

"Watch us." Brock said. The sound of his deep voice echoed around the chamber as it rang out our defiance. He spoke with authority; he spoke for all of us. Hissing followed his words, angry hissing. Even the queen seemed to forget to speak through Selena for a while. She hissed right along with the other two. I wondered what they were saying for a moment before I realised it didn't matter. All I had to do was watch. Selena gripped her head in both hands and dropped to the ground. Her face wore a torment of pain now. She was in pain, but not the kind of pain the hybrids had been in before they had died.

The hissing stopped just as the two bodyguard aliens stepped forward to launch their attack on Brock and Delta. It happened so quickly that if they hadn't been ready and waiting for it, they probably would have been dead. Brock had provoked them at exactly the right time.

The queen watched me with her head tilted to one side, in a curious way, as I tried to keep my attention focused on her. The fights raging on either side of me were hard to ignore, on one hand two of the people I had come to care about a lot were in the fights of their lives, on the other hand I was about to be in the fight of mine and there would be no back up this time.

She moved a half a second earlier than I expected and it was nearly a very short fight. But I managed to get out of the way just in time as she launched herself across the five or so metres between us. It wasn't particularly graceful, but it kept me alive as I ducked to the side and she clipped my shoulder with her knee as she came down right where I had been standing. I swung an arm at her but barely even touched her as I just tried to get out of her way.

She stopped advancing mid-step and looked at me curiously again for a moment, as though she couldn't quite work out how I had evaded her. I didn't give her a chance to work it out, though. As soon as she stopped moving, I ran in, crouched low and barrelled straight into her leg. Given that she was halfway through a step, it made her lose her balance momentarily. Unfortunately for me, she didn't go down and she recovered quickly.

She hissed at me to show her displeasure at being outwitted even for a moment and I was sure I wouldn't get that chance again. Tom yelled something through the radio, but I didn't catch it. He didn't repeat it, so I figured it wasn't directed at me and whoever it had been directed at had gotten the message. The queen hissed at me again as she charged me straight on this time. I ducked under her swinging arm and sliced along the side of her lower torso with my left-hand blade.

Even through the fight when I had to be so careful, I couldn't help but admire how elegant and graceful her movements were. Nothing about her walk earlier had indicated she could move like this, although I had fought enough of these things by this stage, I really shouldn't have been surprised. It was like watching a dancer perform her heart out on a stage in front of an audience of a million. When she turned to face me again, her mouth was turned up in a crooked little smile. As though she was finally starting to see me as an actual competitor in the fight. Not just a gnat, as she had called us.

She didn't charge this time. She gestured for me to attack her. Which of course, I wasn't quite stupid enough to do just because of an invitation. Instead, I started circling her. She mirrored me. Every few steps, we would get a little closer together. When I thought there was a chance she wasn't paying her full attention, I feinted to the right. She fell for the feint and I was able to get another small nick into the left side of her torso with my blade. She hissed at me again and tried to swipe at me with her right arm. I ducked again, but she clipped my shoulder blade.

She must have scratched me a little because it stung like hell. None of the other wounds I had received in the past few weeks stung like that. I wondered what other weapons she had at her disposal that I hadn't accounted for. We danced around each other a bit more. Feinting back and forth, trying to land hits on each other.

"Not as easy as you thought, huh?" I asked her in my best singsong voice. I didn't feel like singing, far from it, but I wasn't going to let her know how utterly bone shakingly terrified I was of losing this fight. I knew what losing meant for me, for my team and for our world. It wasn't an option, so I was trying to show her I wasn't scared. I don't know if it worked.

Selena answered me from somewhere close behind the queen.

"Not easy, but more fun if you fight back after all."

I looked at Selena out of the corner of my eye while I kept the other one firmly on the queen. Her face was still the blank mask, twitching with the occasional spasms of what I thought was pain. The queen charged me again and I sidestepped her quickly and stabbed my blade downward.

It connected with her leg, but I lost my grip on it before I could pull it back out and it fell to the ground with a gentle clatter. I pulled another one from the sheath on my leg without even stopping to lament its loss. If I had a chance, I would try and grab it up later; but I think my chances were slim. At least I had drawn blood. The queen got another good swipe at my shoulder. It was painful. I felt the claws go deeper this time.

I could feel the slow seep of blood down my shoulder. The second swipe was much deeper than the first. I could feel the sting of the first one still and the second one on top of it just made the sting worse, but I could feel it as a separate wound. I wondered if she felt any pain from the wounds I had managed to inflict on her.

There were two shallow slices across the left side of her torso now, a slightly deeper one on the right. That one actually looked like it was weeping a little. Added to the shallow stab wound in the upper thigh, I hoped that meant I was holding my own.

There was a lot of hissing around the chamber. I couldn't tell where some of it was coming from and I wasn't going to turn away from the queen to find out. I could hear the occasional grunt of one of the boys, whether in pain or in effort I couldn't tell... I couldn't even tell who was who. I hoped they weren't copping it too badly and that they were giving as good as they got. I still held onto the unrealistic hope we would all get out of here alive.

The queen lunged at me again and I found it a slightly tougher effort to evade her this time. But I managed it and threw my arm out to try and get a hit in as I moved. I think I missed, but as I swung my arm around, I lost my balance and I went down on one knee. My exhaustion was starting to show and I was sure as hell feeling it.

I managed to right myself before the queen decided to try and press her advantage. I tried to look around me and find out what I could from the other fights. I didn't manage to see anything before the queen pressed this new advantage of my distraction. I saw it out of the corner of my eye as Tom shouted into the radio.

"Boss, look out!" We were both too slow for me to react quickly enough to avoid injury this time.

She managed to use her claws to put great rending holes into my middle back and around my side. My god did it hurt. I screamed in agony and thrashed wildly for a moment with both arms like a crazed wounded animal before I managed to calm myself enough to think.

The queen had backed up a bit and was holding her side and her arm. My crazed thrashing must have made contact somehow. I looked at my blades to check and saw that one of them had blood on it. So at least her attack had cost her, maybe not as much as it had cost me, but something was better than nothing and I would take it.

I pressed what little advantage I had and rushed in again. The wounds on my back were screaming at me. The queen put her arm up to block me and one of my blades became embedded deeply into the flesh. Before I could yank it out again, she raised her foot and kicked me square in the stomach. I lost my grip on the blade as I flew backwards across the chamber before landing in a heap on the floor. The combination of the kick and the landing knocked the wind completely out of me, leaving me struggling to get my breath back.

The queen started to advance on me, and I once again had to accept I may very well not survive what was coming. Delta and the bodyguard he was fighting moved across her path and blocked her view of me for a moment. Suddenly I was yanked backwards behind what I would have taken for a tree if I hadn't known we were on a ship.

Before I could turn to thank Tom – who I assumed was the one helping me – I heard an angry hissing and Tom's voice clearly through the radio.

"Where's Boss? She just disappeared."

I turned just in time to avoid the swinging arm of the bumpy alien I had come across earlier. I flinched and tried to back further away from it, but I was stalled as my back pressed against something solid. It raised its hand again to try and swipe at me and I ducked down and rolled away as far and as fast as I could. I managed to evade it by some miracle and in the process, I rolled right over one of the blades I had dropped.

I reached out and grabbed it and tried to climb to my feet as quickly as I could. All the while, my head on a swivel, watching for a sign of the queen or of this new threat I faced alongside her. I heard the hissing coming up on me before I saw either of them. They approached me from either side. Slowly but determinedly. They were matching each other's pace as they approached me. I was going to be trapped between them, but at least I wasn't cornered.

I couldn't fight them both at once though, so I would have to choose which was the bigger threat to me right now and keep the other one at bay while I did. I decided on the queen. She was bigger, faster, and stronger and in my mind, much more of a threat. I hoped I was right.

As I charged the queen, I realised she was completely ready for me. So, I pulled one of my old moves and dropped into a slide, which took me straight under her. I sliced at both legs with my once again double-bladed hands as I slid and felt a grim satisfaction when they both bit home and did some damage.

I turned in my slide once I was clear of her body, so when I came to a stop again; I was facing both of them and neither one was at my back. She turned a little slower than she had previously moved, but still faster than I would have liked. As she did, I saw what I can only describe as an evil glint in her eyes. She had the same eyes as the others, but at the same time, they were different. Maybe it was the way she held herself or maybe my subconscious was seeing something my conscious brain wasn't but her eyes looked more intelligent somehow. Which made her scarier.

I focused a moment too long on her eyes, but because of it, I learned something. This alien, this queen, was smarter than all the other aliens put together. And she was playing with me. It was a game she expected to win. I could see the confidence in her eyes and the way she held herself.

Her game was coming to an end now. I could see the anger rising in her. Her stature had changed, as well as her eyes and the set of her mouth. I wasn't going to have a lot of time to think through my moves anymore. She was done playing. And she had back up, I didn't.

Everything around me went quiet. There was an insistent buzzing in my ears. My view became tunnel vision, focused on the queen. My brain went into auto-pilot mode and everything else ceased to exist. I ran at the queen again. She must have thought I was going to slide again because she shifted her stance and lowered herself a little, obviously realising it would make it harder for me. Instead, I jumped when I got near her, another thing she hadn't been expecting. I saw the confusion briefly in those intelligent eyes of hers. I slammed my blade down into one of those huge spikes. I let it go once I was sure it was stuck in there and grabbed hold of the spike itself and used my momentum and all of my body weight to pull it downwards.

She screamed in agony and rage as I raised my feet to aid me in pulling on the spike. She tried to spin sharply to throw me off and succeeded somewhat. I was ready to let go anyway, but I landed badly and tripped over my own feet as I overbalanced. I gave up trying to stand and dropped completely into a roll to get out of the way before turning to see what damage I had done. The spike was dangling down the queen's back and she was spitting, shrieking and hissing violently. Blood was spraying from the torn spike as she spun around in pain.

I gathered myself for one last rush. I charged toward her as fast as my legs would carry me. My ankle was hurting a lot. I realised I must have twisted it as I landed. So, my run was slowed considerably. But suddenly I was intercepted by the other alien. It tried to grab at me, but I ducked under its arms and kept running. It watched my limping progress thoughtfully for a moment before coming after me.

It overtook me and stopped in front of me again. It swiped its arms down to try and grab at me again. It was trying to sweep me bodily off the ground. We were quite close to the queen now, so I took inspiration from every single stupid fighting movie I had ever seen in my life and stepped high so that one foot landed on one of its arms. Then the next step on the other, then a third step on its shoulder and launched myself over its head and onto the queen's back (which was conveniently facing me as she spun around in anguish).

As I landed on her back, I grabbed onto another of her spikes to steady myself. I tried with my other hand to push my blade into the back of her neck. But the skin was too taught and she chose that moment to become completely aware of my presence and I lost my grip on the blade. She spun more violently, trying to throw me off, but I held on. I managed to wrap my legs around her chest, which was stupid and dangerous and I knew she would rip them to shreds with her claws, but it was the only way I was going to be able to hold on. At least she couldn't reach to bite me.

I was right about my legs being torn to shreds. She started in on them as soon as she realised she couldn't shake me off. My attention was torn between trying to stay on her back and keeping an eye on the other alien to make sure I didn't cop it from everywhere. I was removed from the pain I was feeling at this moment.

The other alien was trying to get through the queen's thrashing to try and get me off her back. I reached for the last blade I had sheathed at my thigh. But as I was trying to get a good grip on it, the queen gave a particularly violent thrash and I was forced to let it go halfway out of the sheath as I reached for something to grab hold of to secure myself.

I cursed loudly and repeatedly as my hand closed on something I was able to grasp. It was only as it pulled free and I almost dropped it that I realised it was the neck spike of the queen I had partially removed earlier. I almost dropped it, but made a split decision to hold onto and use it. I knew it was sharp because I had been snagged by one earlier on.

Once I was sure I had a solid grip on the spike with all my remaining strength, I slammed it straight down into the – now bare – back of her neck. It sunk in right up to my hand. No need for a twist as it was wide and round, and I heard the tell-tale pop of the spinal cord severing. As she started to fall, I flung myself as hard as I could away from both her and the other alien that I knew was waiting to take me out at the first opportunity.

32

I can honestly say I did not stick the landing. I landed on my side on the hard floor of the ship. I quickly spun to look around and see where the other alien was. In my hurried search, I didn't see it, but I did manage to take in Brock standing across the other side of the room. I forced myself to scan the room again, a little slower and more thoroughly while listening for the sound of attack coming up from behind me.

Finally, I spotted it. It was crouched down on the ground with its hands on either side of its head. It was hissing weakly and seemed to be exerting pressure on its skull. I quickly looked around again and found the bodyguard Brock had obviously been fighting, doing the same thing. I kept scanning as I clumsily tried to gain my feet. I saw Selena in almost the same position. The only difference was she was crunched up laying on her side, also holding her head and hissing.

I gave up trying to stand as my legs couldn't find their way under me. Instead, I crawled over toward the alien. I tried to stay far enough that it wouldn't be able to reach me if it lashed out again. I made my way clumsily – and not so quietly – around behind it. At any moment, I expected it to start attacking me again. Instead, it just kept holding its head and hissing. It almost sounded as though it was in great pain.

I felt no pity for it. These things had killed so many people, they had tried to take over our planet. There was no way I was going to let it happen to anyone else. With remorse I hated myself for feeling, I unsheathed my blade and swiped it roughly across the back of its neck. Twisting it as I went. I felt disgustingly satisfied at the pop of the spinal cord and the sight of the alien crumpling to the ground.

I didn't stay to waste any time or pity on it. Instead, I crawled over to Selena. She was still curled in the foetal position on the ground. I rolled her over to face me. I wanted to see if there was anything of the human left in her. She had been under the queen's control for a long time and I didn't know how that whole thing worked. She looked up at me with the same blank expression she had worn the whole time.

Her breath was coming in fits and starts. Although I could see no physical injuries, from what I could tell, she seemed to be dying. I didn't know what to do. I wanted to call for Tom, but my voice stuck in my throat. Suddenly, she took a deep breath and some life came to her eyes for a moment.

"Thank you." She said with a trembling whisper. It was the last thing she ever said. Her eyes glazed over and became empty. Not the blank look she had worn before, but the empty hollow look of death. I felt a tear slide down my cheek silently as I reach over gently and closed her eyes so I wouldn't have to see that emptiness anymore.

I looked around me again as I reached gingerly for my headset.

"Priest... Tom, Brock, Delta? Is everyone okay?" I asked tentatively.

Suddenly, I felt a presence behind me. I looked up carefully, gripping the handle of my blade in case I needed to defend myself again, though from this position I doubted I had much of a chance.

"You won't be needing that." Brock's rough voice came from behind me. It showed the level of exhaustion he was feeling. His voice was usually like silk. "Can you walk?"

"I don't know, my legs are pretty busted up." I told him, gesturing down to my torn and bleeding legs. He knelt and examined them gently. I tried and failed to hold back my hiss of pain as he gently pulled back the fabric of my ripped pants.

"Sorry," he said, looking me in the eye. "I have to move you. It's going to hurt a bit more, okay?"

I nodded in response and managed to stifle a scream as he picked me up off the ground and pulled me gently to his chest. I laid my head on his shoulder as he walked slowly across the room towards two vague shapes I could see through my half-closed eyelids.

"Brock?" I asked him. "Where is Delta?"

"He's over here. Priest is seeing to him..." Seeing the fear and apprehension on my face, he hurriedly told me, "He's alive. But he got knocked around pretty badly. The one he was fighting flattened him and left him for dead. Then came over to me. I had just beaten the one I was fighting. It jumped me... and then you killed the queen... and it just fell to the ground, covering its head as though it was in excruciating pain."

"What did you do with it?" I asked him.

"I killed it..." he paused for a moment and then continued, "I just couldn't leave it alive. After everything they have done to our people, our planet..." He stopped talking.

"Yeah, I understand," I told him. "I felt the same."

Brock stopped and gently lowered me to the ground.

"Priest, got another patient for you."

Tom looked over at me from where he was shining a light in Delta's eyes. He winced as he saw my ruined legs. Delta wasn't moving.

"Is he okay?" I asked.

"He will be. His brain is just taking a little rest." His tone was that of a doctor trying not to say too much. I was about to remind him I was a grown woman and the leader of a fighting unit and that he should just be straight with me when he threw me off with a question of his own.

"You still got spare pants in your pack?" He asked me.

"No..."

"Pity, you're going to need them." And he used the scissors I hadn't seen in his hand to cut the cuffs off my pants. Then he ripped both legs wide open, exposing the damaged skin to get a better look. It looked bad and where the fabric pulled off the skin, fresh blood began to pool and I screamed from the pain. Tom quickly jabbed a needle into my leg, and I felt the warmth of the morphine start flowing through me.

"Tyne, I'm going to have to stitch some of these up now. But the rest don't need stitches. I can just dress those until we get you back to base, then have a real doctor check them over."

"Okay, do what you gotta do. I'm alright." I told him. Trying to sound more confident in my ability to handle the pain than I felt. Brock came and sat behind me. He positioned himself so I was seated between his legs and wrapped his arms around me in a strong hug. I leaned into him to brace myself against the pain I knew was coming.

Tom took his time stitching my wounds. There were quite a few of them. When he was finished, he set about wrapping them in bandages, so my lower half looked rather like a mummy. I had to laugh. At the same moment, Delta groaned. I realised Tom had waved some smelling salts under his nose while he gave me a moment.

"Delta mate, you okay?" Brock asked him.

"No... Yes... I don't know... Everything hurts. My head feels like it's been split in half." Came the slow, drawn-out reply.

Tom had finished wrapping my legs now and he was throwing all his rubbish off to the side of us, then he gently removed my boot so he could check my ankle, which was swollen and sore. He strapped it tightly and declared me done as Brock replied to Delta.

"Your head hasn't been split in half, but you were clocked pretty hard. You've been out for about fifteen minutes. Just don't try and get up until we can help you. You're probably going to be wobbly."

"You're going to be okay, though. We'll get you out of here shortly." I added.

"Get up? Honey, I can't even open my eyes. Where's Priest?" he said, again slowly.

"I'm here Delta. I'll check you out properly in a minute, just finishing up with Boss."

Delta didn't say anything else, just lay there and waited. Tom finished my ankle and then moved over to Delta.

"You don't have any cuts or abrasions, but you have a wicked concussion. I checked that before I woke you up. I'm not going to do it again now. A bright light in your eyes isn't going to help you much. I can give you a small dose of morphine for the pain, but I can't risk knocking you out again until your head has had time to heal. In the meantime, I think it'll be safe to move both of you. I want to get out of this ship... this place is giving me the creeps." Tom told Delta as he checked around to make sure he hadn't left anything important behind.

"Yeah, me too," said Brock. "Time to go."

Brock stood carefully and slowly from behind me and reached down to help me up off the ground. He did it slowly and gently. My cut pant legs waved around me, but the bandages were thick and the morphine was still running through my system, so I didn't feel any pain from that. Legs still stung a bit though, but more importantly, I could stand. Once I was upright, he made sure I was steady and then proceeded to help Tom lift Delta gingerly from the ground.

Once we were all upright, Tom slung his medical pack onto his back and pulled my arm gently over his shoulder so he could aid me in walking out of the ship. Brock did the same with Delta. I briefly lamented that it wasn't Brock's strong arms holding me upright as we stumbled our way through the maze we all hoped led us back out of this ship, but I quickly let go of it, because there was no way Tom would have been able to support that much of Delta's weight.

It took us nearly thirty minutes to slowly stumble our way through the maze. We rested a few times on our journey. Delta was still fighting his concussion and my legs were getting more painful by the minute. But eventually, after what felt like a lifetime of wandering, we saw sunlight trickling through an opening. And we walked out of the ship into the late afternoon sun of the clearing.

The sight that greeted us as our eyes adjusted to the sun after the dim lighting of the inside of the ship was blood and bodies. I looked around desperately, searching for any sign of the rest of my team. I only had to hunt for a moment before I saw them over at the far side of the clearing, away from all the bodies. They were all grouped around a couple of lumps on the ground.

My heart was in my throat as I tried to hurry my way over to them to see what was going on. Cain saw us first and hurried over to help, Abel half a step behind him. Cain walked straight up to me and Tom and swept me gently up into his arms, taking note of my bandaged legs. Abel jumped on the other side of Delta and helped Brock support him over to the group. Tom rushed away as soon as I was secure in Cain's arms.

"Hey little sister," he greeted me as he walked, "I take it you won?"

I nodded, unable to trust my voice. Cain walked quickly, but careful not to jostle me too much.

"Is everyone okay?" I finally managed to ask him. I was terrified of the answer, but I needed to know.

"We're all alive..." he paused and took a deep breath. "Sundance has a broken arm and I think his shoulder is going to need surgery this time. It's completely dislocated and floppy. It'd be funny if he wasn't in so much pain. But Priest has all the drugs." He paused for a second before continuing. "Cam has a nasty gash on her face and another on her neck. Techie has done some damage to his left hand and one of his legs. Butch has a few scratches and bruises and is currently sporting a seriously wicked black eye." He stopped talking and fear suddenly gripped me through the middle.

"Cain. Where's Rush? Is she okay?" He didn't answer me straight away and I looked at his face in time to see a tear gently fall down his cheek.

"The aliens all fell down ... we were barely holding on and then all of a sudden, they all fell. Holding their heads and hissing... and so did Rush. She was curled up in the foetal position, hands on her head. She was hissing, and her face looked like she was in agony. She stayed like that for a while. Then she stopped. She stopped breathing. She stopped everything... I started CPR straight away and we got her breathing again, but she's not waking up."

I didn't realise we had stopped walking and were standing over the group of people. Brock and Abel had lowered Delta back to the ground and Tayler was holding a damp cloth to his head and talking to him quietly. Brock was watching me. I realised he must have heard Cain informing me of Rochelle's condition.

He came over and helped Cain lower me to the ground next to Rush. I put my hand out to her. Her skin felt cool, but I found the reassuring thud of her pulse in her wrist. I looked to Tom for help, or advice, or anything.

"Talk to her." He said to me gently. "I'll be here, but I gotta check out the others, okay?" I nodded my head and then turned back to look at Rush. I felt Brock's reassuring hand on my shoulder and Delta reached out from where he was laying and touched my knee. I took a deep breath, trying not to think about Selena, about what might be happening.

"Hey Rush, hey sweety. We won. We killed the queen. I killed the queen. She's gone," I took another deep breath, "I know it hurts honey, but you have to wake up. We need you to wake up." Tears were streaming down my face now. I had already thought I'd lost her once on this mission and now it looked like I might be losing her again. I didn't know how to handle it.

I sensed there were less people around watching us. I didn't know what they were doing, but I heard vague movements around me. I felt Brock lean forward so his mouth was at my ear and whispered so low that it wouldn't matter if they had all been sitting there silently listening in. They still wouldn't have heard it.

"Will her to hear you. Concentrate. She could communicate with you in your head and hear your thoughts. Talk to her in there. Maybe she still has those powers." He didn't have to say anything else.

I concentrated as hard as I could and willed Rochelle to hear me. I said the same things again I had said before, but I said them in my head and I begged her to answer me. I don't know how long I sat there talking to her. But the movement around me was slowing to a halt before I thought I heard something. I was on the verge of passing out from the effort of staying upright.

Suddenly I heard it. It was barely a whisper and it was inside my head. But I was sure I had heard Rochelle saying my name. I waited a moment, breath held. Brock froze behind me. Alert to my sudden stillness. Then I heard it again. Stronger this time. It was definitely Rush's voice saying my name. I switched back to verbal communication, squeezing her hand as I did.

"Hey Rush, come back to me, sweetheart. We need to head home in victory together." I waited only another moment before I felt her fingers tighten on mine and a gentle moan came out of her throat.

Brock's arms tightened around my waist as he tried not to jostle me with his own excitement.

"Well, that has to be the biggest headache I ever had." Rochelle's voice was husky but grew stronger with every word. Every syllable.

"Rush? You okay?" I asked her stupidly.

"Yeah. Water? Does anyone have any water?" Tom gently reached under her head and lifted it to help her have a sip of water. Then let her rest again. Suddenly, her eyes flew open and she looked straight at me. "Tyne. We did it. You did it. You killed her. She's dead and the hive is dead. And we won."

The others had gathered back around at the sound of her voice. I sat with tears streaming down my face, nodding my head enthusiastically, not really able to speak. She threw her hand up into the air and grasped hold of the first one to meet it – Cain's – and against Tom's protests, pulled herself to her feet.

"Wow. I feel amazing!" She had a broad grin on her face as she jogged a lap of the clearing and then ran another at full speed. "Really amazing," she repeated as she came back to us. "Can we go home now?" she asked us. We all laughed – even Delta – and we made ready to leave. Someone had gone out of the clearing and collected our packs from where we had left them.

Rush hunted quickly through mine and declared that I was correct about having no more pants. Tom had given me another shot of morphine and a dose of antibiotics to be on the safe side. Before telling me I'd just have to live without them.

They loaded Delta and me onto litters they had constructed while I had been sitting with Rush trying to wake her up. There wasn't enough room in the clearing for a helicopter to land to pick us up, so we were going to have to try and find somewhere else. Cam and Daniel had consulted their maps and gadgets and they found a clearing big enough for what we needed.

We marched long into the night. Rochelle was practically bouncing off walls. She had more energy than anyone had a right to after what we had been through. We rested for a while around eleven thirty and set off again before first light. Around mid-morning, we called in the cavalry.

"Home 51, this is Team Leader. I repeat Home Base, this is Team Leader." I spoke into the open channel on the radio.

"Copy Team Leader, this is Home 51. Boy are we glad to hear from you." Skipp's relief was evident through his voice.

"Report, mission accomplished. I repeat, mission accomplished. We found an alien ship in the forest where they were based. We managed to infiltrate the ship and eliminate the threat found inside."

"Copy that, threat eliminated... you got the bitch. Where are you? We'll organise extraction." Skipp replied. I could hear the smile in his voice.

"Standby for coordinates from Techie." I signed off and gestured for Daniel to take over. We gave them the coordinates of the clearing we were heading for and Skipp told us transport would be there soon. They were coming to get us.

We could hear the thud of the rotor blades before we walked through the trees. It had taken us a few minutes longer to reach the clearing than we had planned. They had arrived before us. It was a glorious sight to see them waiting for us. General Korby was standing outside the helicopter in preparation for our arrival. He looked worn out and stressed.

He seemed to instantly relax when he saw us walk through the trees; he even smiled. The pilots were cheering from where they were standing behind him. As we broke through the trees, they started applauding us. The applause included full blown cheering after a moment. They ran over to us, still cheering. They brought stretchers to replace the makeshift litters we were using.

"Which one of you is Team Leader?" General Korby asked loudly. Brock pointed to me as I raised my hand. He walked over to me and looked down on me laying on the stretcher. "You... are an amazing young woman." He told me with a smile on his face. "An amazing woman. Well done, congratulations. Let's get you all back to base and checked out. I'm really impressed with all of you. You should all be very proud of what you have accomplished." His grin threatened to split his face in half. "Let's get these people loaded up." Delta and I were moved to stretchers and the pilots and their assistants took over, carrying us to the helicopters.

Delta, Brock, Rush, Tom, Cain and I were loaded into one helicopter. Tayler, Aiden, Cam, Daniel and Abel were in the other. The heavy thud of the blades as we lifted off was one of the most comforting sounds I had ever heard. The General sat up the front of our helicopter and turned to us as we headed back over the forest toward the base.

"Thought you'd want to see this," he said and gestured ahead to where the alien ship we had left behind sat in the clearing. He gave a signal to the pilot and with a sharp zinging noise two missiles shot off from the sides of the helicopter, another two appeared from the sides of the other one, before all four of them thumped heavily into the clearing and the ship below.

It went up in a ball of flame. We felt the heat of it even through the closed doors of the helicopter. We didn't hang around to see the aftermath. The helicopters both banked to the side and headed directly back toward the base. We had a slightly longer flight ahead of us to get back than we'd had on the way out here. Rochelle and I held hands as she sat on the floor next to the stretcher I had been transferred to. I fell asleep before we had been flying another five minutes.

Against all the odds, we had survived, not whole or uninjured, but we were all here alive. My team, the Snipers, the Priest, the Hunters, the Half Hybrid and me the Boss. We really had made it.

Epilogue

I'm organising my pack, ready for the next mission. This one was supposed to be an easy one. Simple search and destroy. It shouldn't be too difficult. Hopefully, there won't be any surprises.

In the six months since I had killed that queen, there had been quite a few missions. Rochelle and I had decided to stay in America. We had talked about it for a long time before we made our decision. They – whoever does these things – searched for our families. They weren't able to find them. They had sent someone out to the farm, but the only thing they found there was blood, a lot of blood. So, we have to assume our families didn't survive the attack.

So we had decided to stay. We stayed on the base. My injuries took a few weeks to heal. There had been a few that needed to be re-opened and cleaned out again. Tom had apologised about a thousand times. So, a week in the hospital ward on base and then a few weeks back in my barracks. Brock came to see me every day. We have gotten to know each other really well and a month ago he told me for the first time that he loved me. We live together on the base now. And the General is actually happy for us.

Rochelle ended up with Cain. They are taking things slowly, but they seem happy. They live with Aiden in the cabin next door to Brock and me. Rochelle is still faster and stronger than she was before. Her eyes are still different. The irises are still deep black. She can still sense the aliens a mile away and she is still the best at pointing us toward them when we are hunting.

We can still speak with each other in our minds. The team knows about it, but we haven't shared that information with General Korby or Skipp or anyone else on the base. We agreed amongst ourselves it was probably something they didn't need to know. We didn't want them turning Rochelle into some kind of experiment. She keeps trying to speak to everyone else periodically with her mind, but so far, no luck. Our working theory at the moment is because she and I were already closer than sisters before all this started. At least we'll always be able to find each other if something happens. It's better than a phone.

As for the others. Well, Tom joined the army so he could stay with us. But he wasn't entirely happy – though he never said anything we could tell – so we sought out the church higher ups and got him un-excommunicated. So, he is our official priest as well as our medic. Oh, he's also back finishing nursing school.

Aiden has no lasting injuries from his shoulder. He did end up needing surgery and they are keeping an eye on it, but they think he will be fine. His bite from the hybrid doesn't seem to have developed any long-term side effects. They think he got sick from infection and was probably due to the dirtiness of the hybrid's mouth rather than any kind of poisoning like Rochelle suffered. Between the shoulder and the broken arm, his recovery took around the same time as mine, so we re-joined the team at the same time.

Delta had a serious concussion, but he didn't need surgery and all his scans came back clean. He was released from the hospital ward the next morning and was back with the team a week later. Tayler stayed with him. They are not together in the traditional sense, but they are still close.

Daniel and Cam made their relationship official. We were all thrilled for them. They got married three months ago (Tom performed the ceremony). Cam is currently stuck on radio duties back on base when we go out hunting or on other missions, due to the fact she is going to have a baby. We miss her out in the field, but we get by. They offered to replace her out there, but we declined.

We get sent out on a lot of missions, some big, some smaller. Lately we've been hunting a lot. There are quite a lot of aliens and hybrids (and probably familiars) still hiding out throughout America. And we suspect at least two more hives somewhere in the world, which means two more queens.

They have gone to ground at the moment, trying to stay under the radar and hide from us, we think. People are starting to rebuild. From the information we have been able to gather, we estimate almost half of the world's population was killed or taken during the first series of attacks. We think the aliens also know this. Part of their reason for hiding might be to preserve their food source. But every now and then, we get word an alien or even a couple of hybrids were feeding in an area. We have gone in and taken them out.

I have seen almost a quarter of the world this way and there is a chance I will see a good deal more of it before this job was done. It's exciting to see so many different places. I hope one day when all this is over and all the aliens are dead, I can maybe go back and see them again for myself. I hope the cultures survive the rest of this war so they are still there to learn about in the future.

Hunting and information gathering make up the majority of our missions. We feel as though we are getting close to something. We are cautiously optimistic that we may have found another hive. But we need more information before we can make a definite plan to eliminate it. In the meantime, we hunt and we learn and we wait. And we watch. We watch the planet to find signs and we watch the sky against the aliens getting reinforcements.

We will keep fighting until it's over. We are Delta Team and we will win our planet back from these things no matter what it takes.

We are Delta Team.

Shawline Publishing Group Pty Ltd

www.shawlinepublishing.com.au

SHAWLINE
PUBLISHING
GROUP

Lightning Source UK Ltd.
Milton Keynes UK
UKHW040636070622
404060UK00001B/132